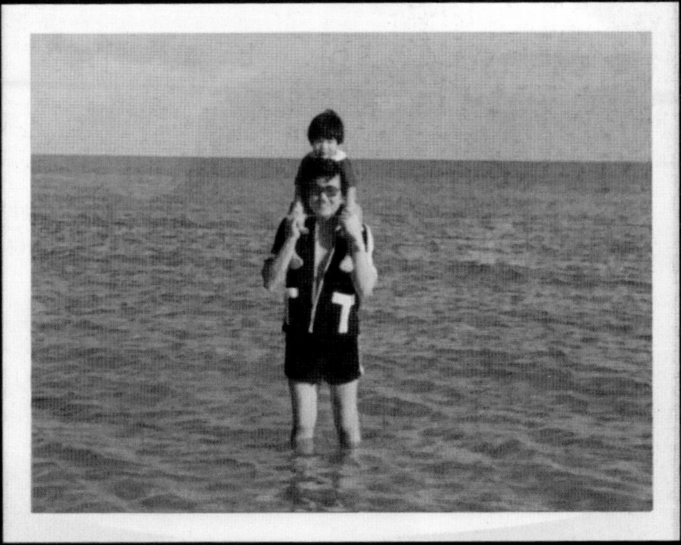

FOR DAD

(OCTOBER 27, 1943 - APRIL 27, 2021)

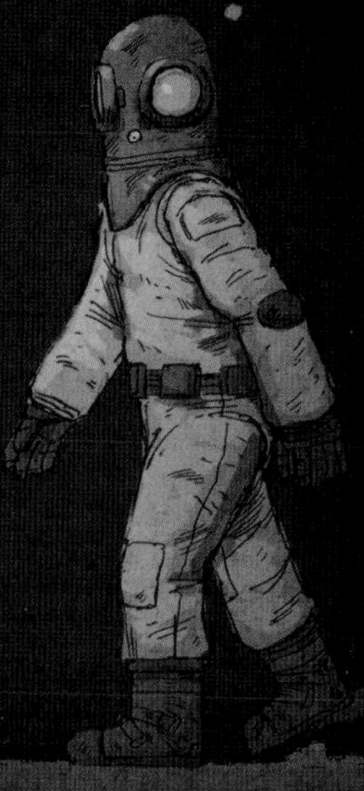

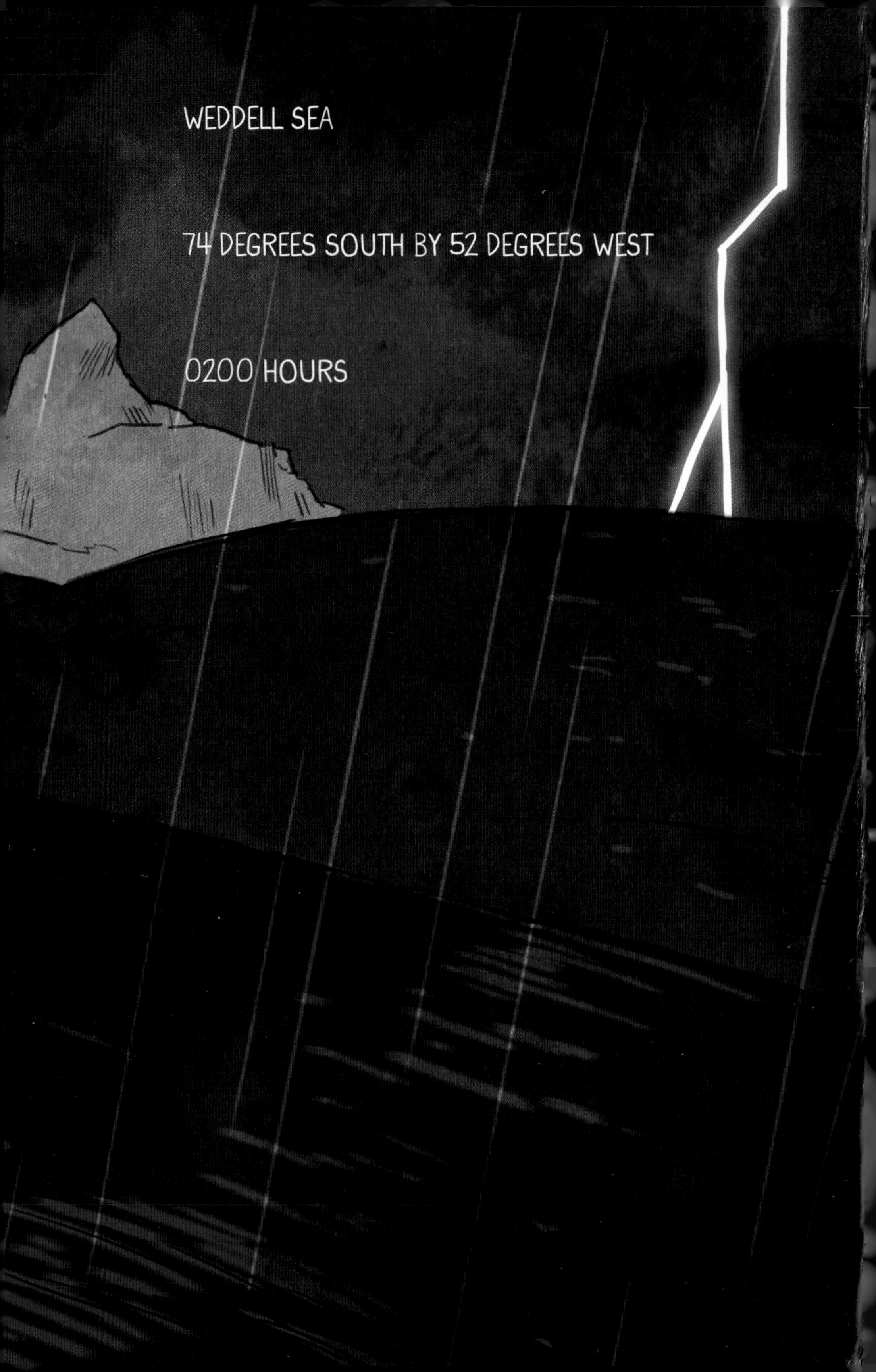
WEDDELL SEA
74 DEGREES SOUTH BY 52 DEGREES WEST
0200 HOURS

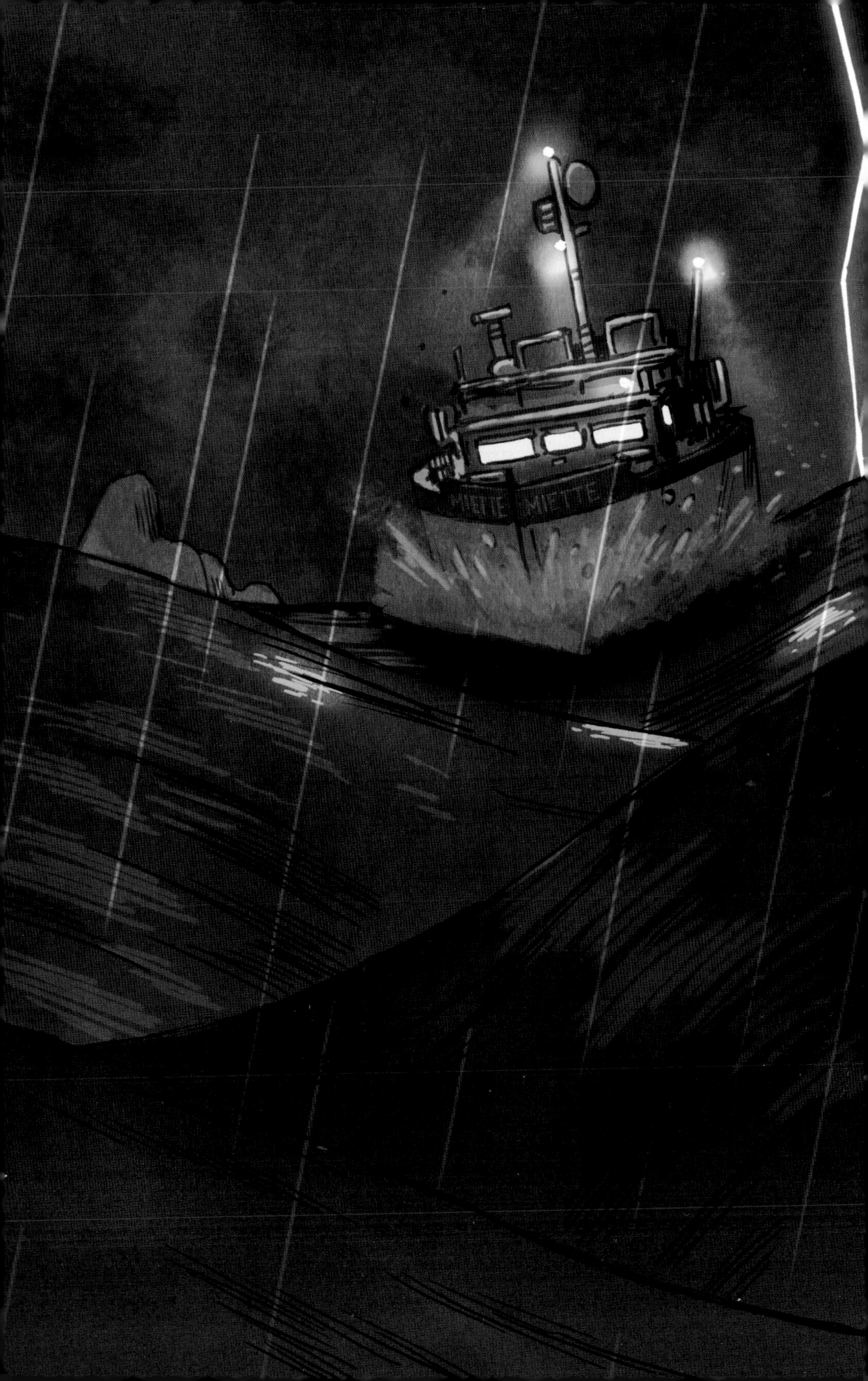

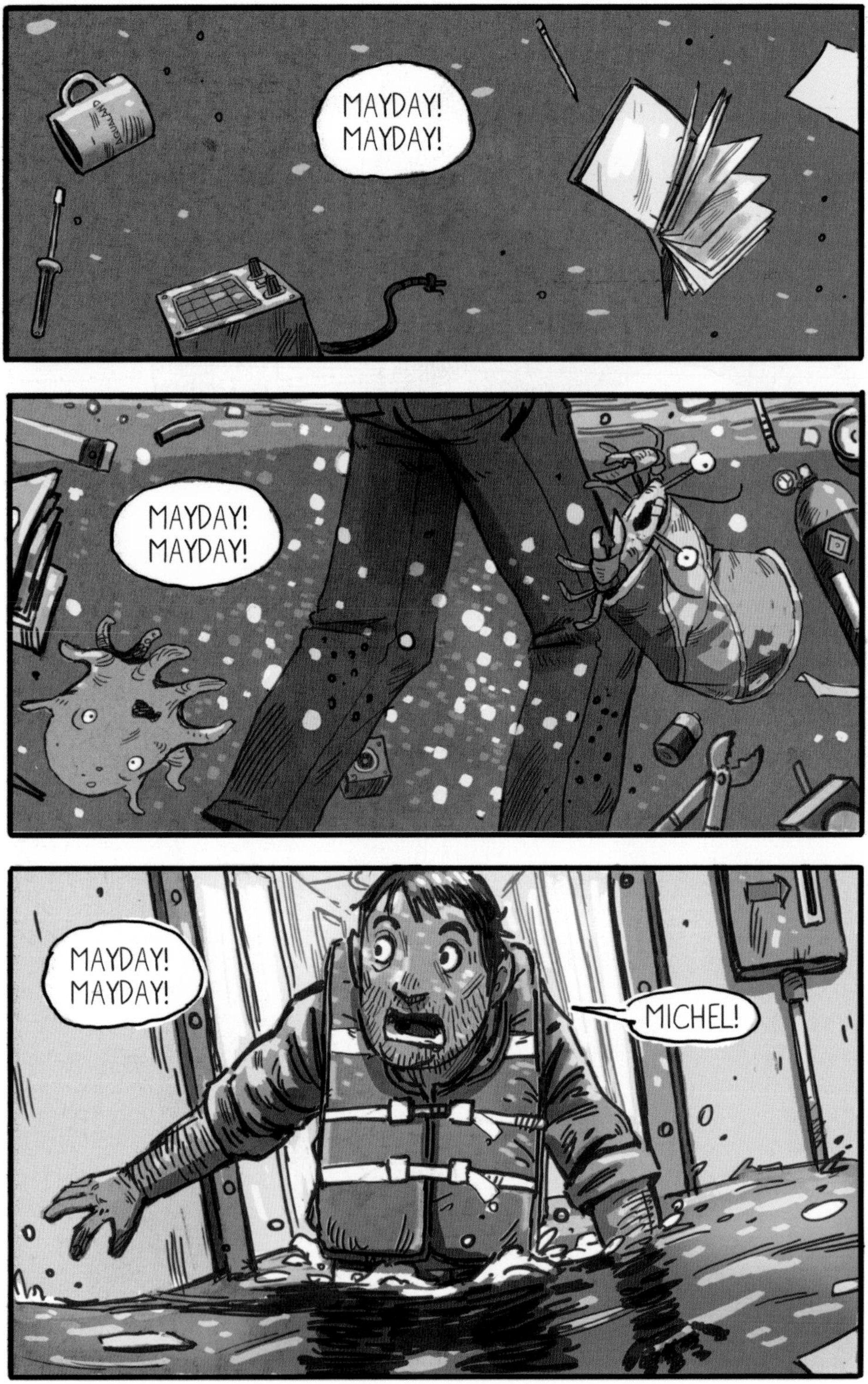
MAYDAY!
MAYDAY!
MAYDAY!
MAYDAY!
MAYDAY!
MAYDAY!
MICHEL!

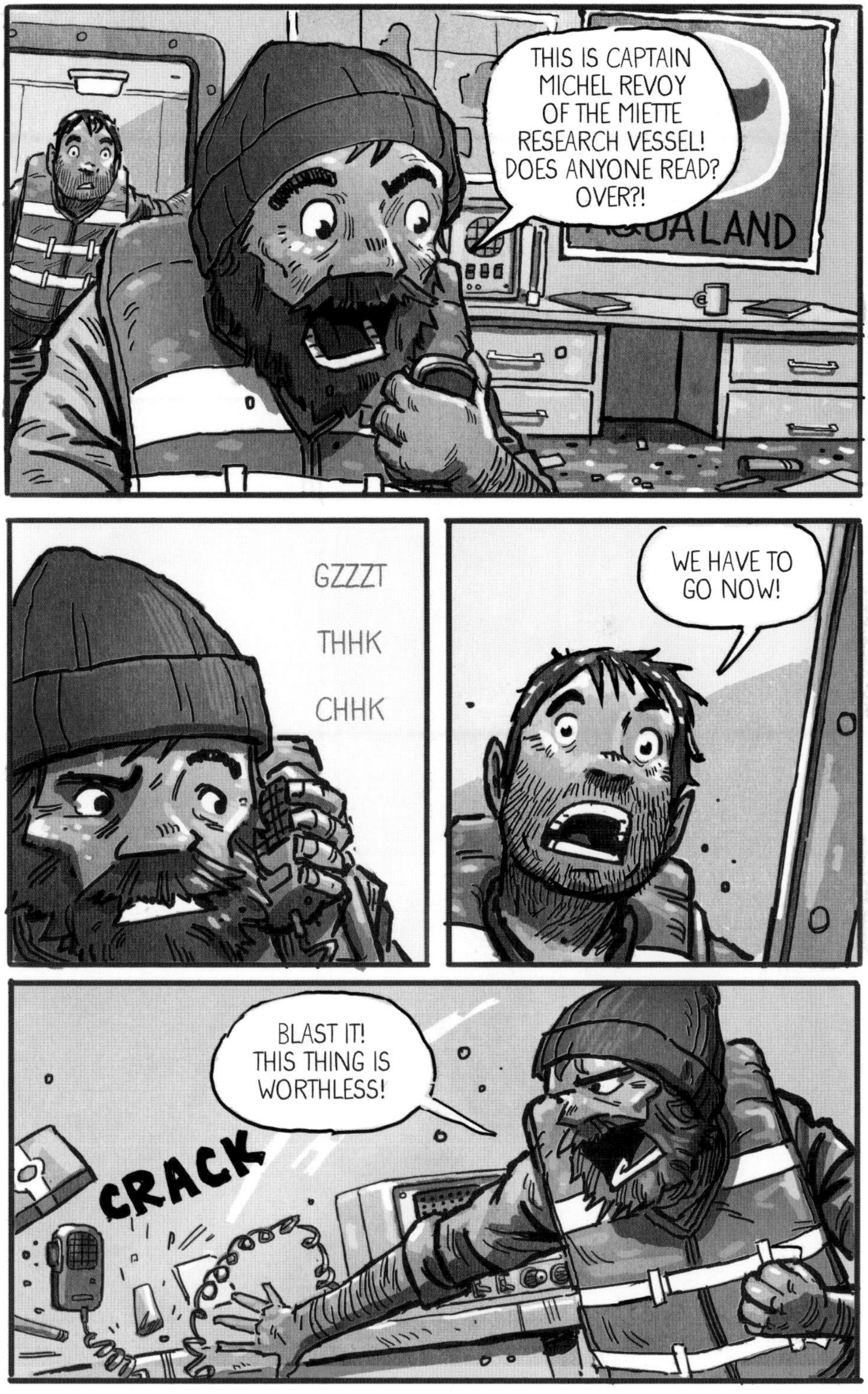
THIS IS CAPTAIN MICHEL REVOY OF THE MIETTE RESEARCH VESSEL! DOES ANYONE READ? OVER?!
AQUALAND
GZZZT
THHK
CHHK
WE HAVE TO GO NOW!
BLAST IT! THIS THING IS WORTHLESS!
CRACK

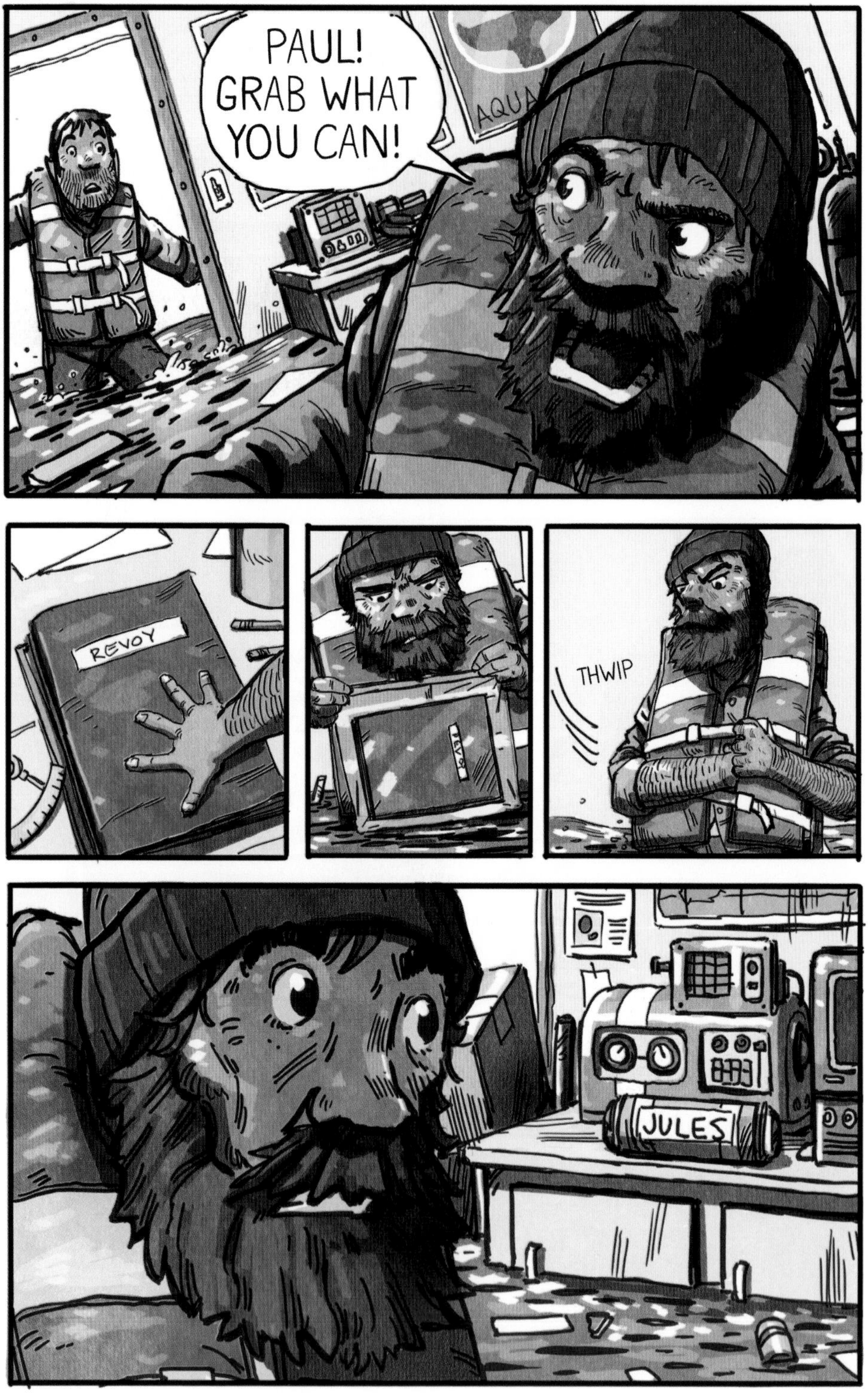
PAUL! GRAB WHAT YOU CAN!
REVOY
THWIP
JULES

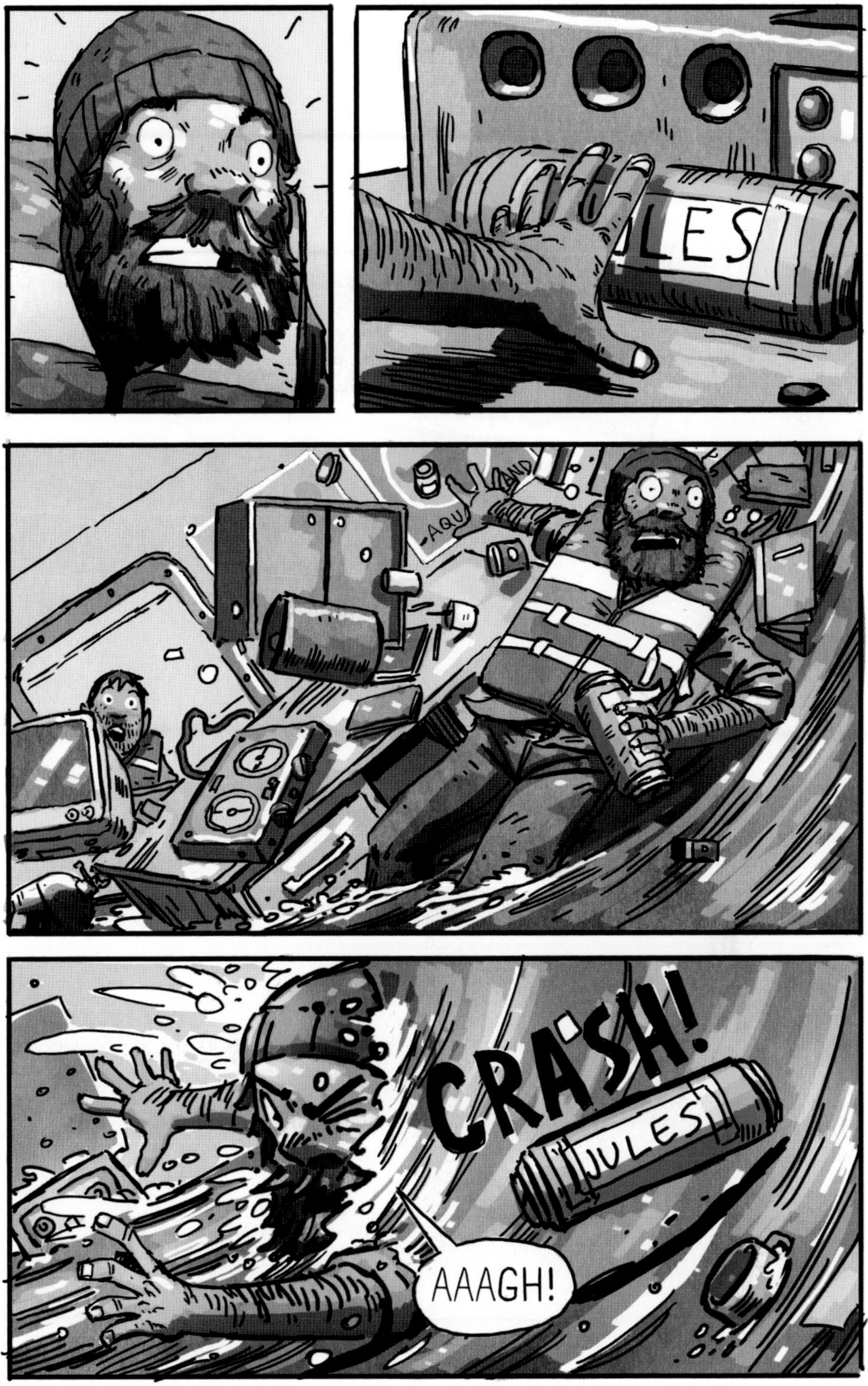
CRASH!
JULES
AAAGH!

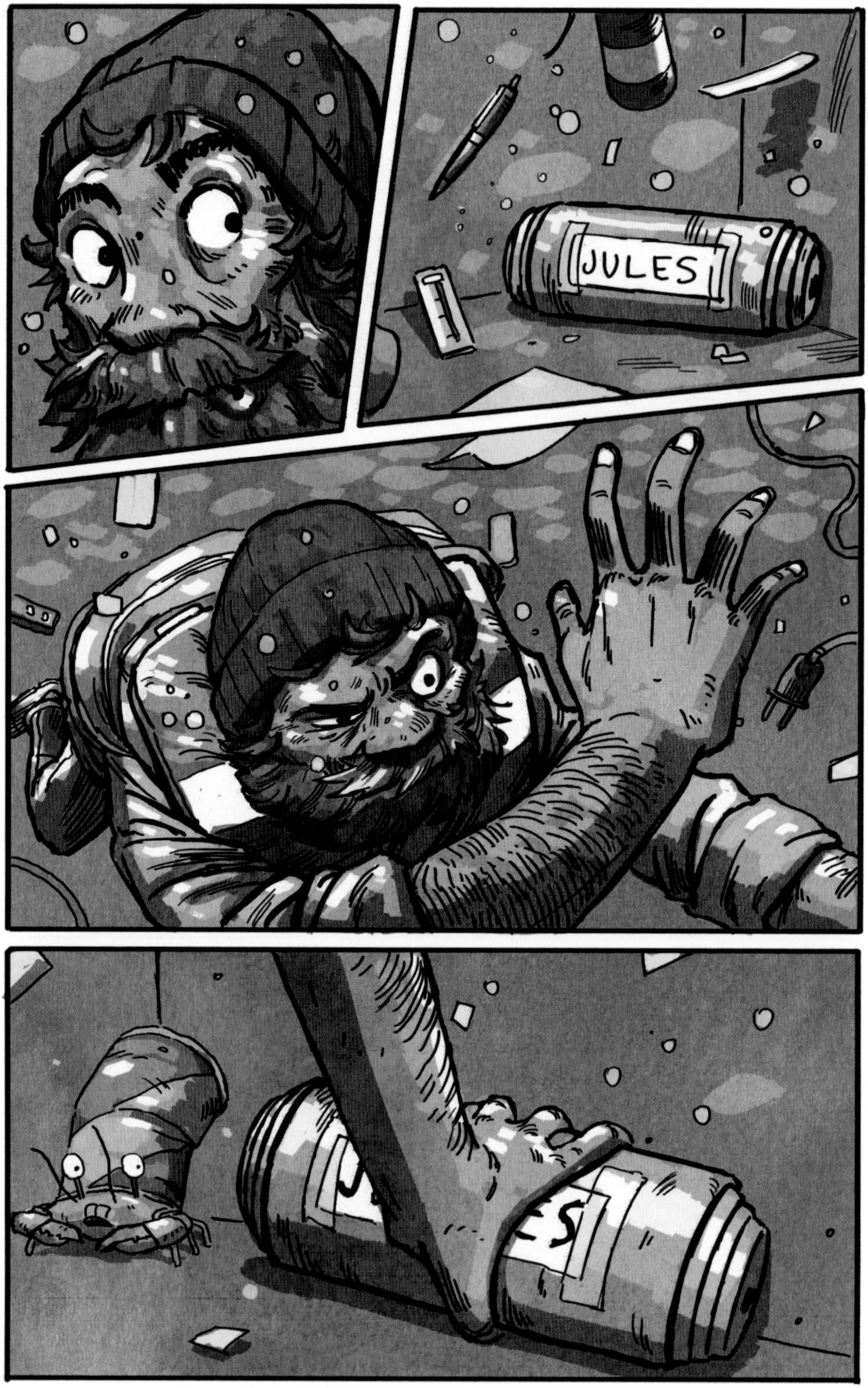
JULES

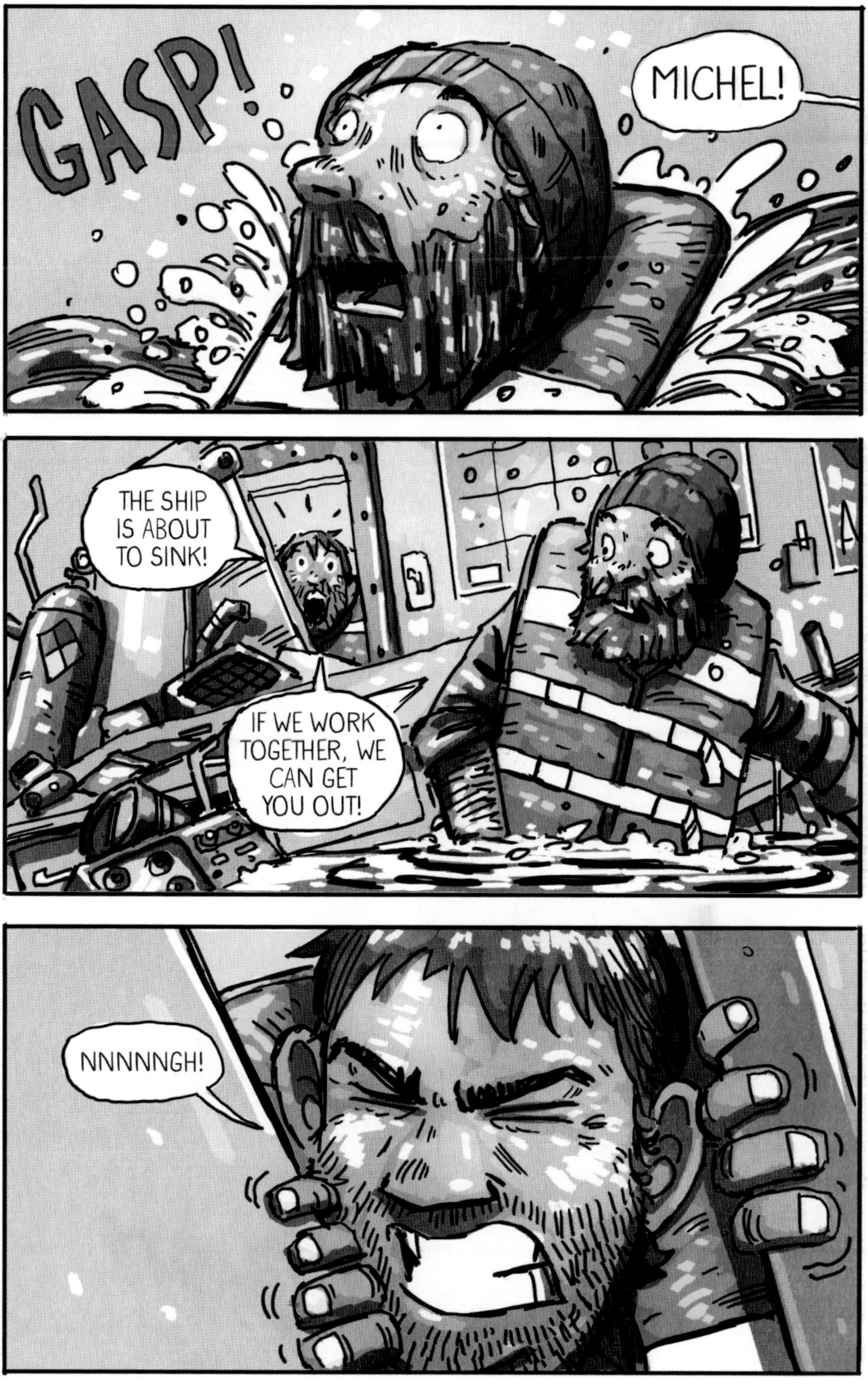
GASP!
MICHEL!
THE SHIP IS ABOUT TO SINK!
IF WE WORK TOGETHER, WE CAN GET YOU OUT!
NNNNNGH!

I'M GONNA GO GET HELP! I'LL BE R—
...PAUL... I'M NOT GOING TO MAKE IT.

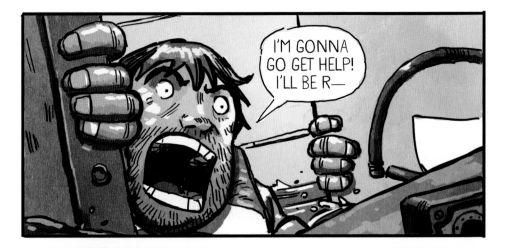

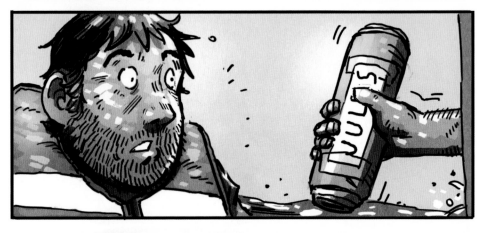

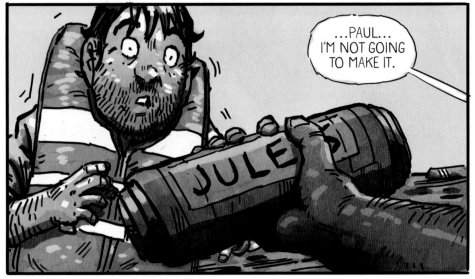

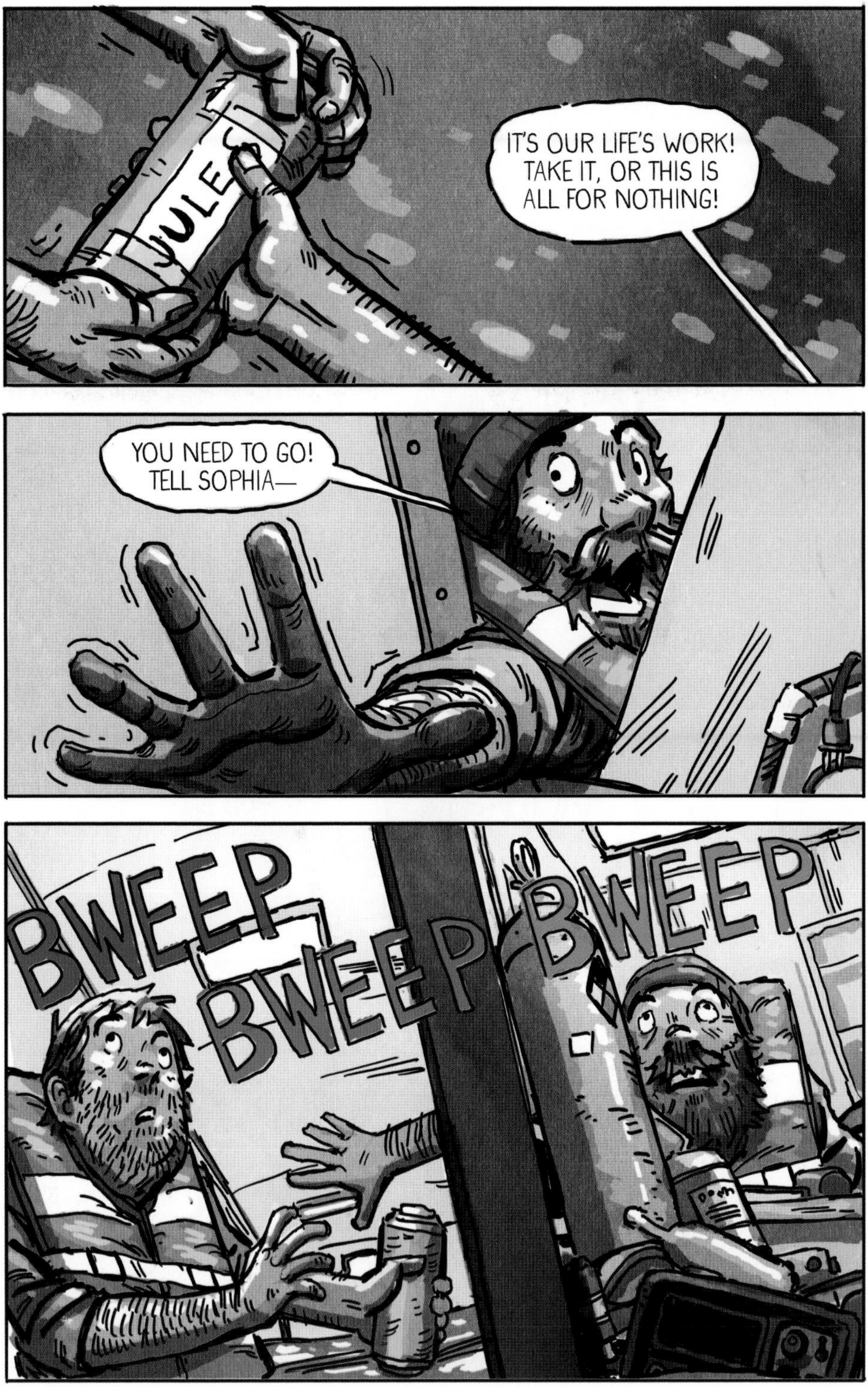
JULES
IT'S OUR LIFE'S WORK! TAKE IT, OR THIS IS ALL FOR NOTHING!
YOU NEED TO GO! TELL SOPHIA—
BWEEP
BWEEP
BWEEP

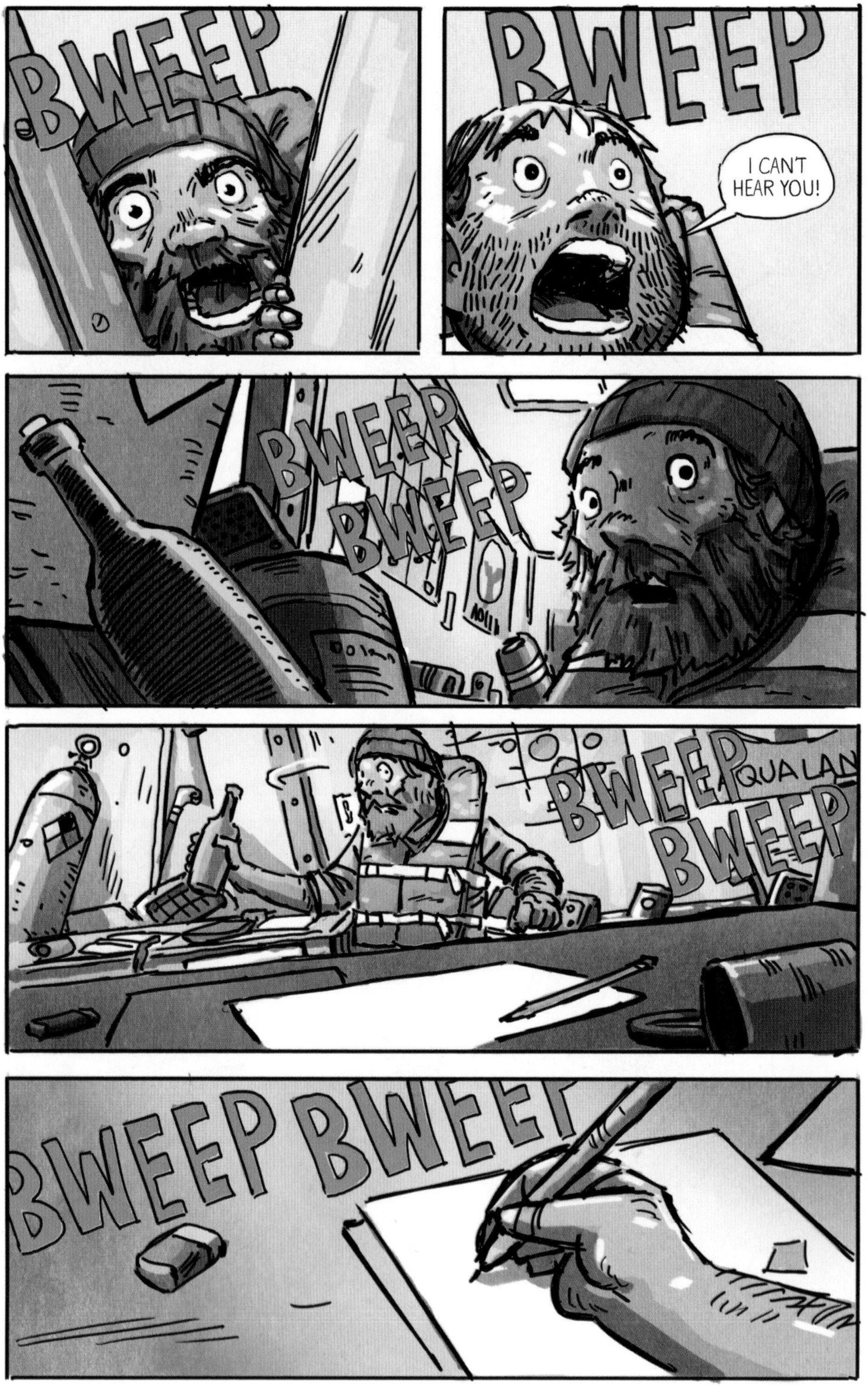
BWEEP
BWEEP
I CAN'T HEAR YOU!
BWEEP
BWEEP
BWEEP
BWEEP
QUALAN
BWEEP BWEEP

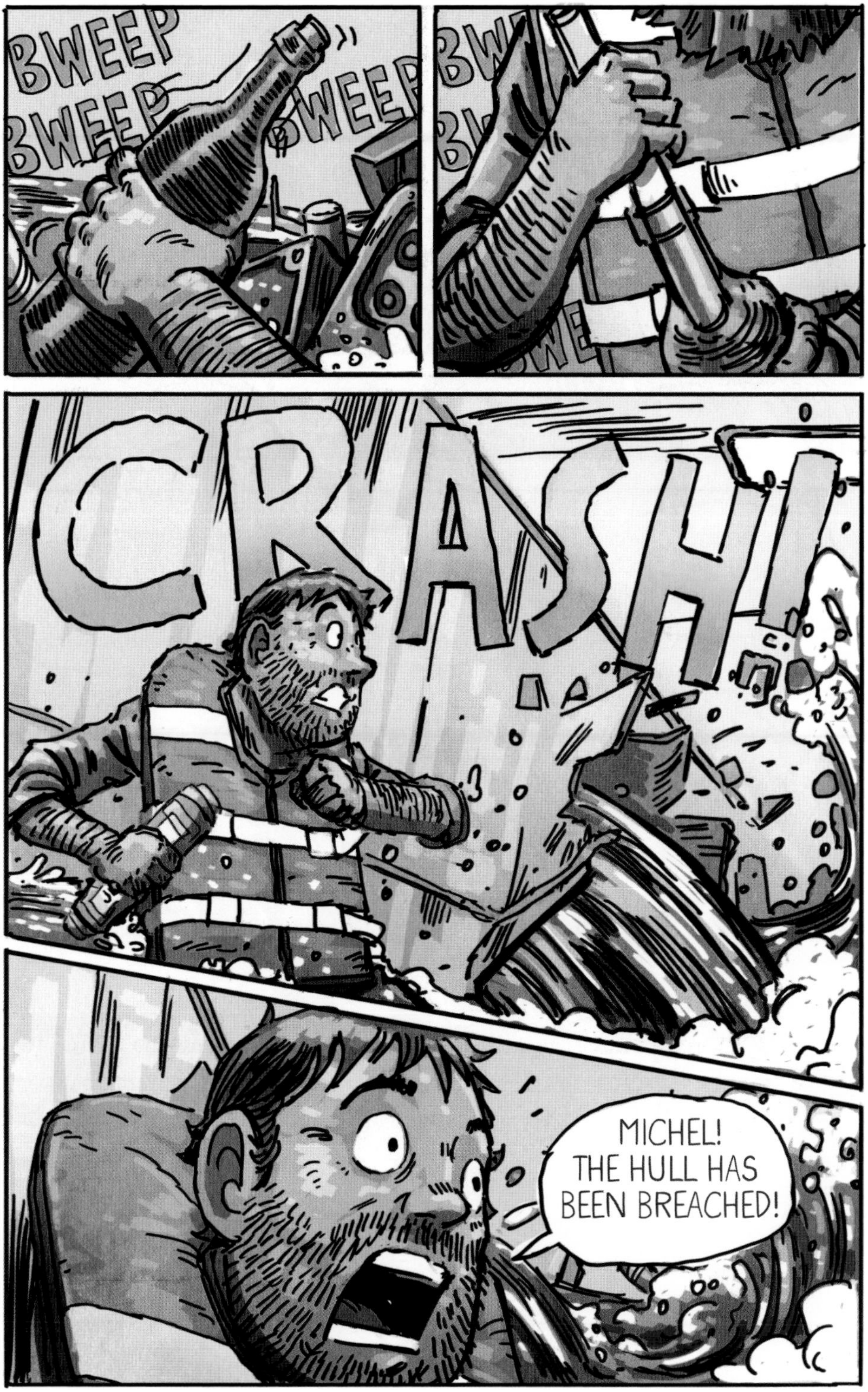
BWEEP
BWEEP
BWEEP
CRASH!
MICHEL! THE HULL HAS BEEN BREACHED!

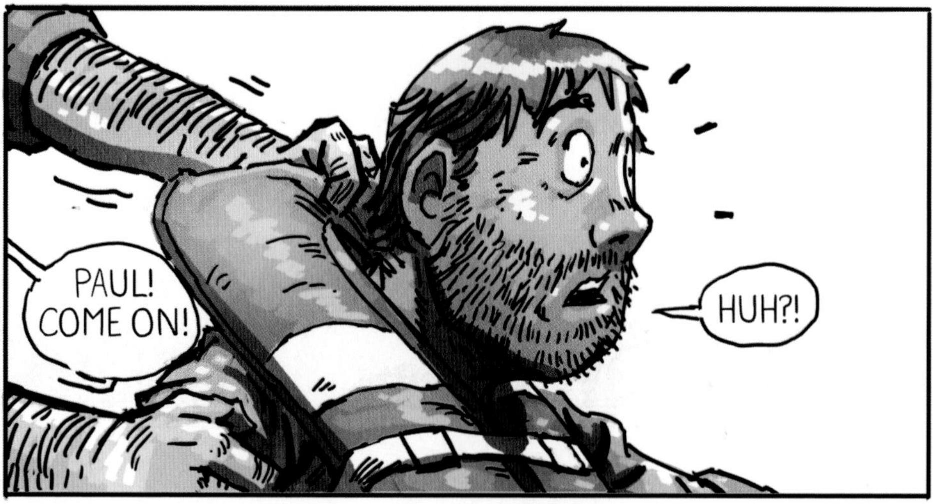
PAUL! COME ON!
HUH?!

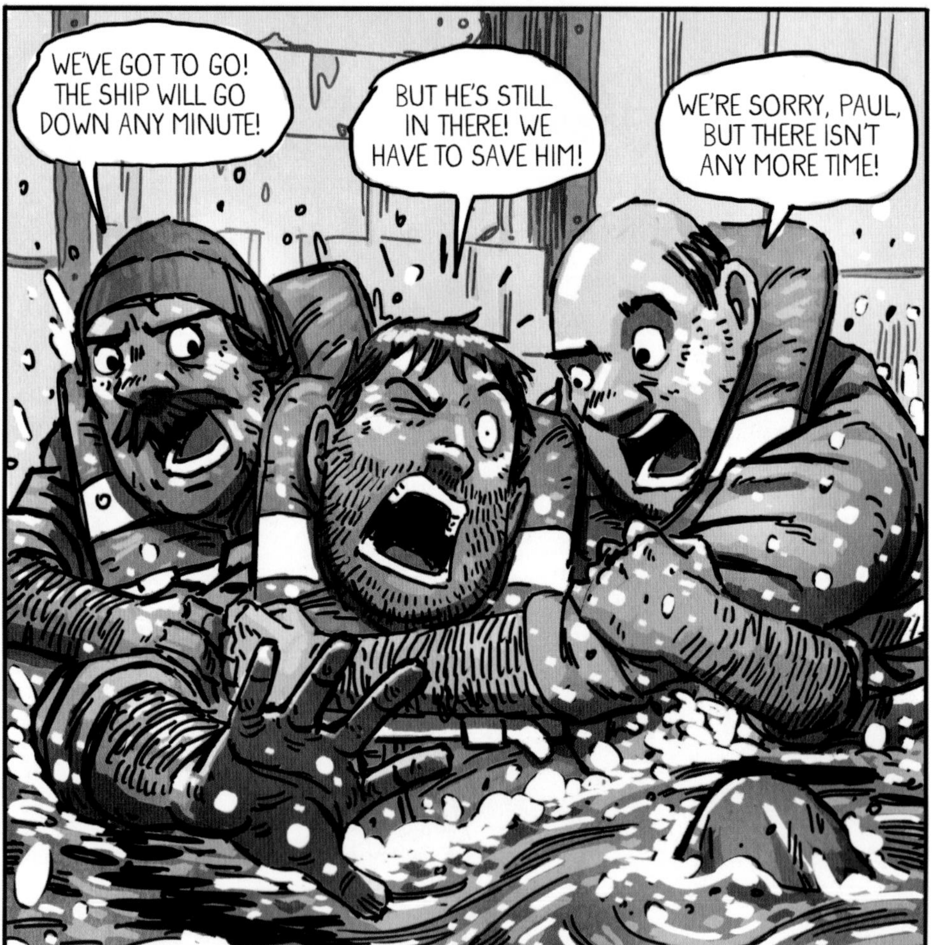
WE'VE GOT TO GO! THE SHIP WILL GO DOWN ANY MINUTE!
BUT HE'S STILL IN THERE! WE HAVE TO SAVE HIM!
WE'RE SORRY, PAUL, BUT THERE ISN'T ANY MORE TIME!

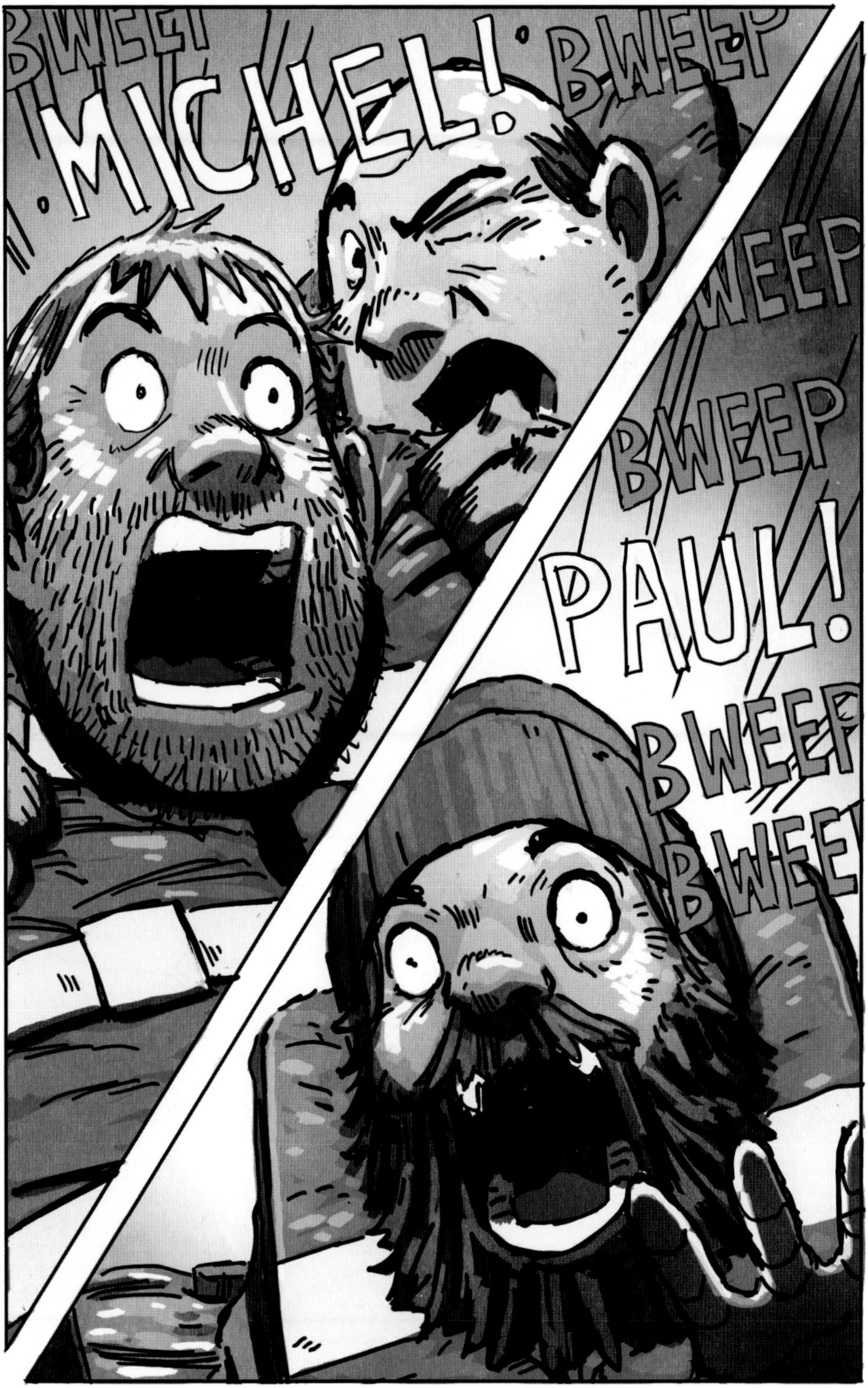
BWEEP
MICHEL!
BWEEP
BWEEP
BWEEP
PAUL!
BWEEP
BWEE

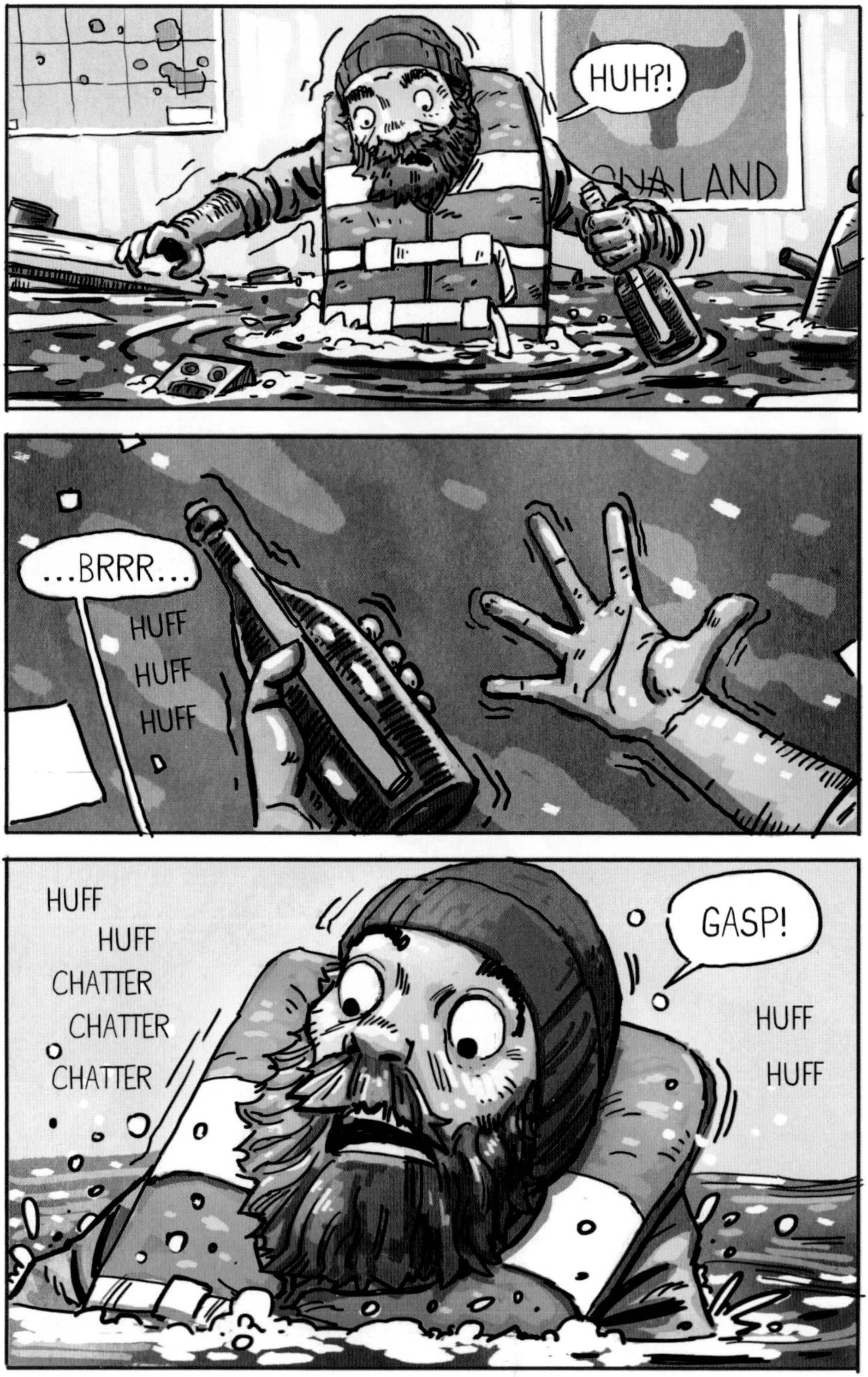
HUH?!
...BRRR...
HUFF
HUFF
HUFF
HUFF
HUFF
CHATTER
CHATTER
CHATTER
GASP!
HUFF
HUFF

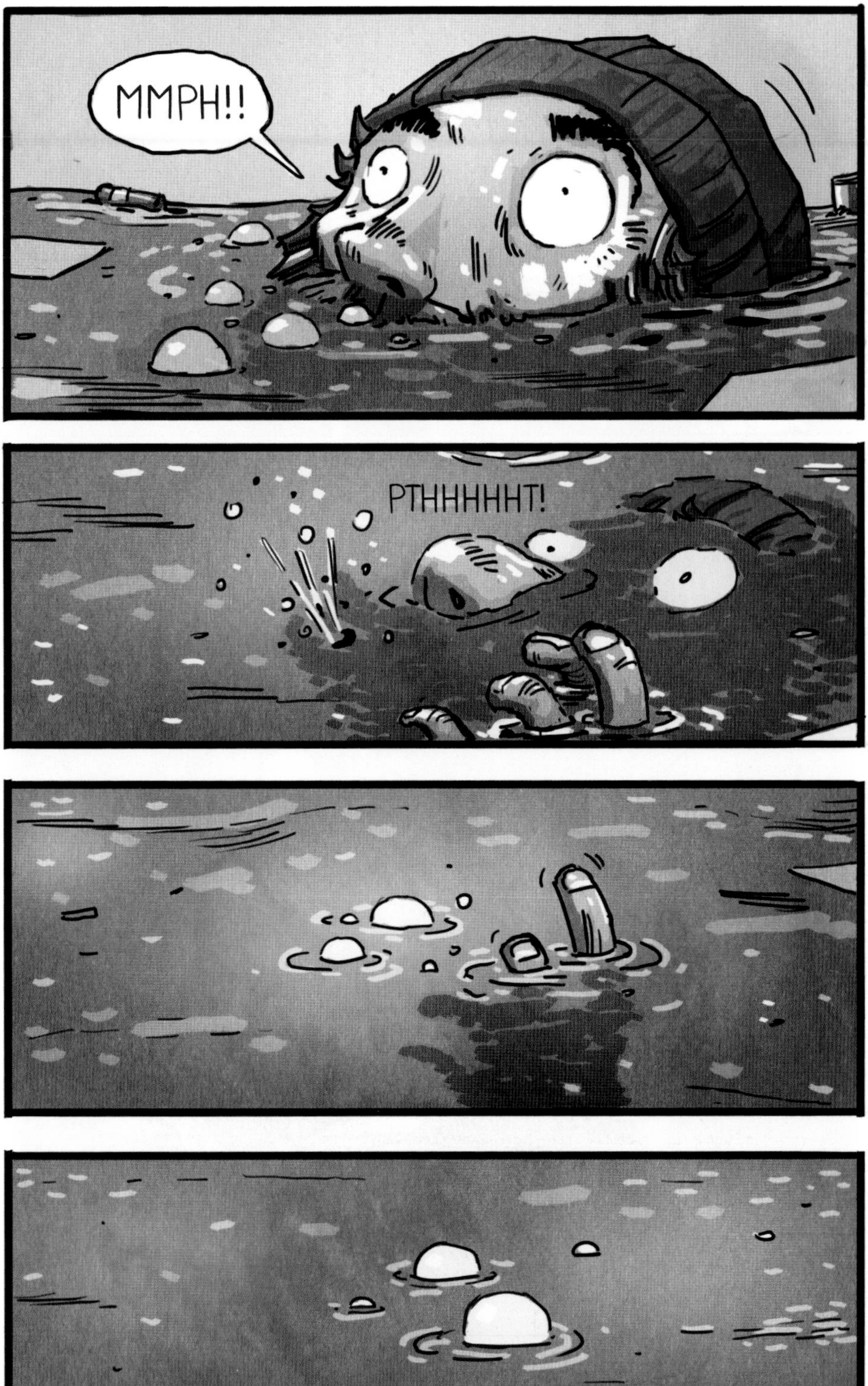
MMPH!!
PTHHHHHT!

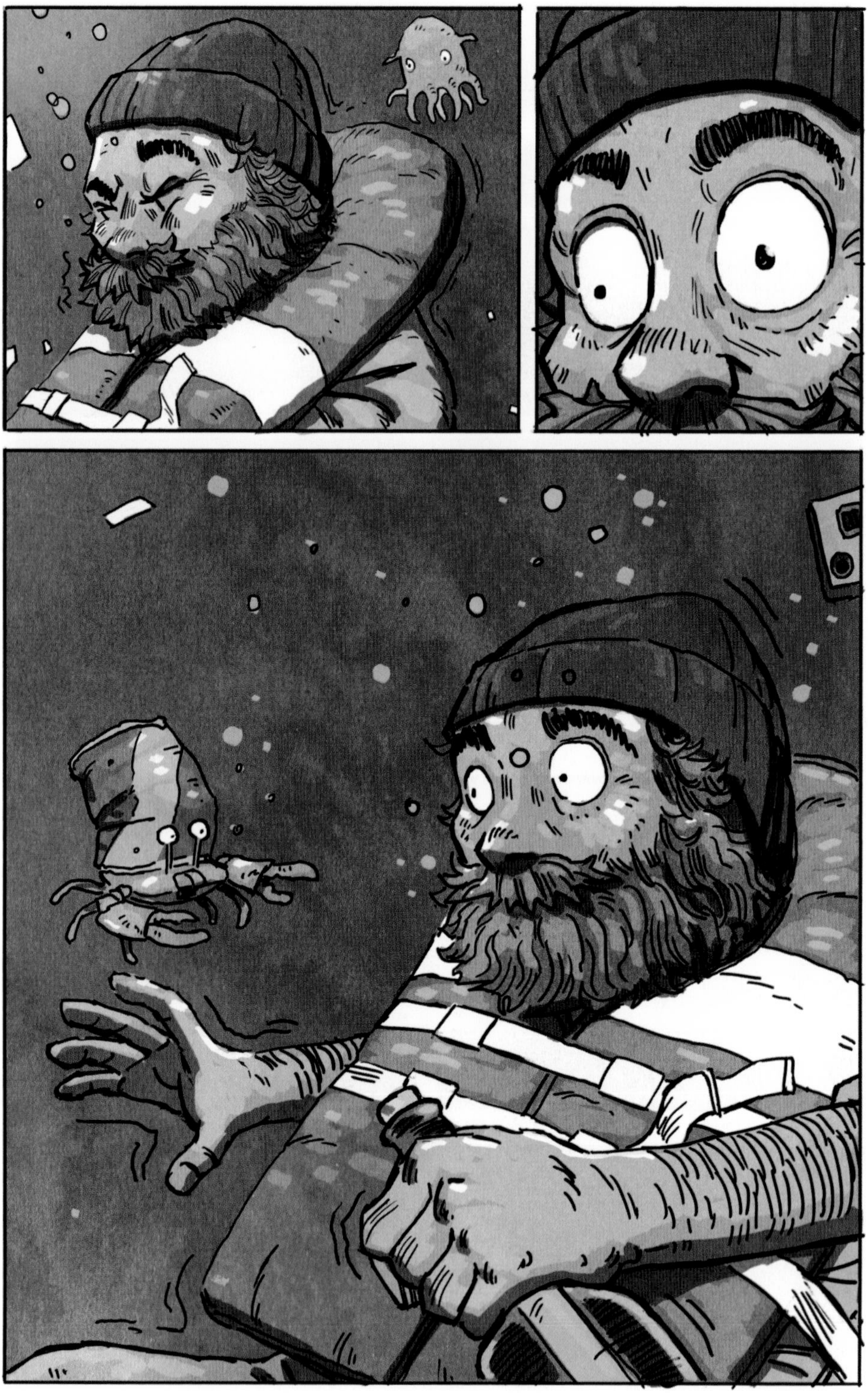

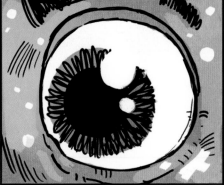

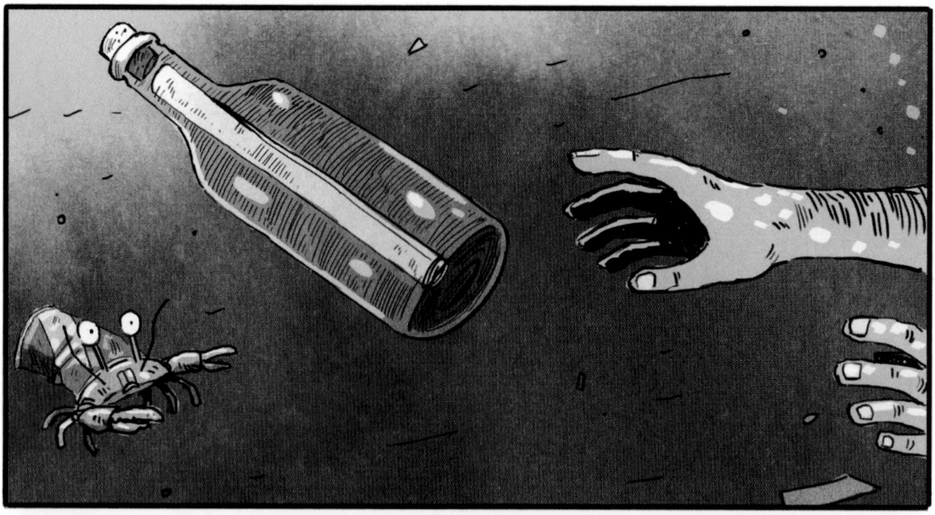

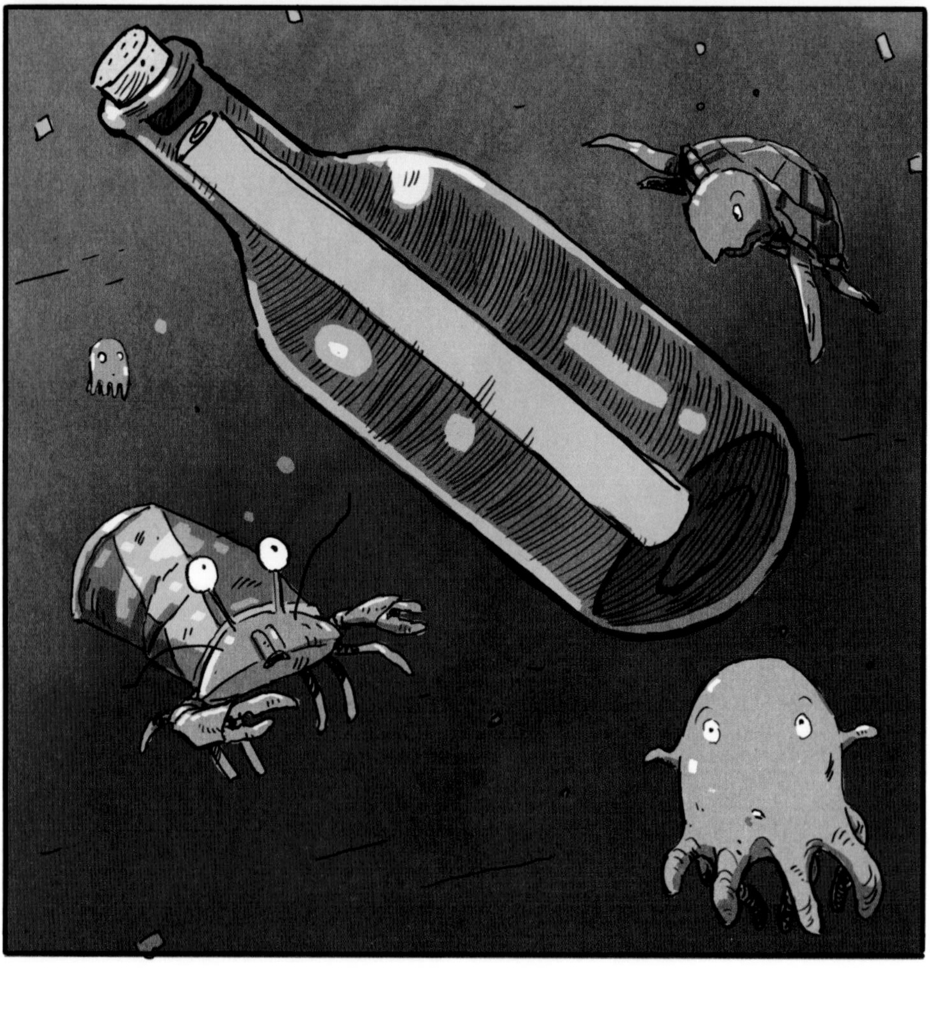

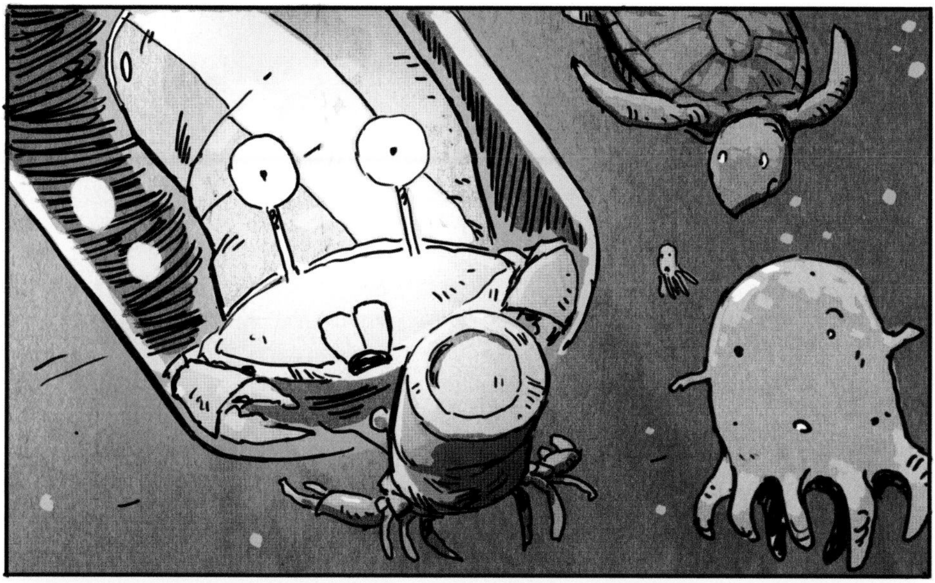

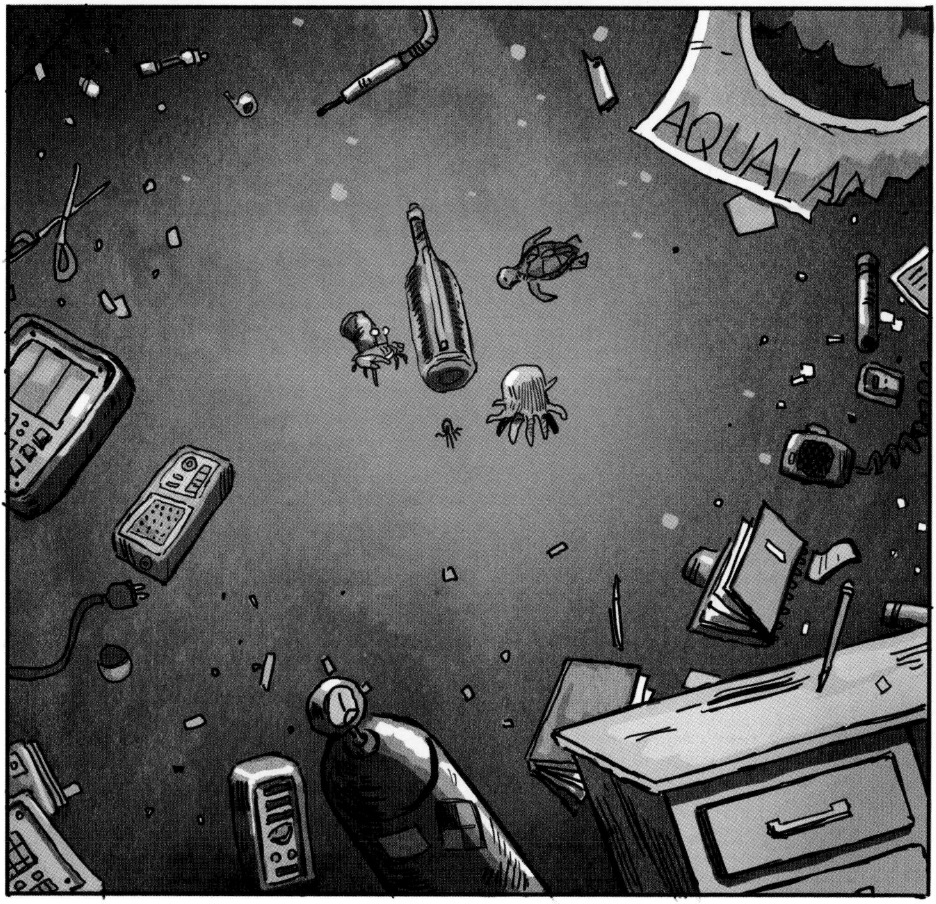
AQUALA

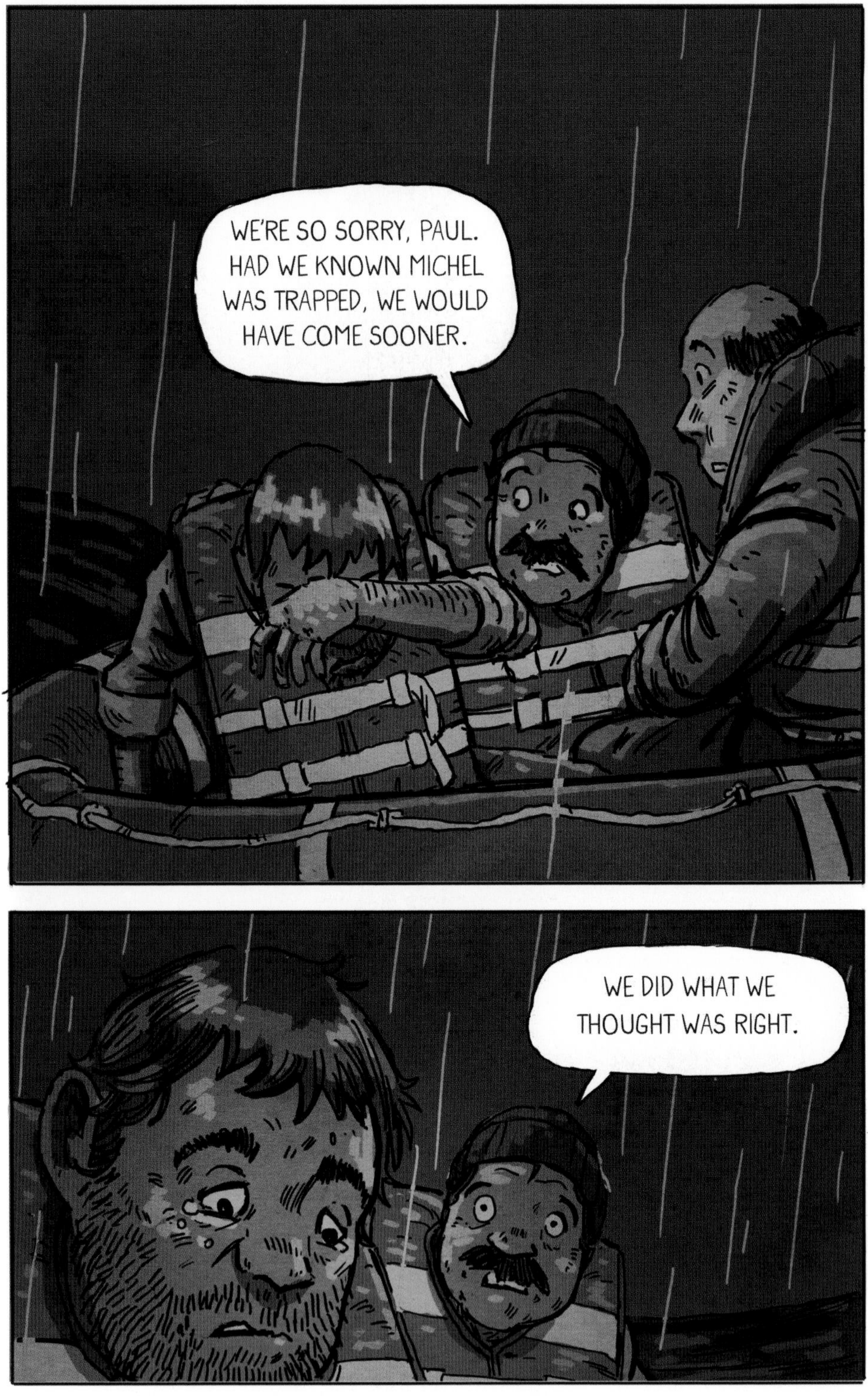
WE'RE SO SORRY, PAUL. HAD WE KNOWN MICHEL WAS TRAPPED, WE WOULD HAVE COME SOONER.
WE DID WHAT WE THOUGHT WAS RIGHT.

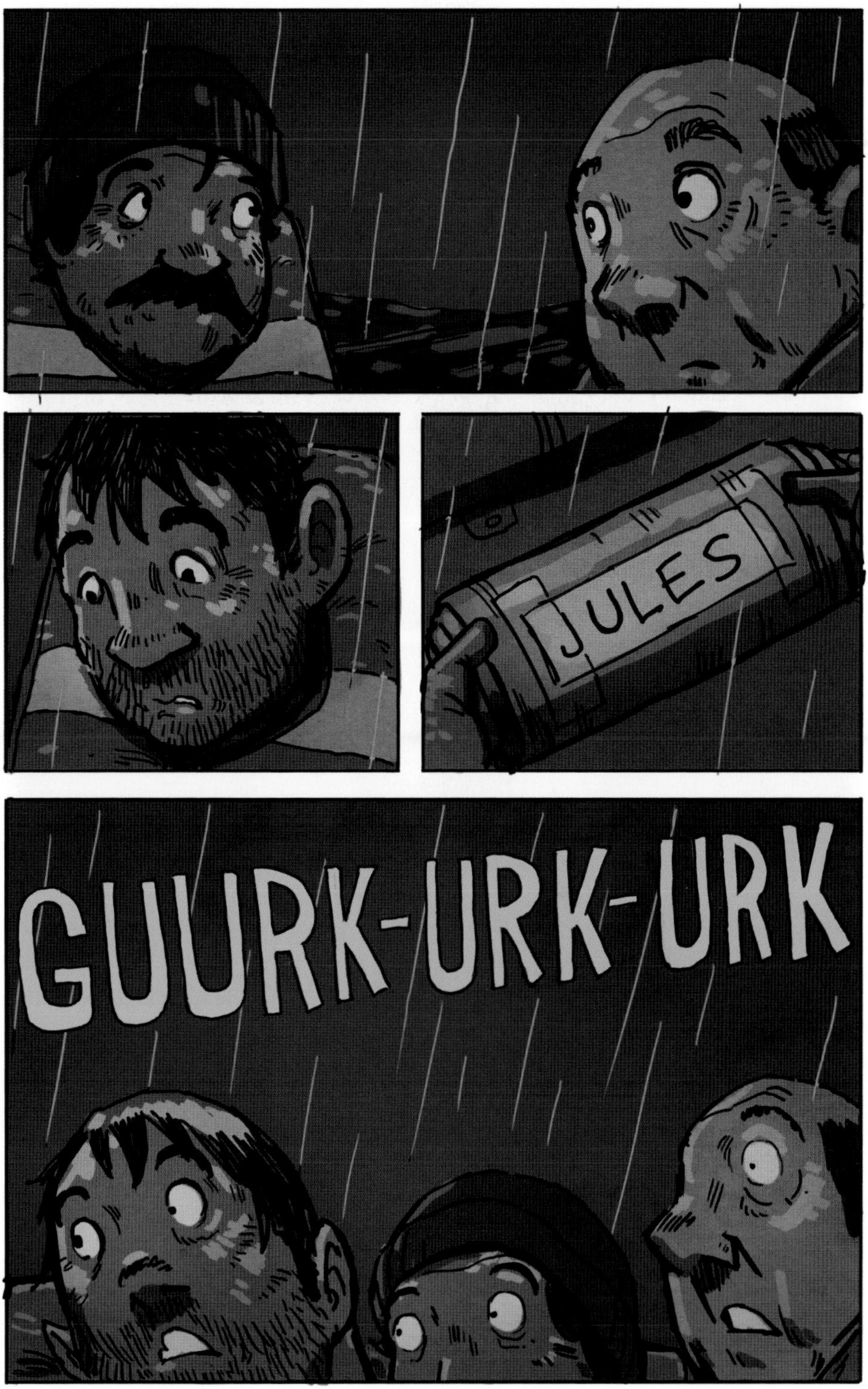
JULES
GUURK-URK-URK

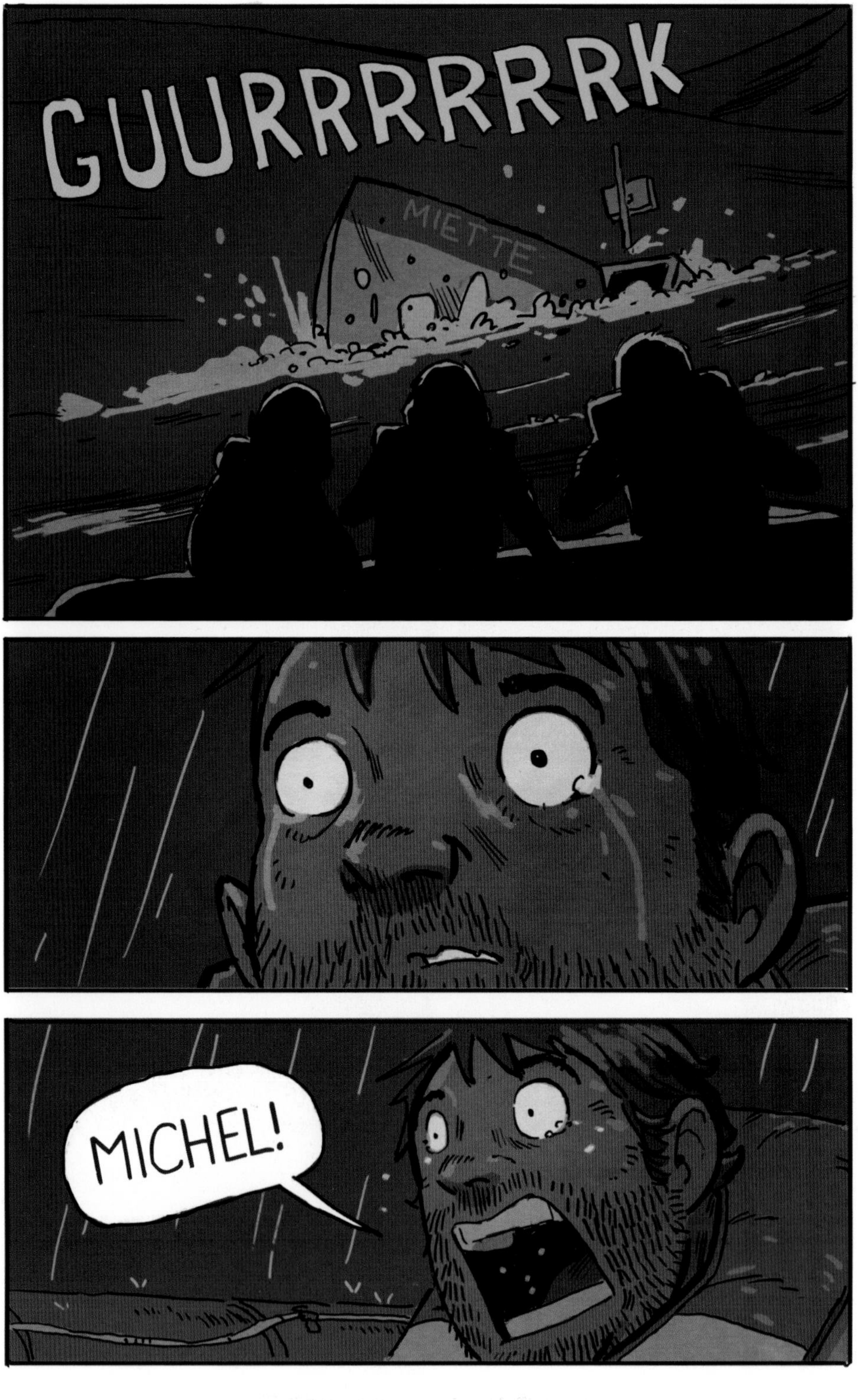
GUURRRRRRK
MIETTE
MICHEL!

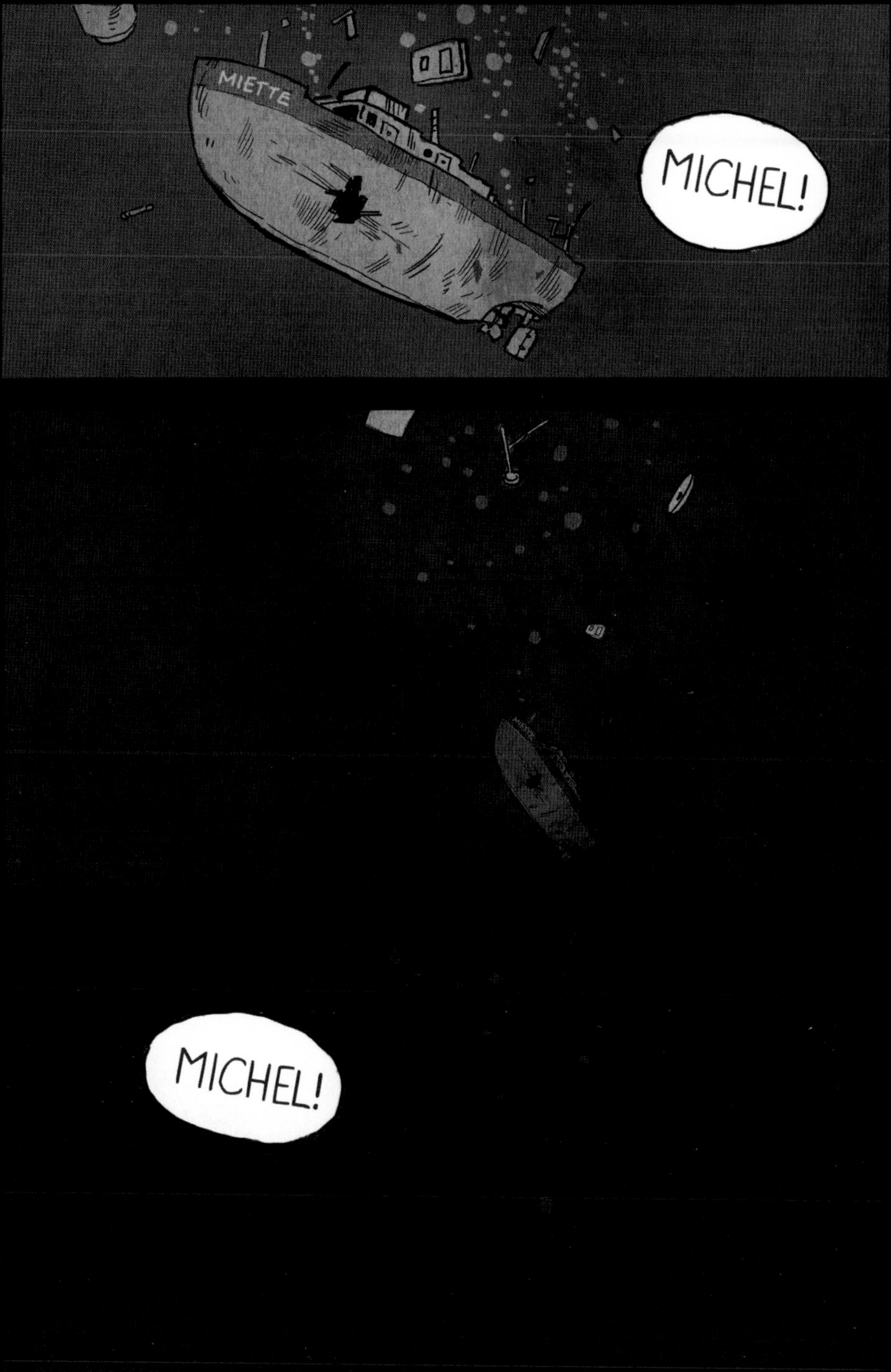
MIETTE
MICHEL!
MICHEL!

THE AQUANAUT

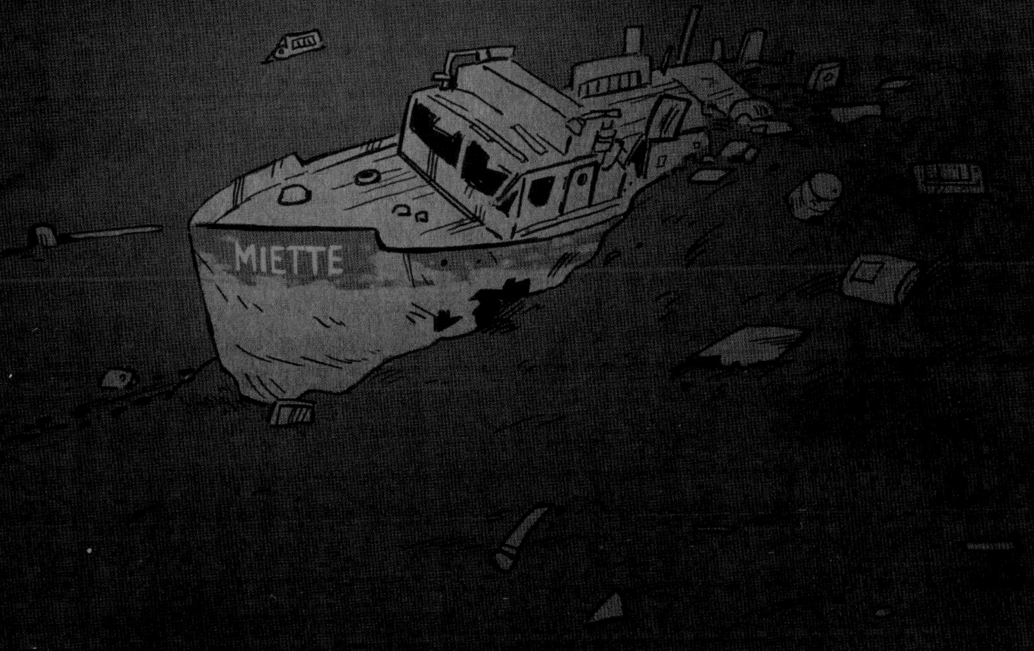
MIETTE

A STORY BY

DAN SANTAT

graphix
An Imprint of
SCHOLASTIC

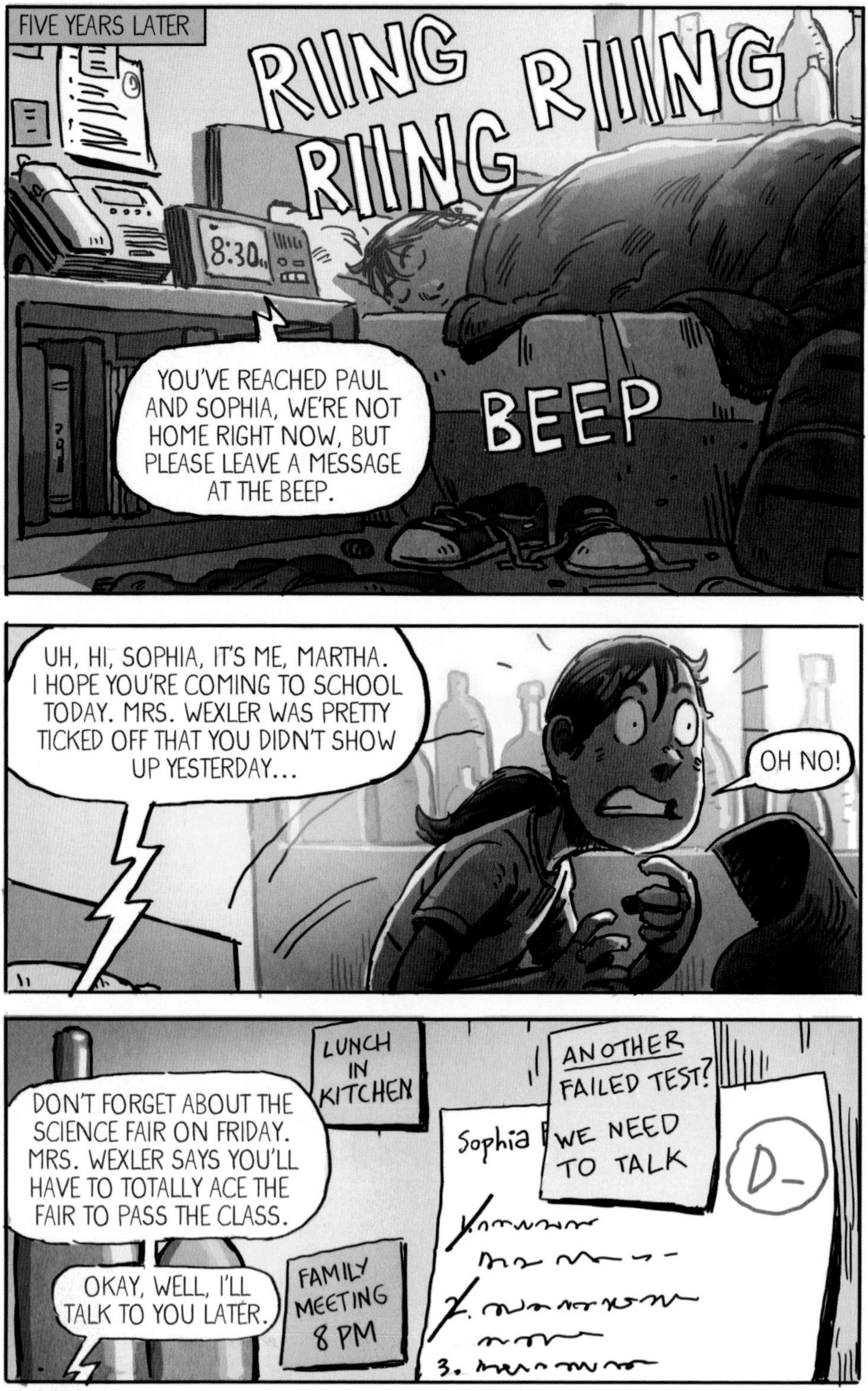
FIVE YEARS LATER
RIING RIING RIIING
8:30
YOU'VE REACHED PAUL AND SOPHIA, WE'RE NOT HOME RIGHT NOW, BUT PLEASE LEAVE A MESSAGE AT THE BEEP.
BEEP
UH, HI, SOPHIA, IT'S ME, MARTHA. I HOPE YOU'RE COMING TO SCHOOL TODAY. MRS. WEXLER WAS PRETTY TICKED OFF THAT YOU DIDN'T SHOW UP YESTERDAY...
OH NO!
LUNCH IN KITCHEN
ANOTHER FAILED TEST? WE NEED TO TALK
Sophia
D-
DON'T FORGET ABOUT THE SCIENCE FAIR ON FRIDAY. MRS. WEXLER SAYS YOU'LL HAVE TO TOTALLY ACE THE FAIR TO PASS THE CLASS.
FAMILY MEETING 8 PM
OKAY, WELL, I'LL TALK TO YOU LATER.

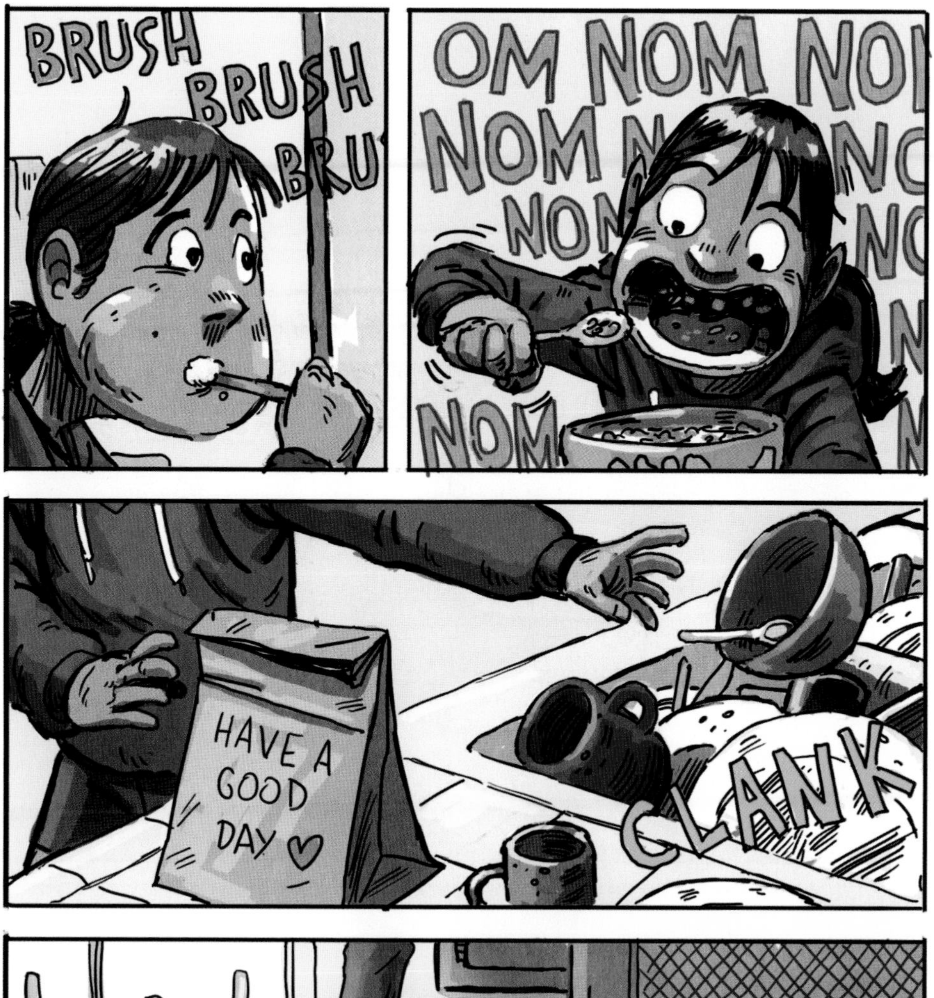
BRUSH
BRUSH
BRU
OM NOM NO
NOM N
NOM
NOM
HAVE A GOOD DAY
CLANK

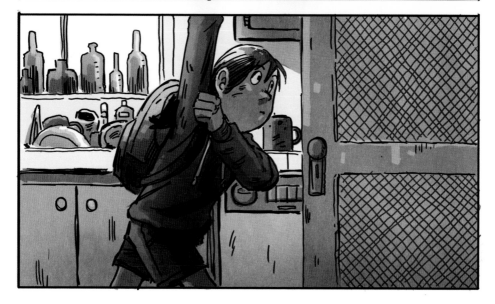

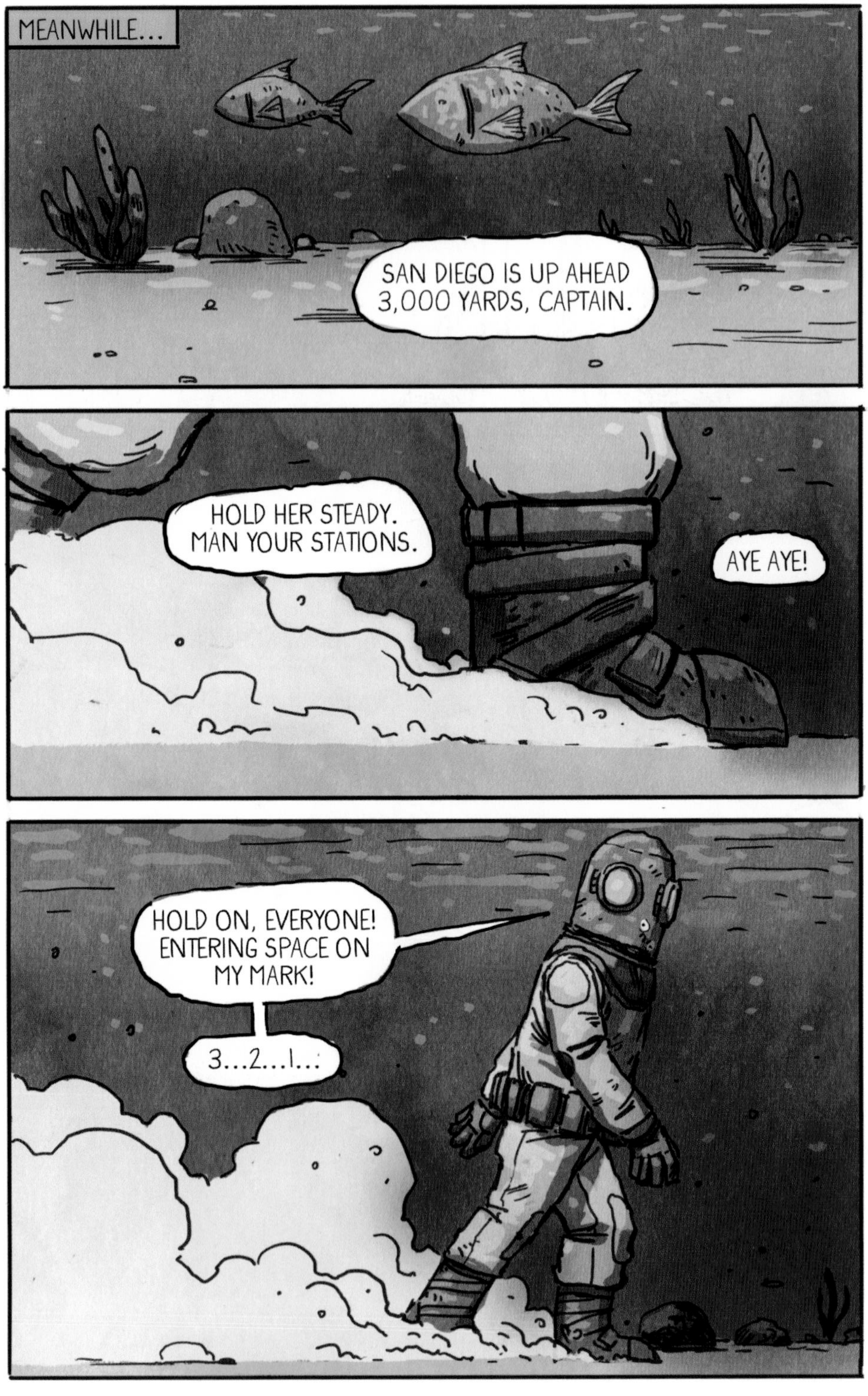
MEANWHILE...
SAN DIEGO IS UP AHEAD 3,000 YARDS, CAPTAIN.
HOLD HER STEADY. MAN YOUR STATIONS.
AYE AYE!
HOLD ON, EVERYONE! ENTERING SPACE ON MY MARK!
3...2...1...

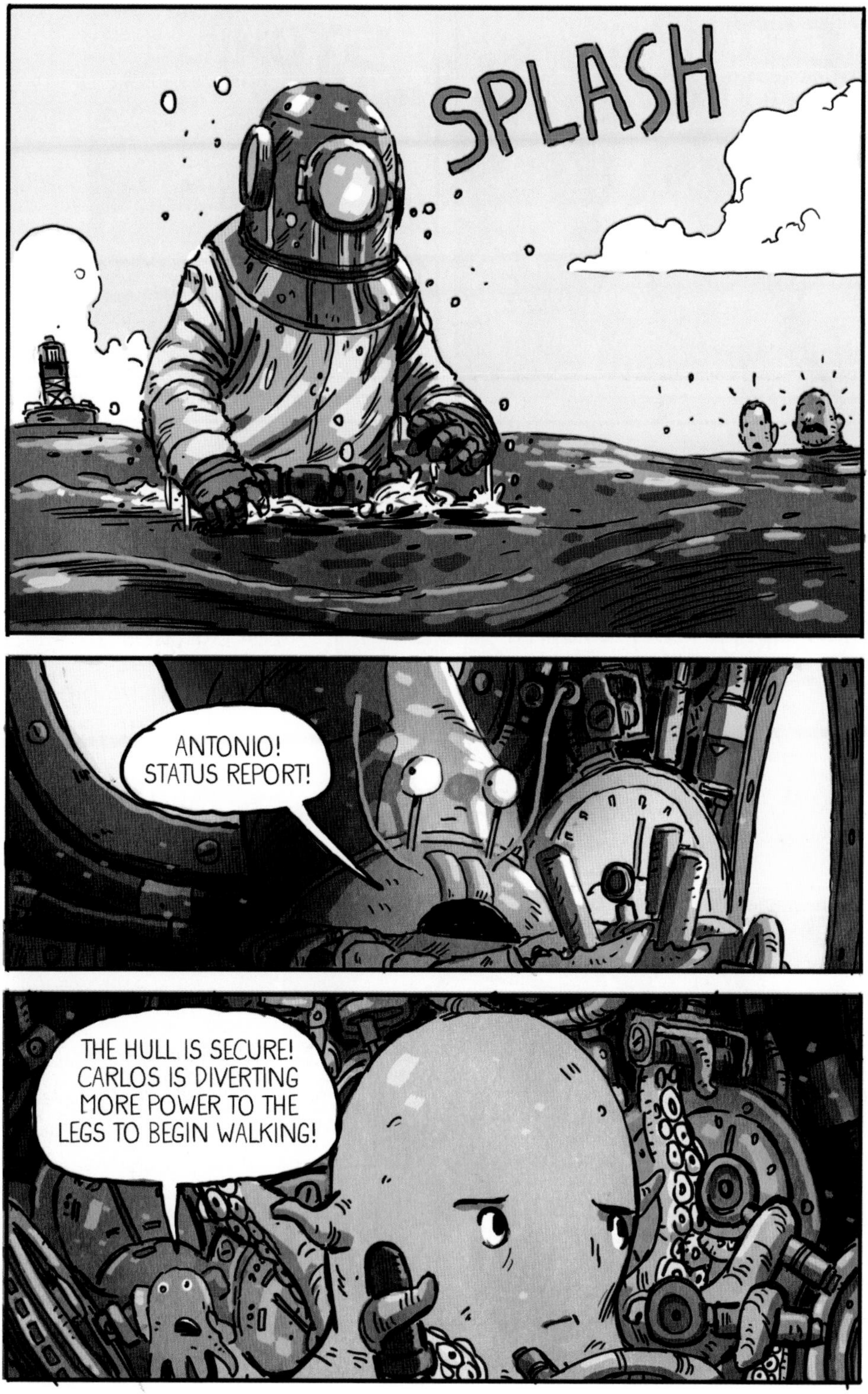
SPLASH
ANTONIO! STATUS REPORT!
THE HULL IS SECURE! CARLOS IS DIVERTING MORE POWER TO THE LEGS TO BEGIN WALKING!

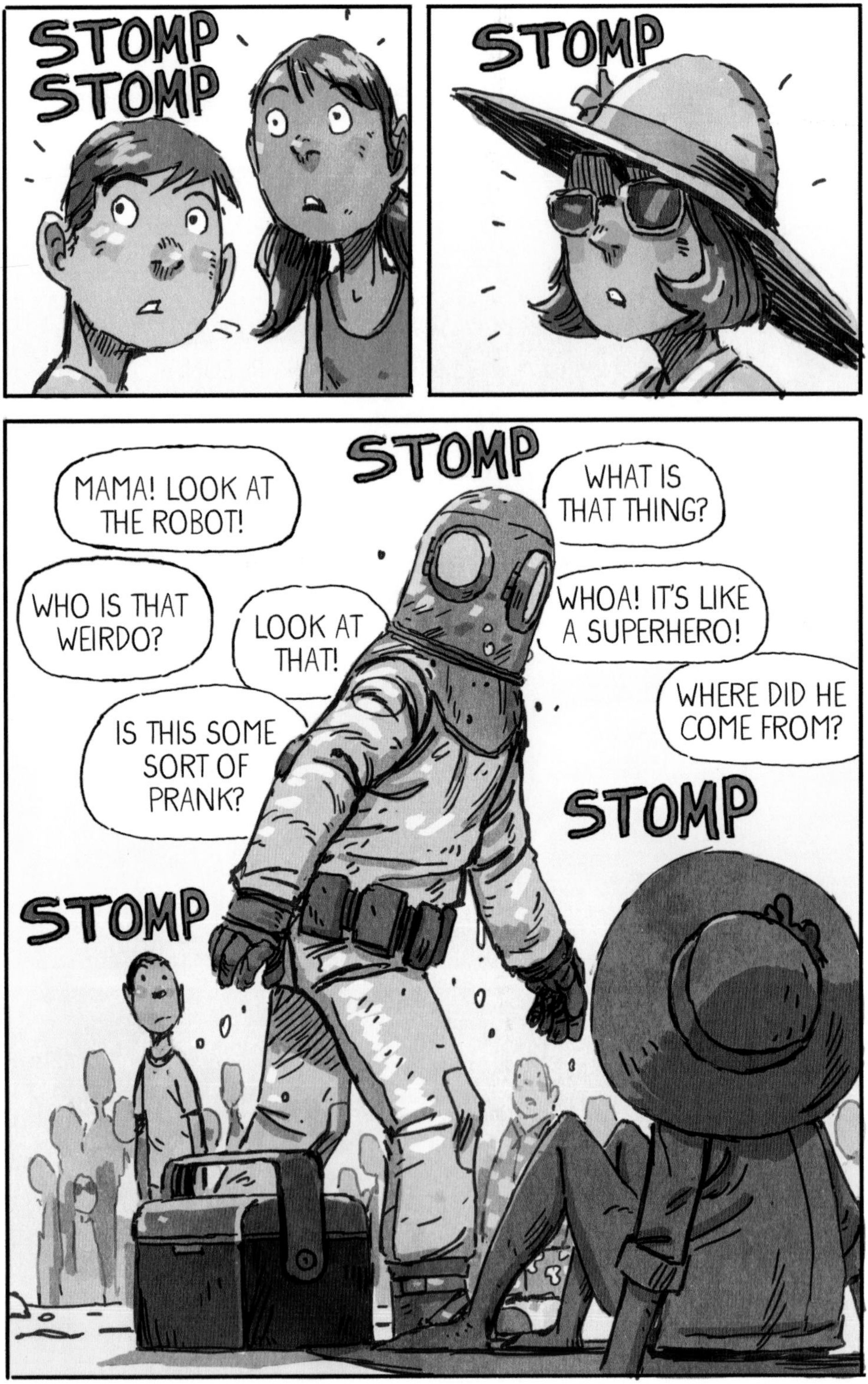
STOMP
STOMP
STOMP
STOMP
MAMA! LOOK AT THE ROBOT!
WHAT IS THAT THING?
WHO IS THAT WEIRDO?
LOOK AT THAT!
WHOA! IT'S LIKE A SUPERHERO!
WHERE DID HE COME FROM?
IS THIS SOME SORT OF PRANK?
STOMP
STOMP

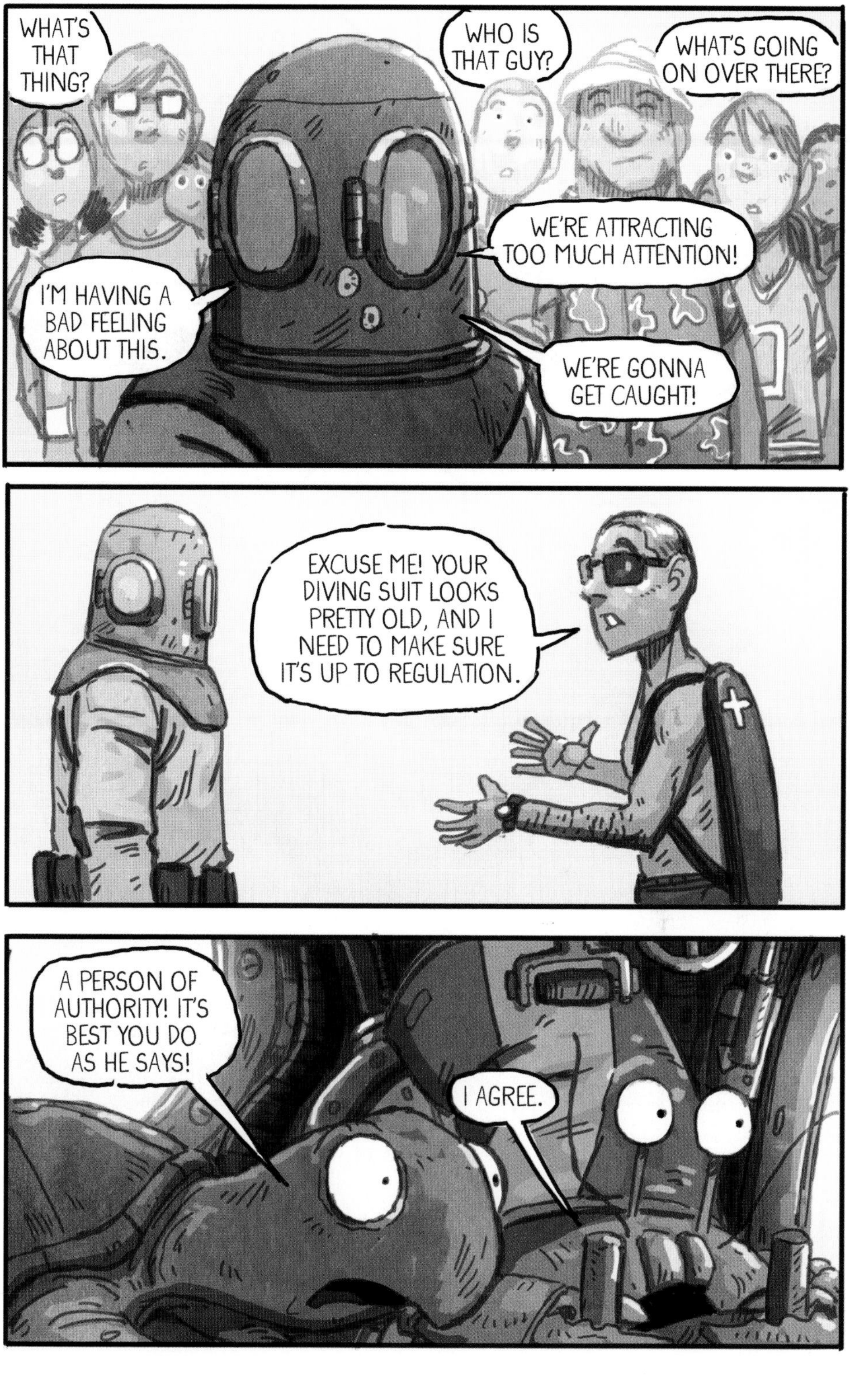
WHAT'S THAT THING?
WHO IS THAT GUY?
WHAT'S GOING ON OVER THERE?
WE'RE ATTRACTING TOO MUCH ATTENTION!
I'M HAVING A BAD FEELING ABOUT THIS.
WE'RE GONNA GET CAUGHT!
EXCUSE ME! YOUR DIVING SUIT LOOKS PRETTY OLD, AND I NEED TO MAKE SURE IT'S UP TO REGULATION.
A PERSON OF AUTHORITY! IT'S BEST YOU DO AS HE SAYS!
I AGREE.

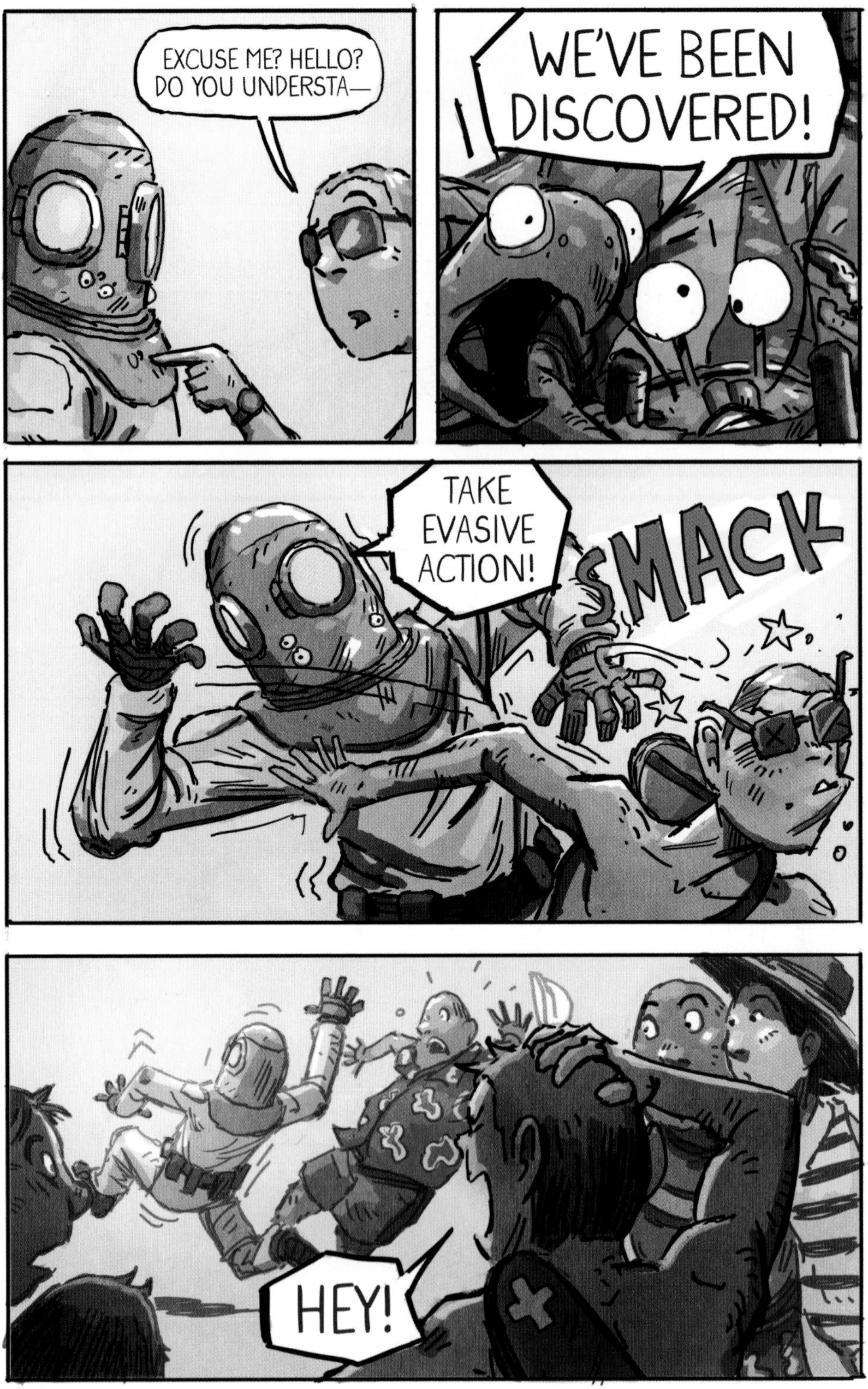
EXCUSE ME? HELLO? DO YOU UNDERSTA—
WE'VE BEEN DISCOVERED!
TAKE EVASIVE ACTION!
SMACK
HEY!

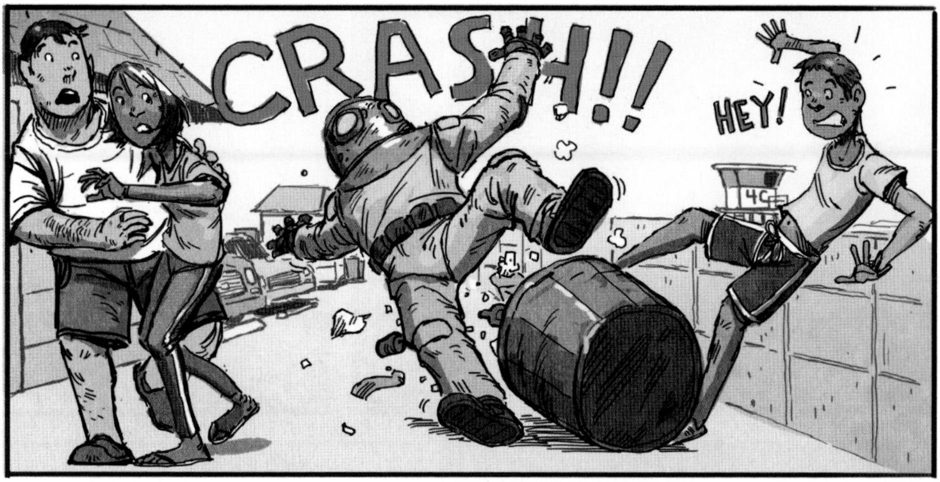
CRASH!!
HEY!

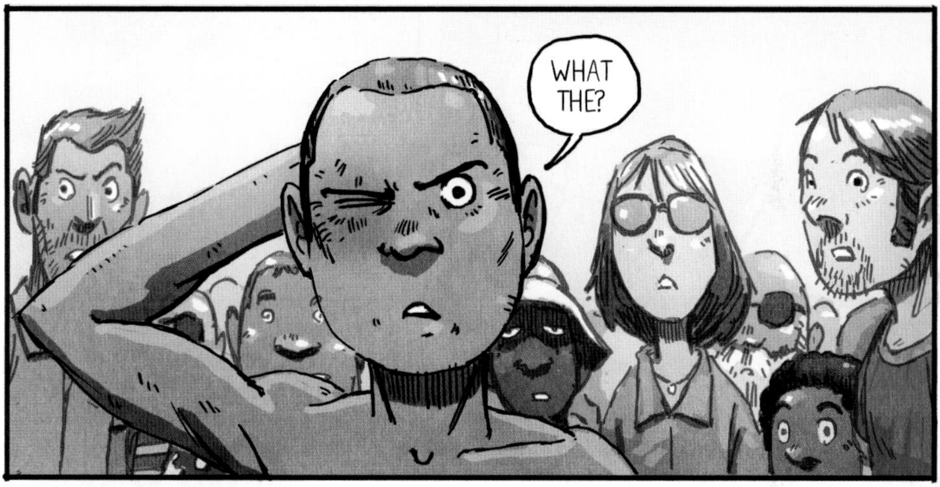
WHAT THE?

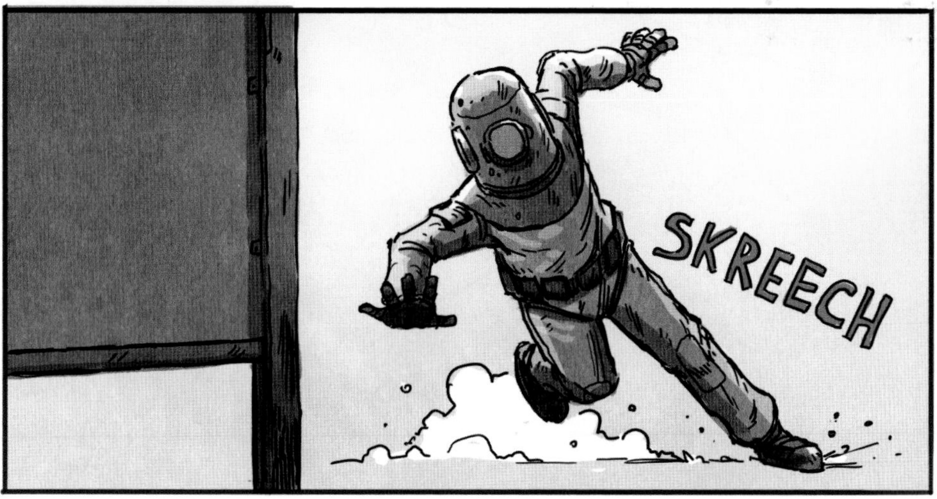
SKREECH

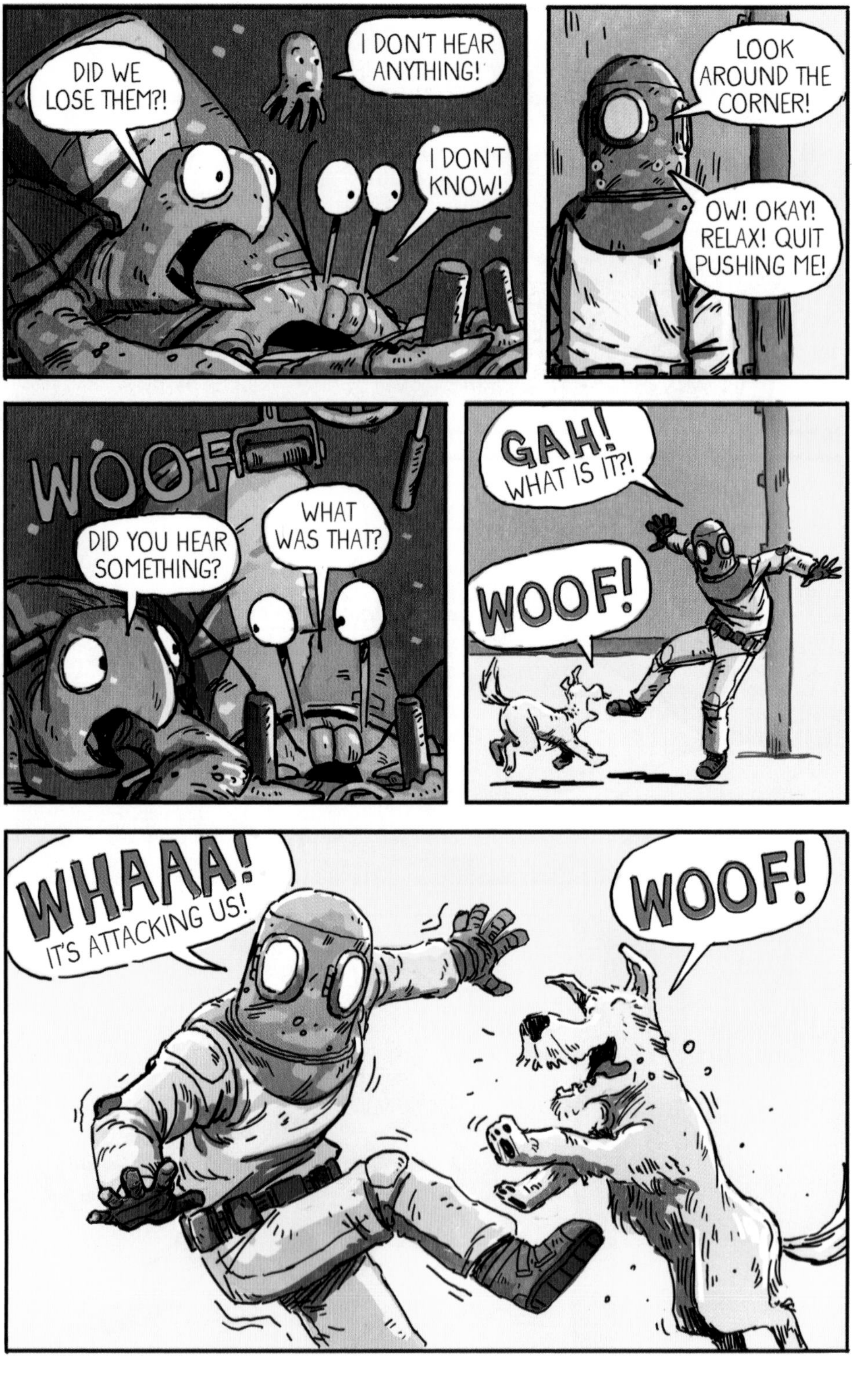
DID WE LOSE THEM?!
I DON'T HEAR ANYTHING!
I DON'T KNOW!
LOOK AROUND THE CORNER!
OW! OKAY! RELAX! QUIT PUSHING ME!
WOOF
DID YOU HEAR SOMETHING?
WHAT WAS THAT?
GAH! WHAT IS IT?!
WOOF!
WHAAA! IT'S ATTACKING US!
WOOF!

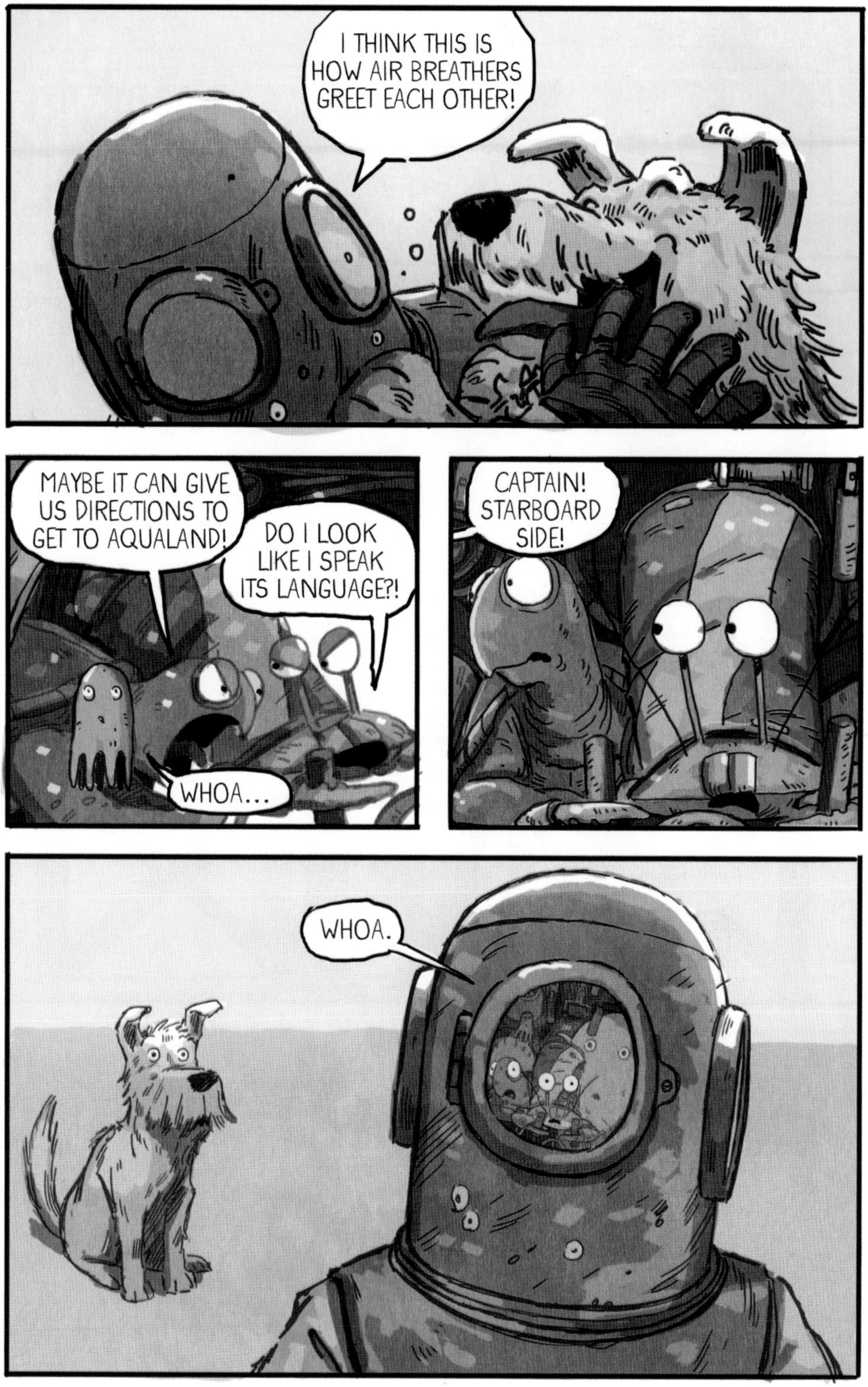
I THINK THIS IS HOW AIR BREATHERS GREET EACH OTHER!
MAYBE IT CAN GIVE US DIRECTIONS TO GET TO AQUALAND!
DO I LOOK LIKE I SPEAK ITS LANGUAGE?!
WHOA...
CAPTAIN! STARBOARD SIDE!
WHOA.

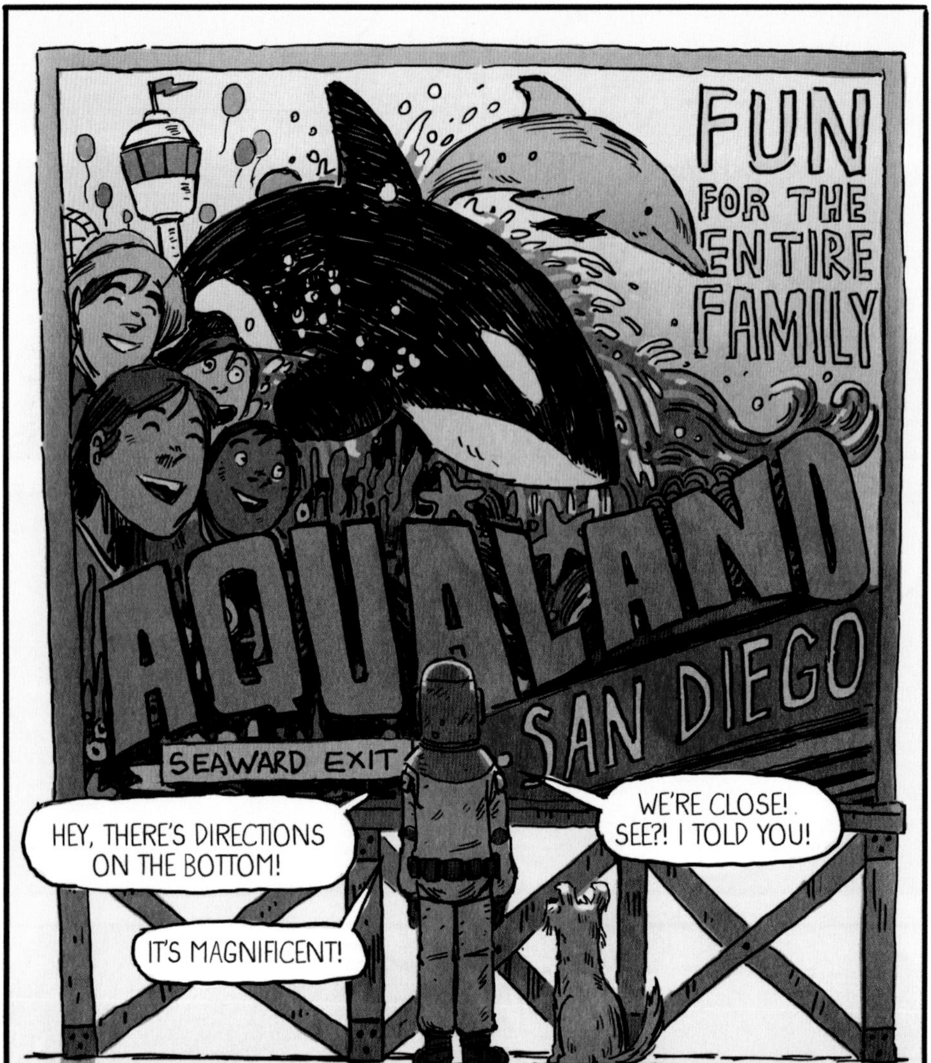
FUN FOR THE ENTIRE FAMILY
AQUALAND
SAN DIEGO
SEAWARD EXIT
HEY, THERE'S DIRECTIONS ON THE BOTTOM!
IT'S MAGNIFICENT!
WE'RE CLOSE! SEE?! I TOLD YOU!

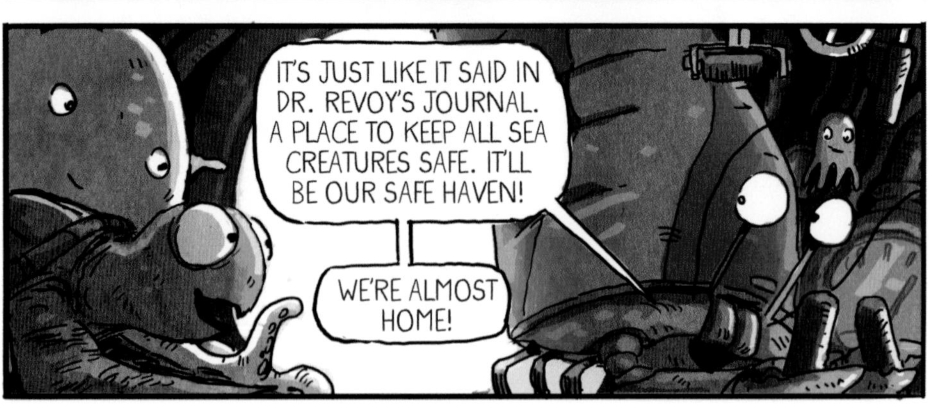
IT'S JUST LIKE IT SAID IN DR. REVOY'S JOURNAL. A PLACE TO KEEP ALL SEA CREATURES SAFE. IT'LL BE OUR SAFE HAVEN!
WE'RE ALMOST HOME!

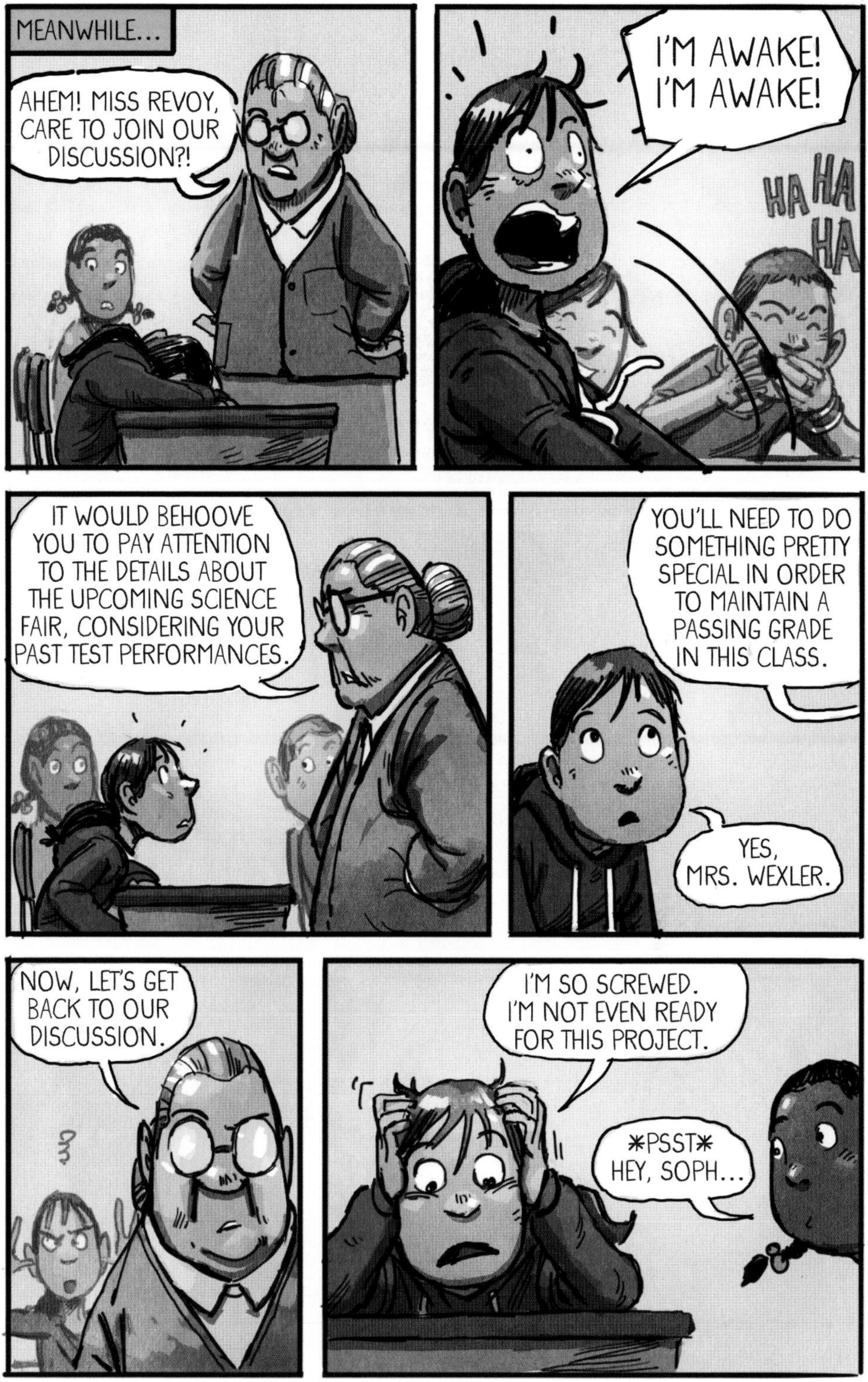

MEANWHILE...
AHEM! MISS REVOY, CARE TO JOIN OUR DISCUSSION?!
I'M AWAKE! I'M AWAKE!
HA HA HA
IT WOULD BEHOOVE YOU TO PAY ATTENTION TO THE DETAILS ABOUT THE UPCOMING SCIENCE FAIR, CONSIDERING YOUR PAST TEST PERFORMANCES.
YOU'LL NEED TO DO SOMETHING PRETTY SPECIAL IN ORDER TO MAINTAIN A PASSING GRADE IN THIS CLASS.
YES, MRS. WEXLER.
NOW, LET'S GET BACK TO OUR DISCUSSION.
I'M SO SCREWED. I'M NOT EVEN READY FOR THIS PROJECT.
PSST HEY, SOPH...

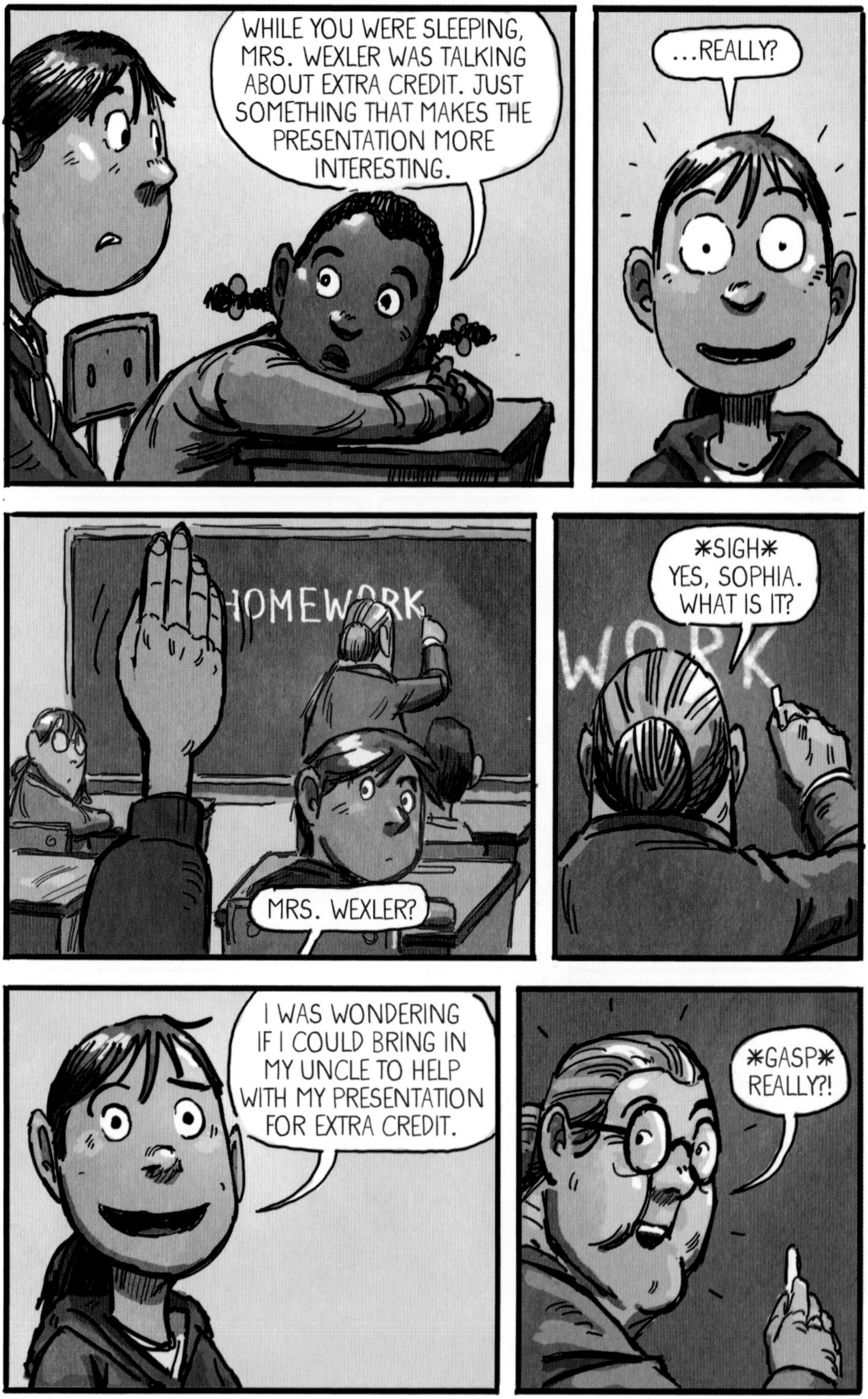

WHILE YOU WERE SLEEPING, MRS. WEXLER WAS TALKING ABOUT EXTRA CREDIT. JUST SOMETHING THAT MAKES THE PRESENTATION MORE INTERESTING.
...REALLY?
HOMEWORK
MRS. WEXLER?
WORK
SIGH YES, SOPHIA. WHAT IS IT?
I WAS WONDERING IF I COULD BRING IN MY UNCLE TO HELP WITH MY PRESENTATION FOR EXTRA CREDIT.
GASP REALLY?!

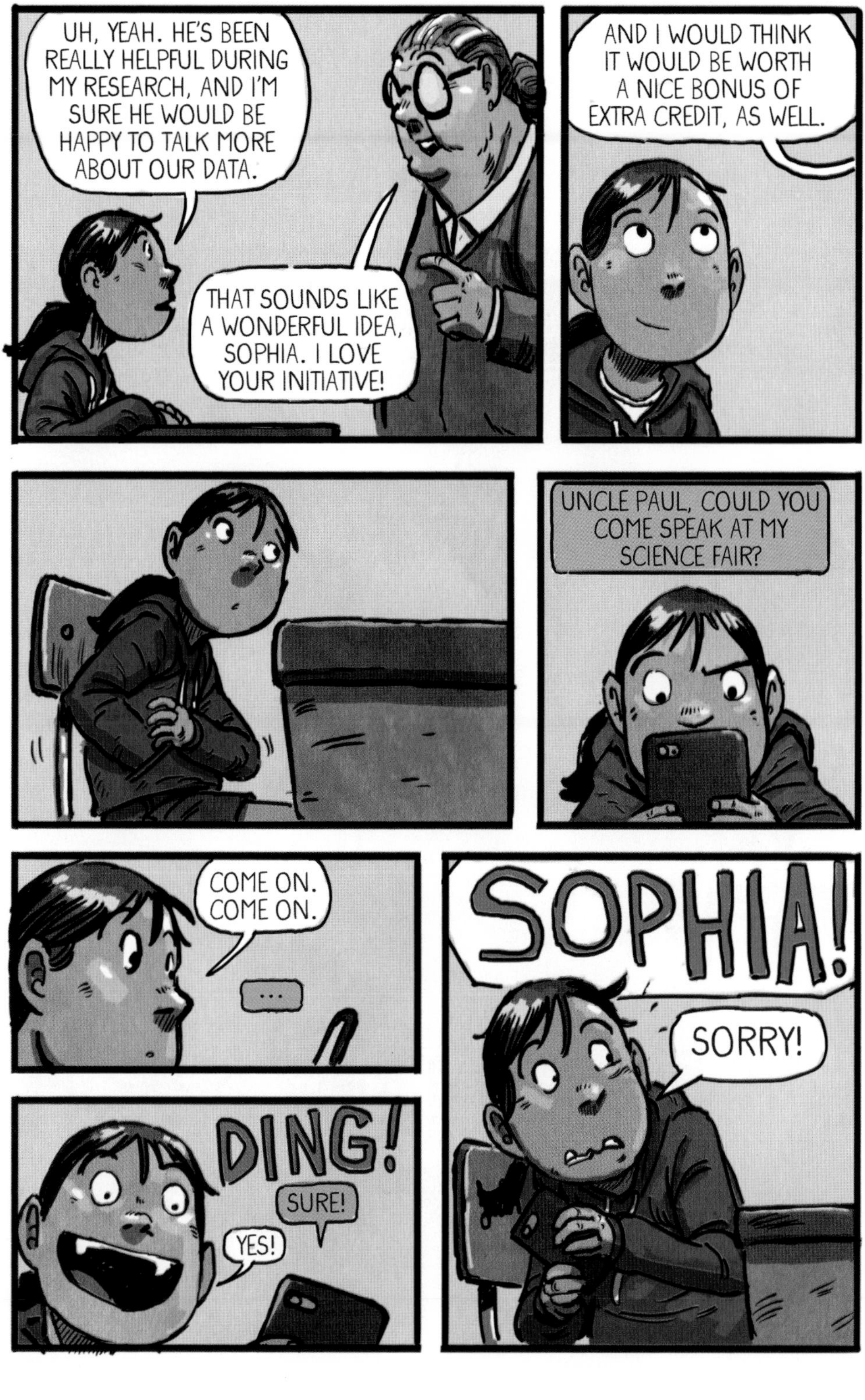
UH, YEAH. HE'S BEEN REALLY HELPFUL DURING MY RESEARCH, AND I'M SURE HE WOULD BE HAPPY TO TALK MORE ABOUT OUR DATA.
THAT SOUNDS LIKE A WONDERFUL IDEA, SOPHIA. I LOVE YOUR INITIATIVE!
AND I WOULD THINK IT WOULD BE WORTH A NICE BONUS OF EXTRA CREDIT, AS WELL.
UNCLE PAUL, COULD YOU COME SPEAK AT MY SCIENCE FAIR?
COME ON. COME ON.
...
DING!
SURE!
YES!
SOPHIA!
SORRY!

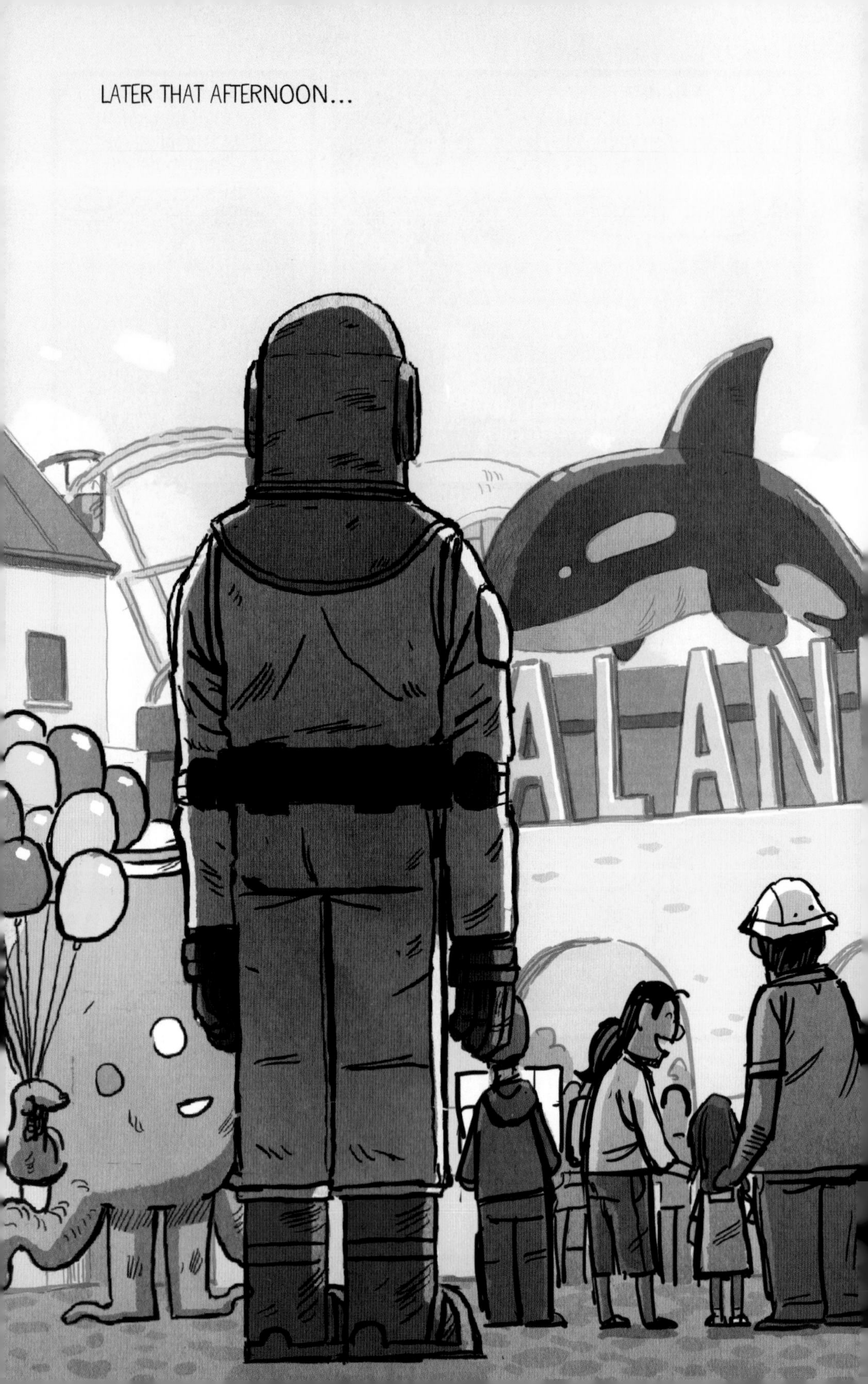
LATER THAT AFTERNOON...

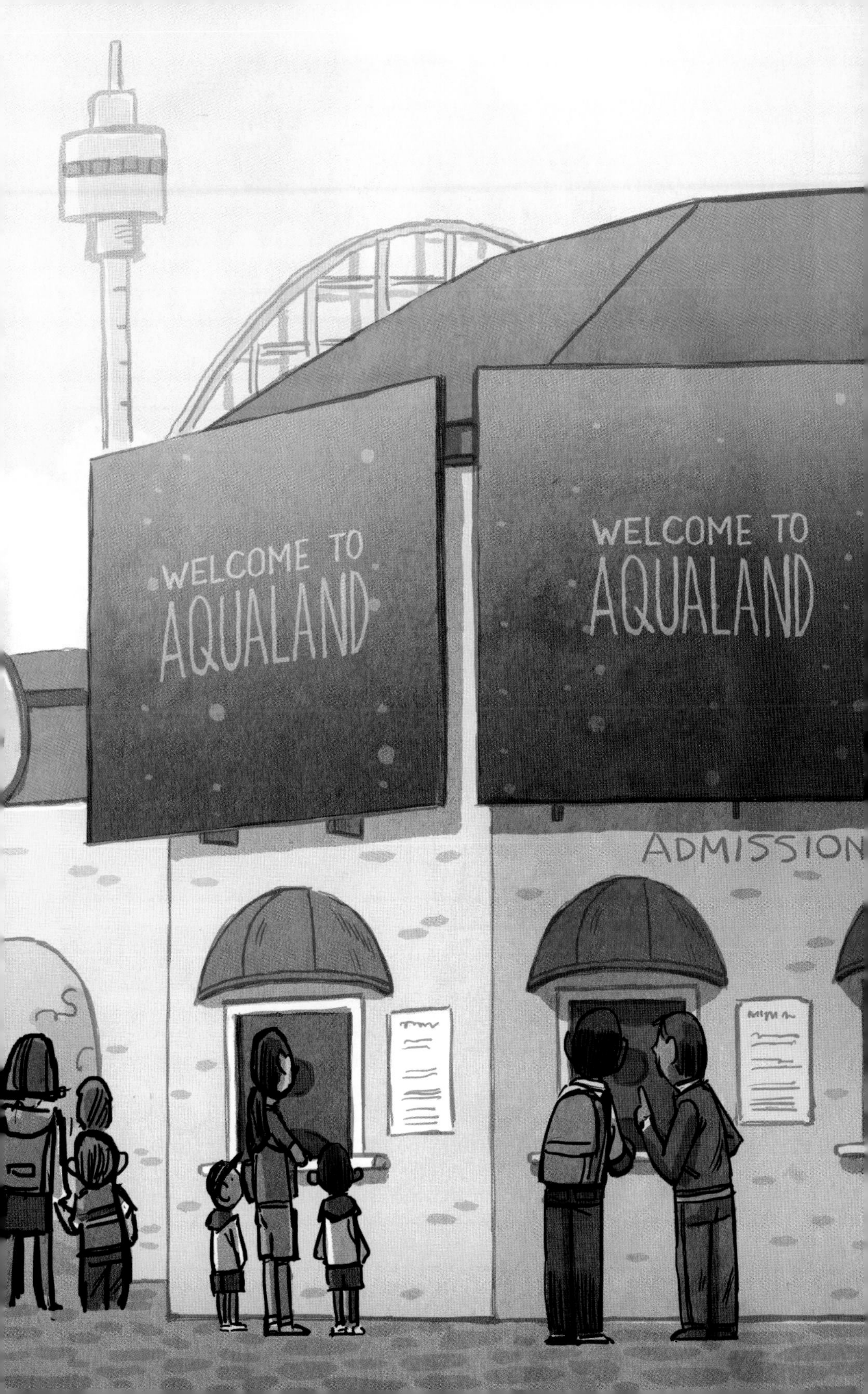
WELCOME TO AQUALAND
WELCOME TO AQUALAND
ADMISSION

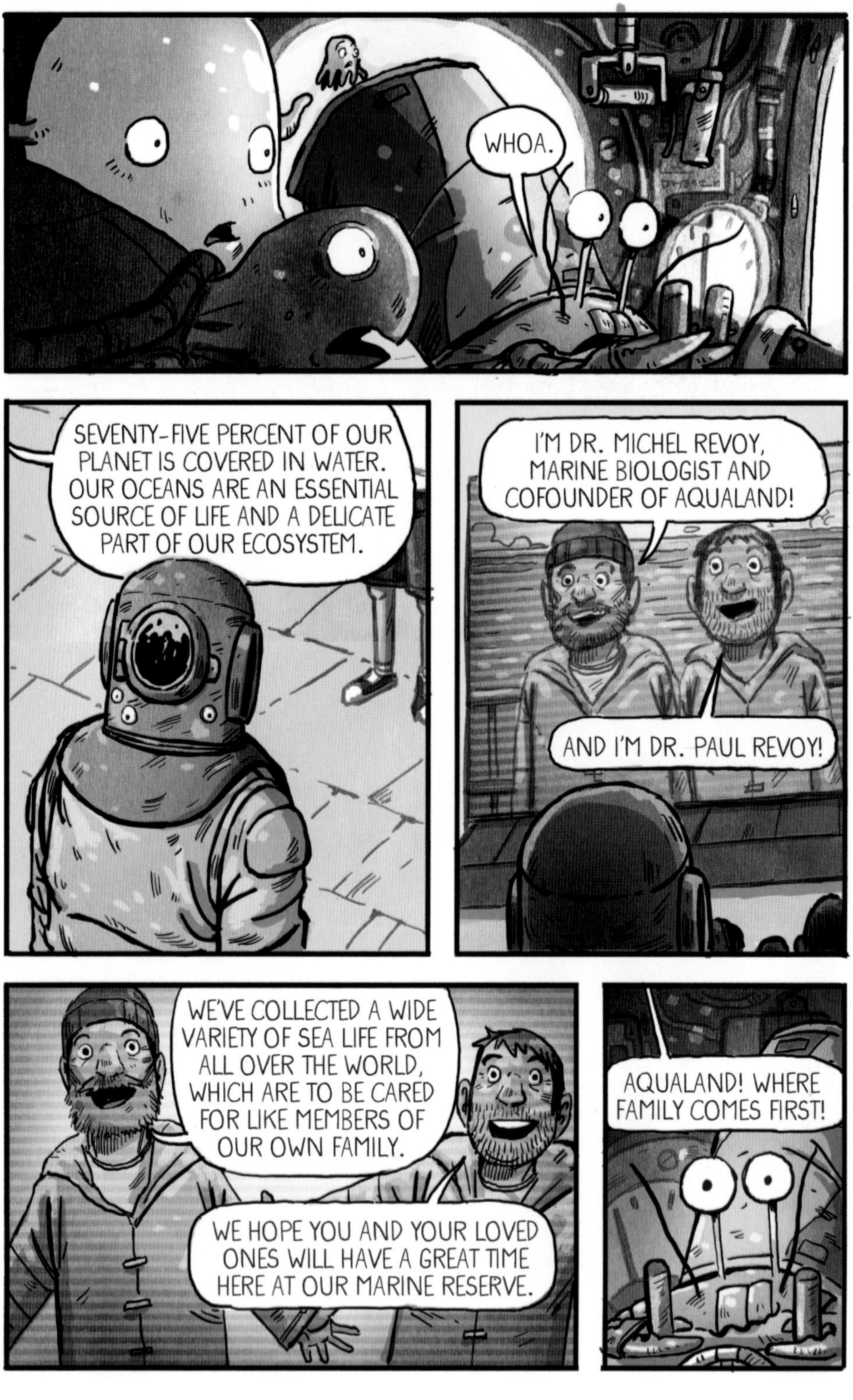
WHOA.
SEVENTY-FIVE PERCENT OF OUR PLANET IS COVERED IN WATER. OUR OCEANS ARE AN ESSENTIAL SOURCE OF LIFE AND A DELICATE PART OF OUR ECOSYSTEM.
I'M DR. MICHEL REVOY, MARINE BIOLOGIST AND COFOUNDER OF AQUALAND!
AND I'M DR. PAUL REVOY!
WE'VE COLLECTED A WIDE VARIETY OF SEA LIFE FROM ALL OVER THE WORLD, WHICH ARE TO BE CARED FOR LIKE MEMBERS OF OUR OWN FAMILY.
WE HOPE YOU AND YOUR LOVED ONES WILL HAVE A GREAT TIME HERE AT OUR MARINE RESERVE.
AQUALAND! WHERE FAMILY COMES FIRST!

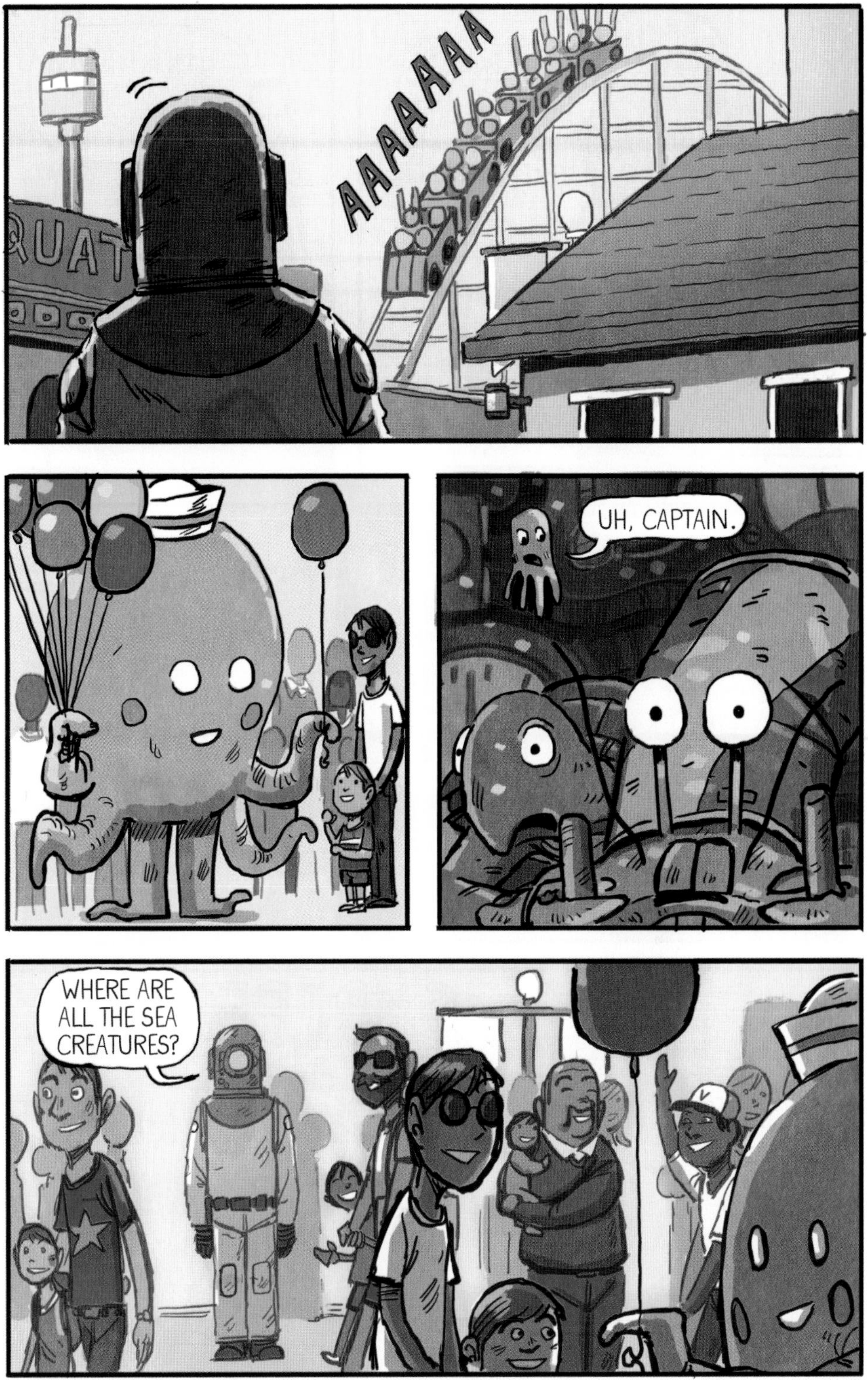
AAAAAAA
QUAT
UH, CAPTAIN.
WHERE ARE ALL THE SEA CREATURES?

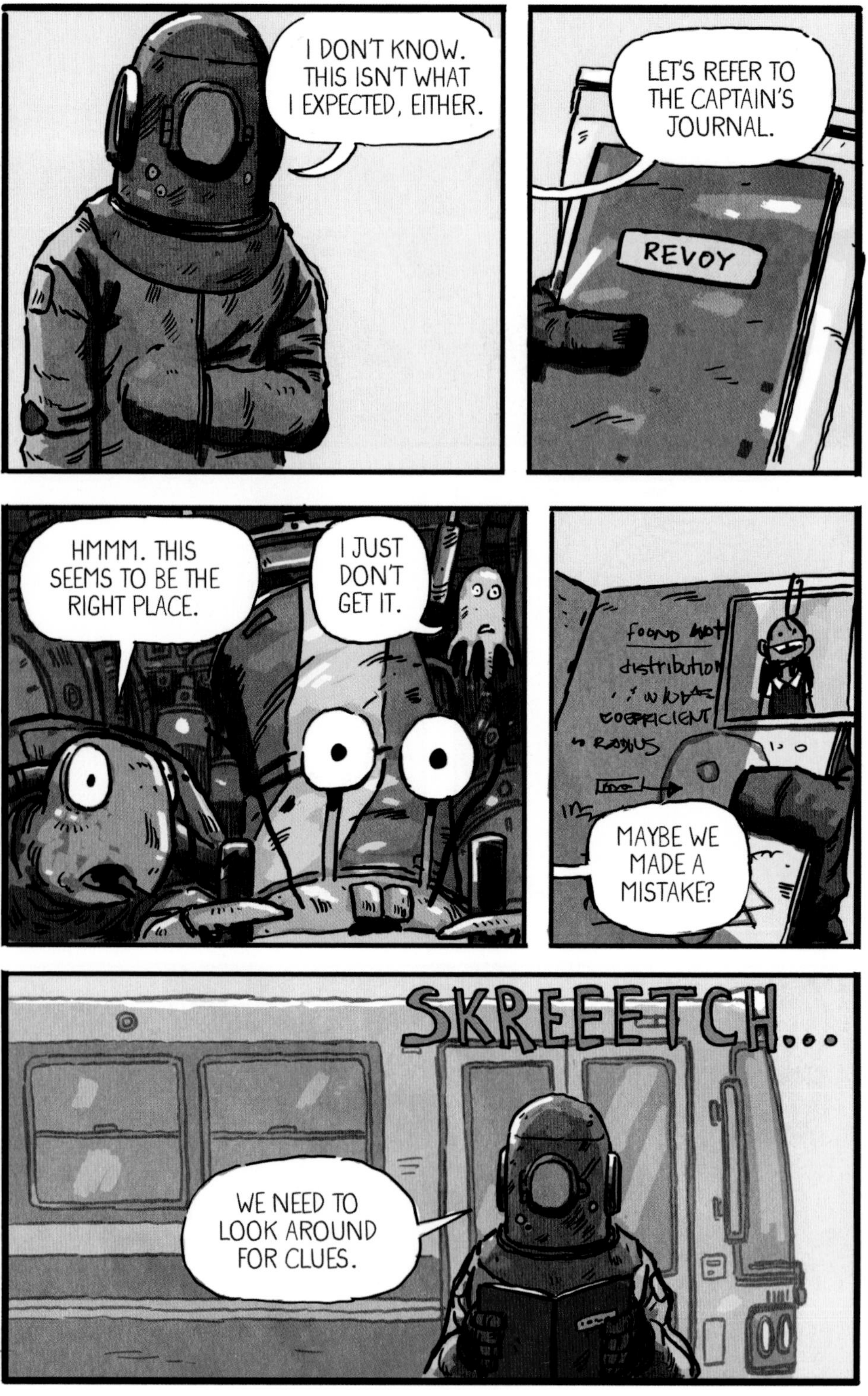
I DON'T KNOW. THIS ISN'T WHAT I EXPECTED, EITHER.
LET'S REFER TO THE CAPTAIN'S JOURNAL.
REVOY
HMMM. THIS SEEMS TO BE THE RIGHT PLACE.
I JUST DON'T GET IT.
MAYBE WE MADE A MISTAKE?
SKREEETCH...
WE NEED TO LOOK AROUND FOR CLUES.

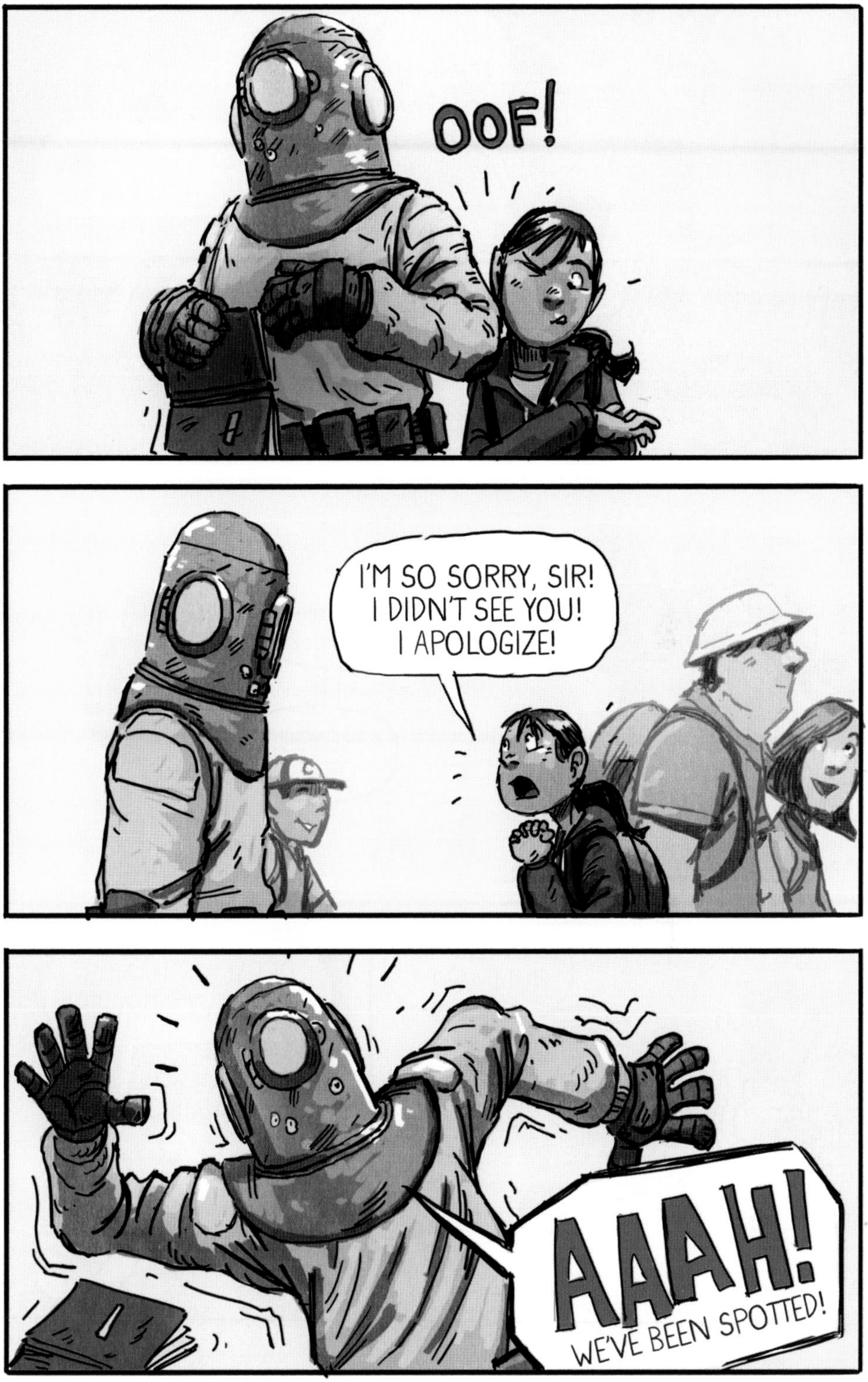
OOF!
I'M SO SORRY, SIR! I DIDN'T SEE YOU! I APOLOGIZE!
AAAH! WE'VE BEEN SPOTTED!

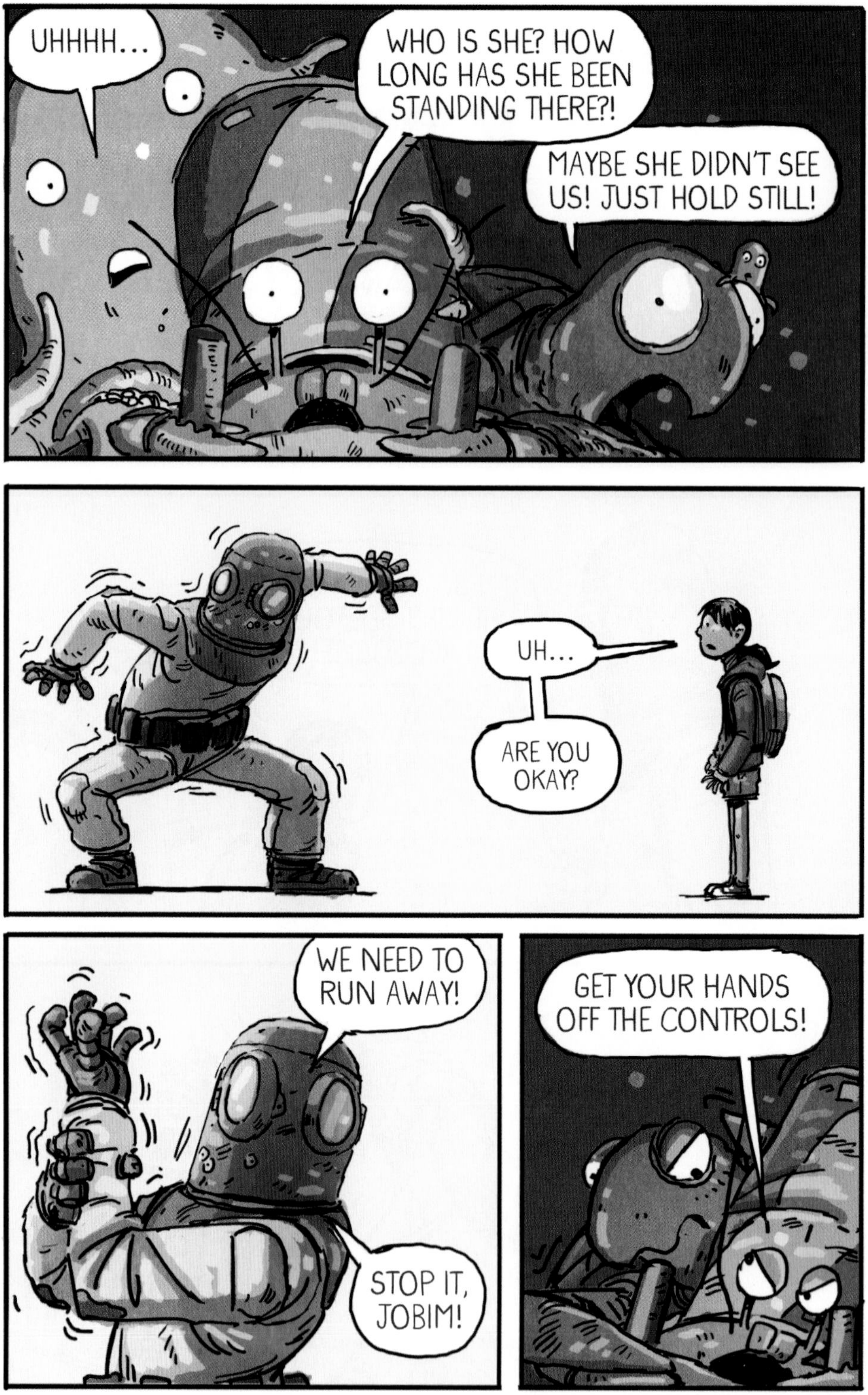
UHHHH...
WHO IS SHE? HOW LONG HAS SHE BEEN STANDING THERE?!
MAYBE SHE DIDN'T SEE US! JUST HOLD STILL!
UH...
ARE YOU OKAY?
WE NEED TO RUN AWAY!
STOP IT, JOBIM!
GET YOUR HANDS OFF THE CONTROLS!

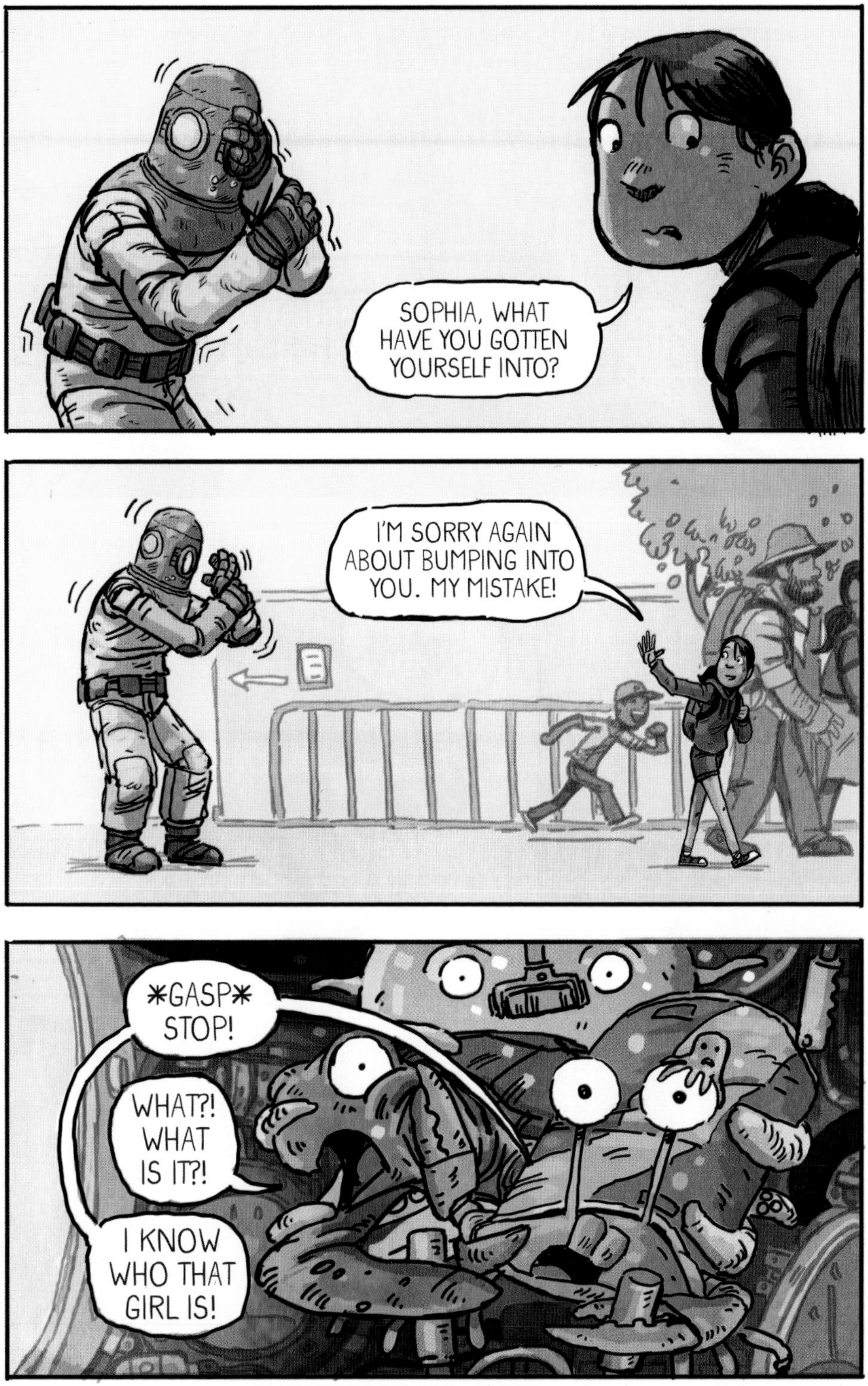
SOPHIA, WHAT HAVE YOU GOTTEN YOURSELF INTO?
I'M SORRY AGAIN ABOUT BUMPING INTO YOU. MY MISTAKE!
GASP STOP!
WHAT?! WHAT IS IT?!
I KNOW WHO THAT GIRL IS!

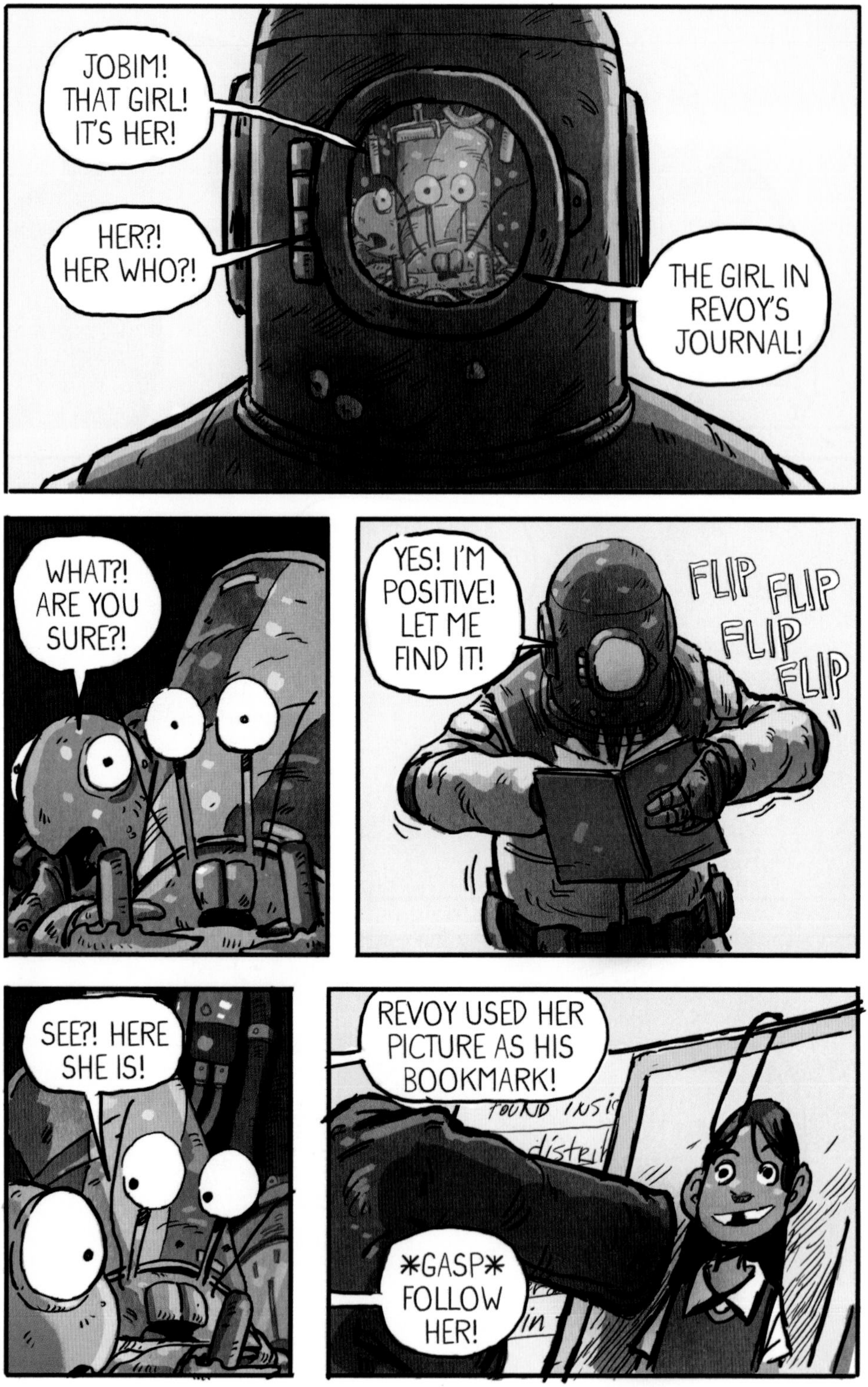
JOBIM! THAT GIRL! IT'S HER!
HER?! HER WHO?!
THE GIRL IN REVOY'S JOURNAL!
WHAT?! ARE YOU SURE?!
YES! I'M POSITIVE! LET ME FIND IT!
FLIP FLIP FLIP FLIP
SEE?! HERE SHE IS!
REVOY USED HER PICTURE AS HIS BOOKMARK!
GASP FOLLOW HER!

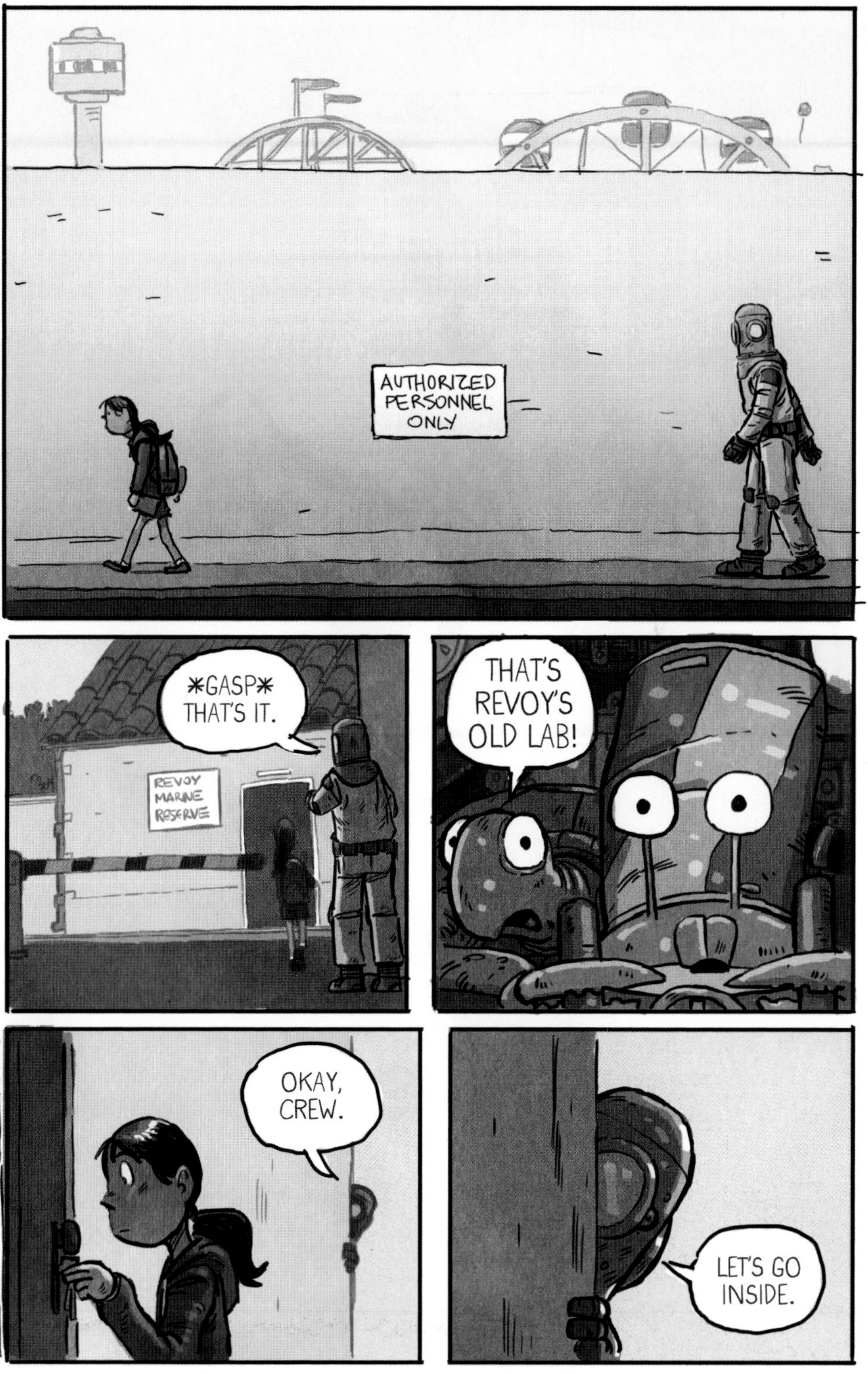
AUTHORIZED PERSONNEL ONLY
GASP THAT'S IT.
REVOY MARINE RESERVE
THAT'S REVOY'S OLD LAB!
OKAY, CREW.
LET'S GO INSIDE.

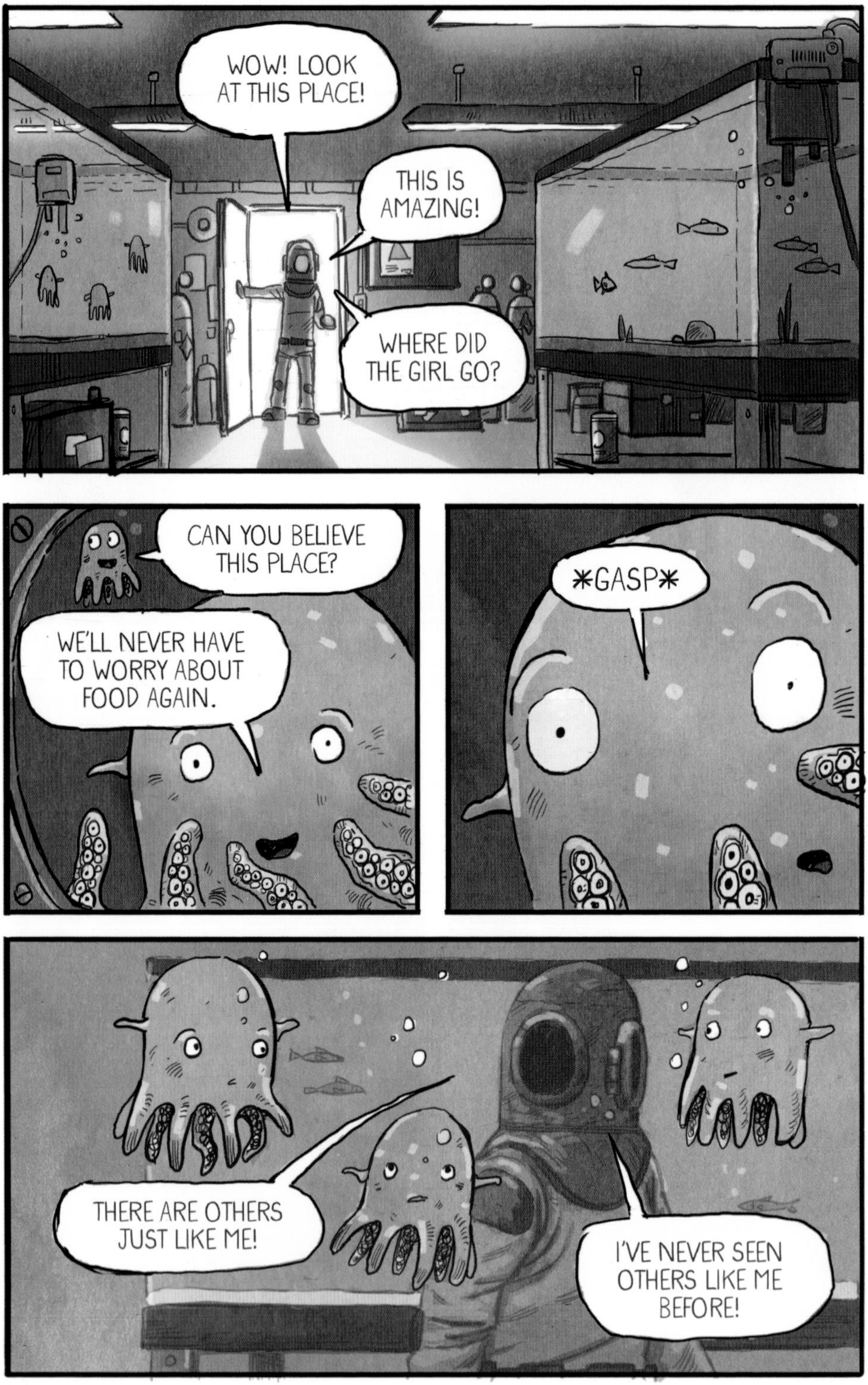
WOW! LOOK AT THIS PLACE!
THIS IS AMAZING!
WHERE DID THE GIRL GO?
CAN YOU BELIEVE THIS PLACE?
WE'LL NEVER HAVE TO WORRY ABOUT FOOD AGAIN.
GASP
THERE ARE OTHERS JUST LIKE ME!
I'VE NEVER SEEN OTHERS LIKE ME BEFORE!

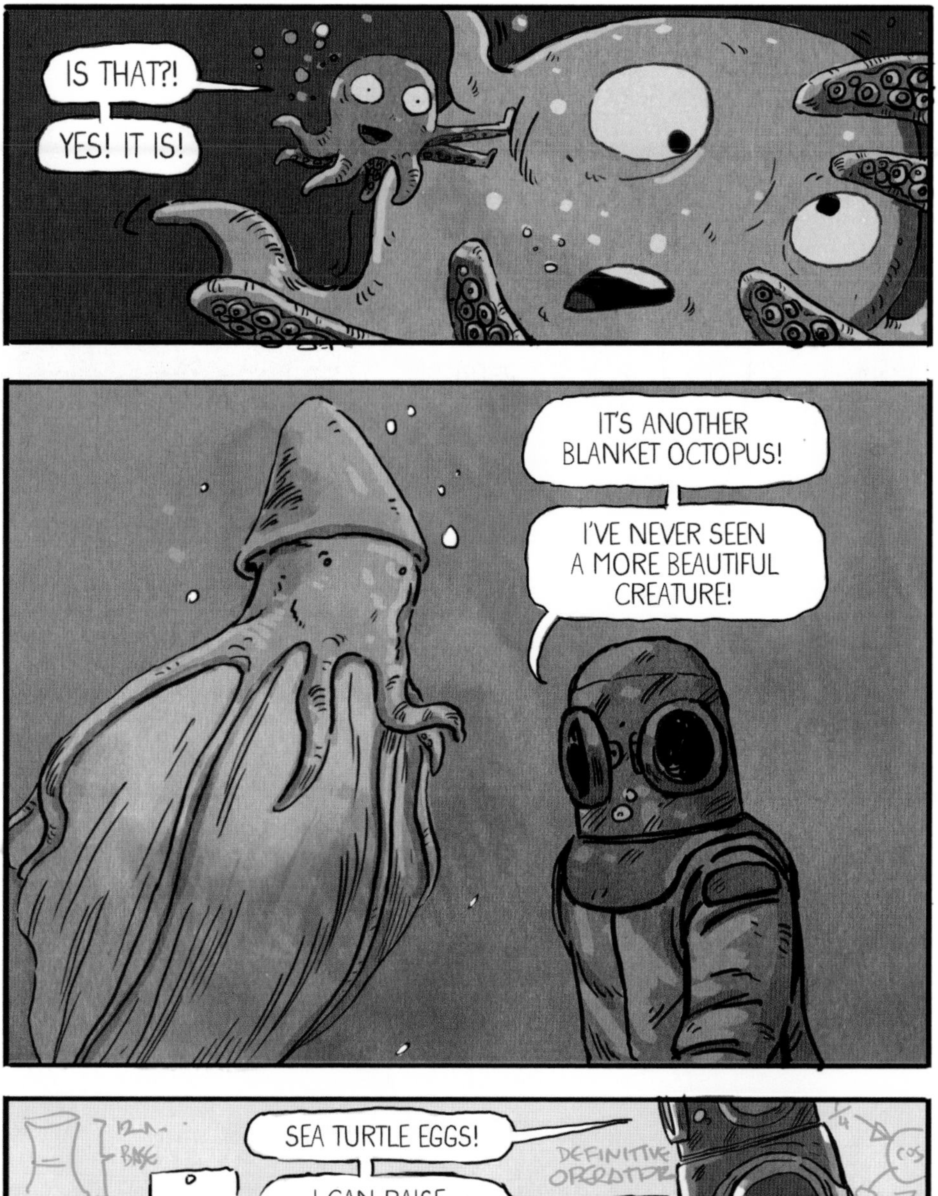
IS THAT?!
YES! IT IS!
IT'S ANOTHER BLANKET OCTOPUS!
I'VE NEVER SEEN A MORE BEAUTIFUL CREATURE!
SEA TURTLE EGGS!
I CAN RAISE OTHERS LIKE ME!

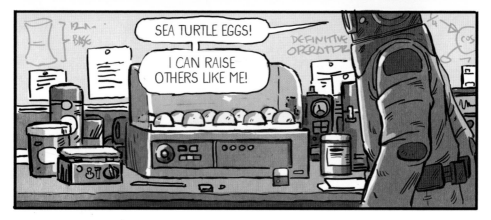

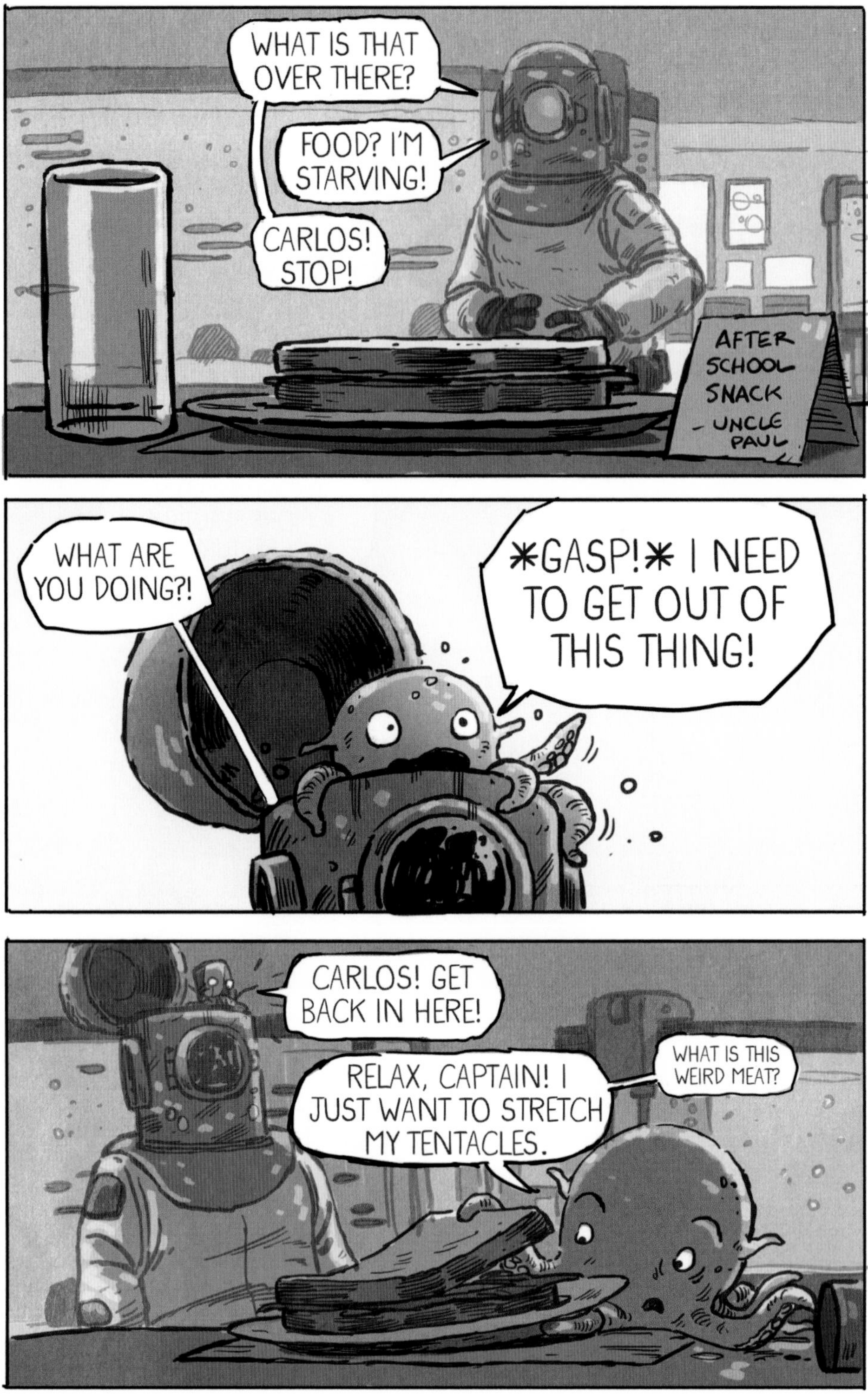
WHAT IS THAT OVER THERE?
FOOD? I'M STARVING!
CARLOS! STOP!
AFTER SCHOOL SNACK - UNCLE PAUL
WHAT ARE YOU DOING?!
GASP! I NEED TO GET OUT OF THIS THING!
CARLOS! GET BACK IN HERE!
RELAX, CAPTAIN! I JUST WANT TO STRETCH MY TENTACLES.
WHAT IS THIS WEIRD MEAT?

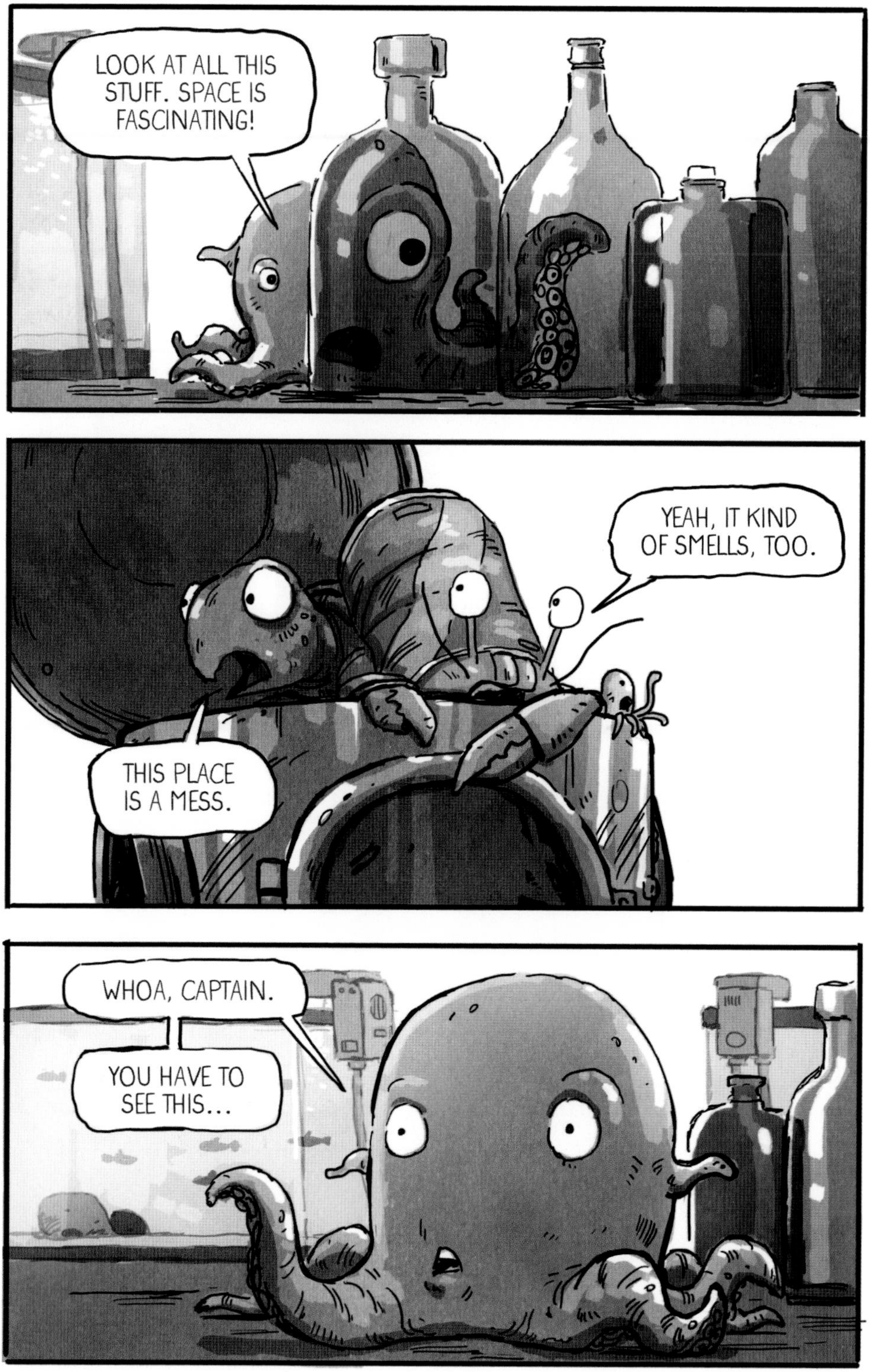
LOOK AT ALL THIS STUFF. SPACE IS FASCINATING!
THIS PLACE IS A MESS.
YEAH, IT KIND OF SMELLS, TOO.
WHOA, CAPTAIN.
YOU HAVE TO SEE THIS...

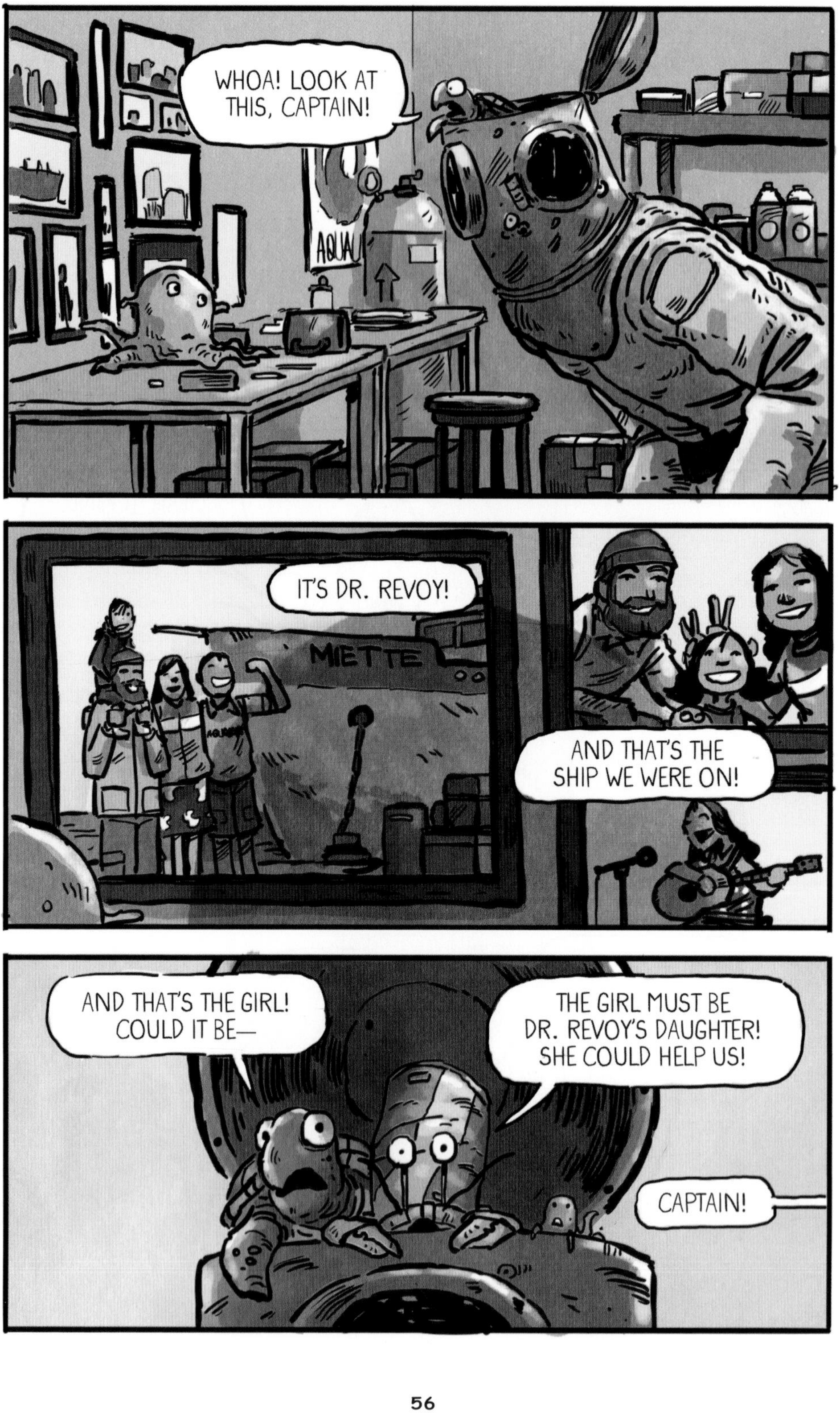
WHOA! LOOK AT THIS, CAPTAIN!
AQUA
IT'S DR. REVOY!
MIETTE
AND THAT'S THE SHIP WE WERE ON!
AND THAT'S THE GIRL! COULD IT BE—
THE GIRL MUST BE DR. REVOY'S DAUGHTER! SHE COULD HELP US!
CAPTAIN!

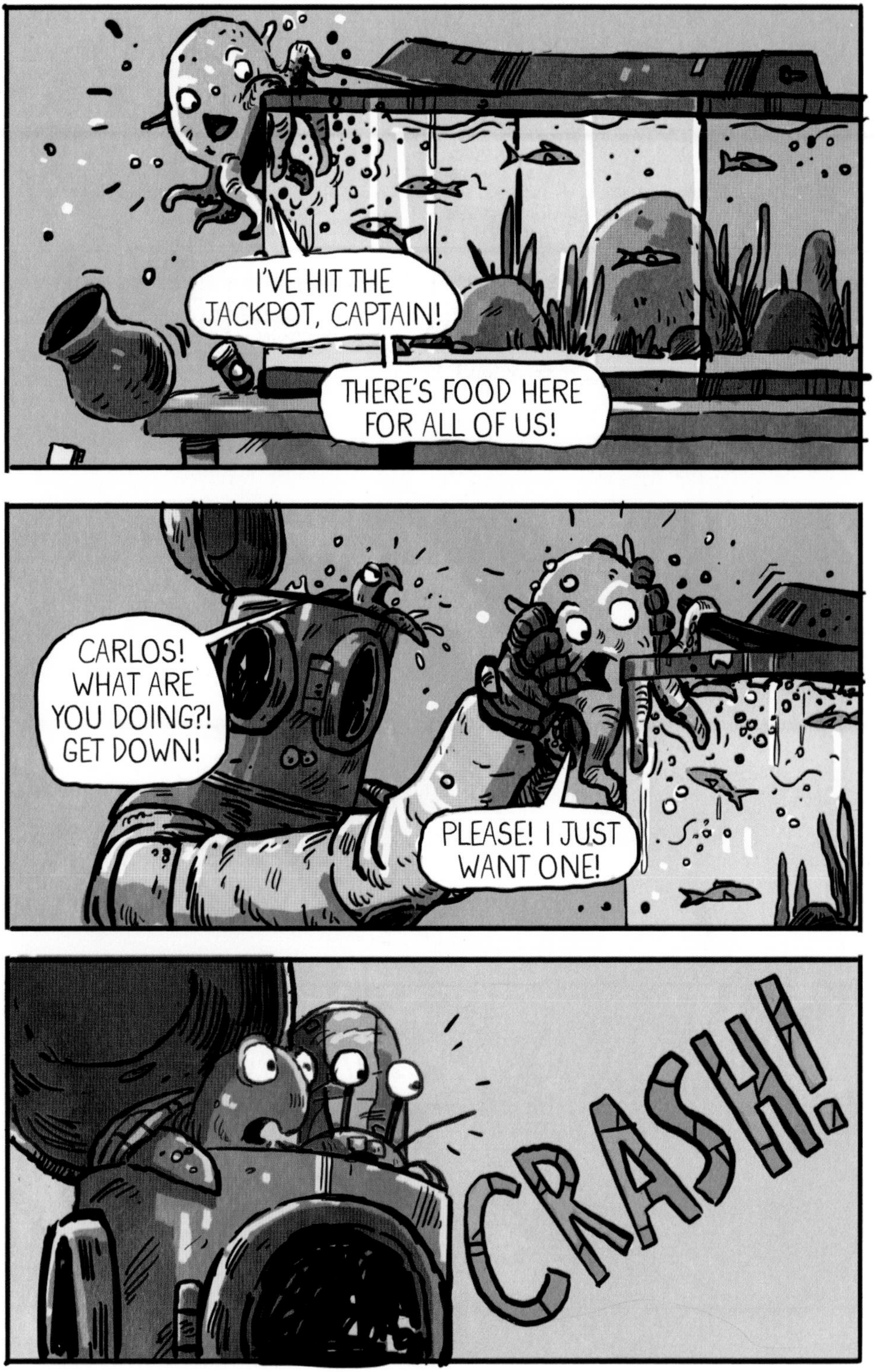
I'VE HIT THE JACKPOT, CAPTAIN!
THERE'S FOOD HERE FOR ALL OF US!
CARLOS! WHAT ARE YOU DOING?! GET DOWN!
PLEASE! I JUST WANT ONE!
CRASH!

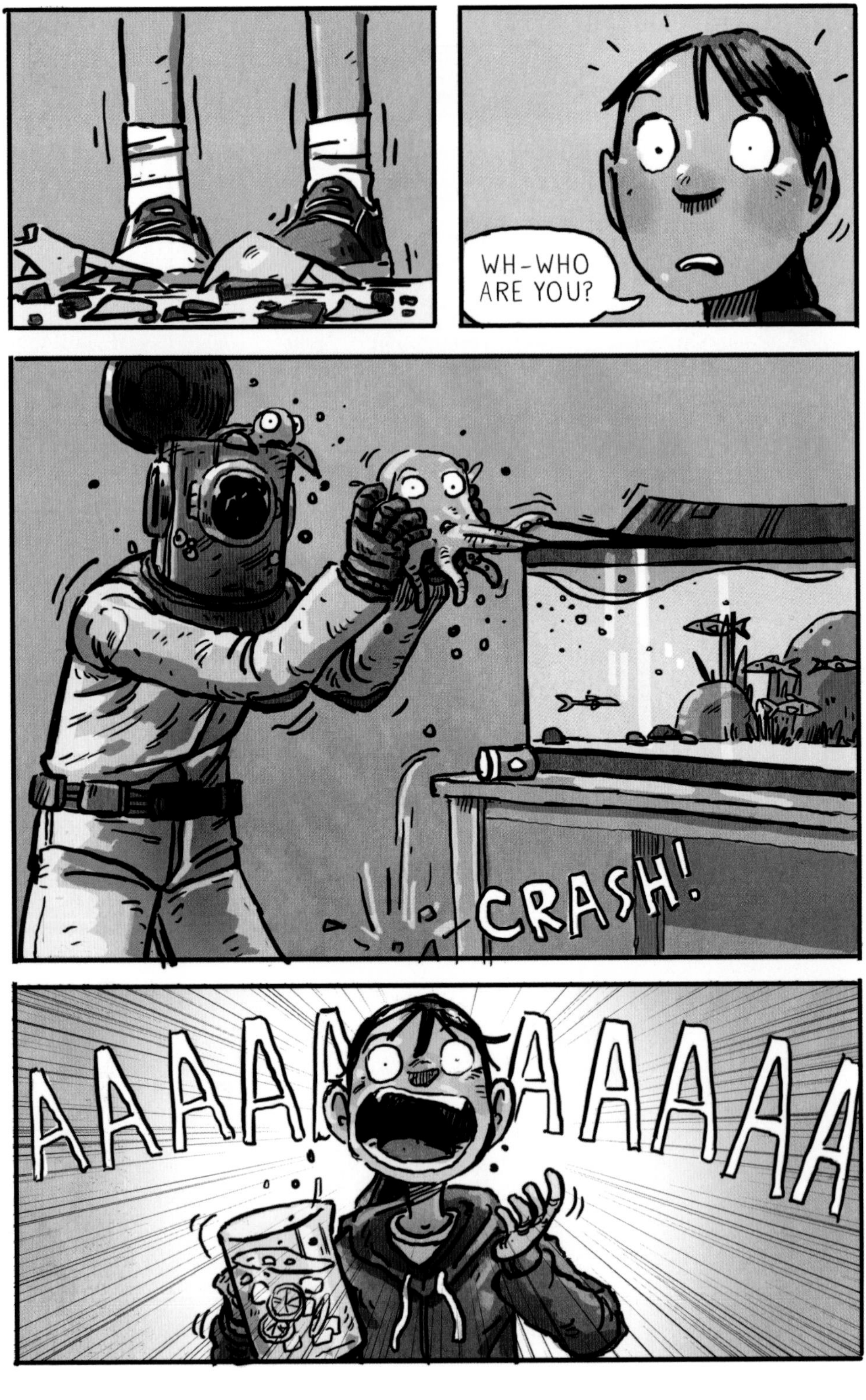
WH-WHO ARE YOU?
CRASH!
AAAAAAAAAA

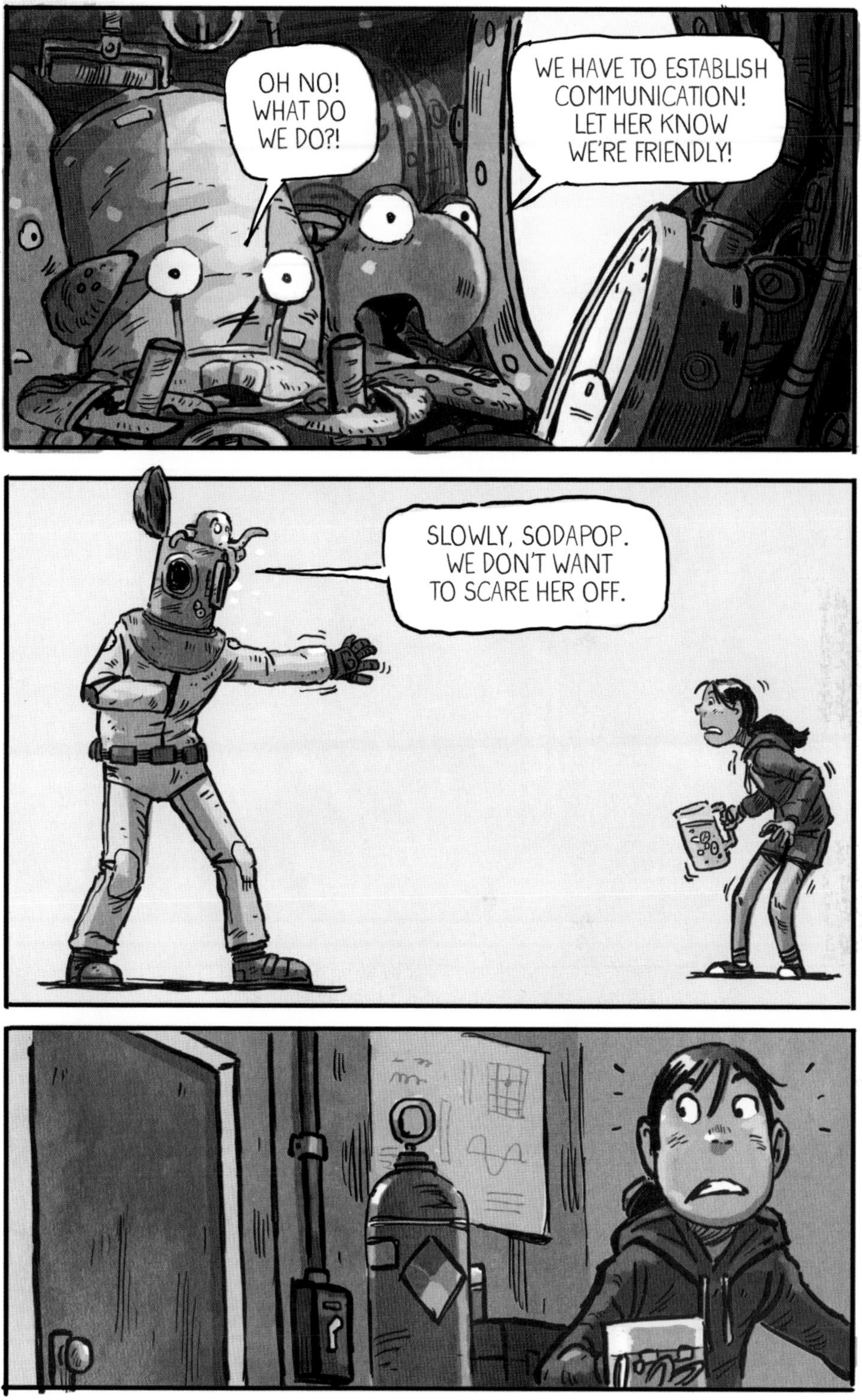
OH NO!
WHAT DO
WE DO?!
WE HAVE TO ESTABLISH
COMMUNICATION!
LET HER KNOW
WE'RE FRIENDLY!
SLOWLY, SODAPOP.
WE DON'T WANT
TO SCARE HER OFF.

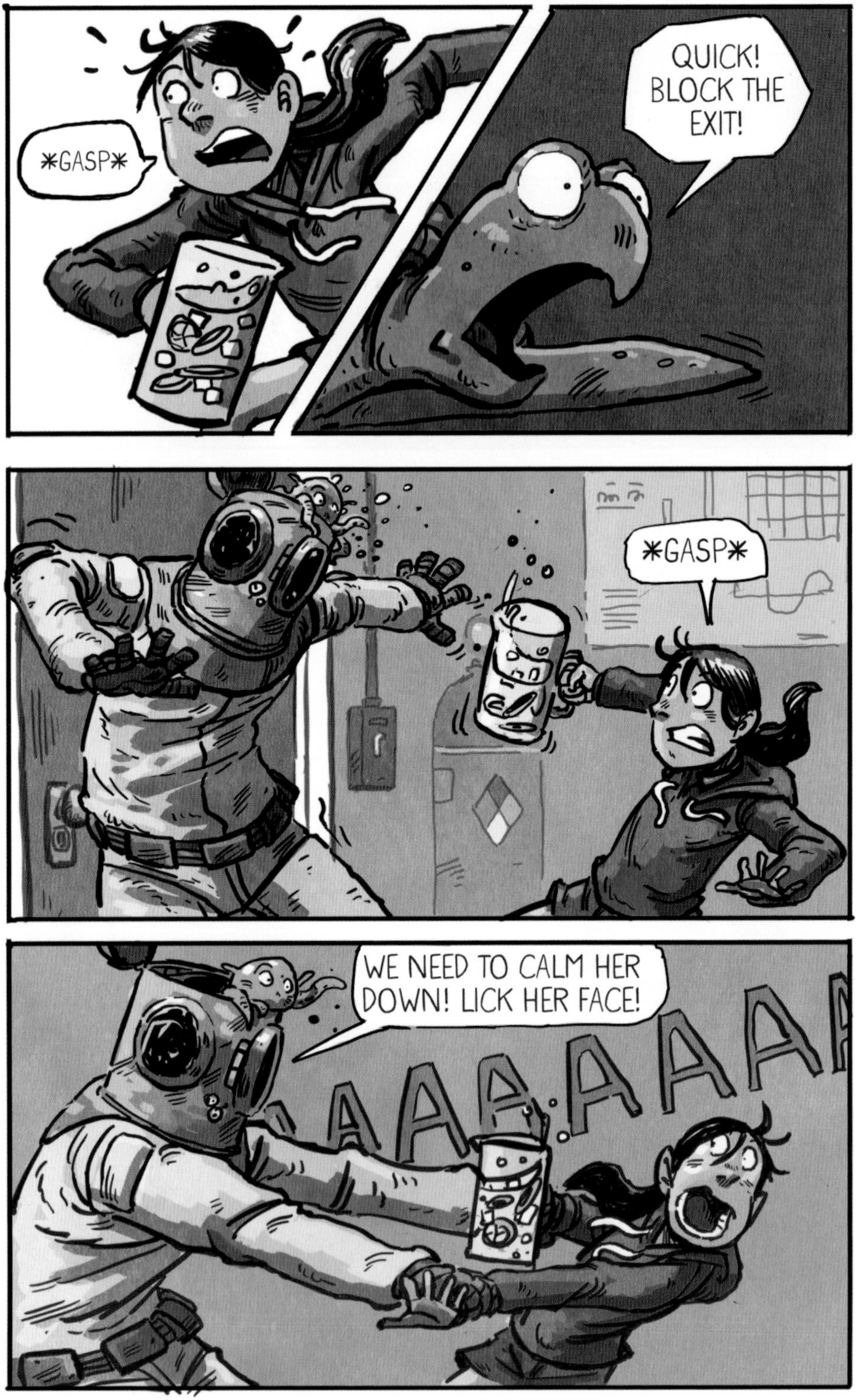
GASP
QUICK! BLOCK THE EXIT!
GASP
WE NEED TO CALM HER DOWN! LICK HER FACE!
AAAAAAAA

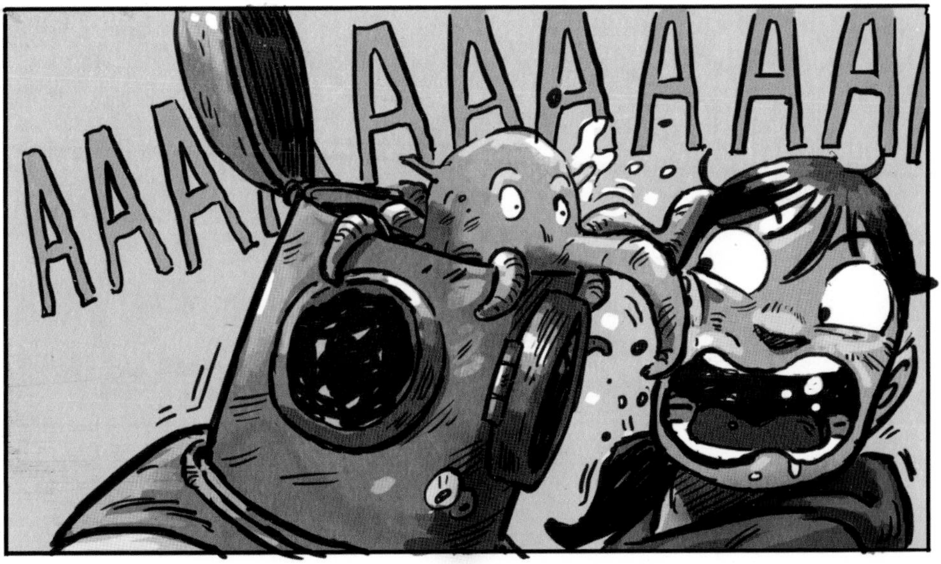
AAAAAAAAAA

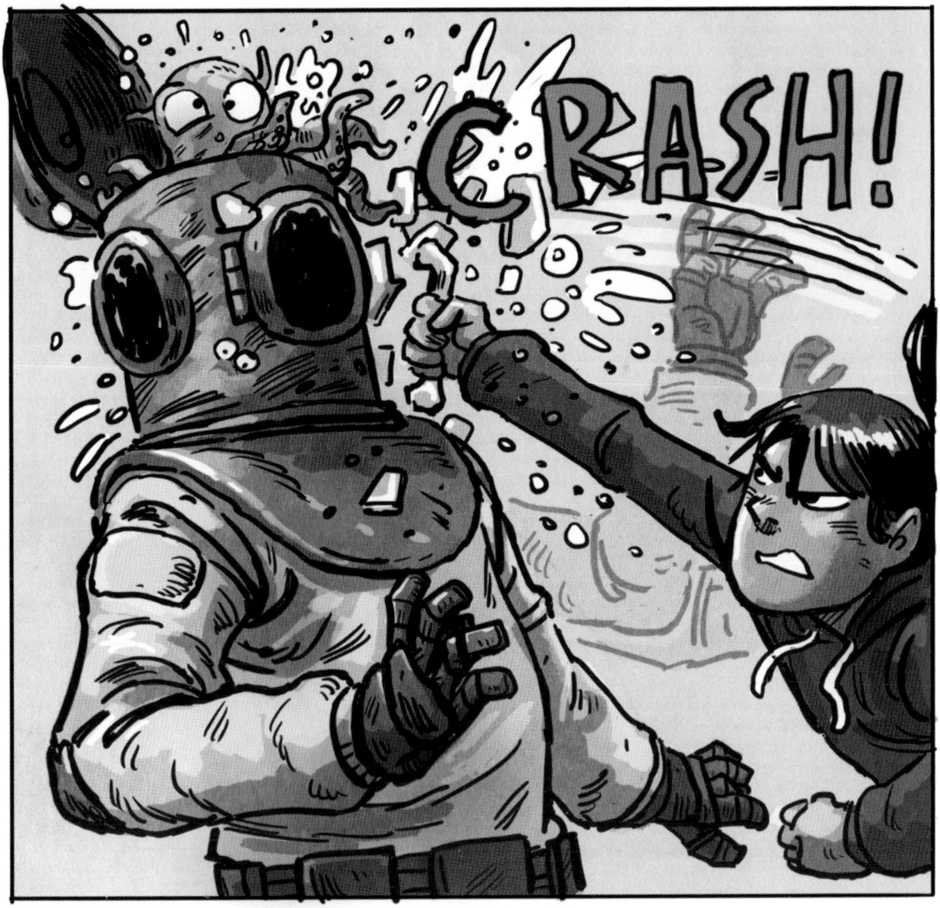
CRASH!

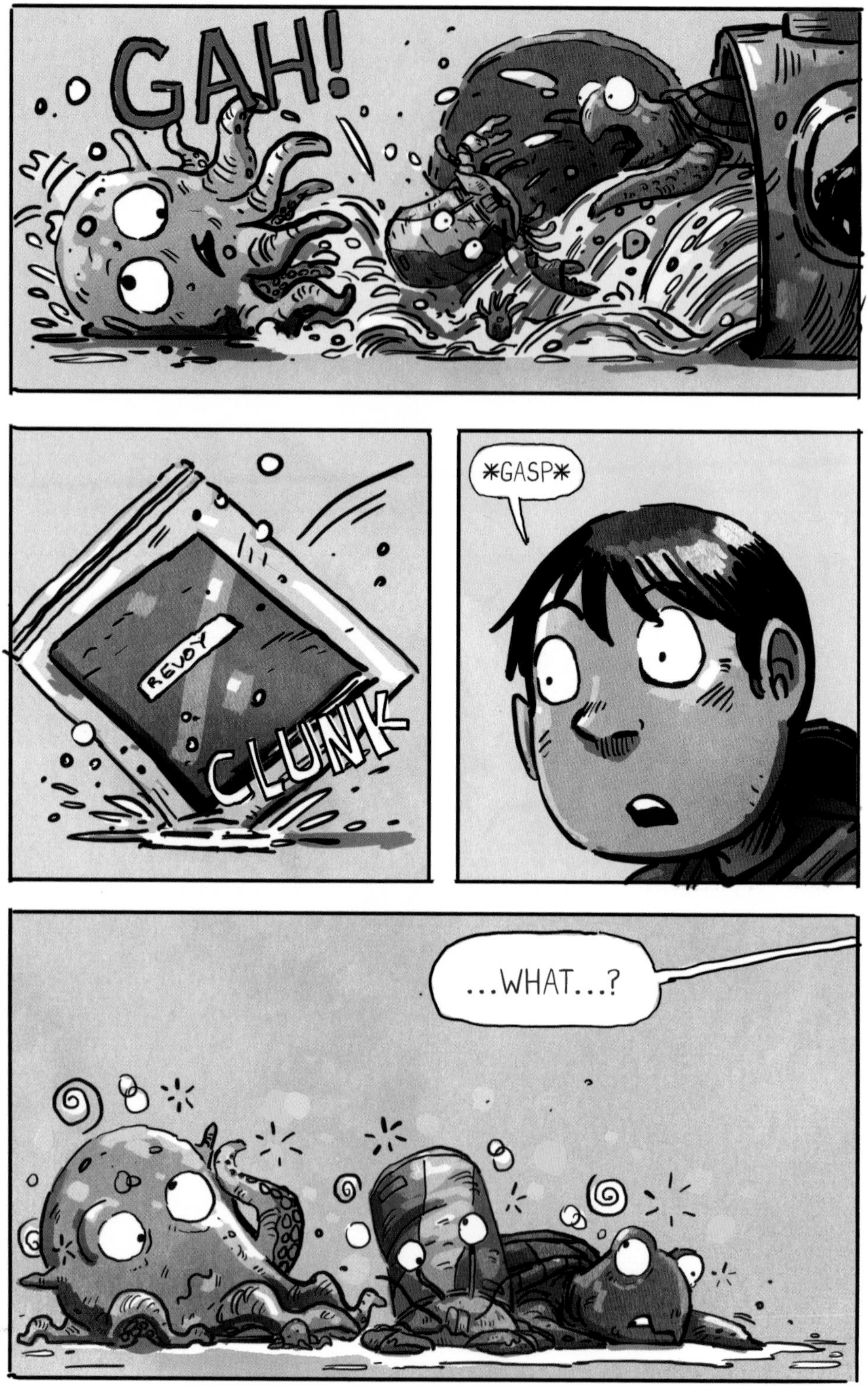
GAH!
REVOY
CLUNK
GASP
...WHAT...?

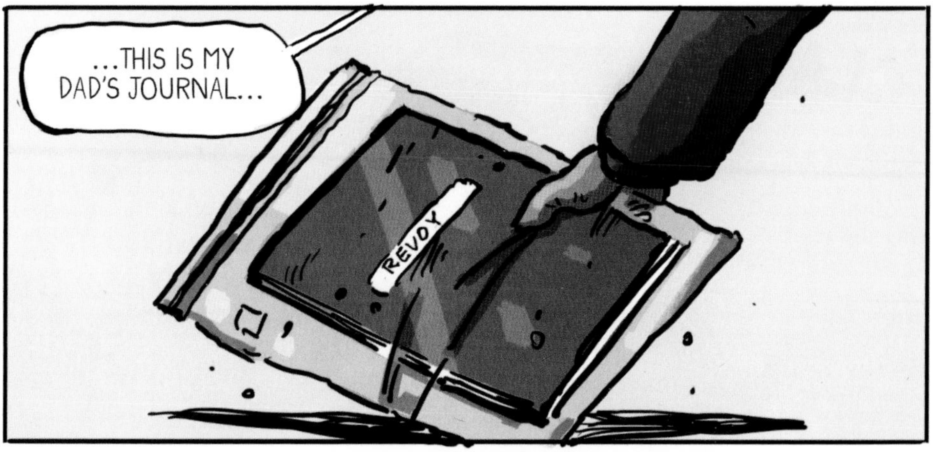
...THIS IS MY DAD'S JOURNAL...
REVOY

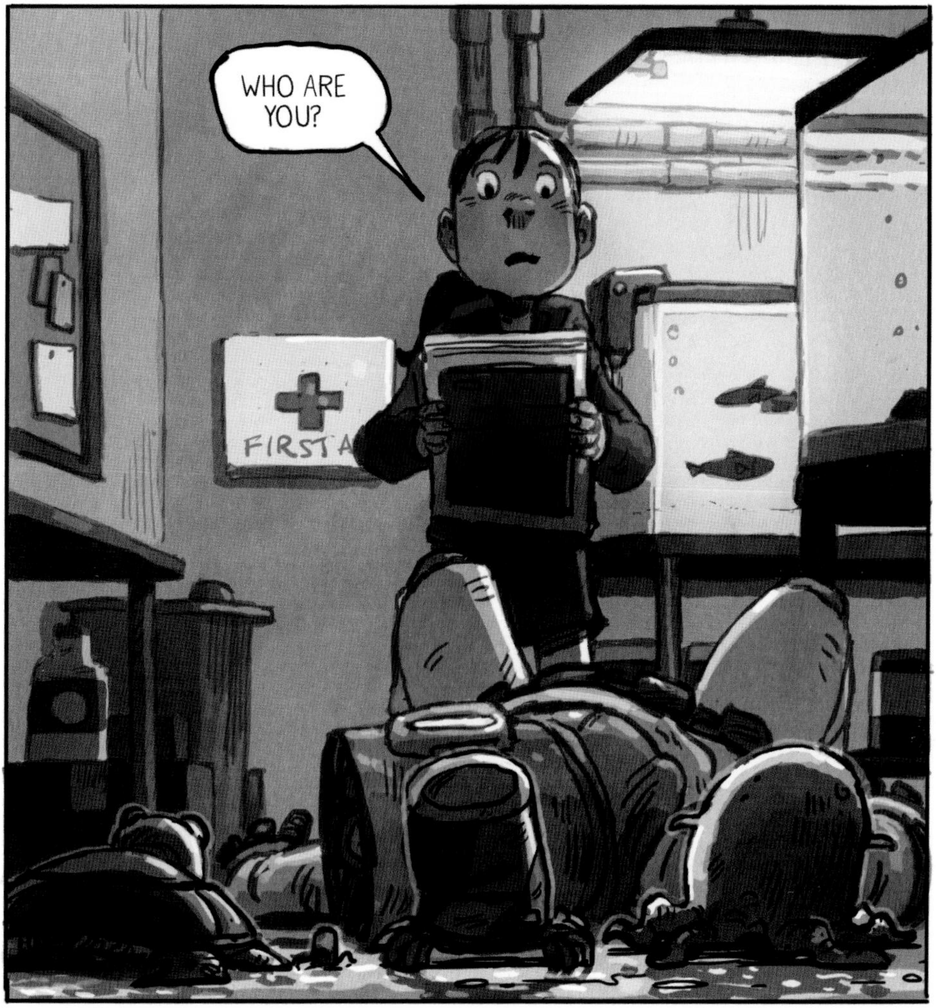
WHO ARE YOU?
FIRST A

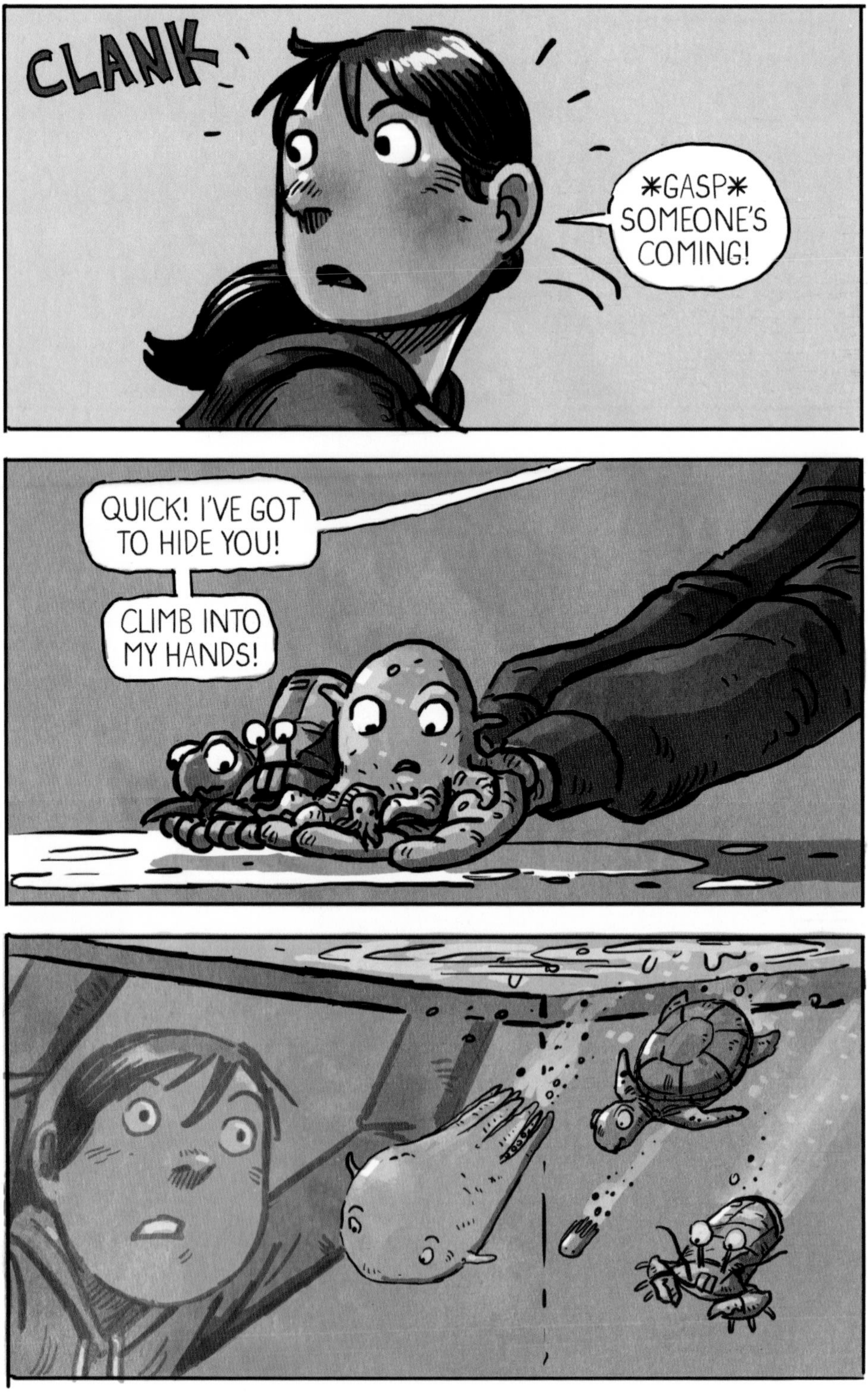
CLANK
GASP SOMEONE'S COMING!
QUICK! I'VE GOT TO HIDE YOU!
CLIMB INTO MY HANDS!

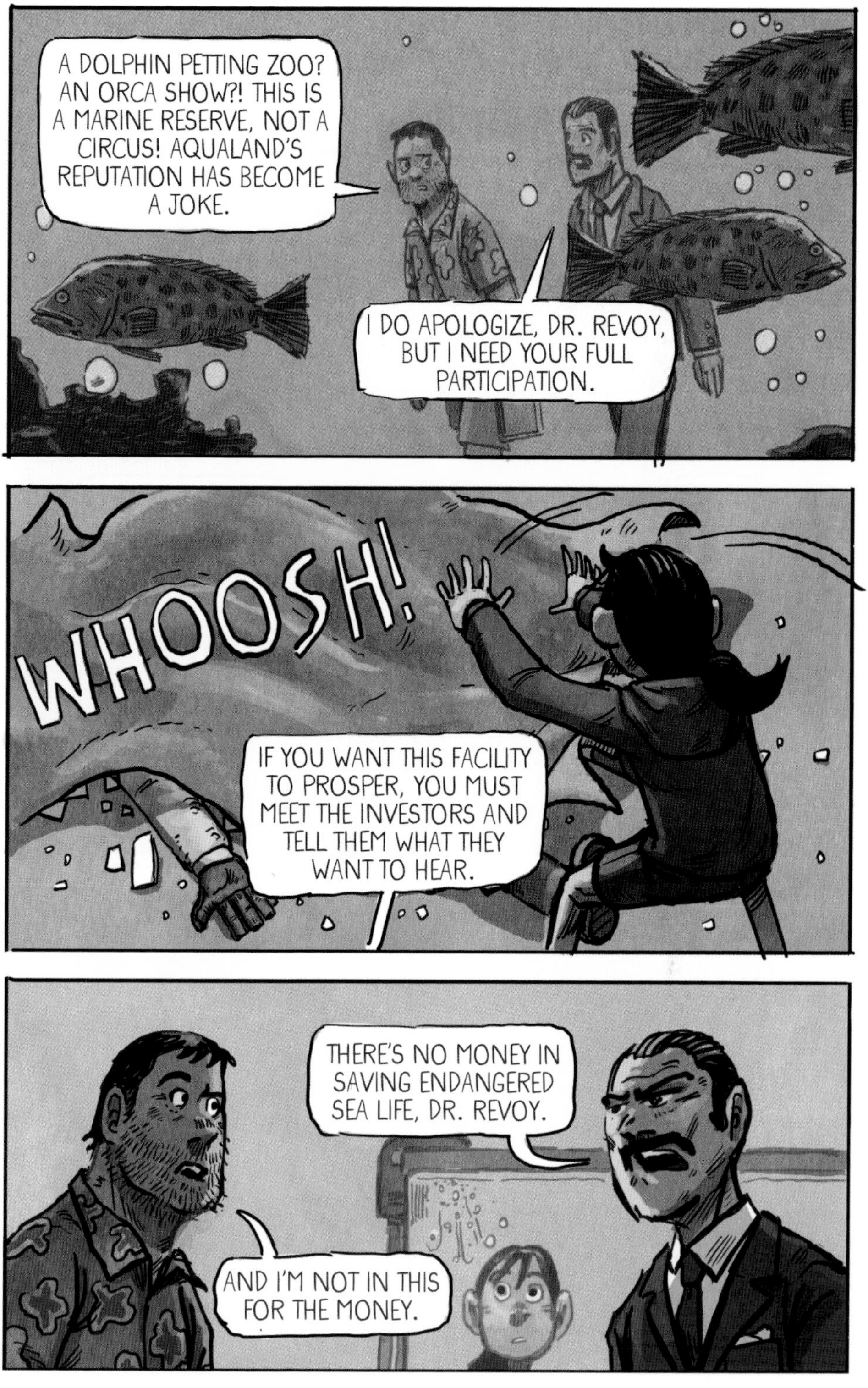
A DOLPHIN PETTING ZOO? AN ORCA SHOW?! THIS IS A MARINE RESERVE, NOT A CIRCUS! AQUALAND'S REPUTATION HAS BECOME A JOKE.
I DO APOLOGIZE, DR. REVOY, BUT I NEED YOUR FULL PARTICIPATION.
WHOOSH!
IF YOU WANT THIS FACILITY TO PROSPER, YOU MUST MEET THE INVESTORS AND TELL THEM WHAT THEY WANT TO HEAR.
THERE'S NO MONEY IN SAVING ENDANGERED SEA LIFE, DR. REVOY.
AND I'M NOT IN THIS FOR THE MONEY.

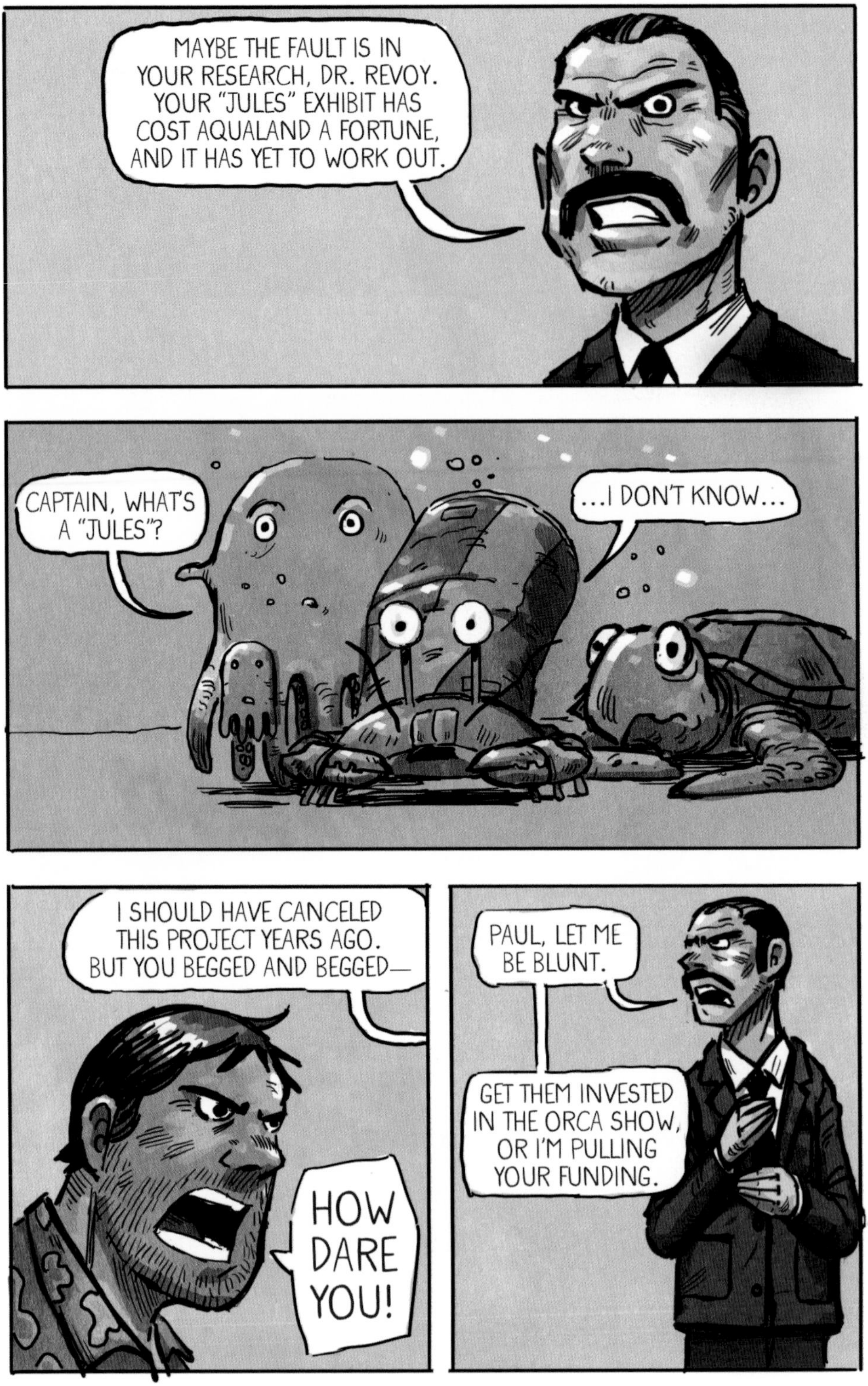
MAYBE THE FAULT IS IN YOUR RESEARCH, DR. REVOY. YOUR "JULES" EXHIBIT HAS COST AQUALAND A FORTUNE, AND IT HAS YET TO WORK OUT.
CAPTAIN, WHAT'S A "JULES"?
...I DON'T KNOW...
I SHOULD HAVE CANCELED THIS PROJECT YEARS AGO. BUT YOU BEGGED AND BEGGED—
HOW DARE YOU!
PAUL, LET ME BE BLUNT.
GET THEM INVESTED IN THE ORCA SHOW, OR I'M PULLING YOUR FUNDING.

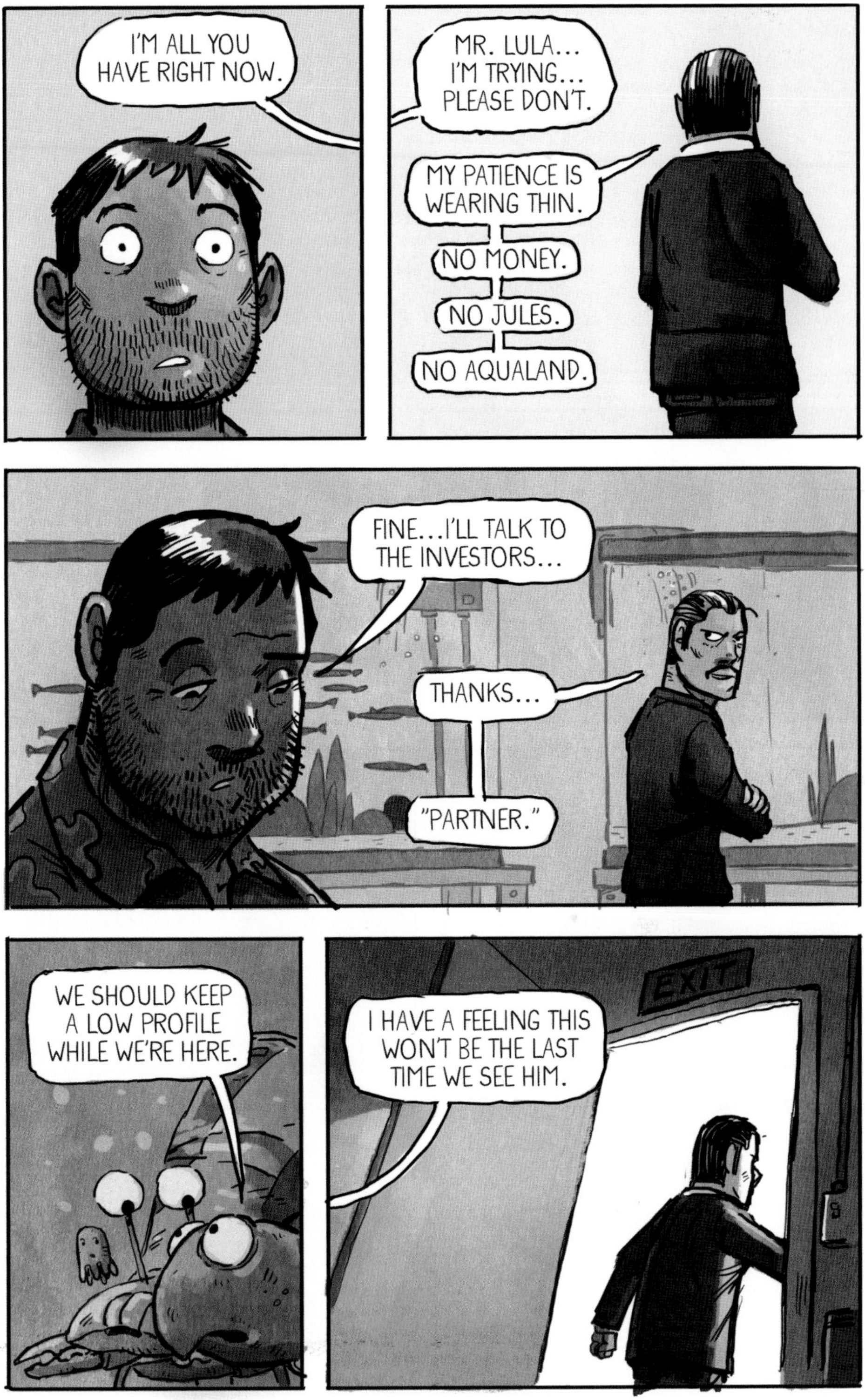
I'M ALL YOU HAVE RIGHT NOW.
MR. LULA... I'M TRYING... PLEASE DON'T.
MY PATIENCE IS WEARING THIN.
NO MONEY.
NO JULES.
NO AQUALAND.
FINE...I'LL TALK TO THE INVESTORS...
THANKS...
"PARTNER."
WE SHOULD KEEP A LOW PROFILE WHILE WE'RE HERE.
I HAVE A FEELING THIS WON'T BE THE LAST TIME WE SEE HIM.
EXIT

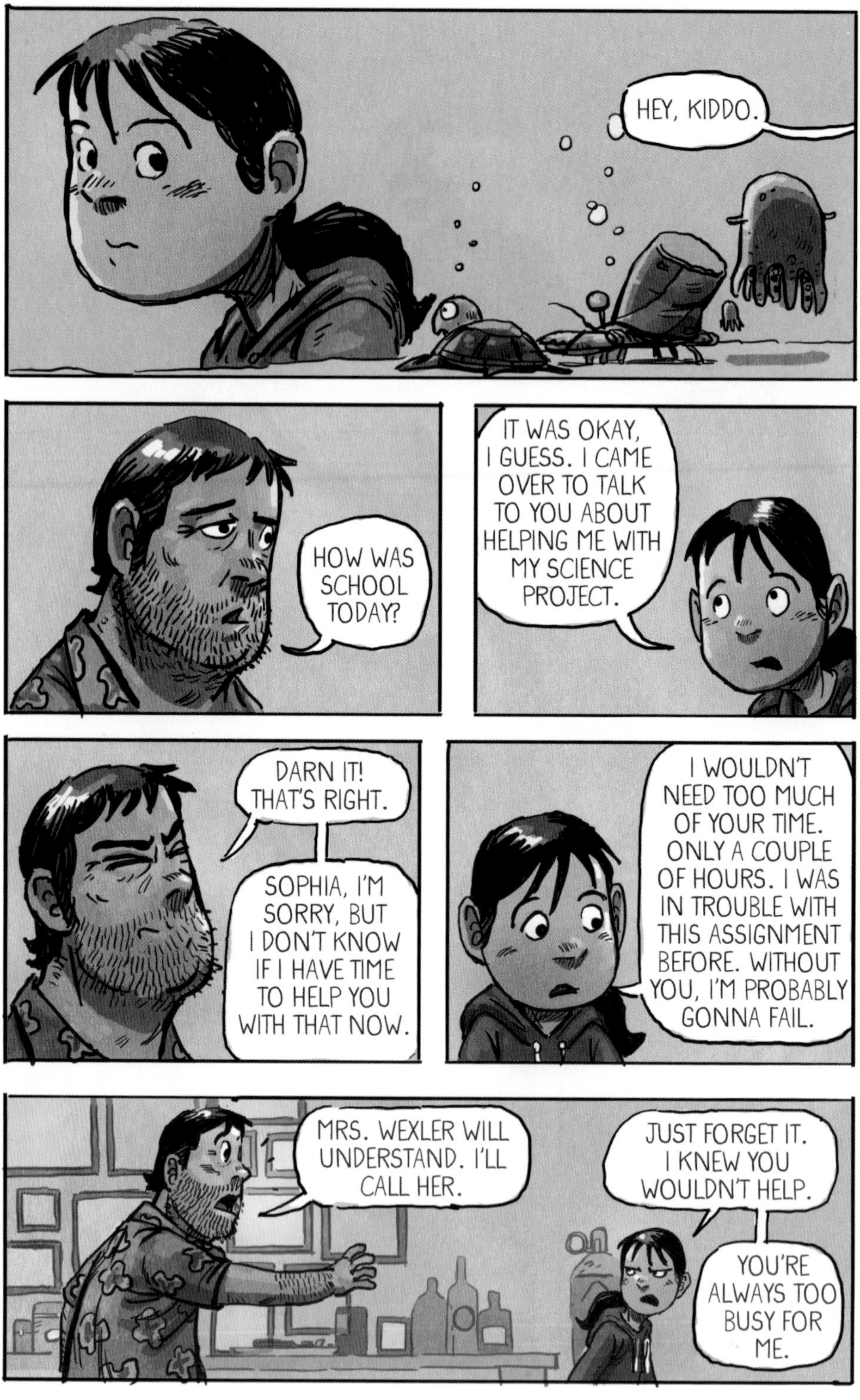
HEY, KIDDO.
HOW WAS SCHOOL TODAY?
IT WAS OKAY, I GUESS. I CAME OVER TO TALK TO YOU ABOUT HELPING ME WITH MY SCIENCE PROJECT.
DARN IT! THAT'S RIGHT.
SOPHIA, I'M SORRY, BUT I DON'T KNOW IF I HAVE TIME TO HELP YOU WITH THAT NOW.
I WOULDN'T NEED TOO MUCH OF YOUR TIME. ONLY A COUPLE OF HOURS. I WAS IN TROUBLE WITH THIS ASSIGNMENT BEFORE. WITHOUT YOU, I'M PROBABLY GONNA FAIL.
MRS. WEXLER WILL UNDERSTAND. I'LL CALL HER.
JUST FORGET IT. I KNEW YOU WOULDN'T HELP.
YOU'RE ALWAYS TOO BUSY FOR ME.

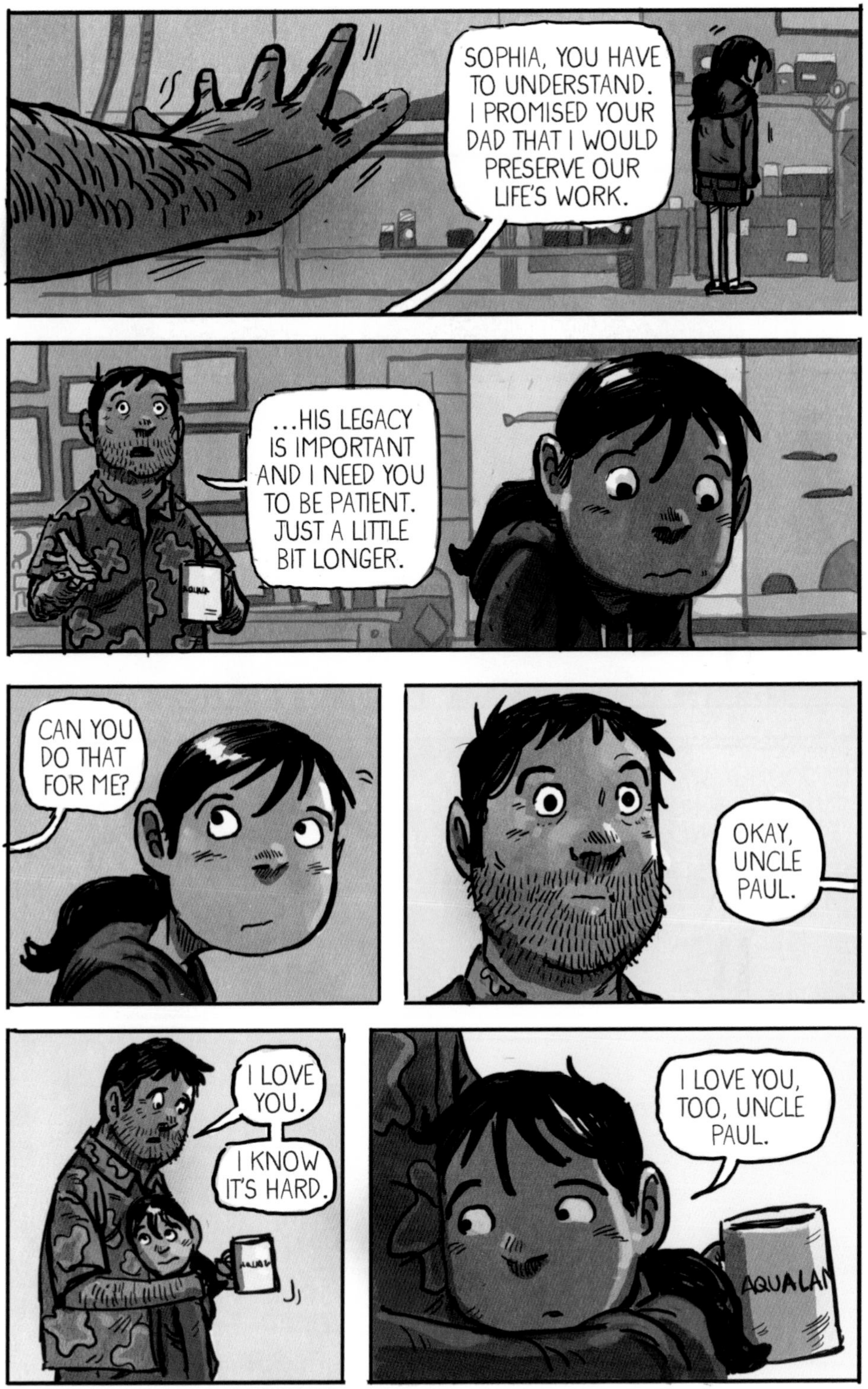
SOPHIA, YOU HAVE TO UNDERSTAND. I PROMISED YOUR DAD THAT I WOULD PRESERVE OUR LIFE'S WORK.
...HIS LEGACY IS IMPORTANT AND I NEED YOU TO BE PATIENT. JUST A LITTLE BIT LONGER.
CAN YOU DO THAT FOR ME?
OKAY, UNCLE PAUL.
I LOVE YOU.
I KNOW IT'S HARD.
I LOVE YOU, TOO, UNCLE PAUL.

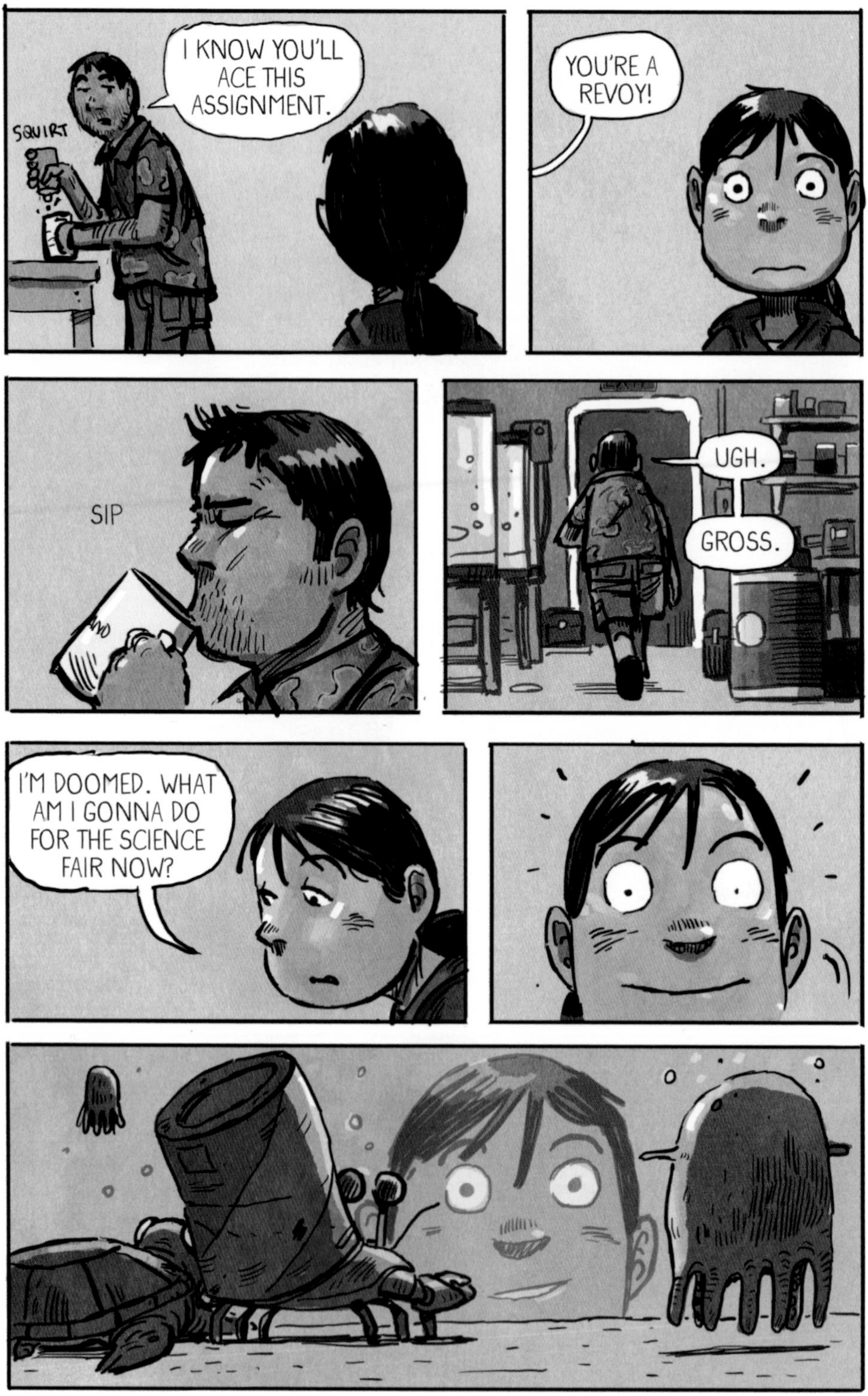
I KNOW YOU'LL ACE THIS ASSIGNMENT.
SQUIRT
YOU'RE A REVOY!
SIP
UGH.
GROSS.
I'M DOOMED. WHAT AM I GONNA DO FOR THE SCIENCE FAIR NOW?

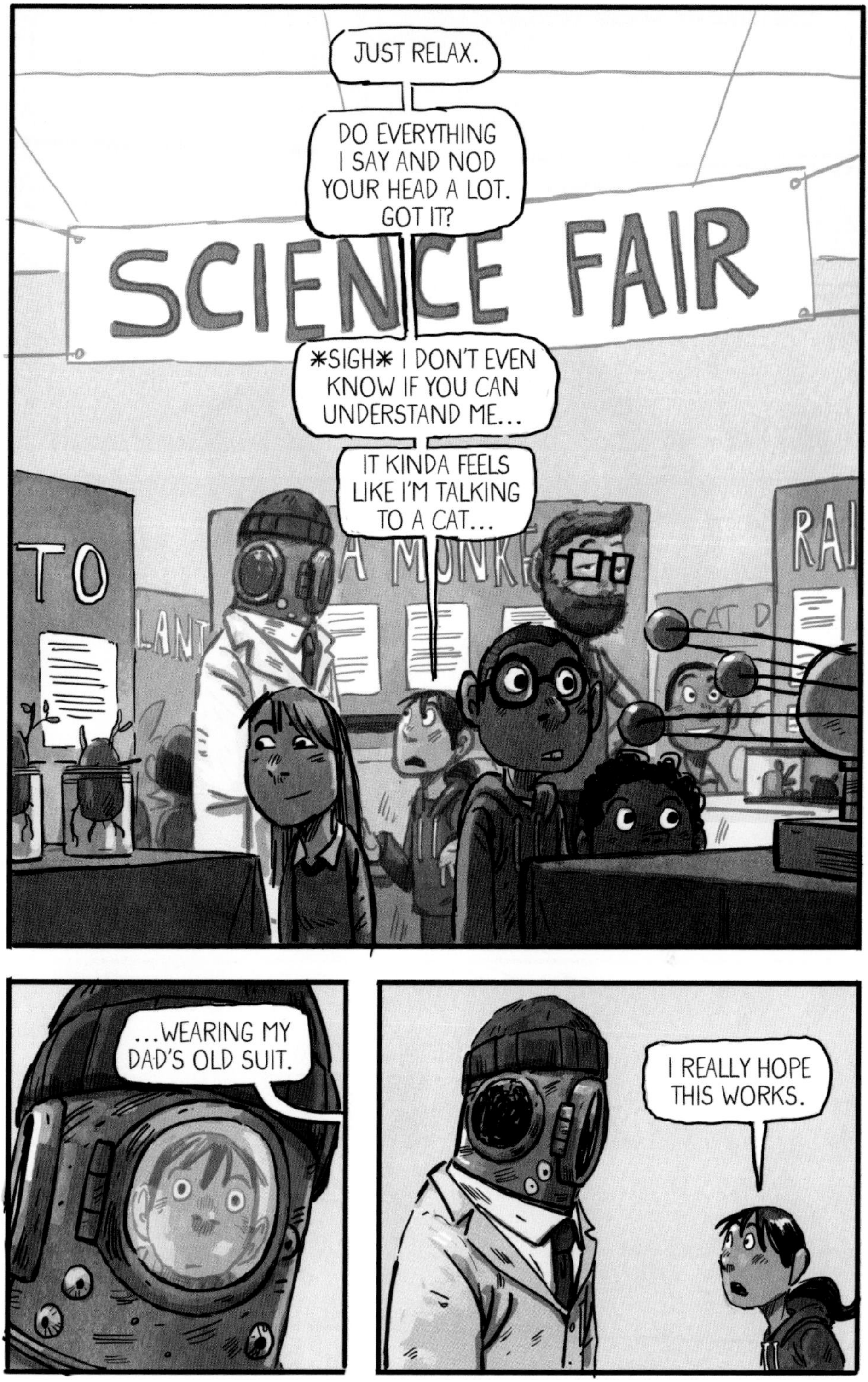
JUST RELAX.
DO EVERYTHING I SAY AND NOD YOUR HEAD A LOT. GOT IT?
SCIENCE FAIR
SIGH I DON'T EVEN KNOW IF YOU CAN UNDERSTAND ME...
IT KINDA FEELS LIKE I'M TALKING TO A CAT...
...WEARING MY DAD'S OLD SUIT.
I REALLY HOPE THIS WORKS.

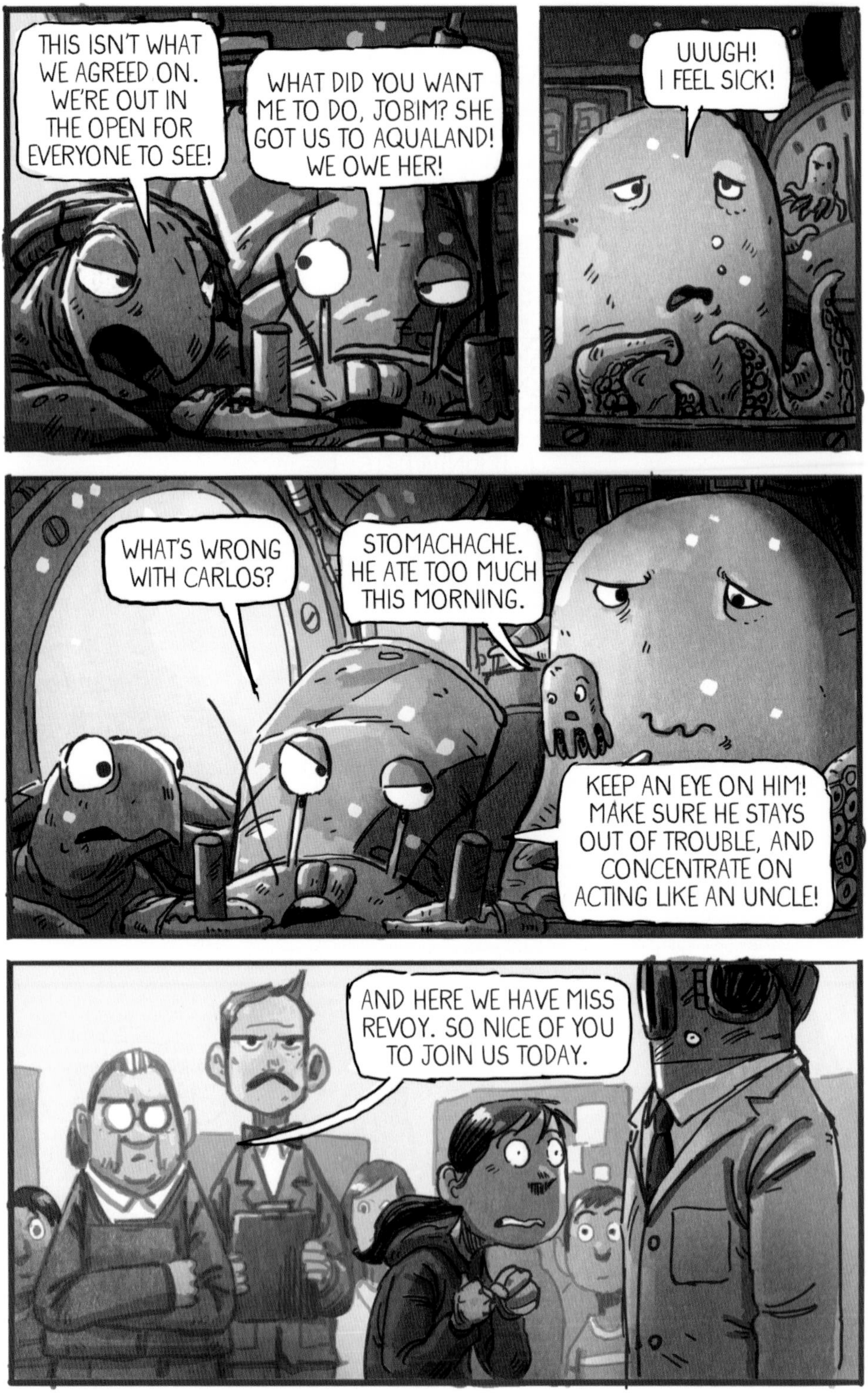
THIS ISN'T WHAT WE AGREED ON. WE'RE OUT IN THE OPEN FOR EVERYONE TO SEE!
WHAT DID YOU WANT ME TO DO, JOBIM? SHE GOT US TO AQUALAND! WE OWE HER!
UUUGH! I FEEL SICK!
WHAT'S WRONG WITH CARLOS?
STOMACHACHE. HE ATE TOO MUCH THIS MORNING.
KEEP AN EYE ON HIM! MAKE SURE HE STAYS OUT OF TROUBLE, AND CONCENTRATE ON ACTING LIKE AN UNCLE!
AND HERE WE HAVE MISS REVOY. SO NICE OF YOU TO JOIN US TODAY.

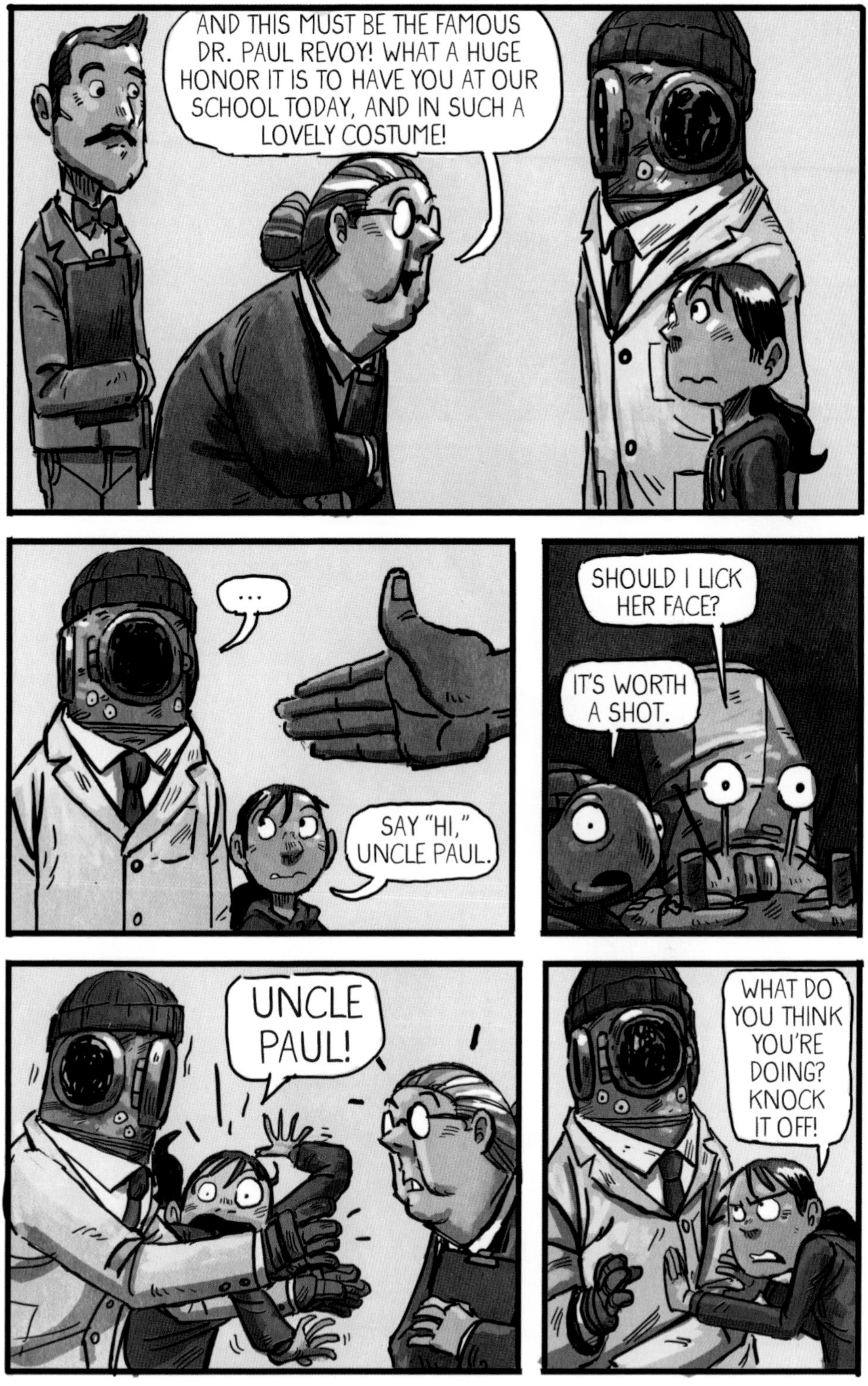
AND THIS MUST BE THE FAMOUS DR. PAUL REVOY! WHAT A HUGE HONOR IT IS TO HAVE YOU AT OUR SCHOOL TODAY, AND IN SUCH A LOVELY COSTUME!
...
SAY "HI," UNCLE PAUL.
SHOULD I LICK HER FACE?
IT'S WORTH A SHOT.
UNCLE PAUL!
WHAT DO YOU THINK YOU'RE DOING? KNOCK IT OFF!

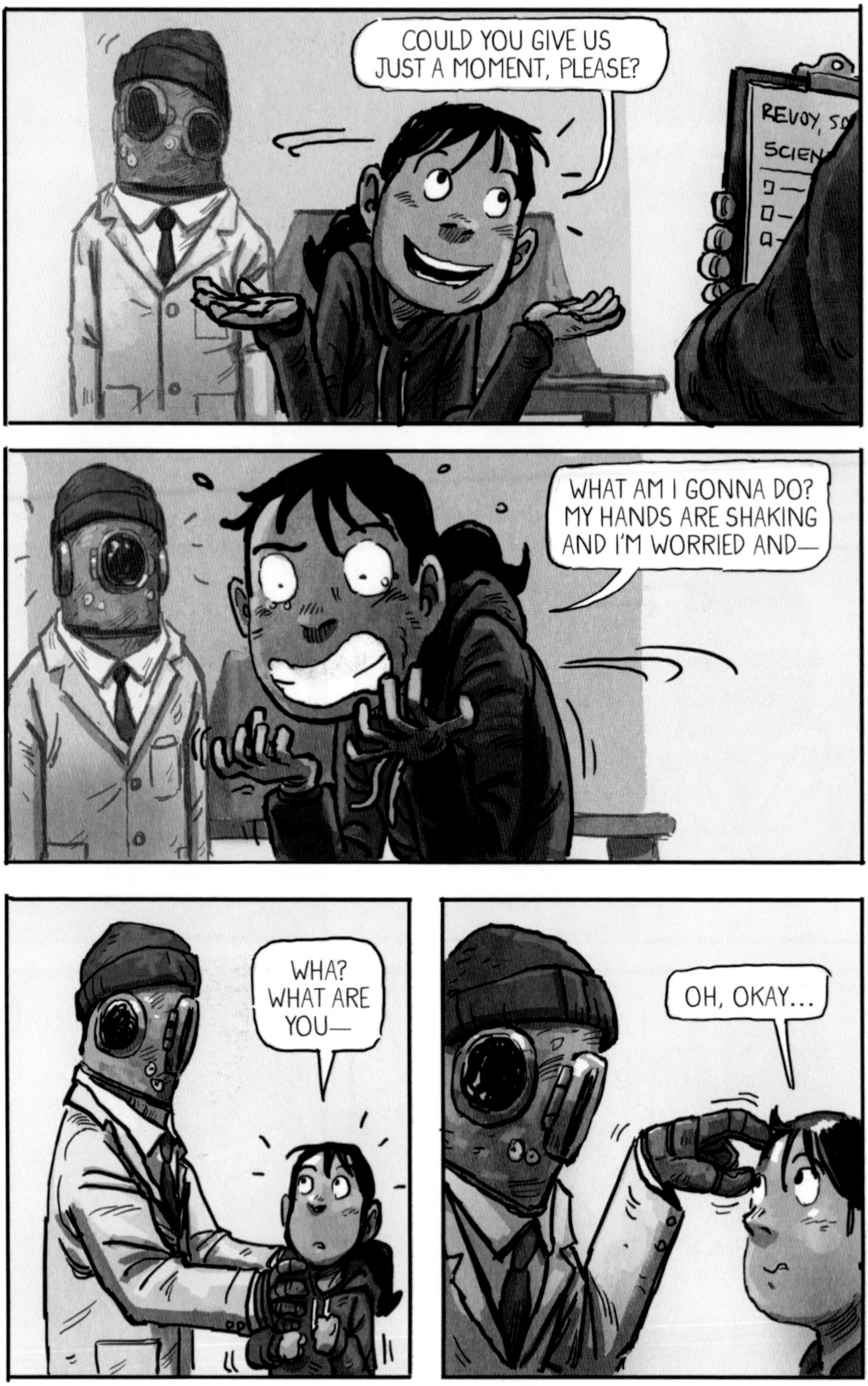
COULD YOU GIVE US JUST A MOMENT, PLEASE?
REVOY, SC
SCIEN
WHAT AM I GONNA DO? MY HANDS ARE SHAKING AND I'M WORRIED AND—
WHA? WHAT ARE YOU—
OH, OKAY...

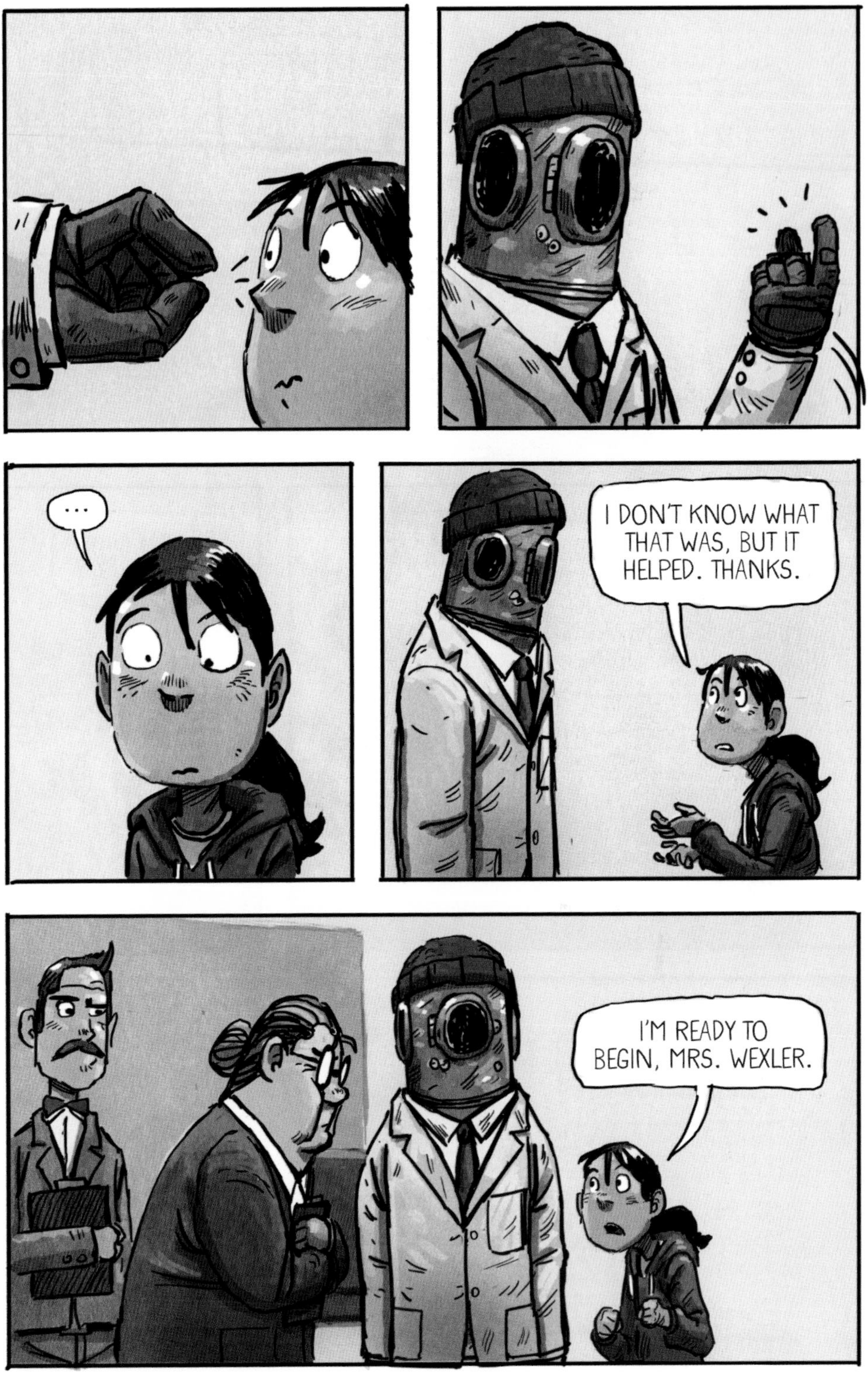
...
I DON'T KNOW WHAT THAT WAS, BUT IT HELPED. THANKS.
I'M READY TO BEGIN, MRS. WEXLER.

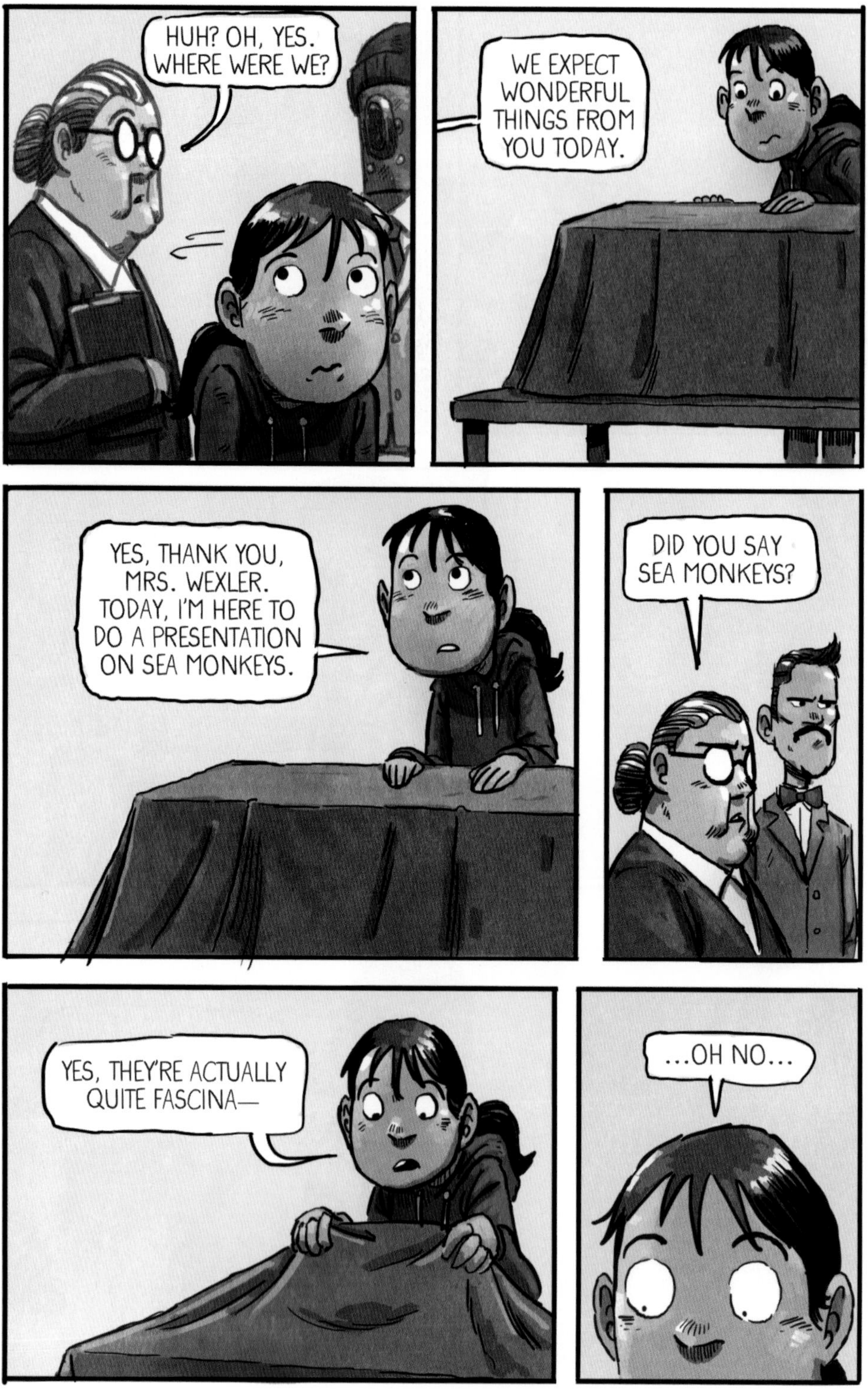
HUH? OH, YES. WHERE WERE WE?
WE EXPECT WONDERFUL THINGS FROM YOU TODAY.
YES, THANK YOU, MRS. WEXLER. TODAY, I'M HERE TO DO A PRESENTATION ON SEA MONKEYS.
DID YOU SAY SEA MONKEYS?
YES, THEY'RE ACTUALLY QUITE FASCINA—
...OH NO...

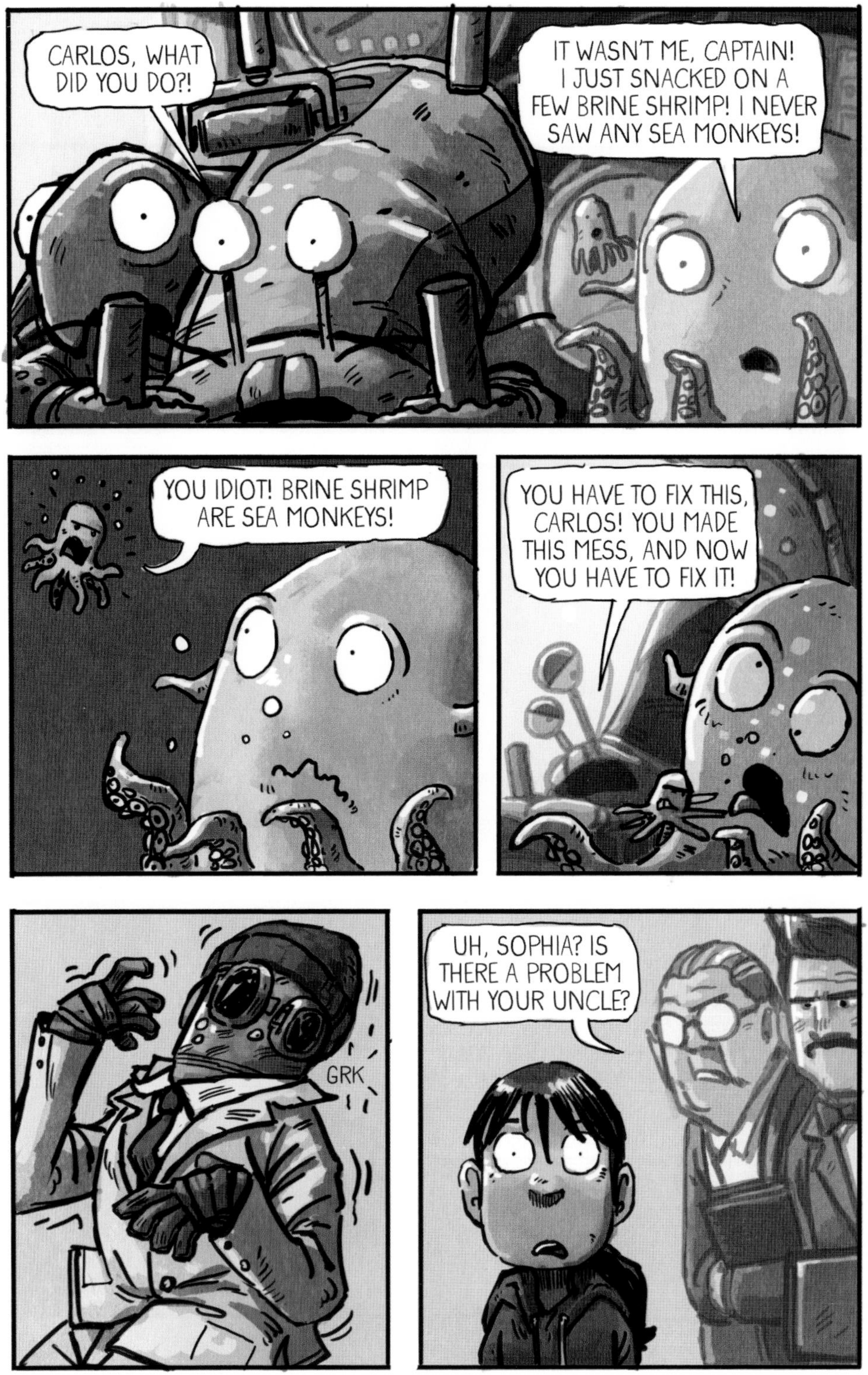
CARLOS, WHAT DID YOU DO?!
IT WASN'T ME, CAPTAIN! I JUST SNACKED ON A FEW BRINE SHRIMP! I NEVER SAW ANY SEA MONKEYS!
YOU IDIOT! BRINE SHRIMP ARE SEA MONKEYS!
YOU HAVE TO FIX THIS, CARLOS! YOU MADE THIS MESS, AND NOW YOU HAVE TO FIX IT!
GRK
UH, SOPHIA? IS THERE A PROBLEM WITH YOUR UNCLE?

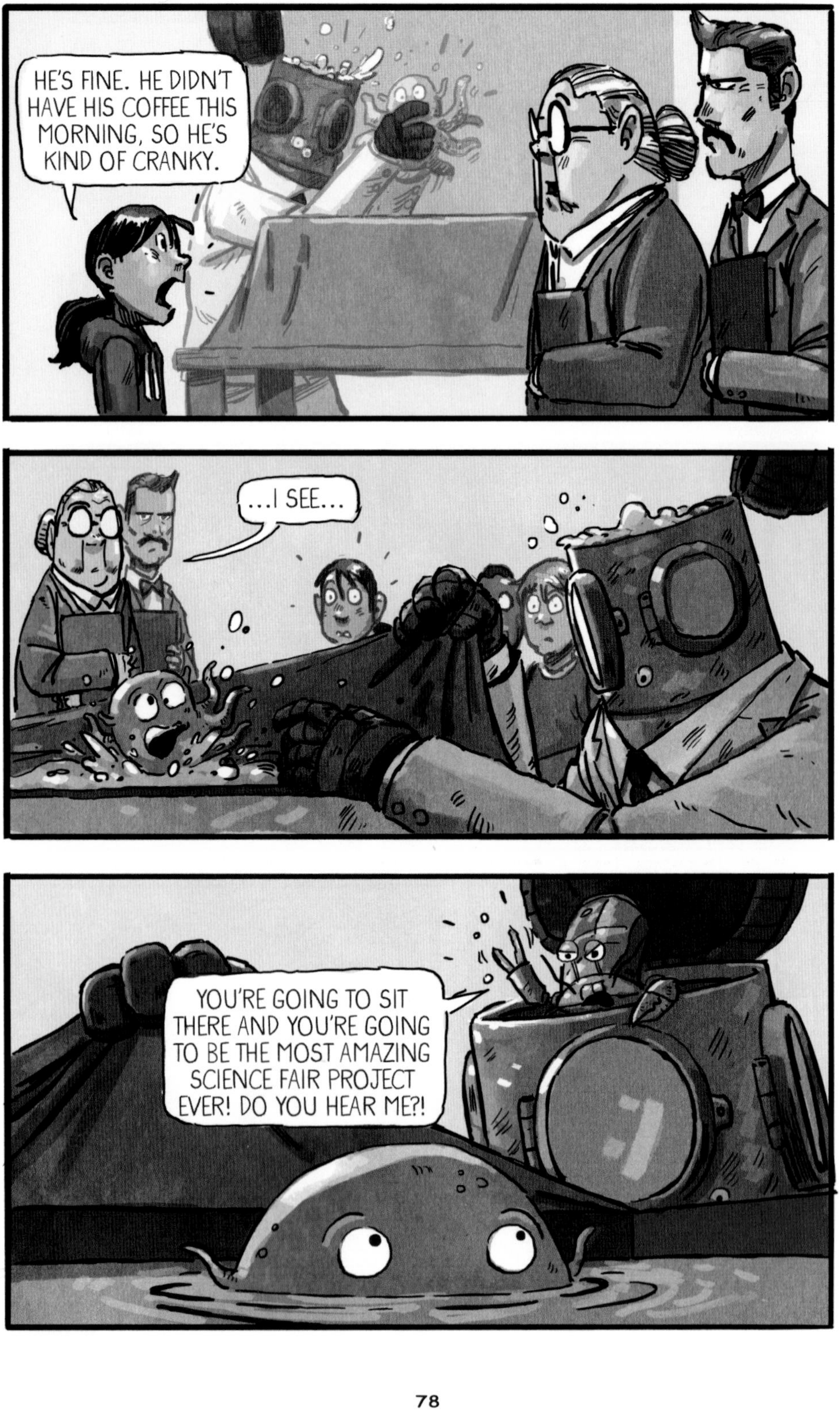
HE'S FINE. HE DIDN'T HAVE HIS COFFEE THIS MORNING, SO HE'S KIND OF CRANKY.
...I SEE...
YOU'RE GOING TO SIT THERE AND YOU'RE GOING TO BE THE MOST AMAZING SCIENCE FAIR PROJECT EVER! DO YOU HEAR ME?!

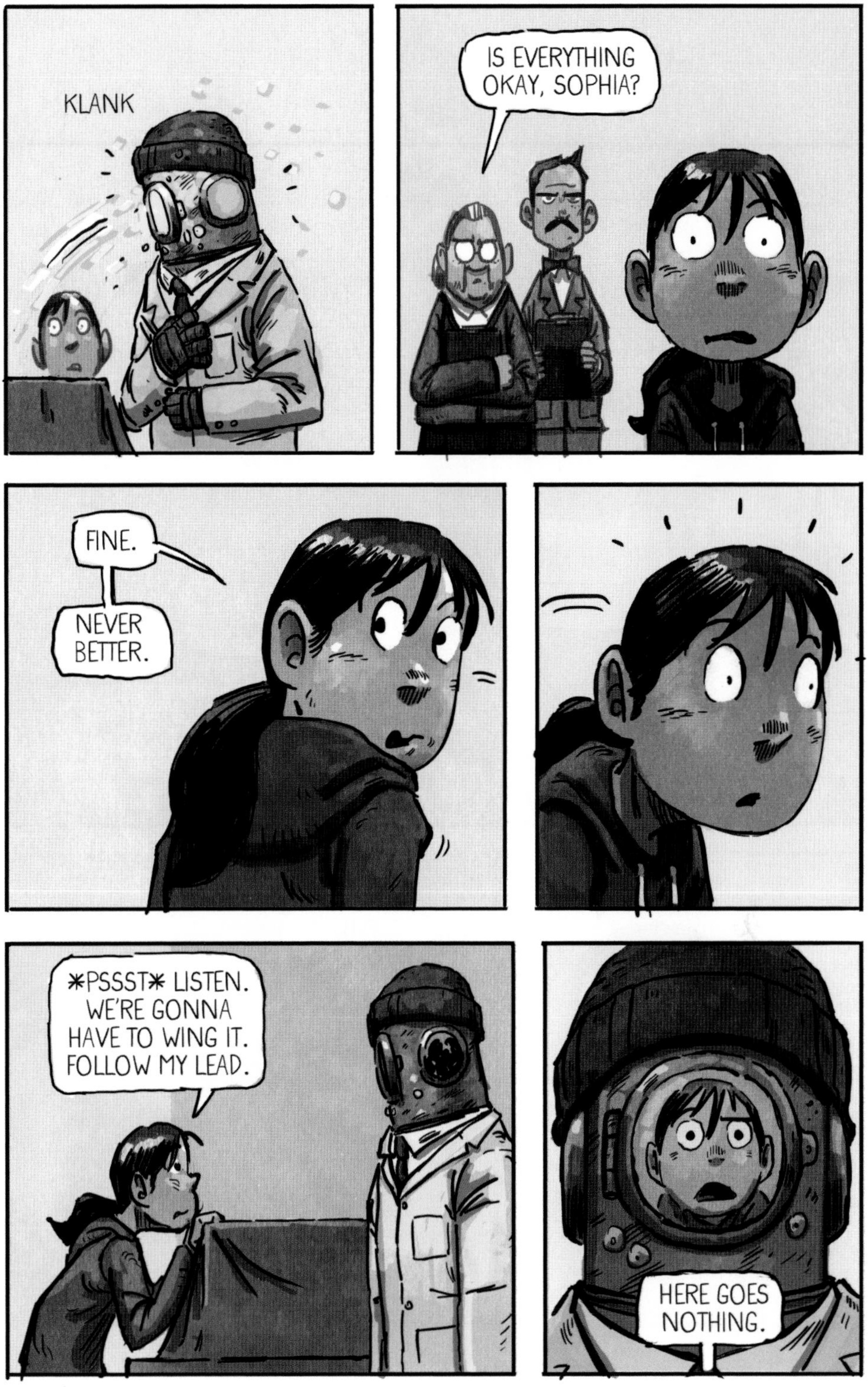
KLANK
IS EVERYTHING OKAY, SOPHIA?
FINE.
NEVER BETTER.
PSSST LISTEN. WE'RE GONNA HAVE TO WING IT. FOLLOW MY LEAD.
HERE GOES NOTHING.

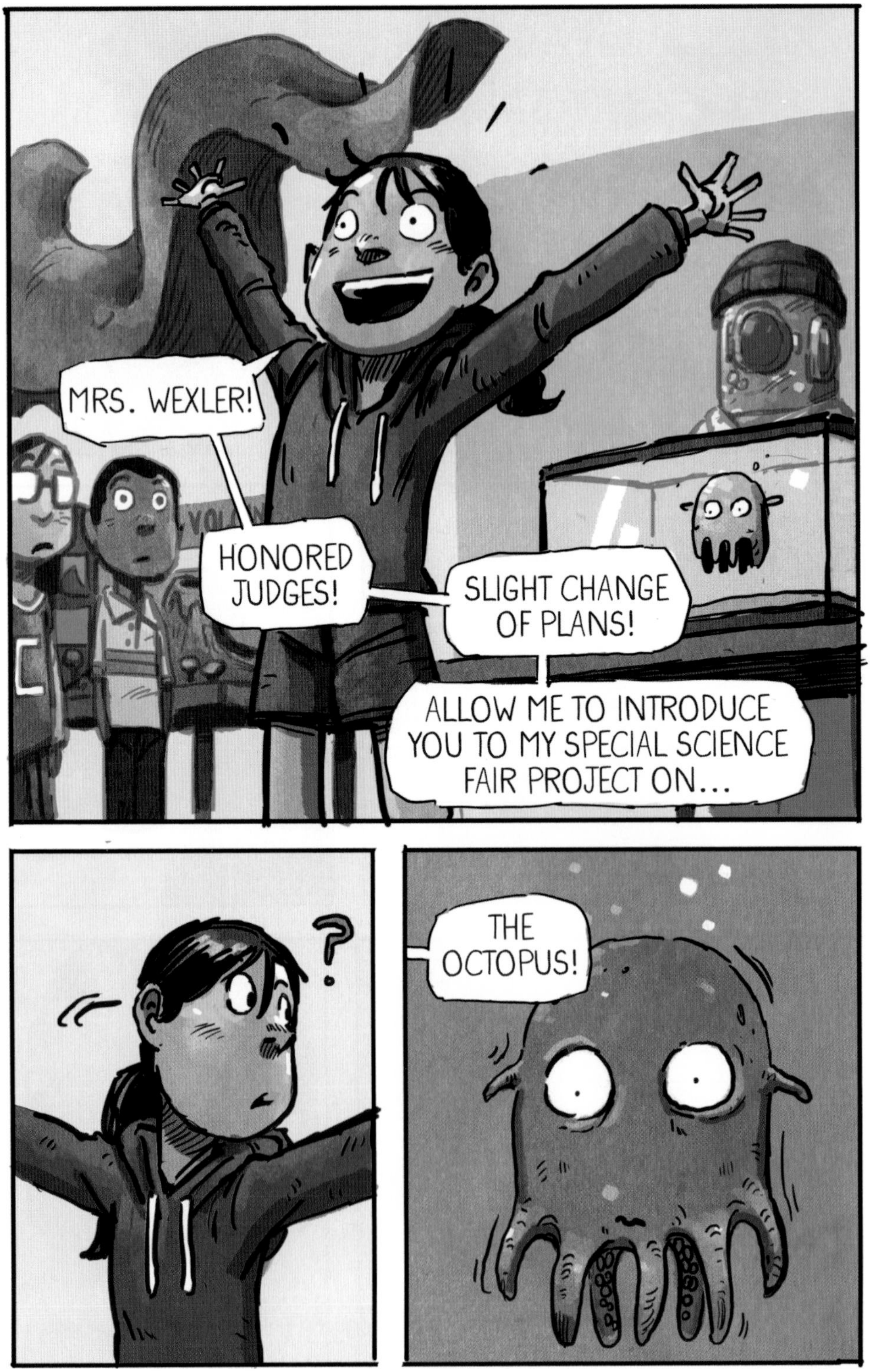
MRS. WEXLER!
HONORED JUDGES!
SLIGHT CHANGE OF PLANS!
ALLOW ME TO INTRODUCE YOU TO MY SPECIAL SCIENCE FAIR PROJECT ON...
?
THE OCTOPUS!

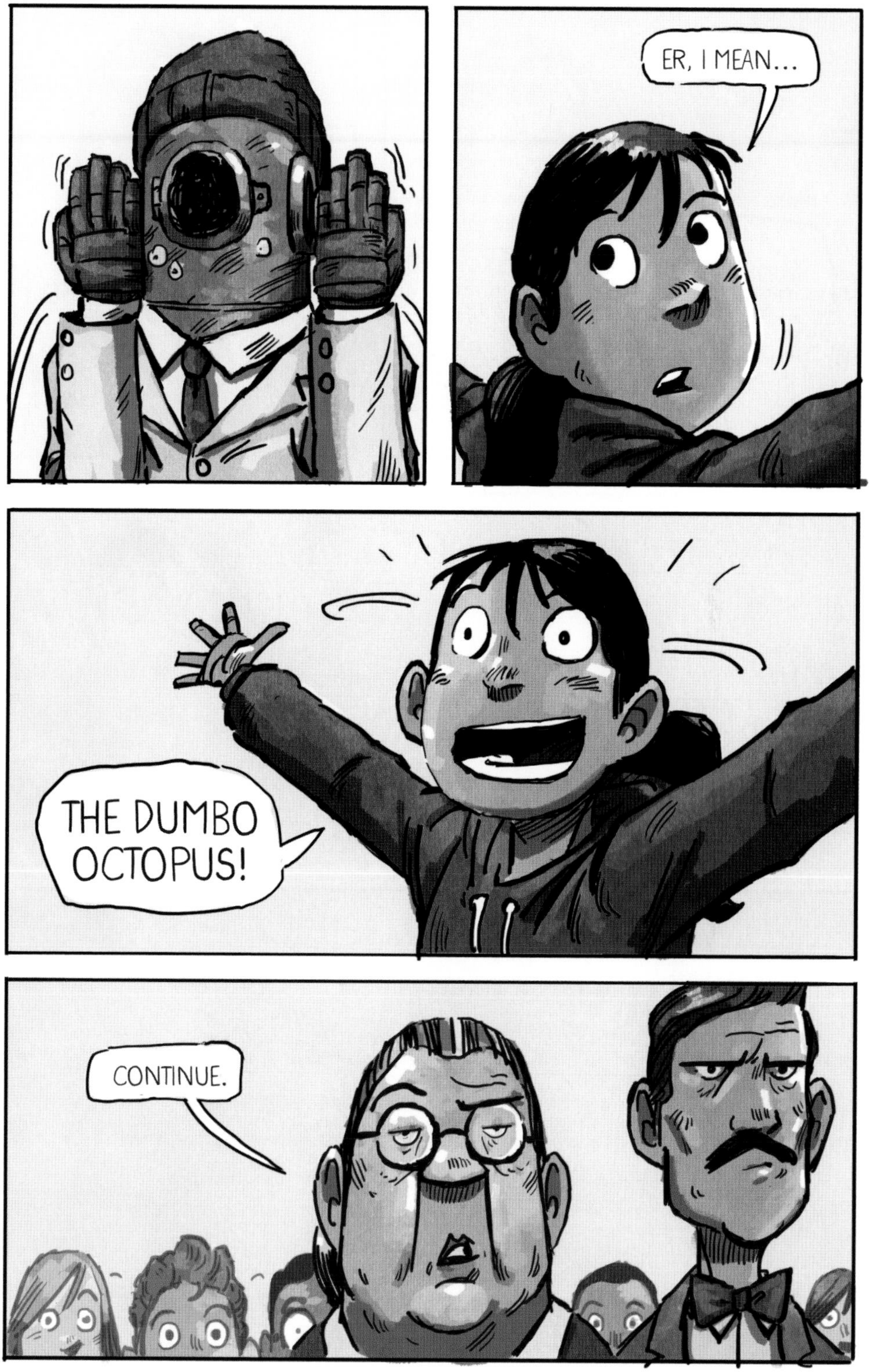
ER, I MEAN...
THE DUMBO OCTOPUS!
CONTINUE.

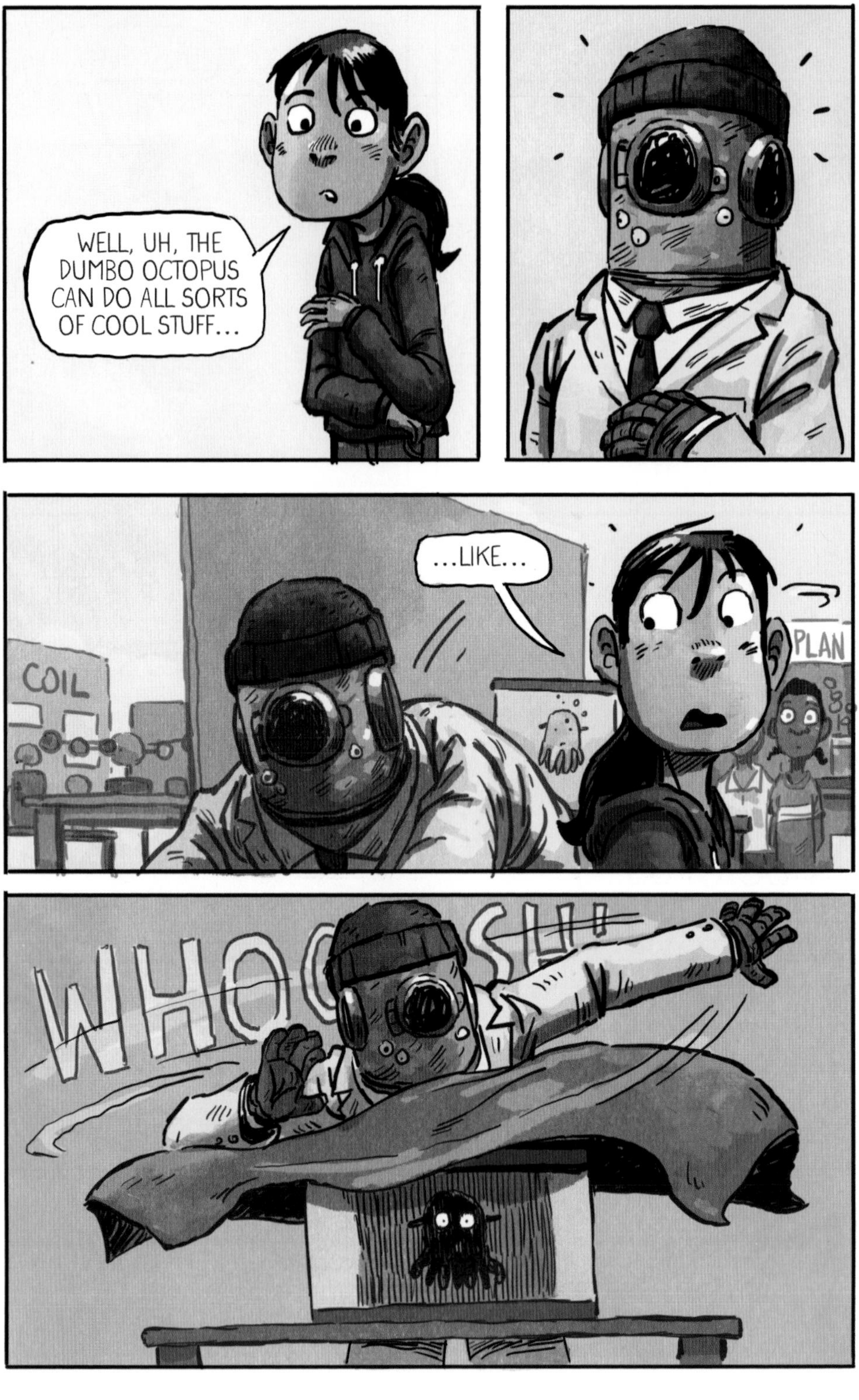
WELL, UH, THE DUMBO OCTOPUS CAN DO ALL SORTS OF COOL STUFF...
...LIKE...
COIL
PLAN
WHOOSH!

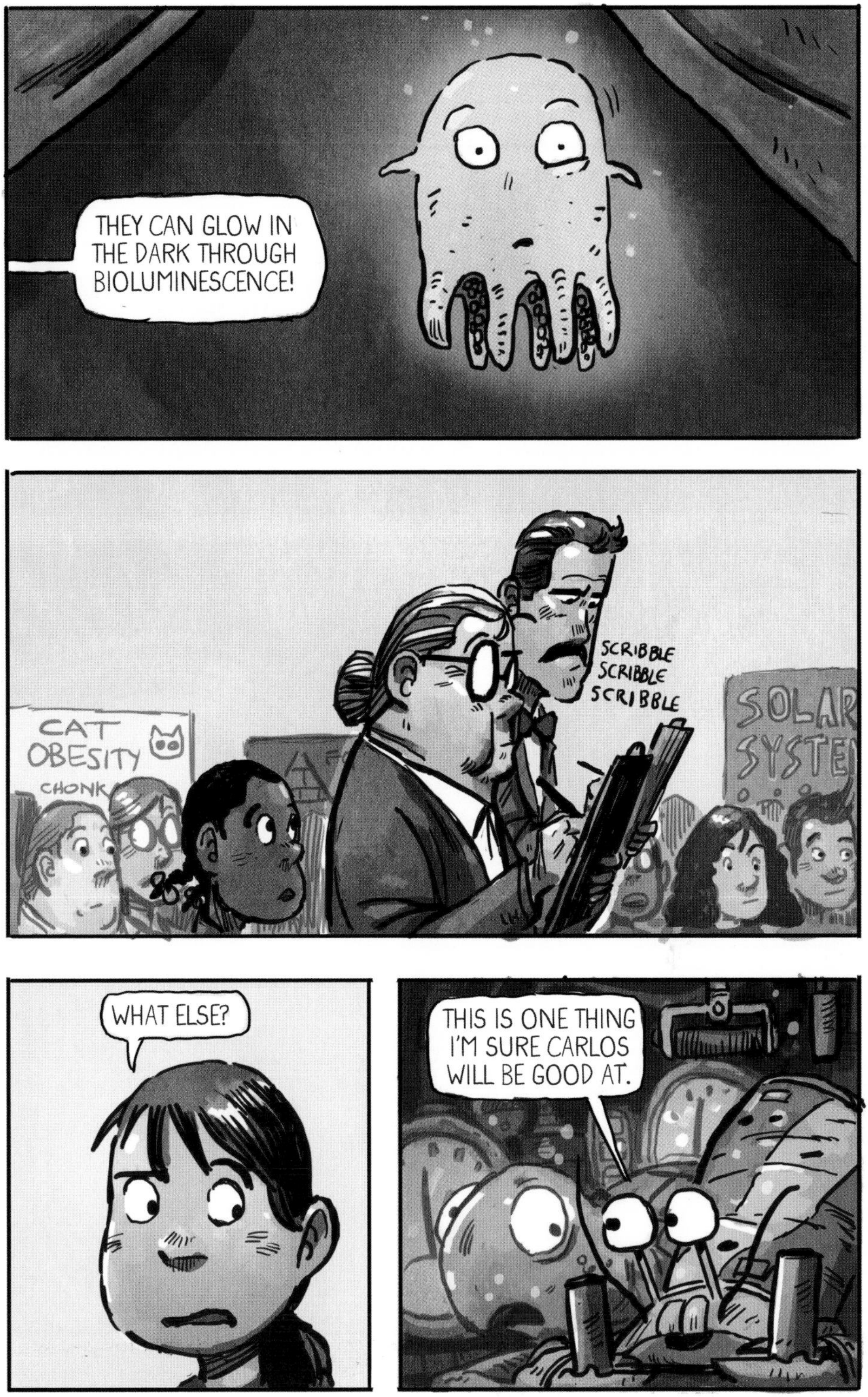
THEY CAN GLOW IN THE DARK THROUGH BIOLUMINESCENCE!
CAT OBESITY
CHONK
SOLAR SYSTEM
SCRIBBLE SCRIBBLE SCRIBBLE
WHAT ELSE?
THIS IS ONE THING I'M SURE CARLOS WILL BE GOOD AT.

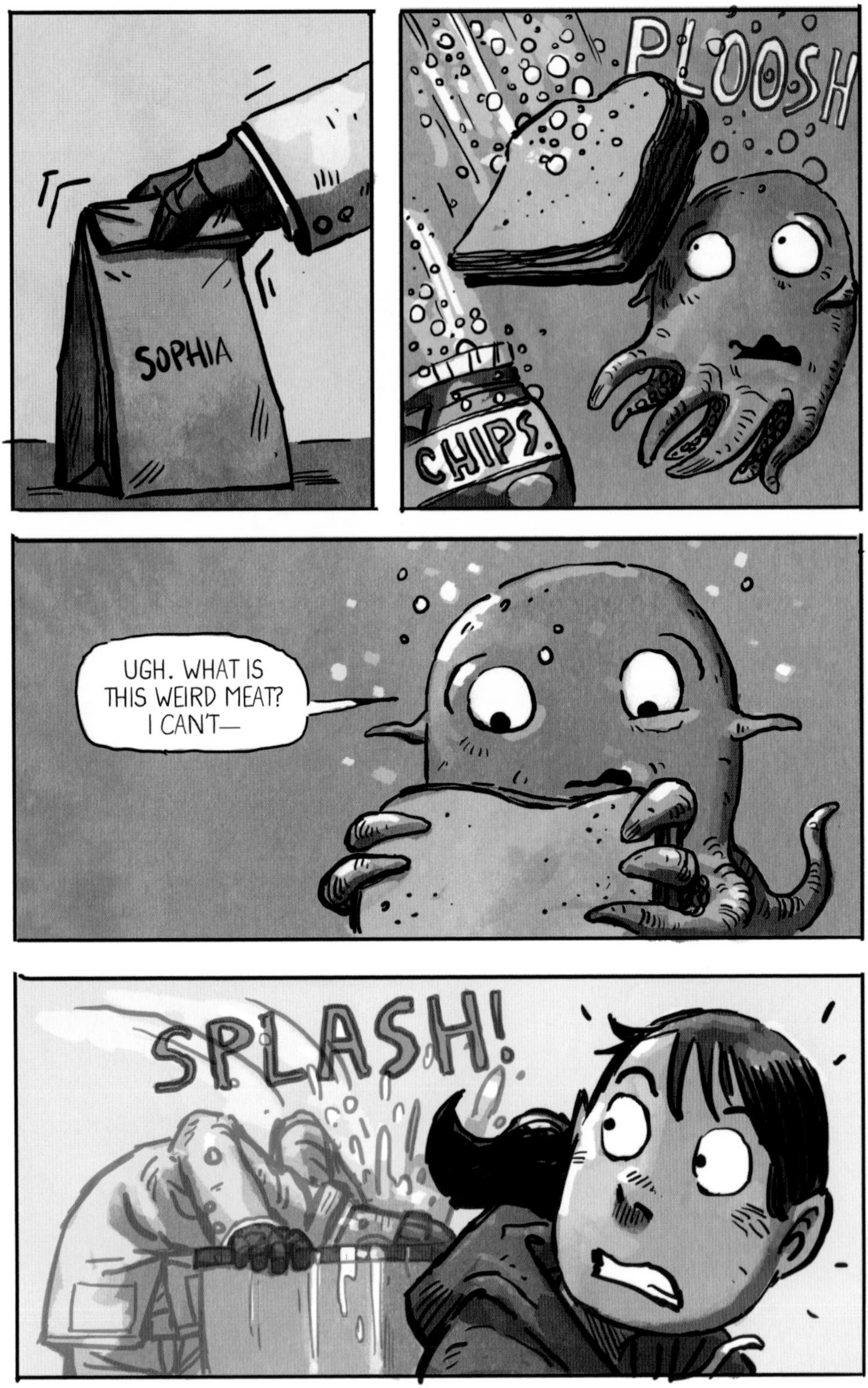
SOPHIA
PLOOSH
CHIPS
UGH. WHAT IS THIS WEIRD MEAT? I CAN'T—
SPLASH!

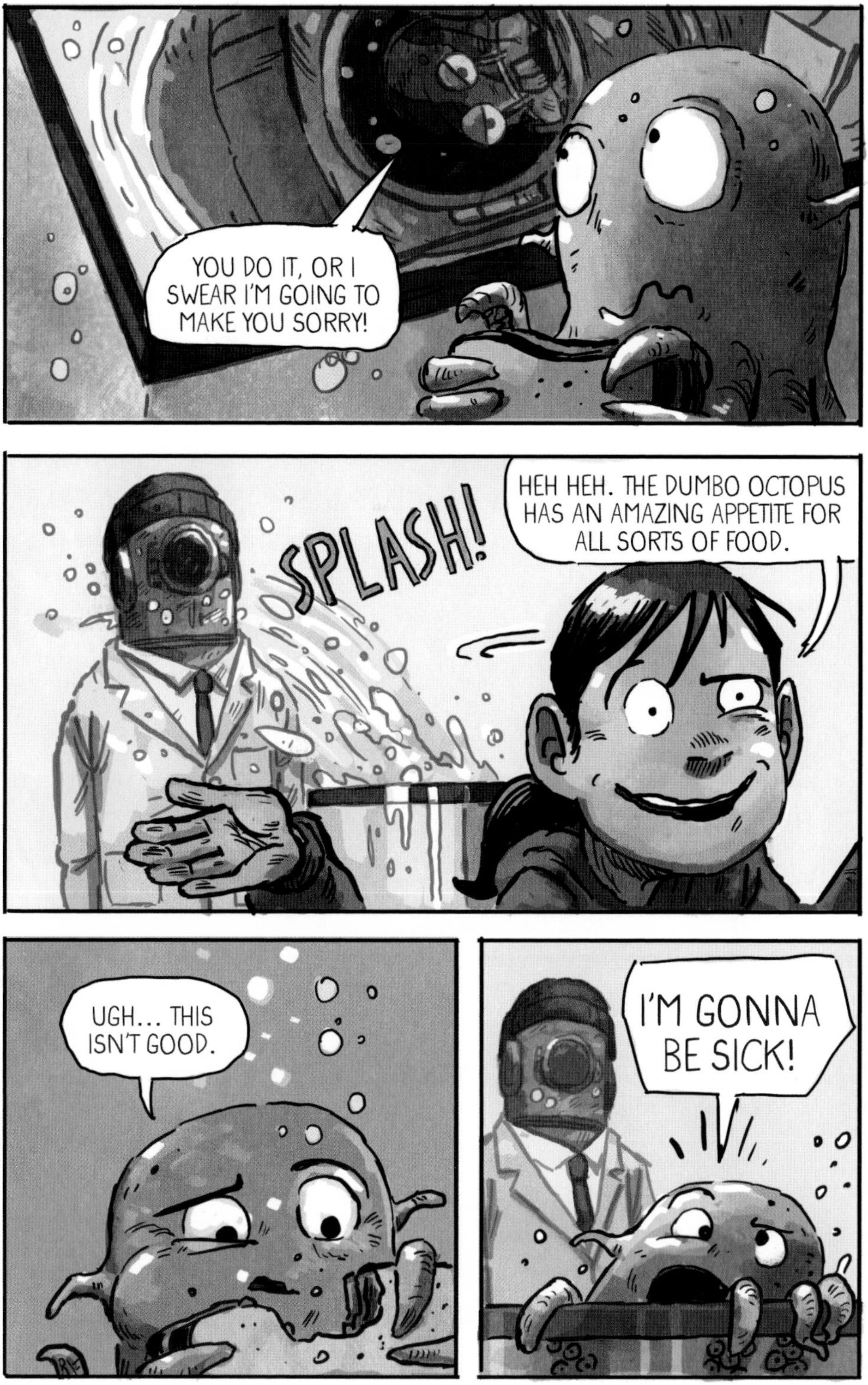
YOU DO IT, OR I SWEAR I'M GOING TO MAKE YOU SORRY!
SPLASH!
HEH HEH. THE DUMBO OCTOPUS HAS AN AMAZING APPETITE FOR ALL SORTS OF FOOD.
UGH... THIS ISN'T GOOD.
I'M GONNA BE SICK!

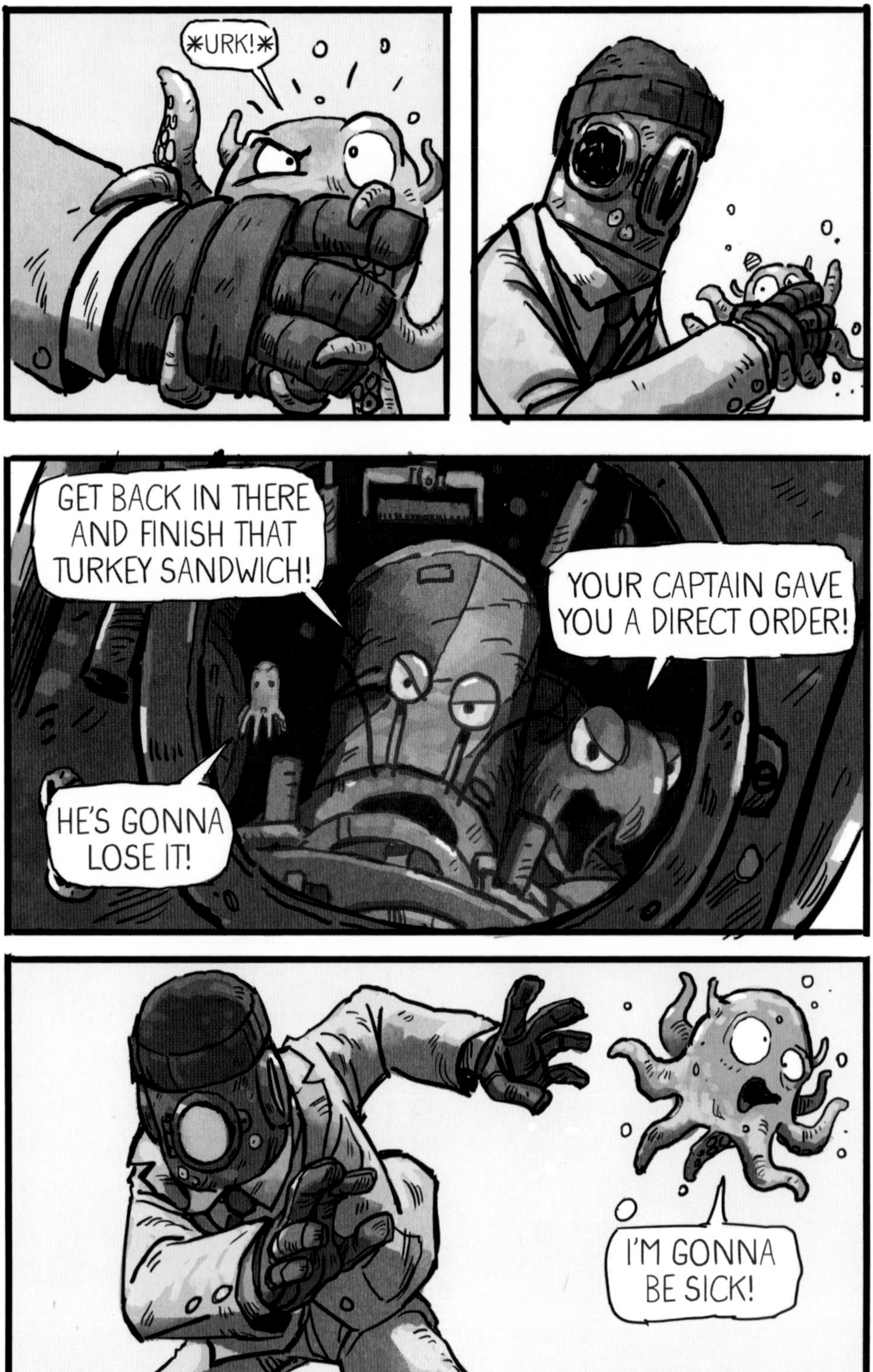
URK!
GET BACK IN THERE AND FINISH THAT TURKEY SANDWICH!
YOUR CAPTAIN GAVE YOU A DIRECT ORDER!
HE'S GONNA LOSE IT!
I'M GONNA BE SICK!

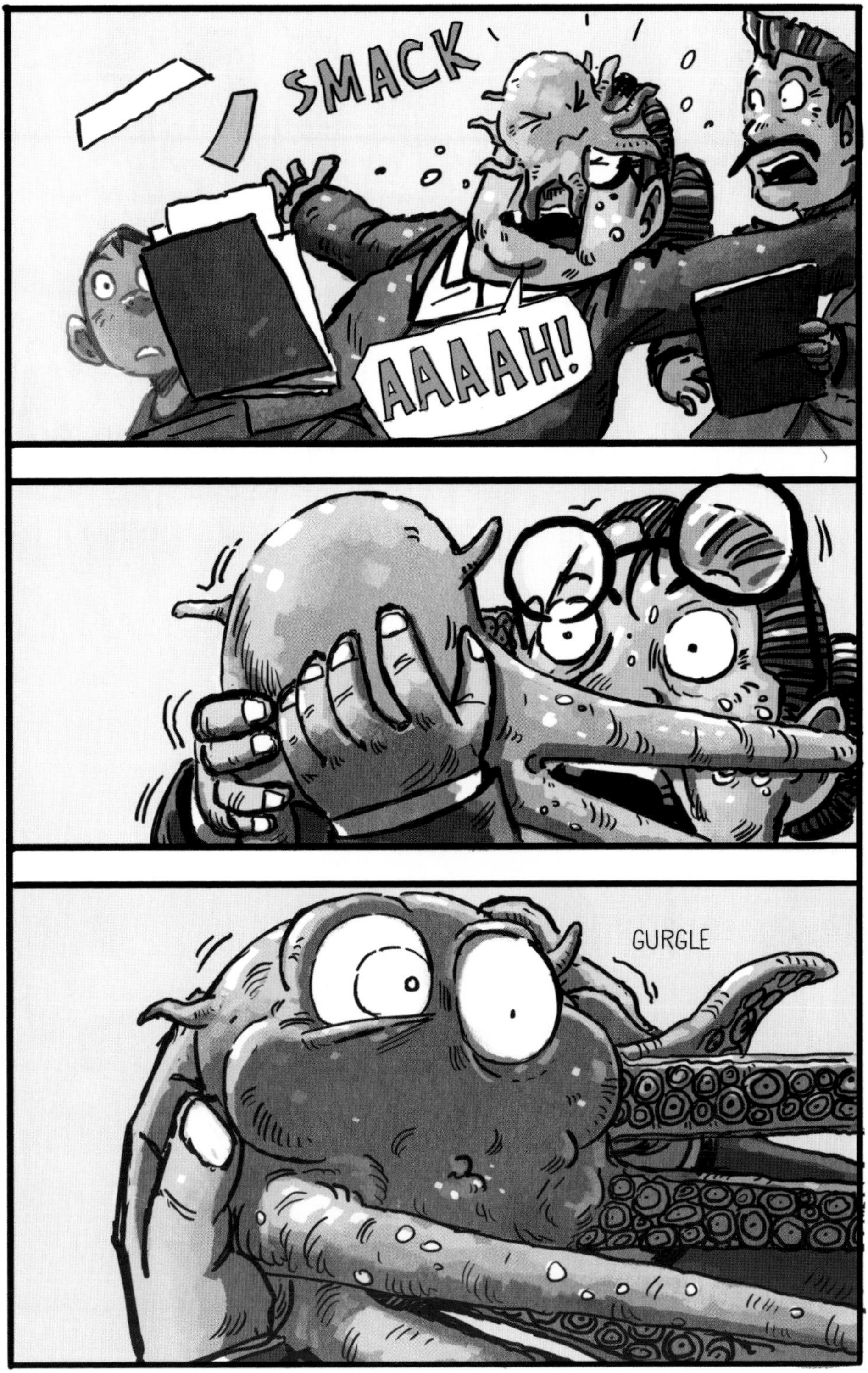
SMACK
AAAAH!
GURGLE

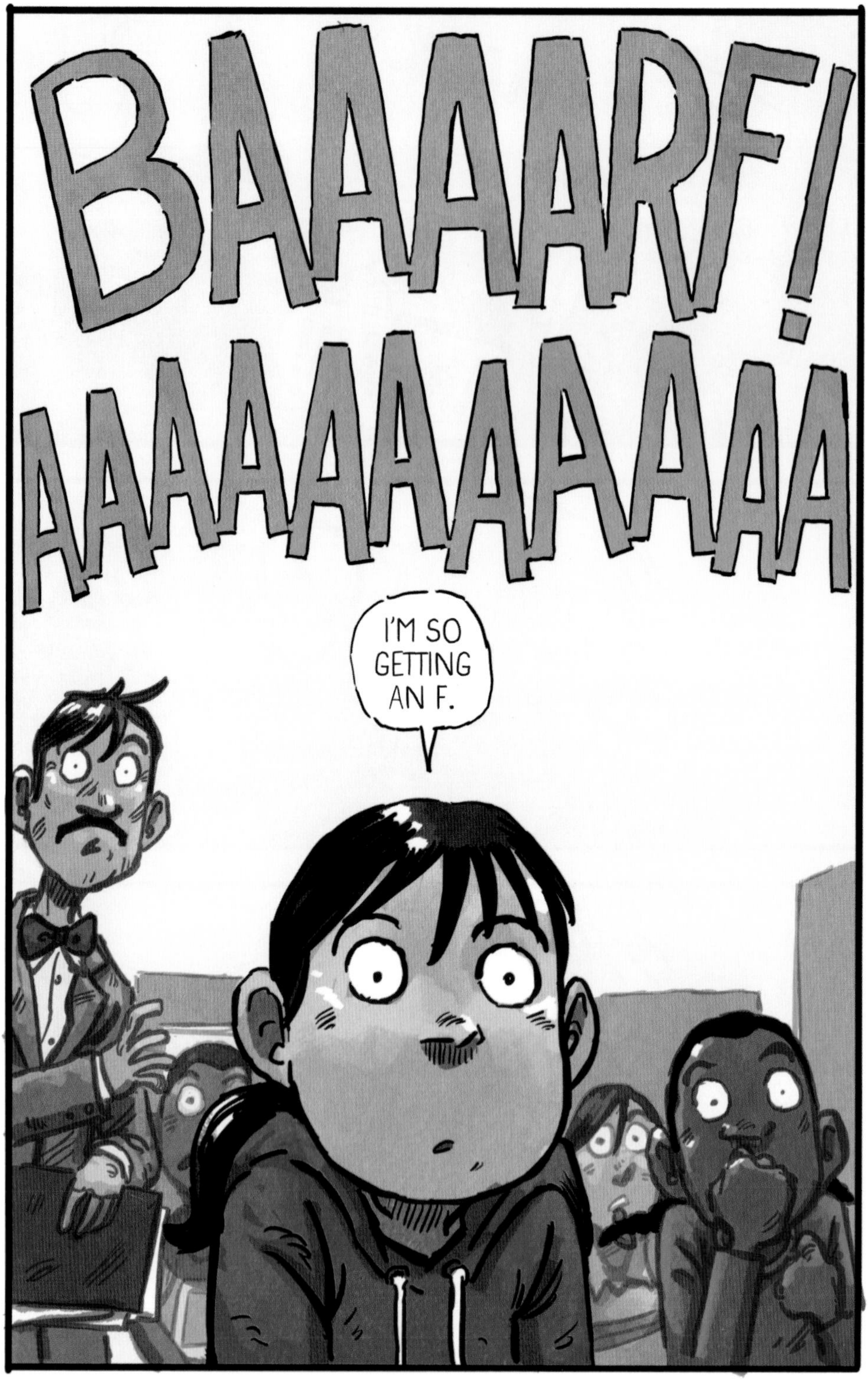
BAAAARF!
AAAAAAAAAAA
I'M SO GETTING AN F.

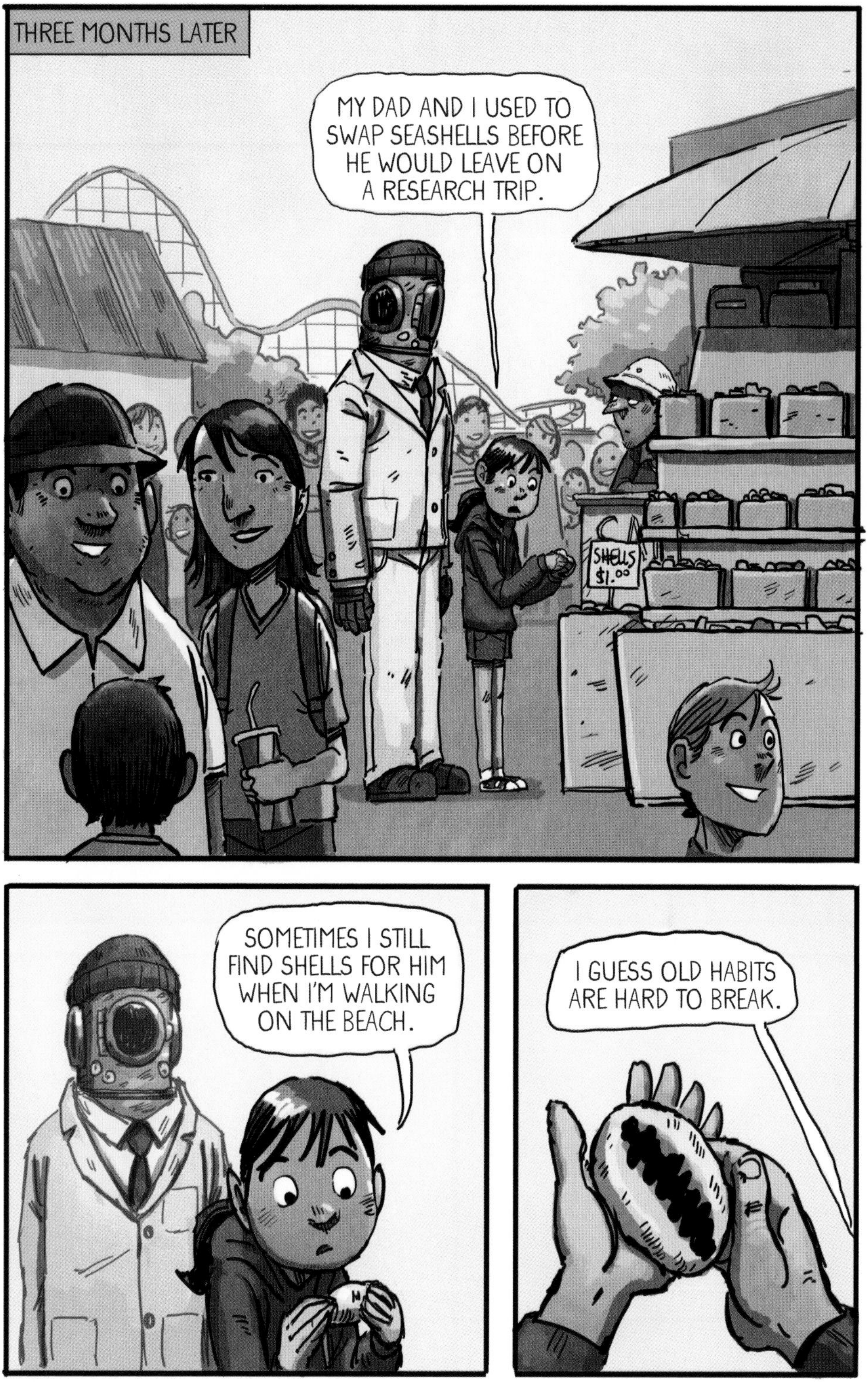
THREE MONTHS LATER
MY DAD AND I USED TO SWAP SEASHELLS BEFORE HE WOULD LEAVE ON A RESEARCH TRIP.
SHELLS $1.00
SOMETIMES I STILL FIND SHELLS FOR HIM WHEN I'M WALKING ON THE BEACH.
I GUESS OLD HABITS ARE HARD TO BREAK.

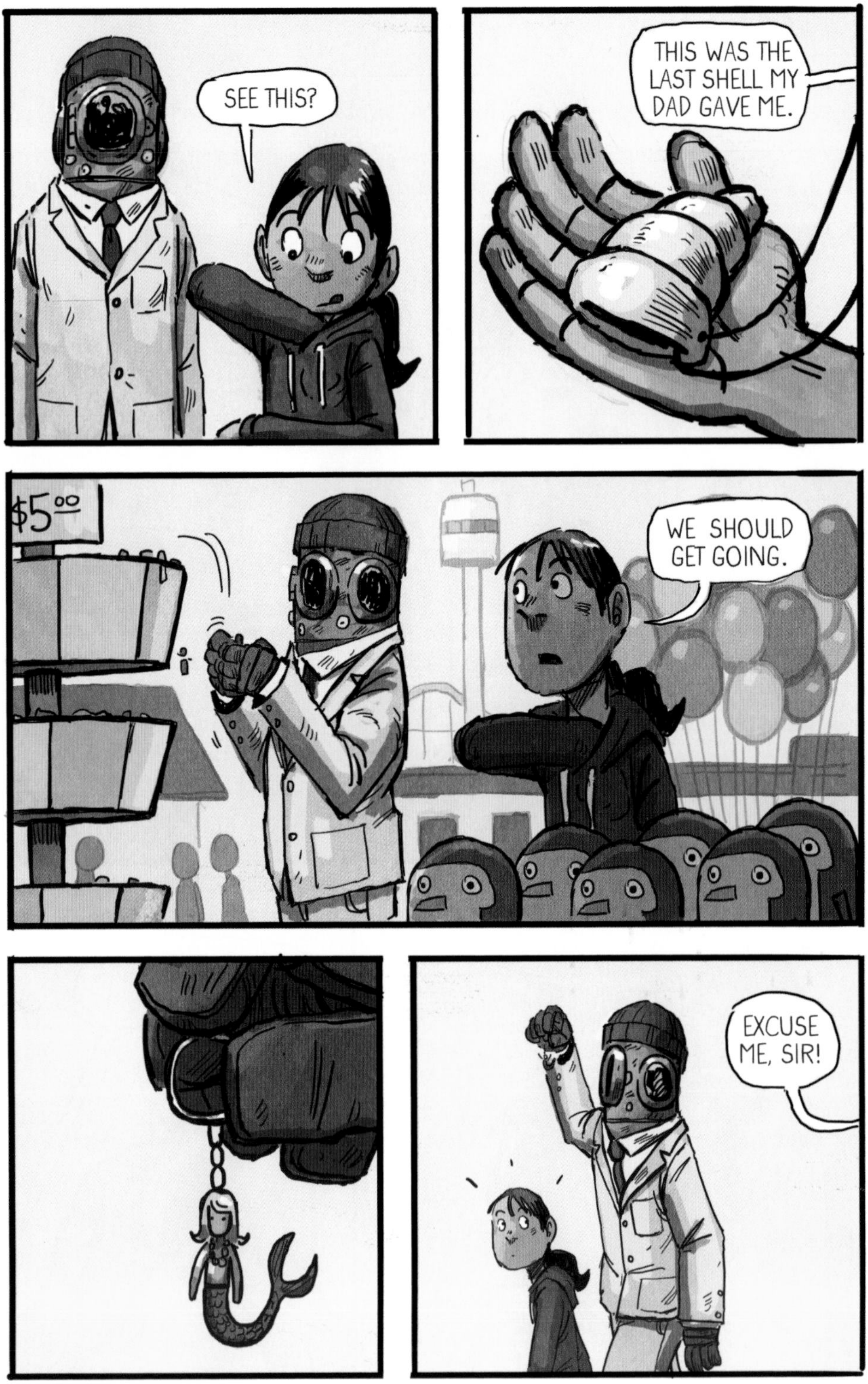
SEE THIS?
THIS WAS THE LAST SHELL MY DAD GAVE ME.
$5.00
WE SHOULD GET GOING.
EXCUSE ME, SIR!

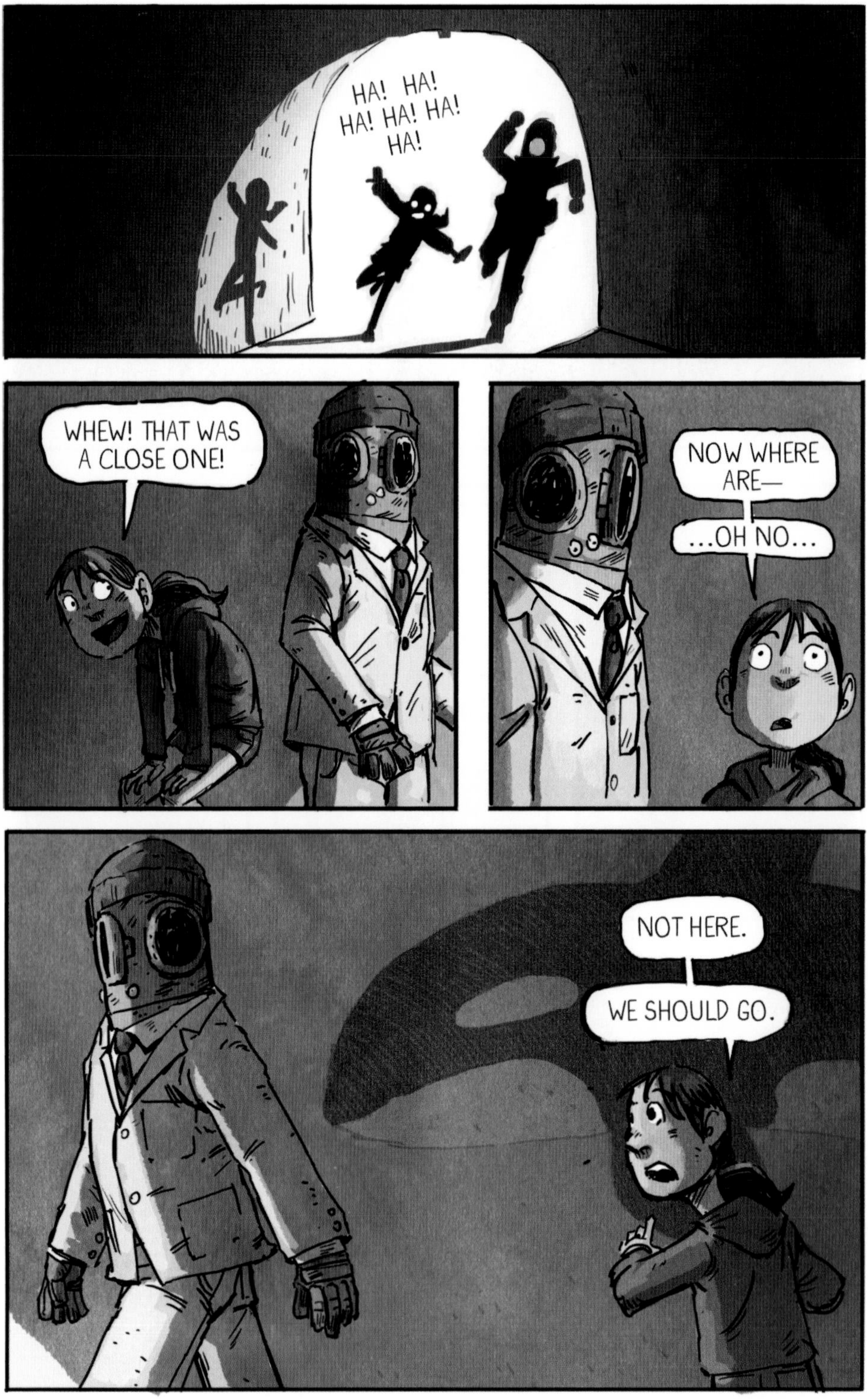
HA! HA!
HA! HA! HA!
HA!
WHEW! THAT WAS A CLOSE ONE!
NOW WHERE ARE—
...OH NO...
NOT HERE.
WE SHOULD GO.

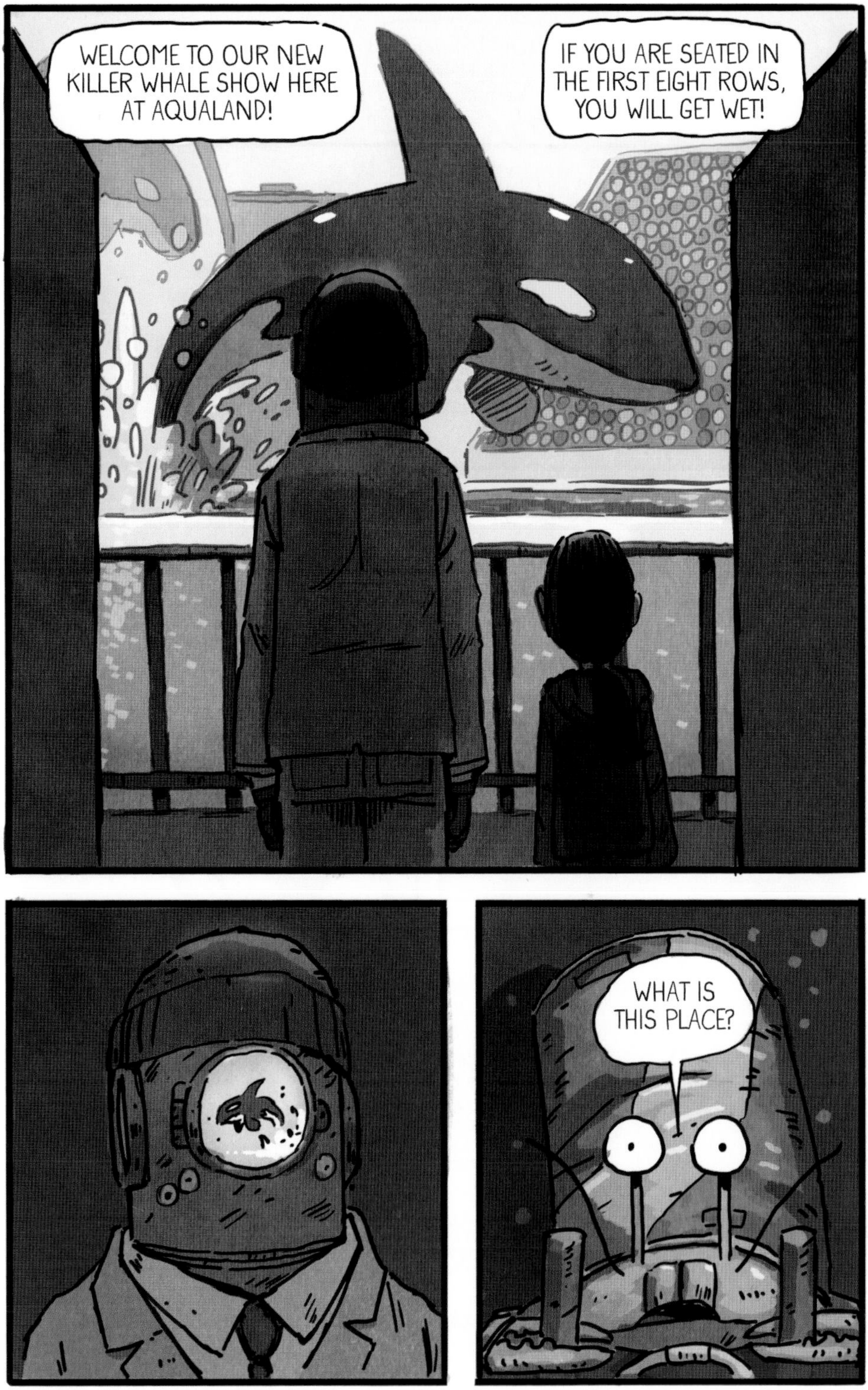
WELCOME TO OUR NEW KILLER WHALE SHOW HERE AT AQUALAND!
IF YOU ARE SEATED IN THE FIRST EIGHT ROWS, YOU WILL GET WET!
WHAT IS THIS PLACE?

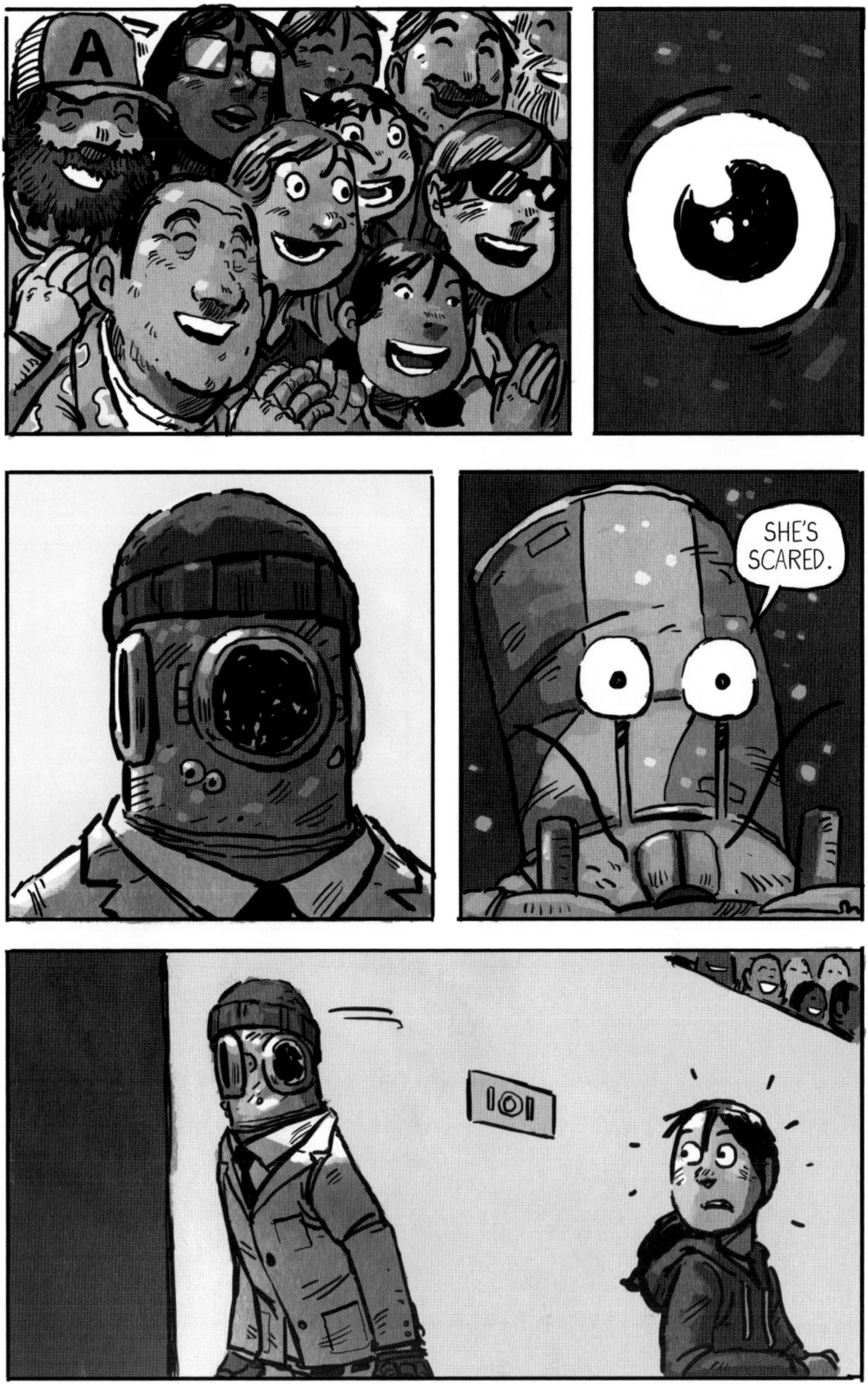
A
SHE'S SCARED.
101

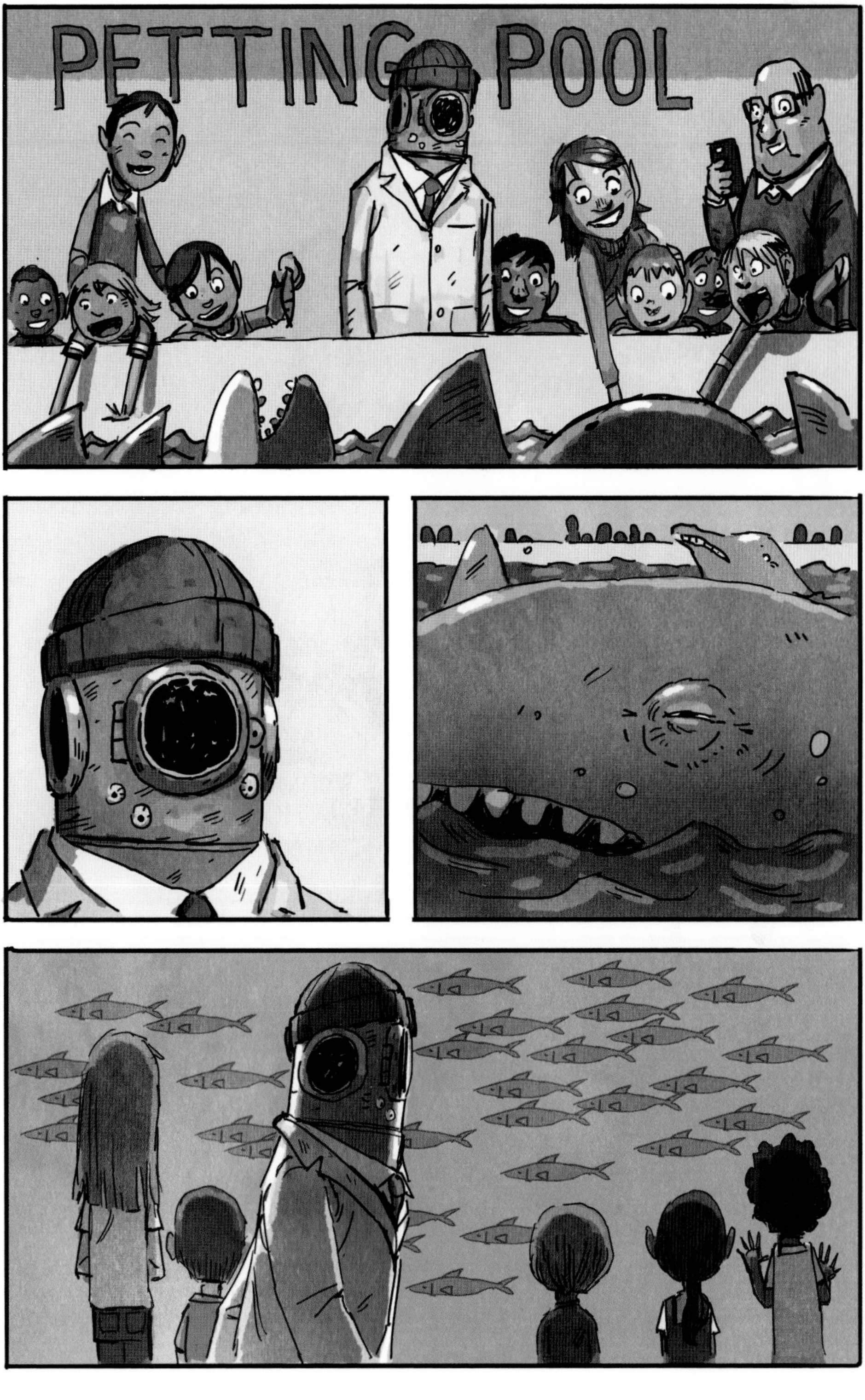
PETTING POOL

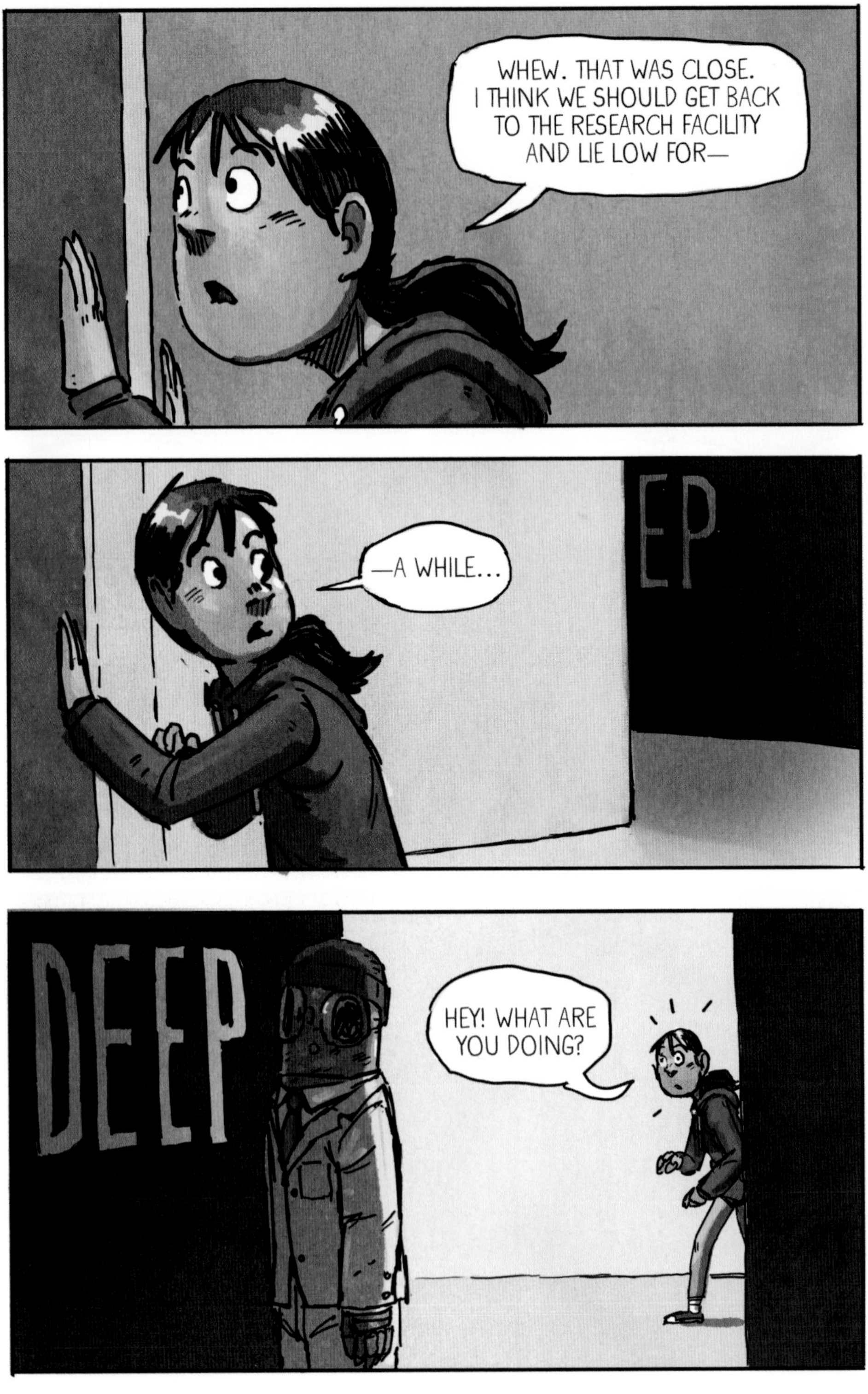
WHEW. THAT WAS CLOSE. I THINK WE SHOULD GET BACK TO THE RESEARCH FACILITY AND LIE LOW FOR—
EP
—A WHILE...
DEEP
HEY! WHAT ARE YOU DOING?

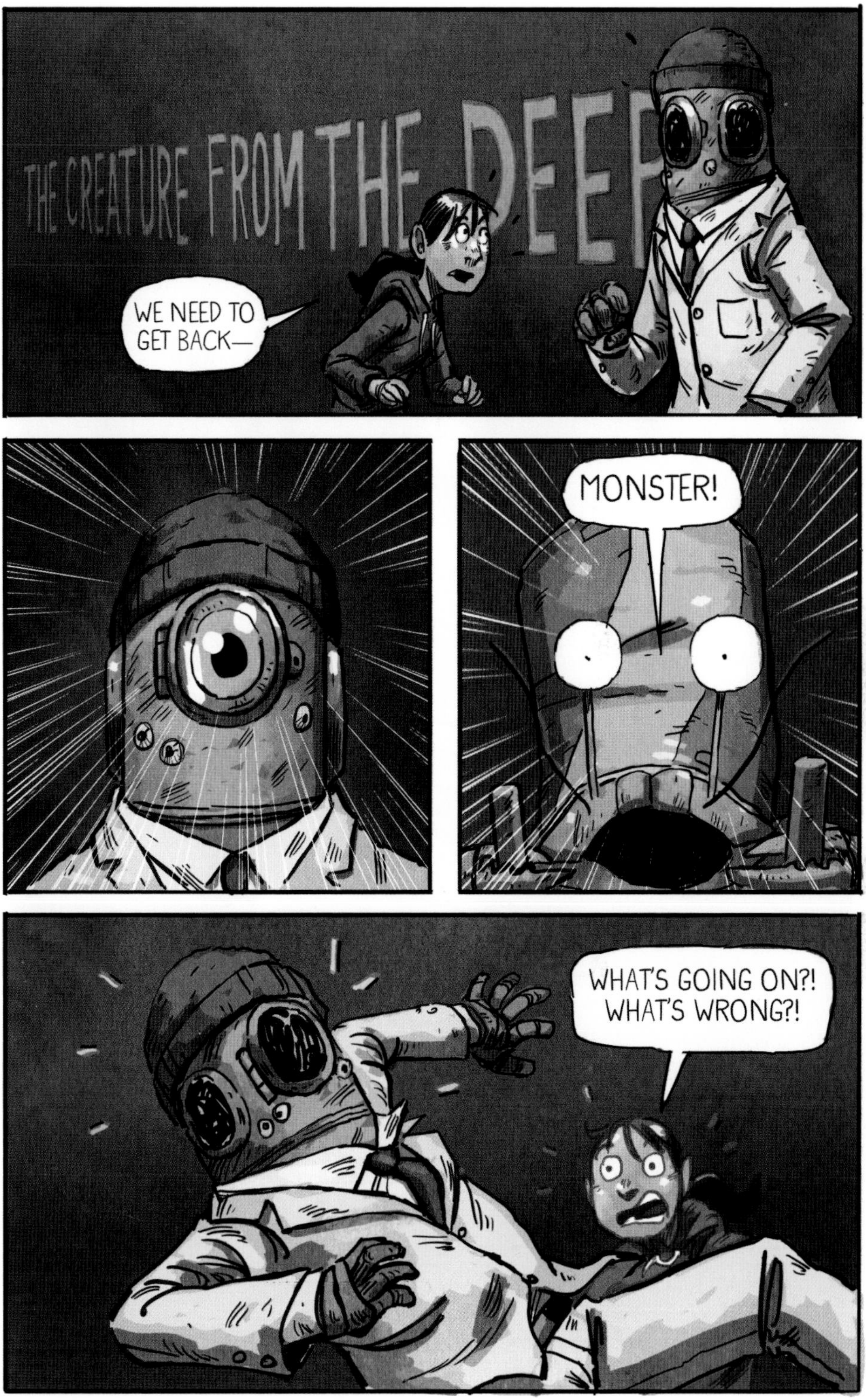
THE CREATURE FROM THE DEEP
WE NEED TO GET BACK—
MONSTER!
WHAT'S GOING ON?! WHAT'S WRONG?!

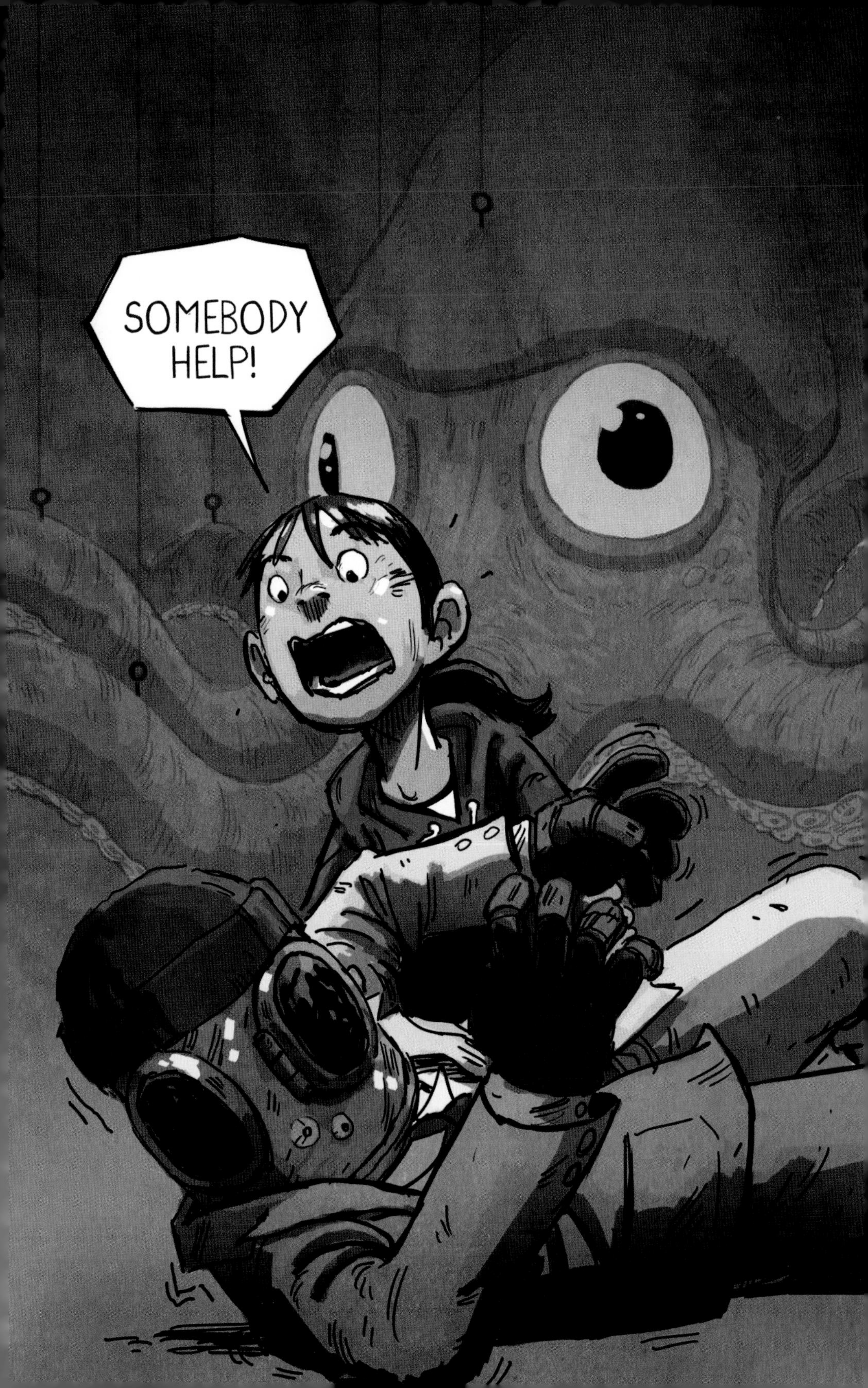
SOMEBODY HELP!

OKAY, SON, YOU CAN
OPEN YOUR EYES NOW...

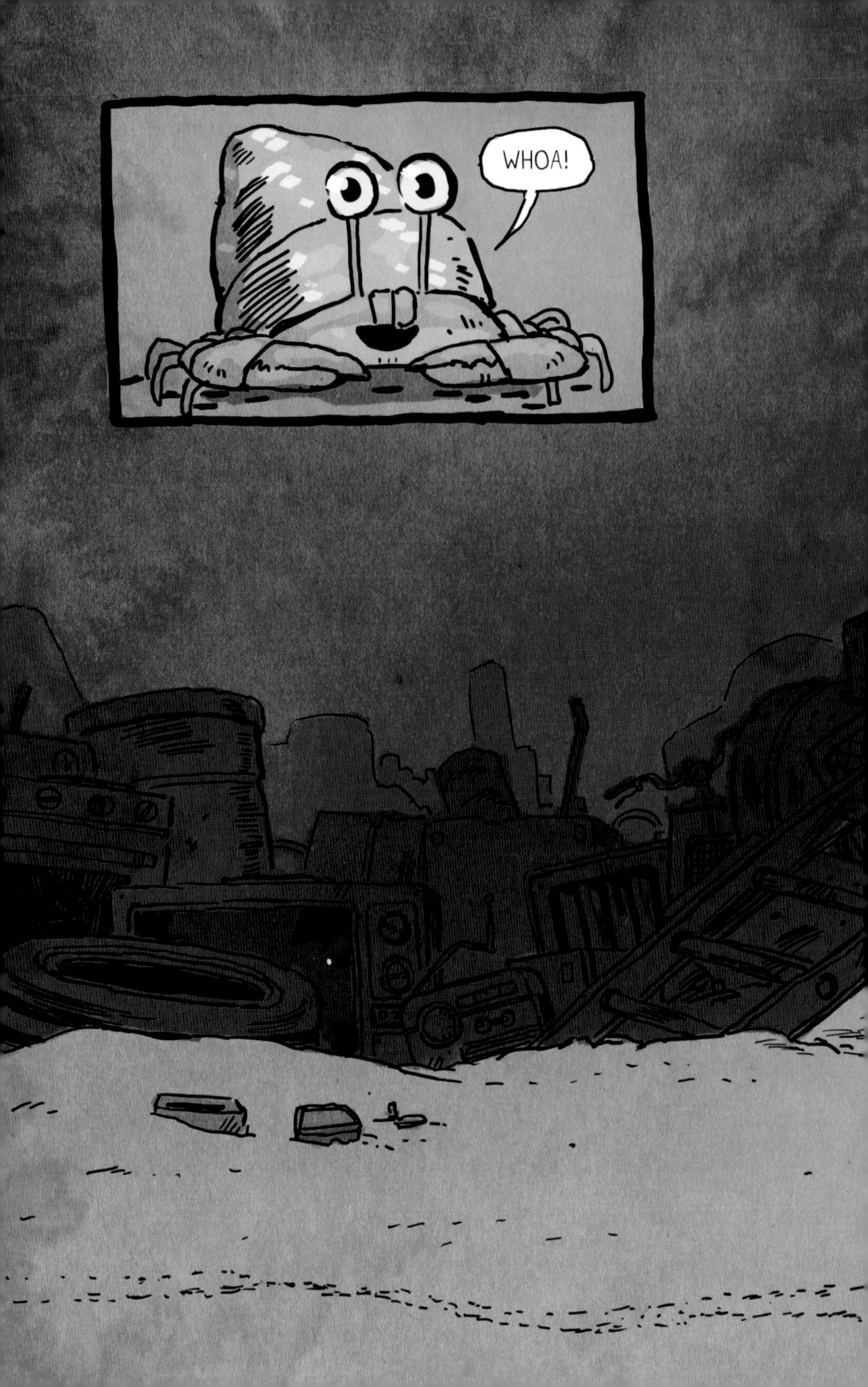
WHOA!

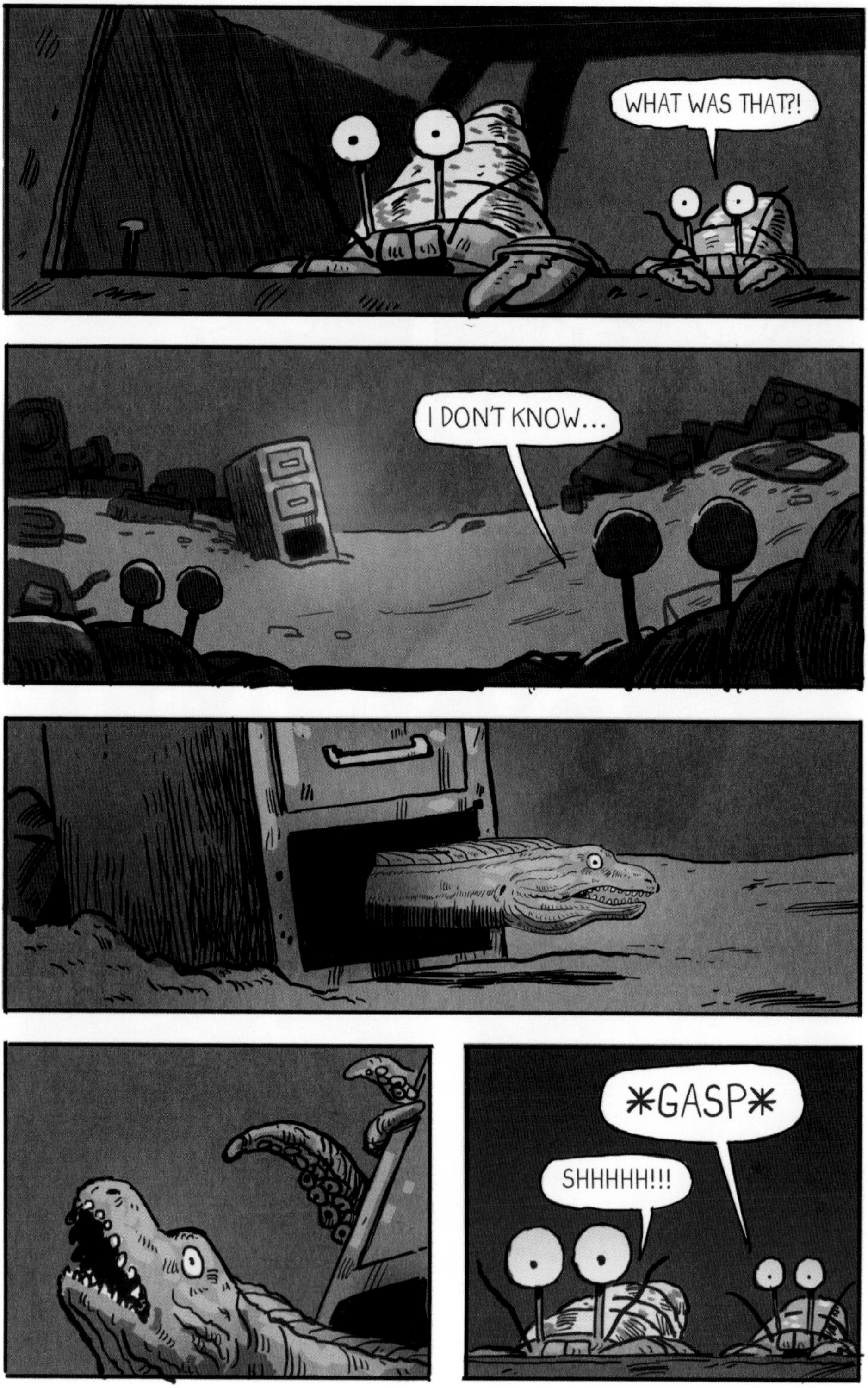
WHAT WAS THAT?!
I DON'T KNOW...
GASP
SHHHHH!!!

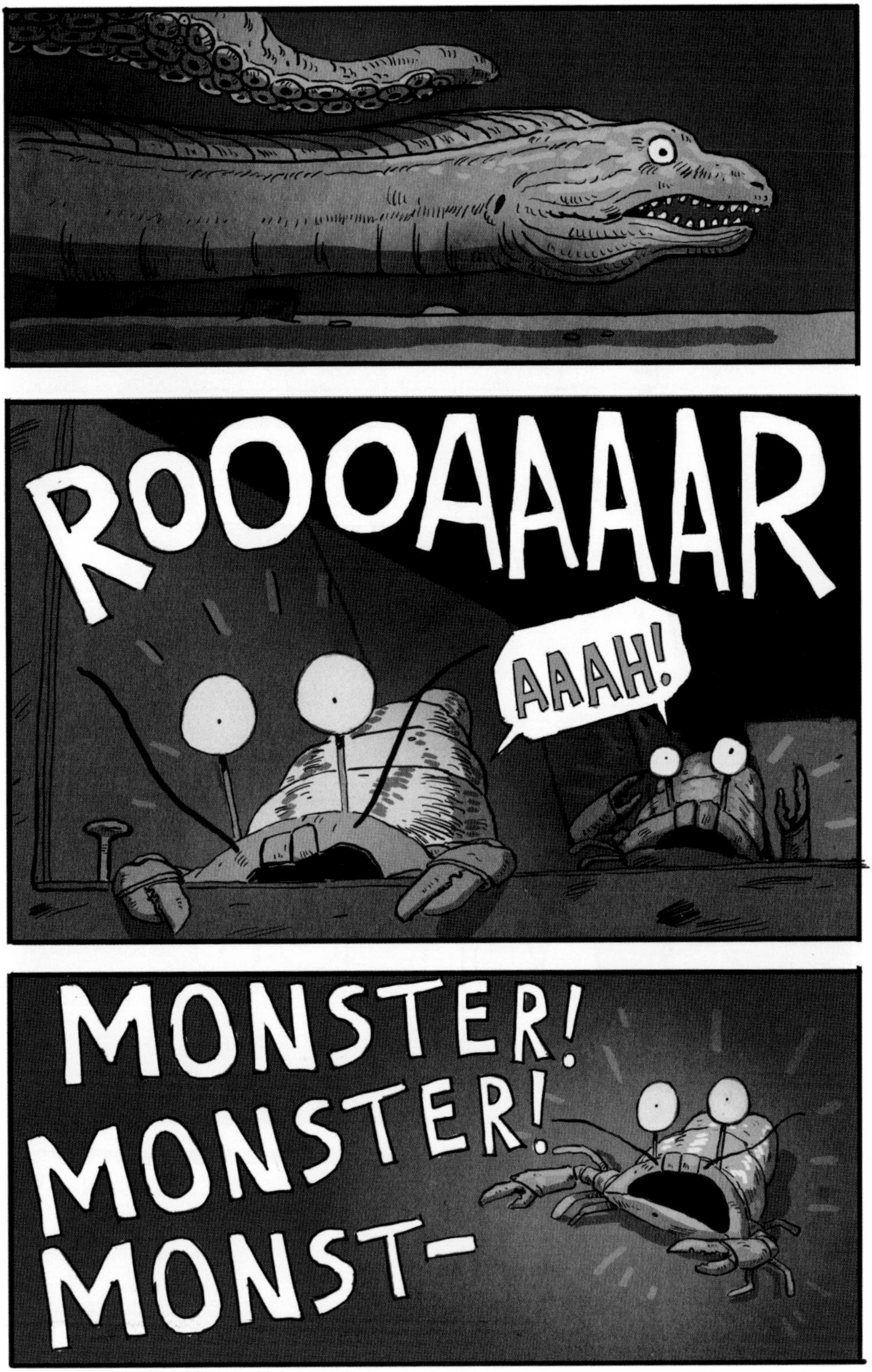
ROOOAAAAR
AAAH!
MONSTER!
MONSTER!
MONST-

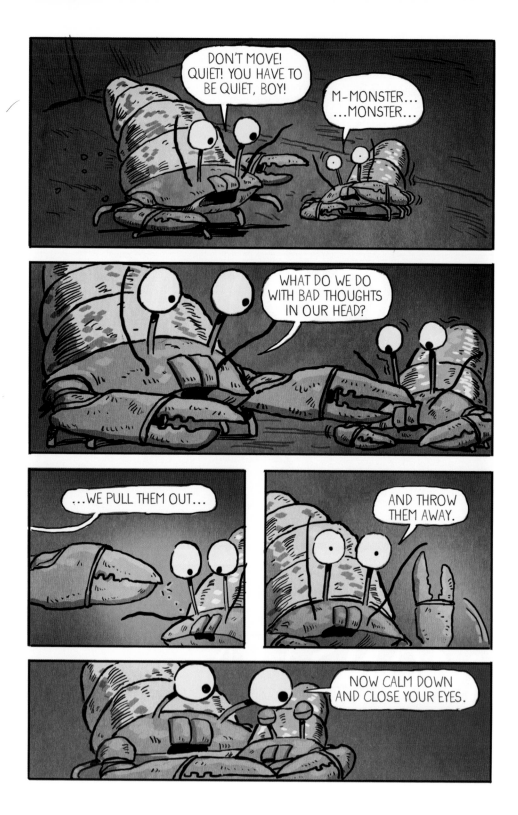

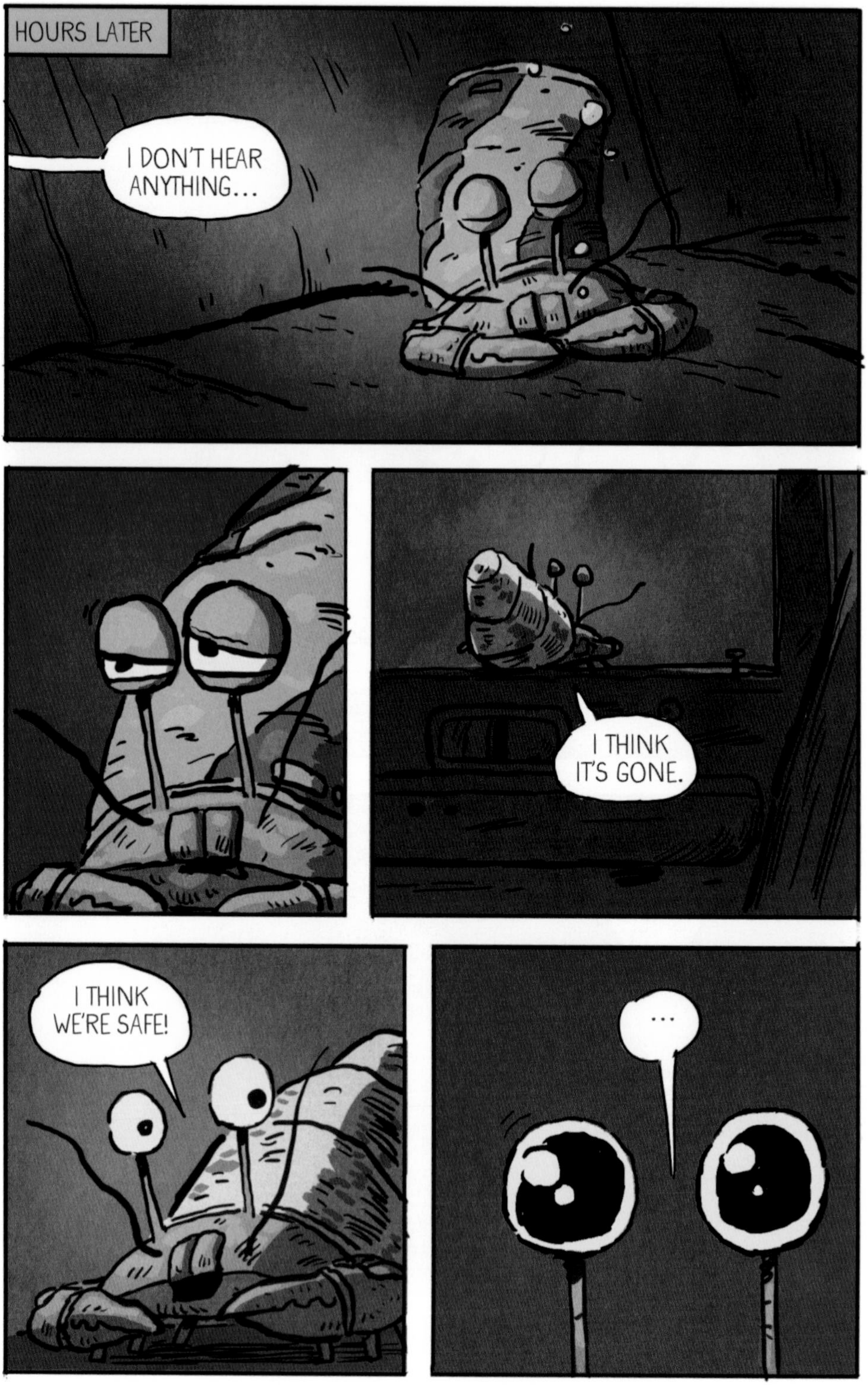
HOURS LATER
I DON'T HEAR ANYTHING...
I THINK IT'S GONE.
I THINK WE'RE SAFE!
...

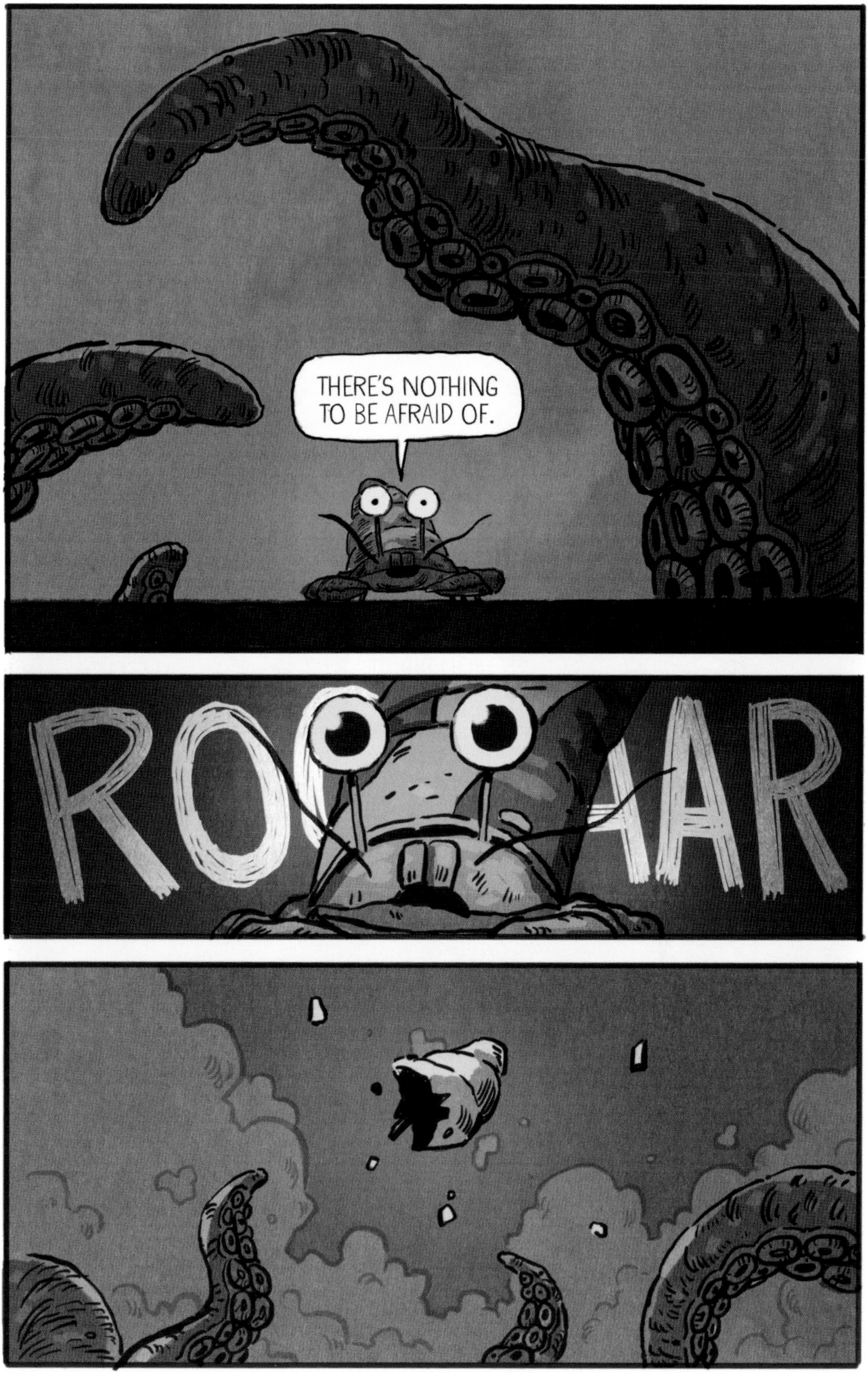
THERE'S NOTHING TO BE AFRAID OF.
ROOOAAR

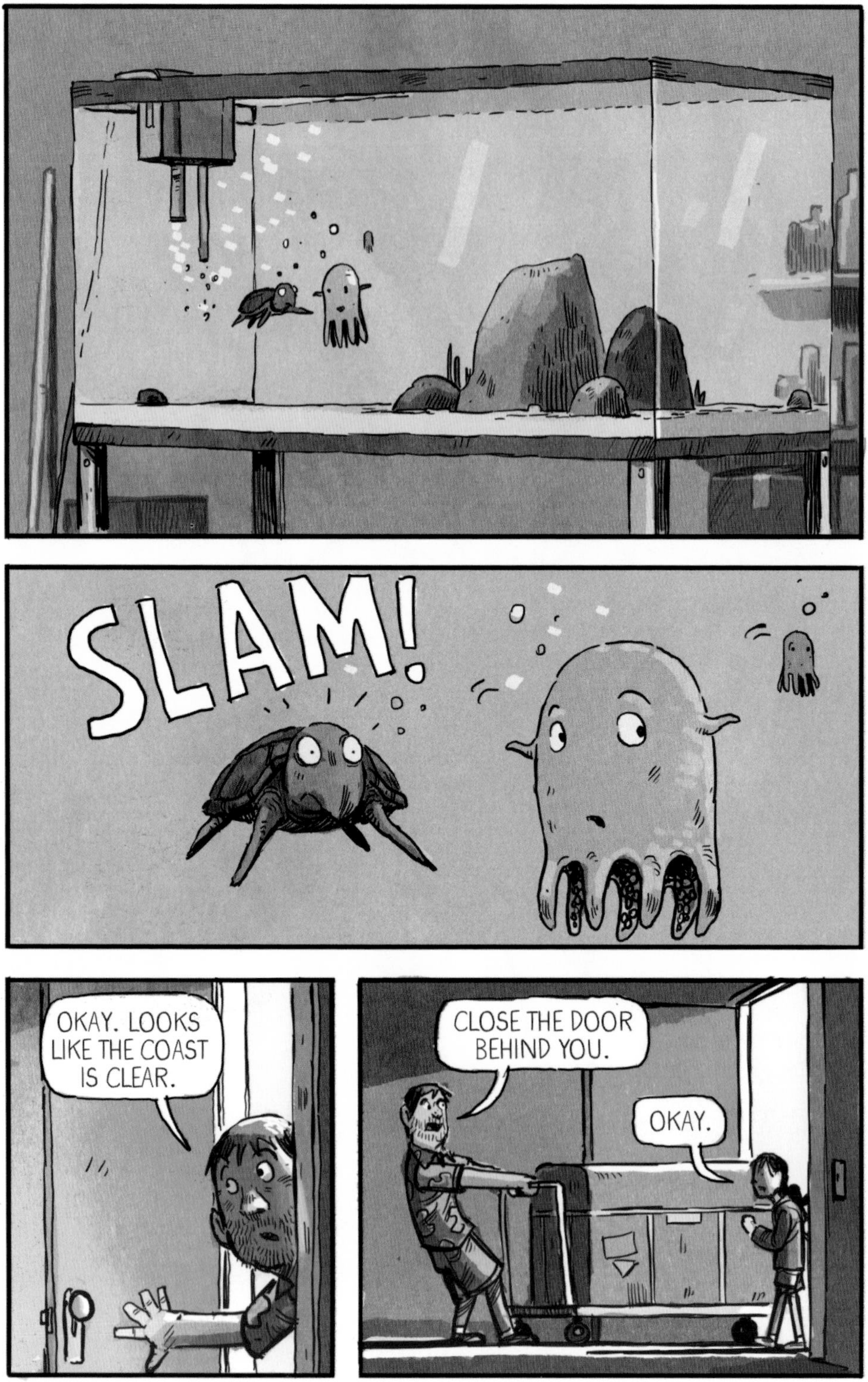
SLAM!
OKAY. LOOKS LIKE THE COAST IS CLEAR.
CLOSE THE DOOR BEHIND YOU.
OKAY.

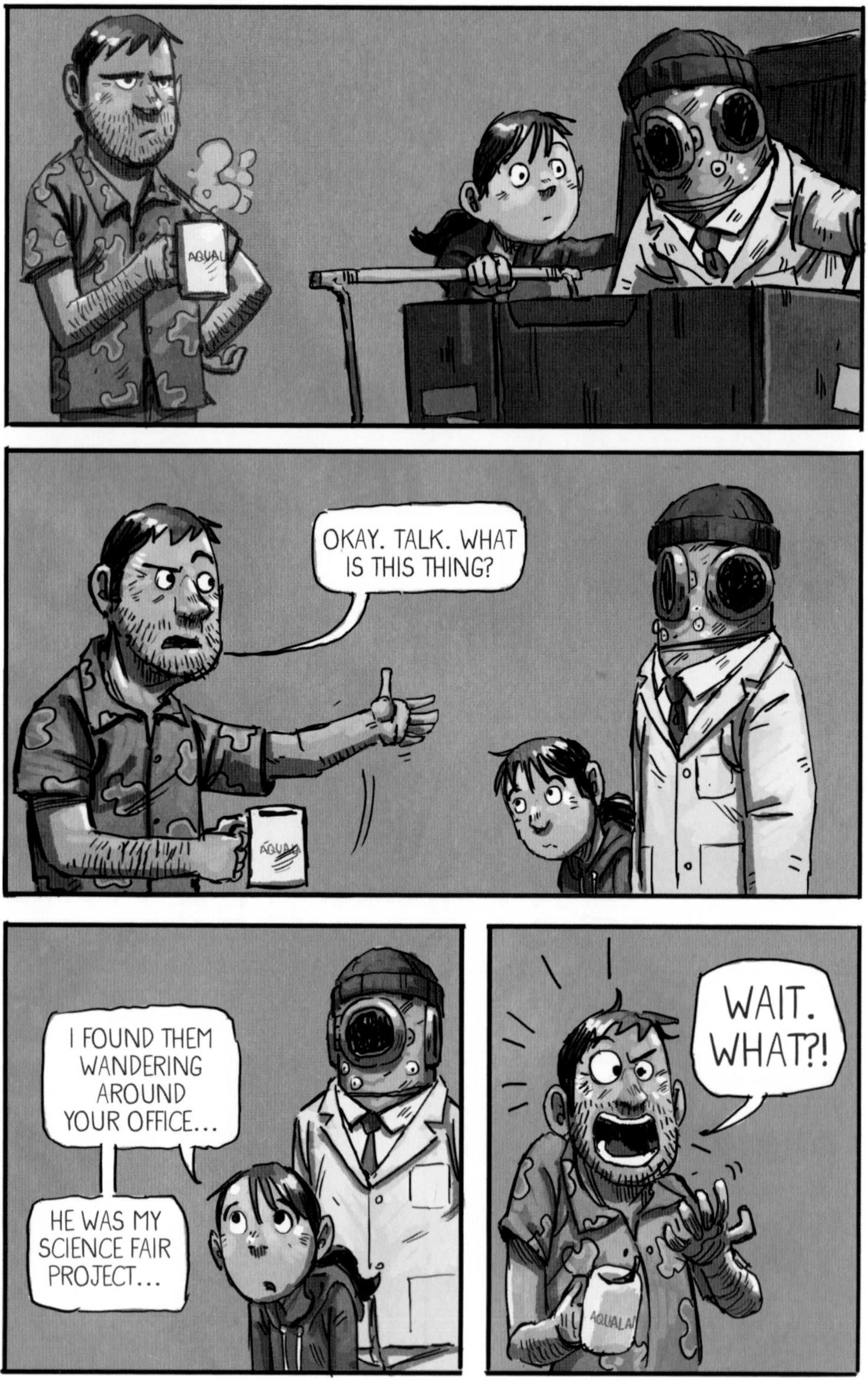
AQUAL
OKAY. TALK. WHAT IS THIS THING?
I FOUND THEM WANDERING AROUND YOUR OFFICE...
HE WAS MY SCIENCE FAIR PROJECT...
WAIT. WHAT?!

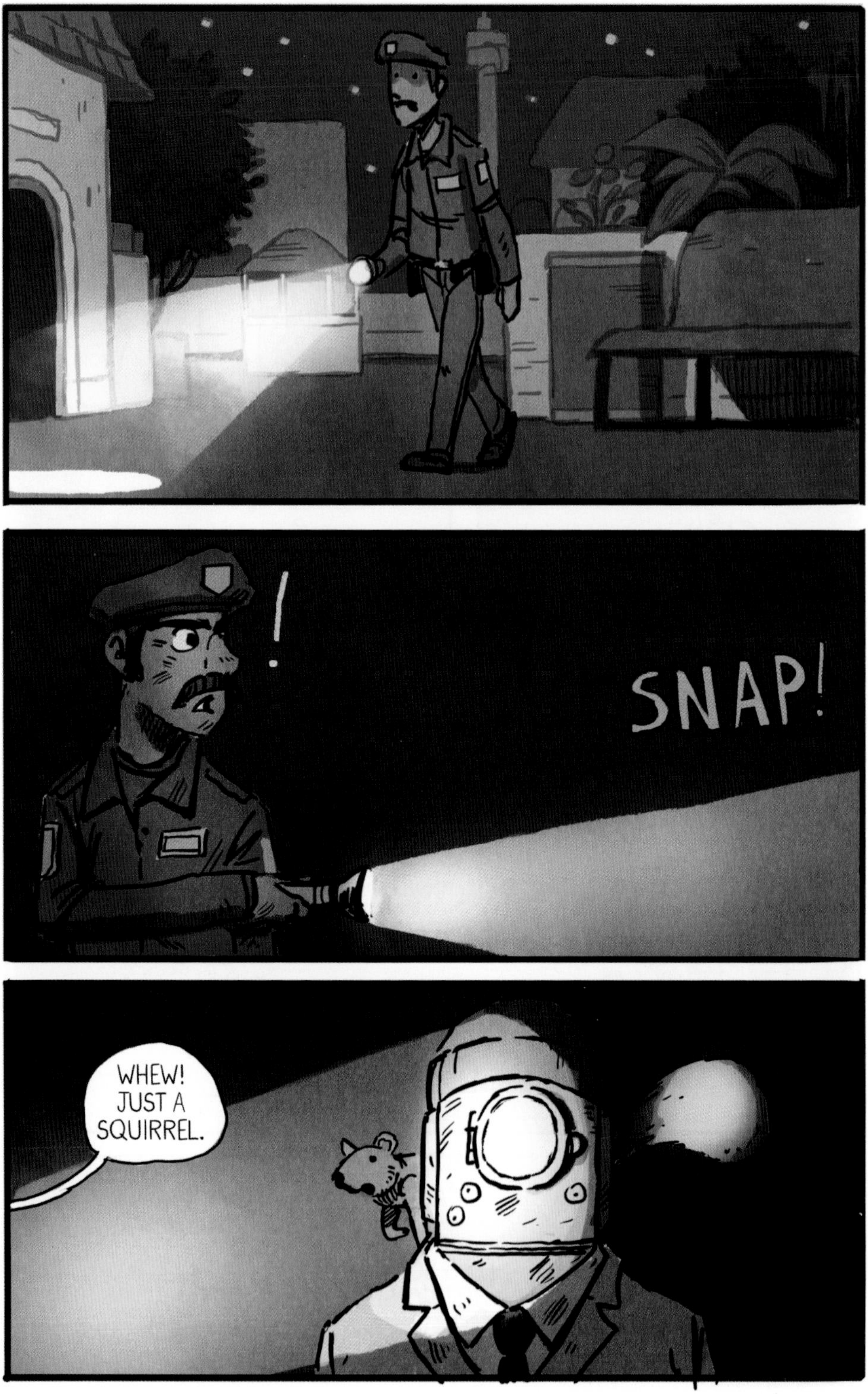
!
SNAP!
WHEW! JUST A SQUIRREL.

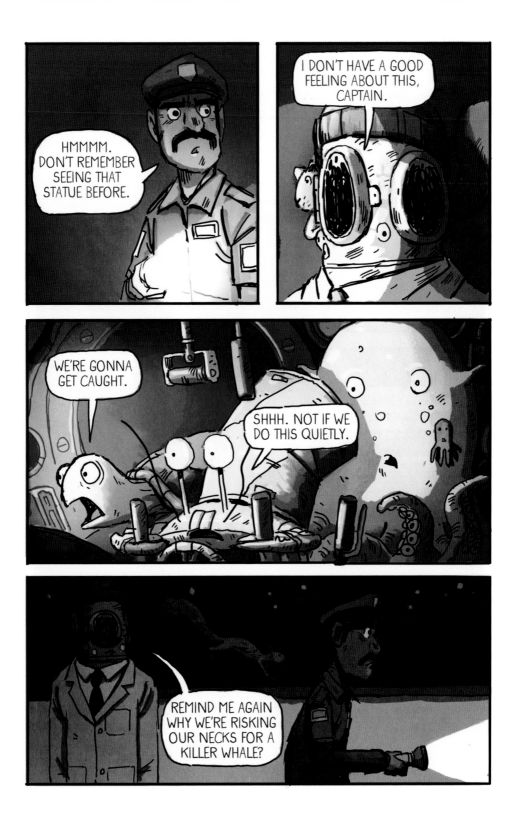

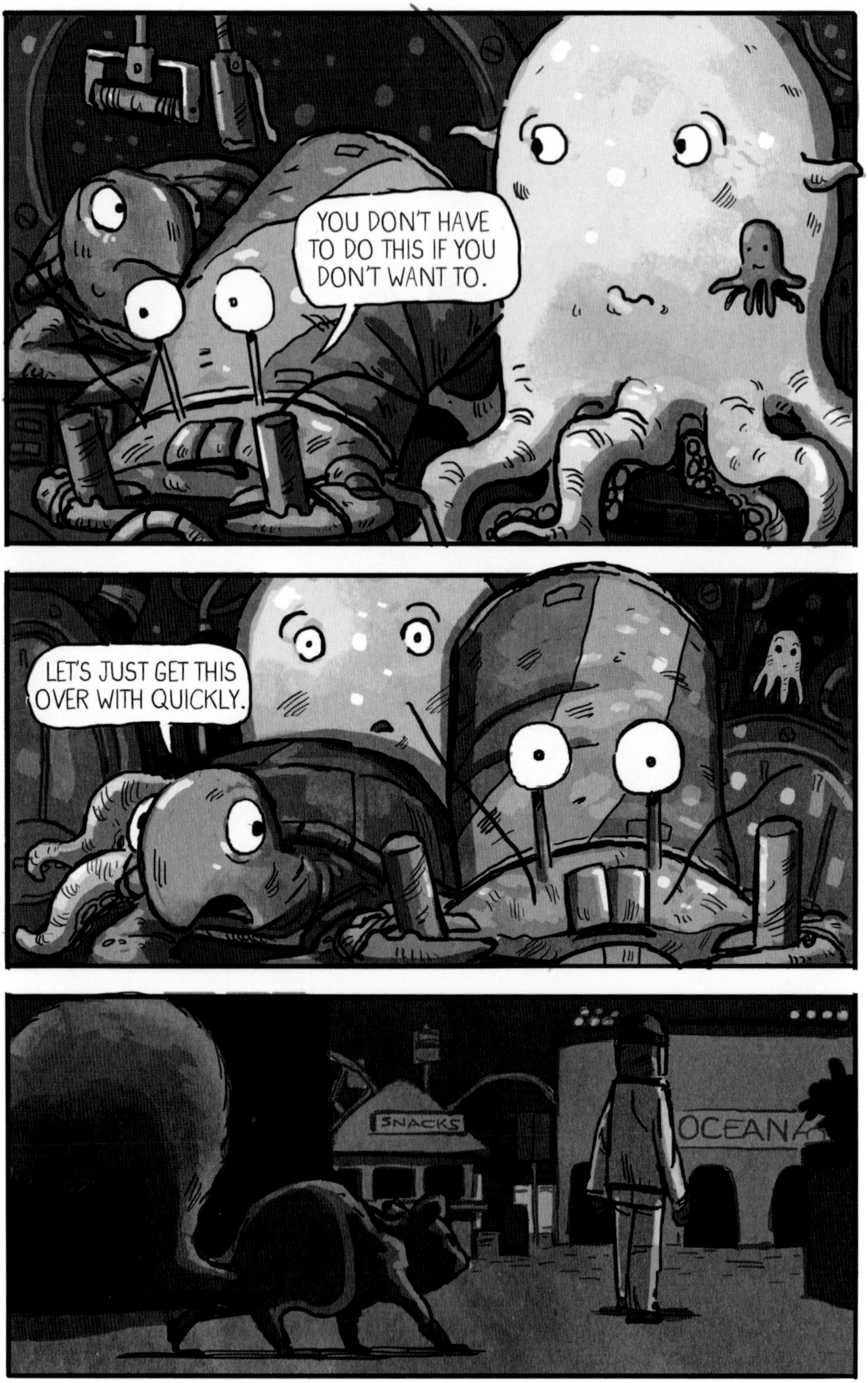
YOU DON'T HAVE TO DO THIS IF YOU DON'T WANT TO.
LET'S JUST GET THIS OVER WITH QUICKLY.
SNACKS
OCEAN

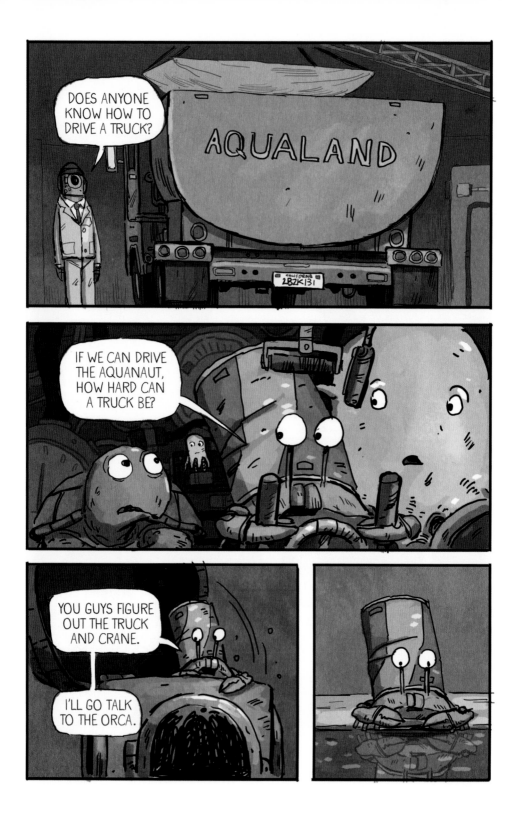

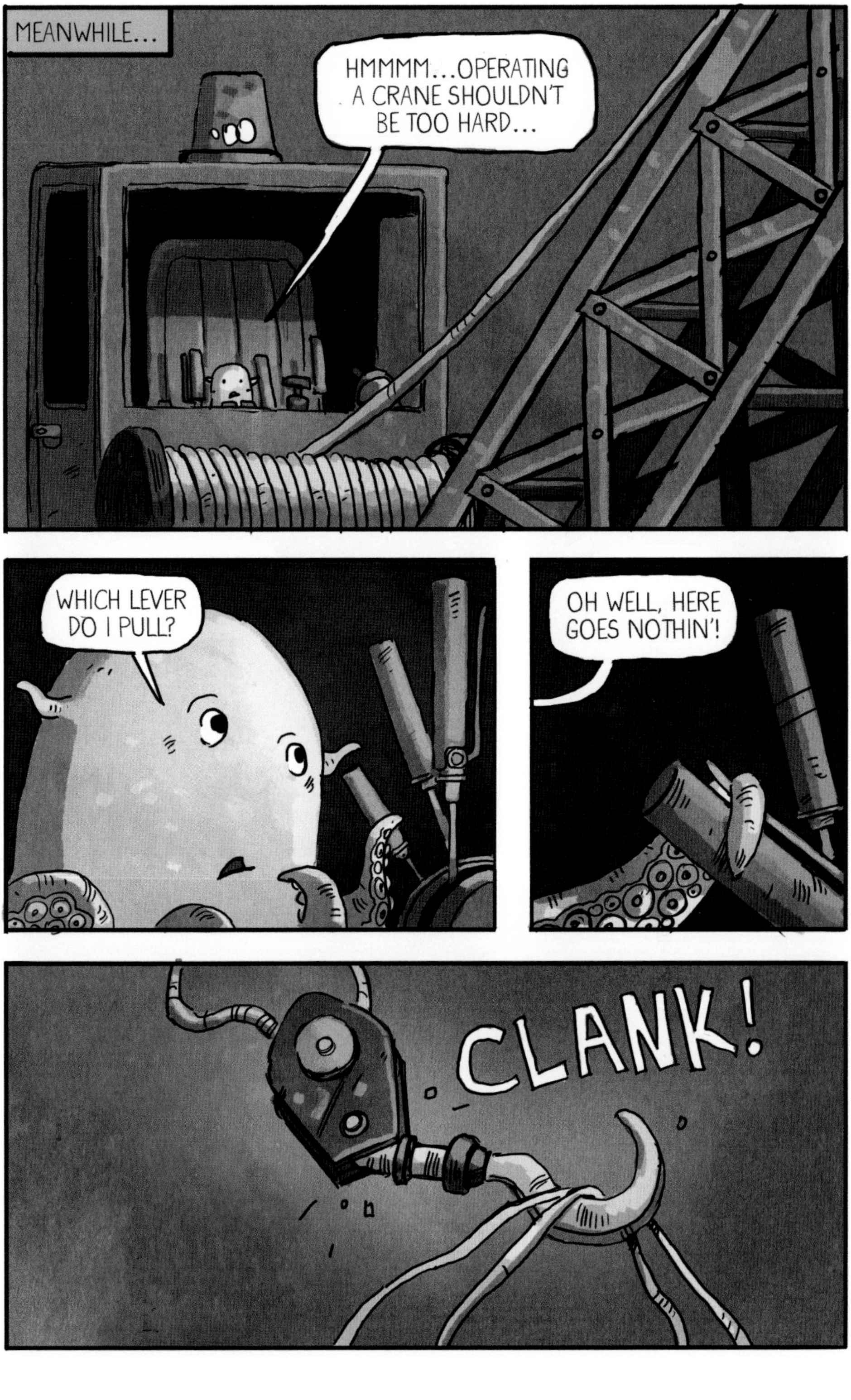
MEANWHILE...
HMMMM...OPERATING A CRANE SHOULDN'T BE TOO HARD...
WHICH LEVER DO I PULL?
OH WELL, HERE GOES NOTHIN'!
CLANK!

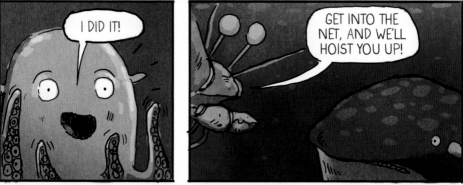

140

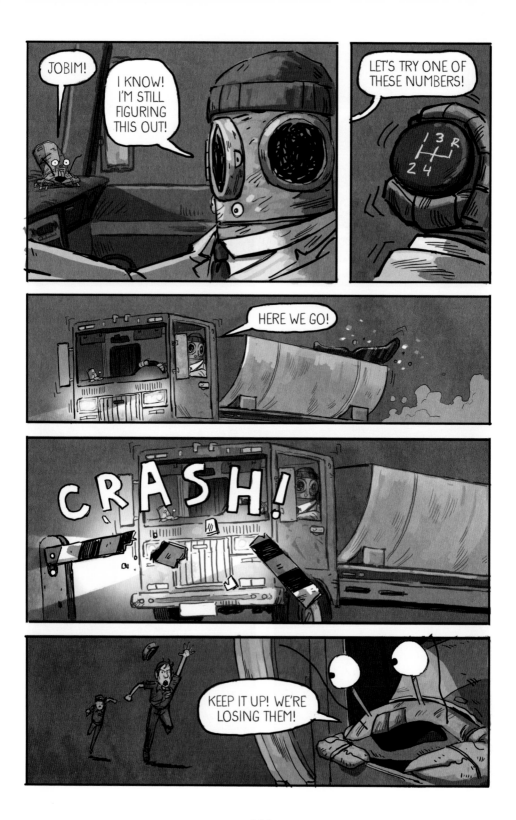

145

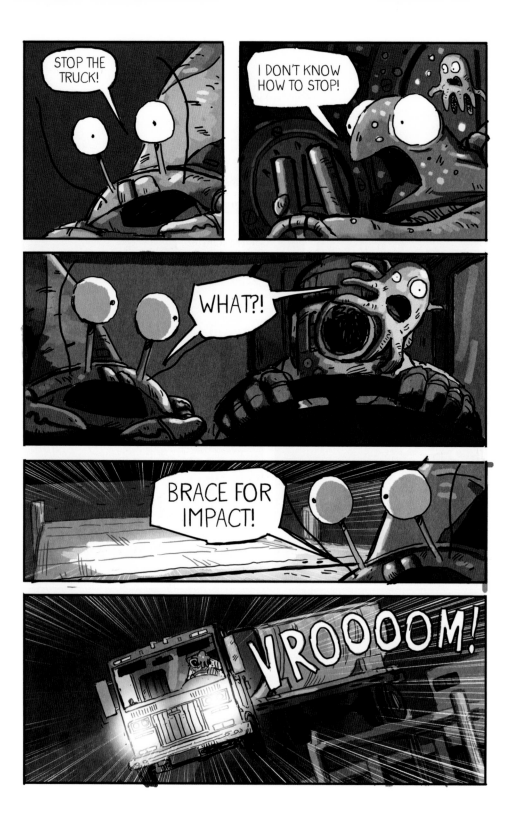

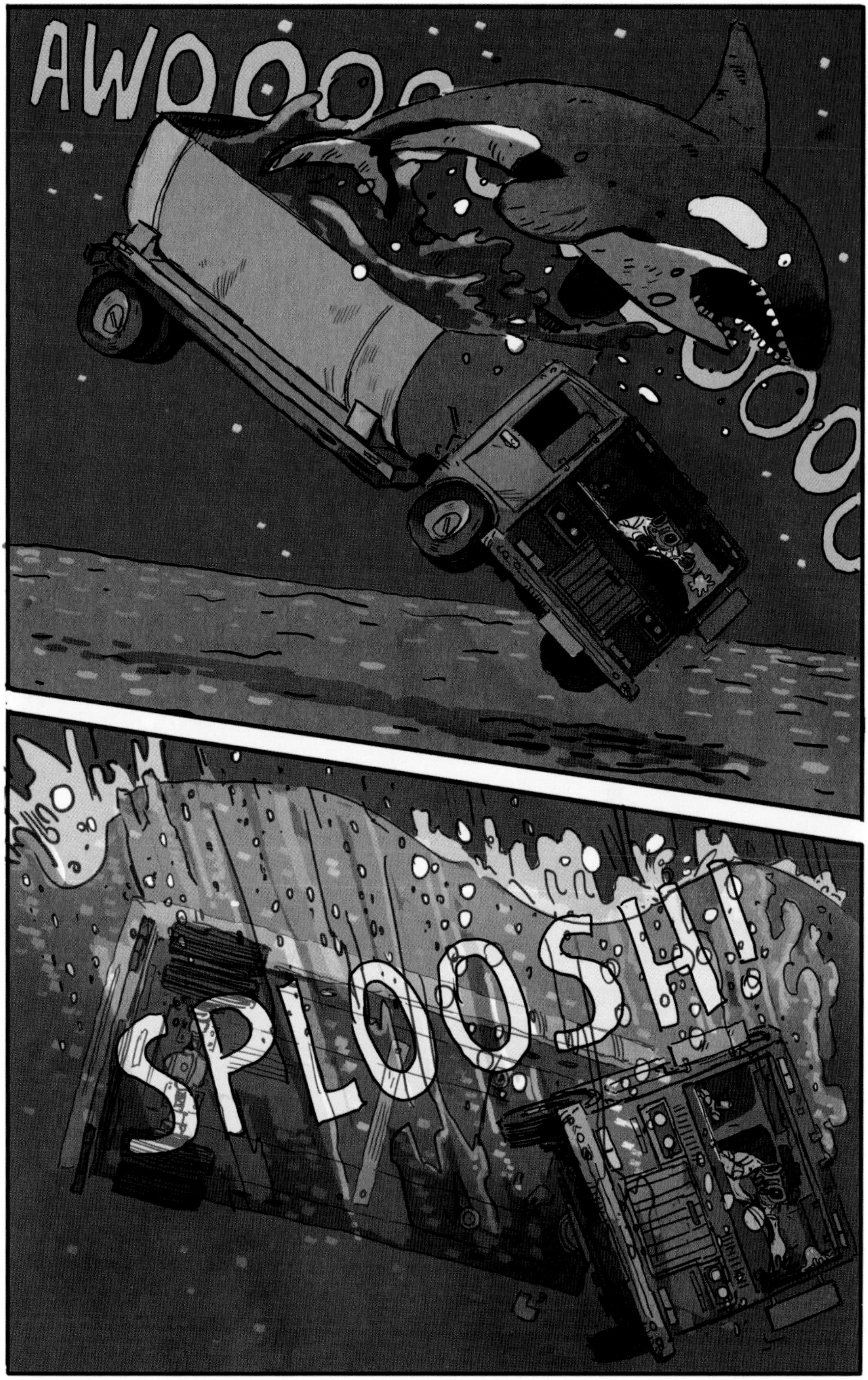
AWOOOOOOOOO
SPLOOSH!

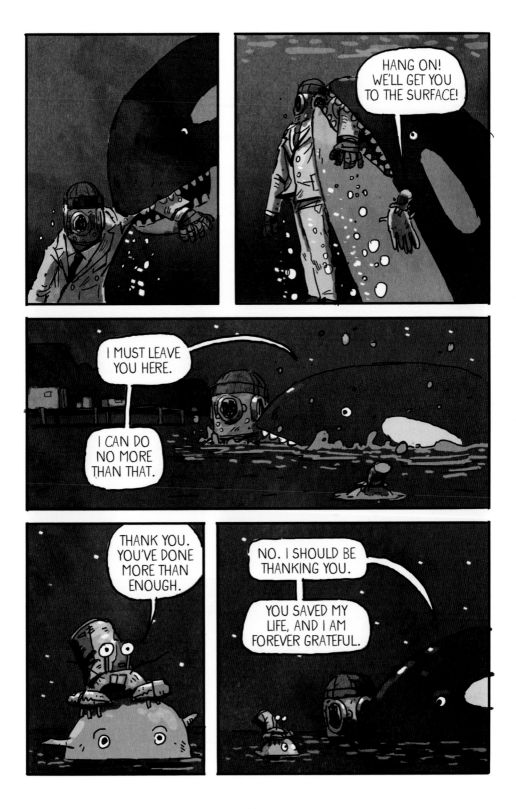

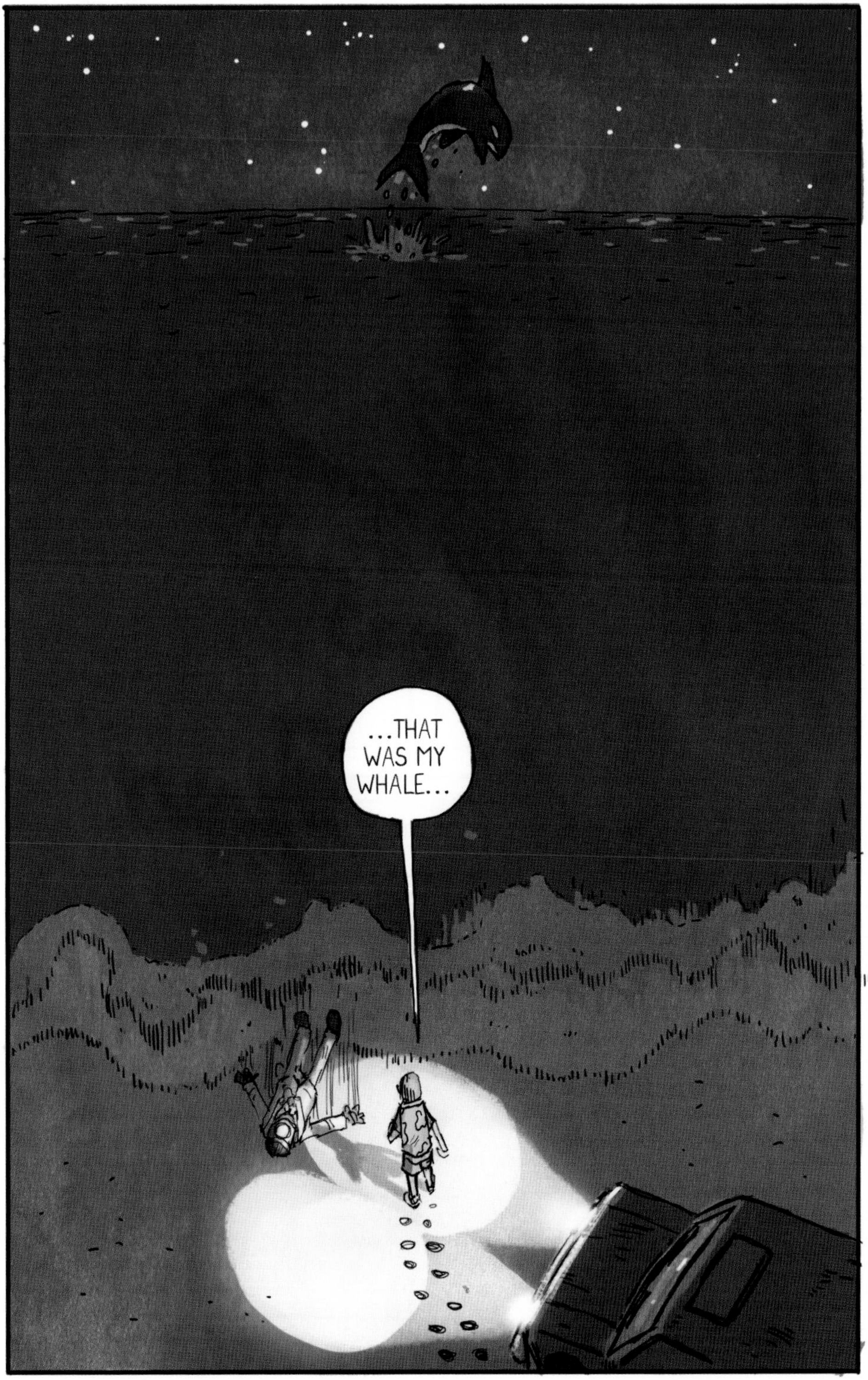
...THAT WAS MY WHALE...

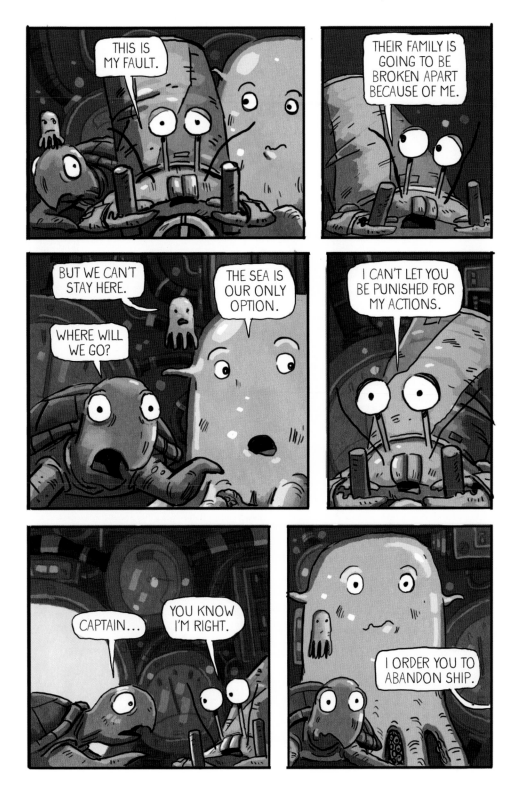

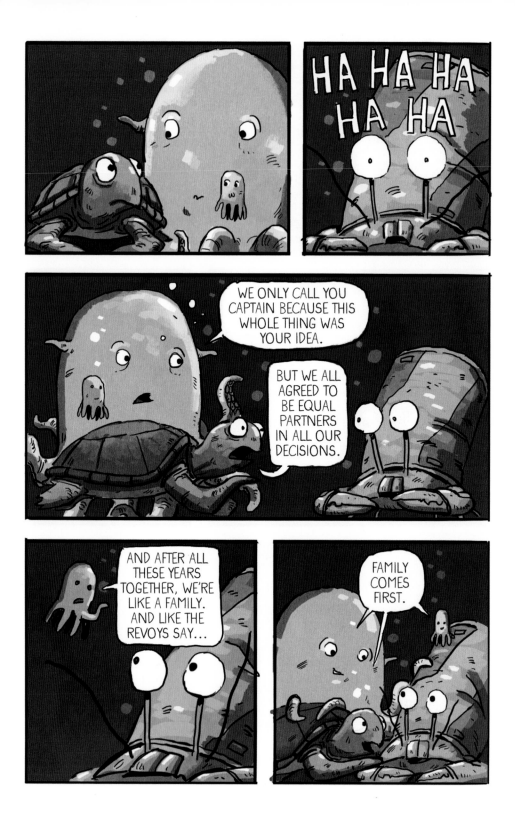

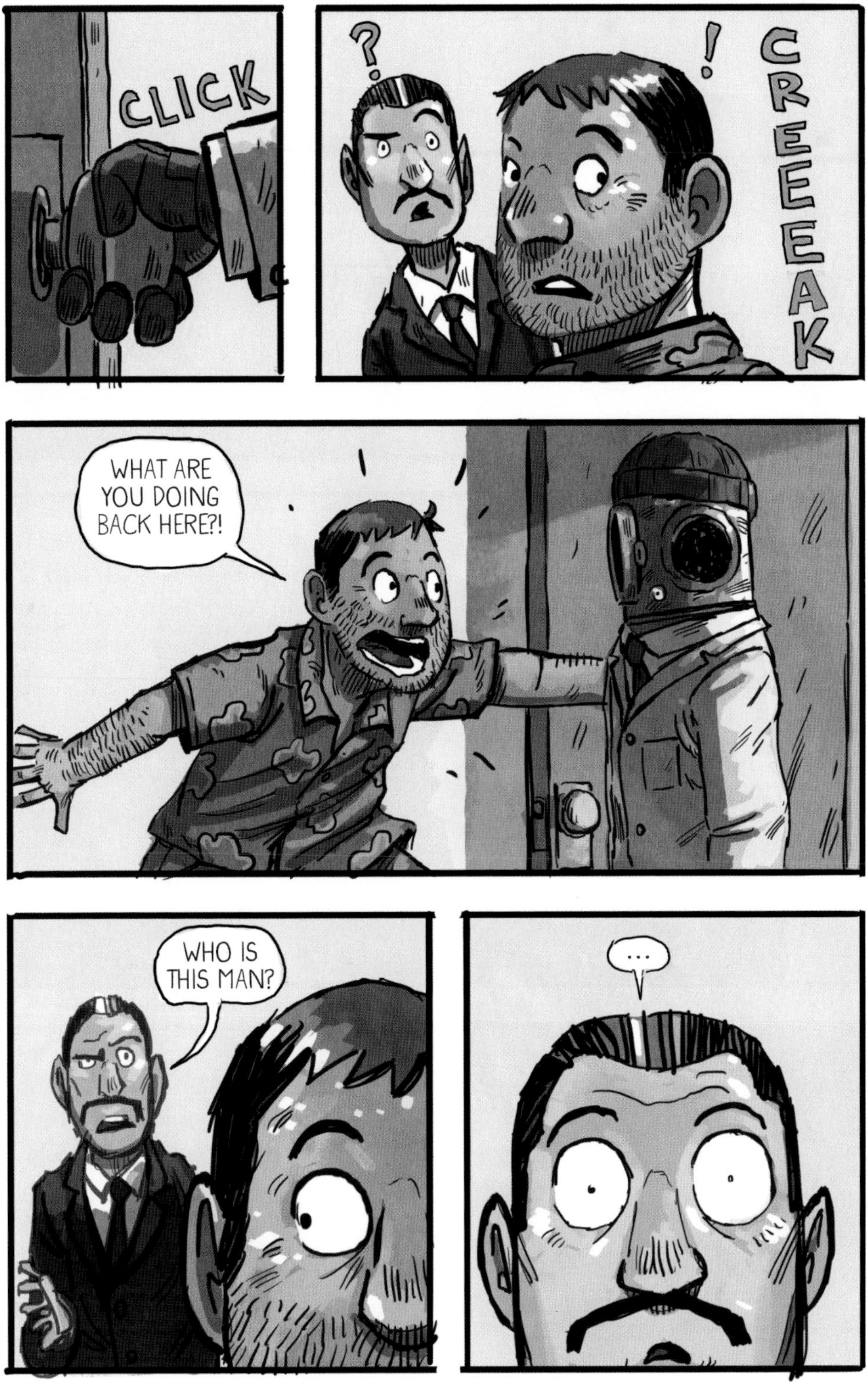
CLICK
?
!
CREEEAK
WHAT ARE YOU DOING BACK HERE?!
WHO IS THIS MAN?
...

165

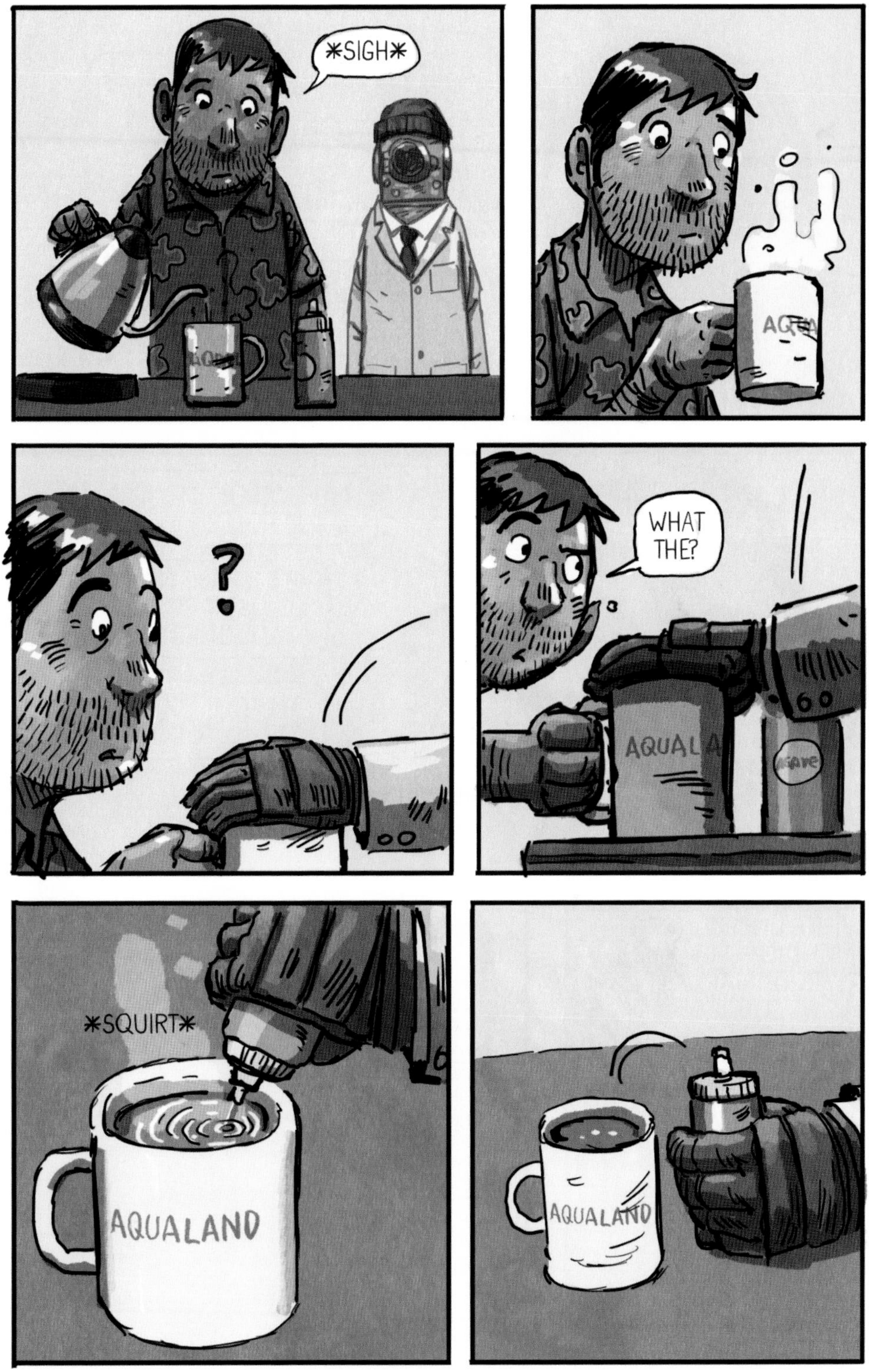
SIGH
WHAT THE?
SQUIRT
AQUALAND
AQUALAND

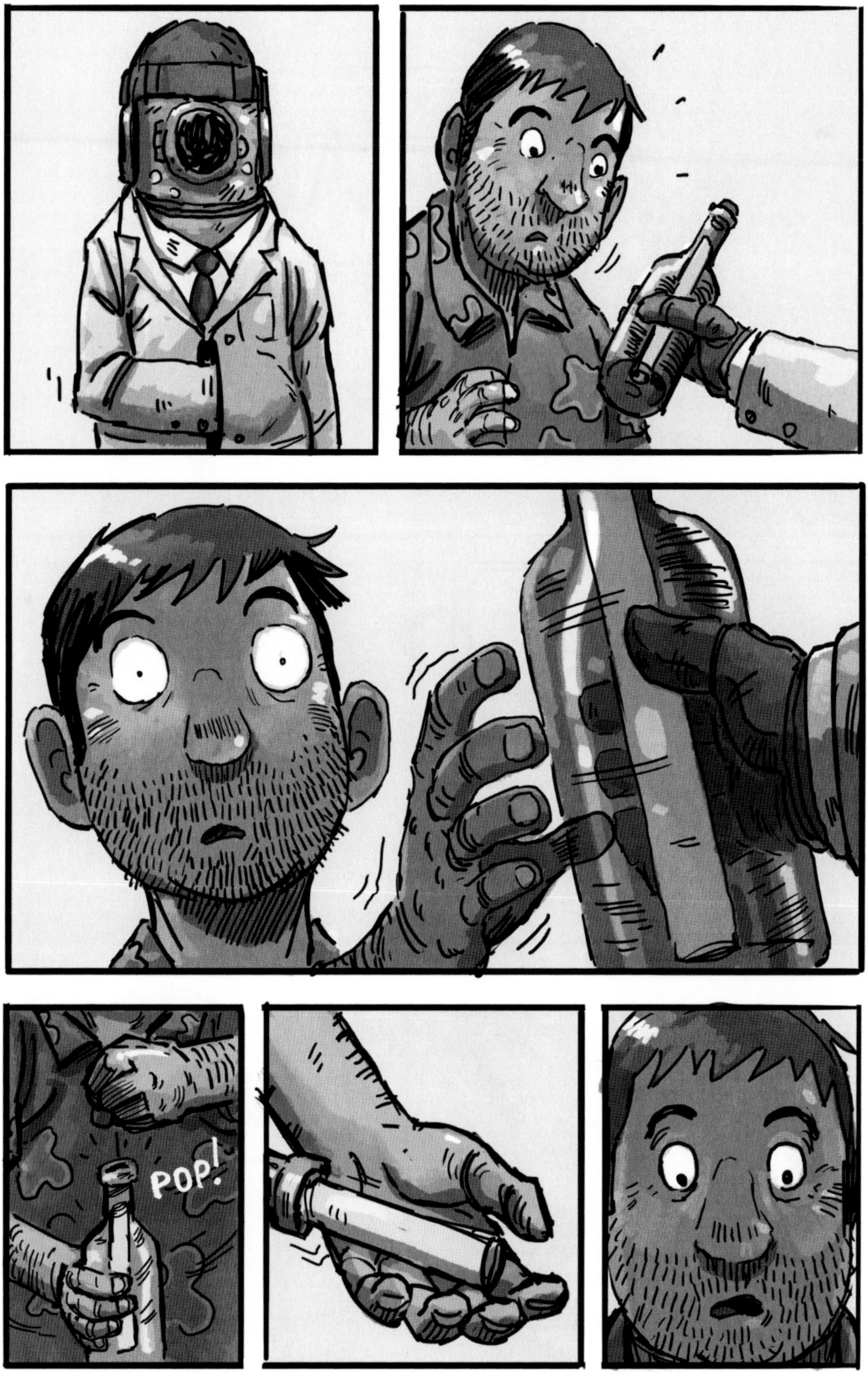
POP!

175

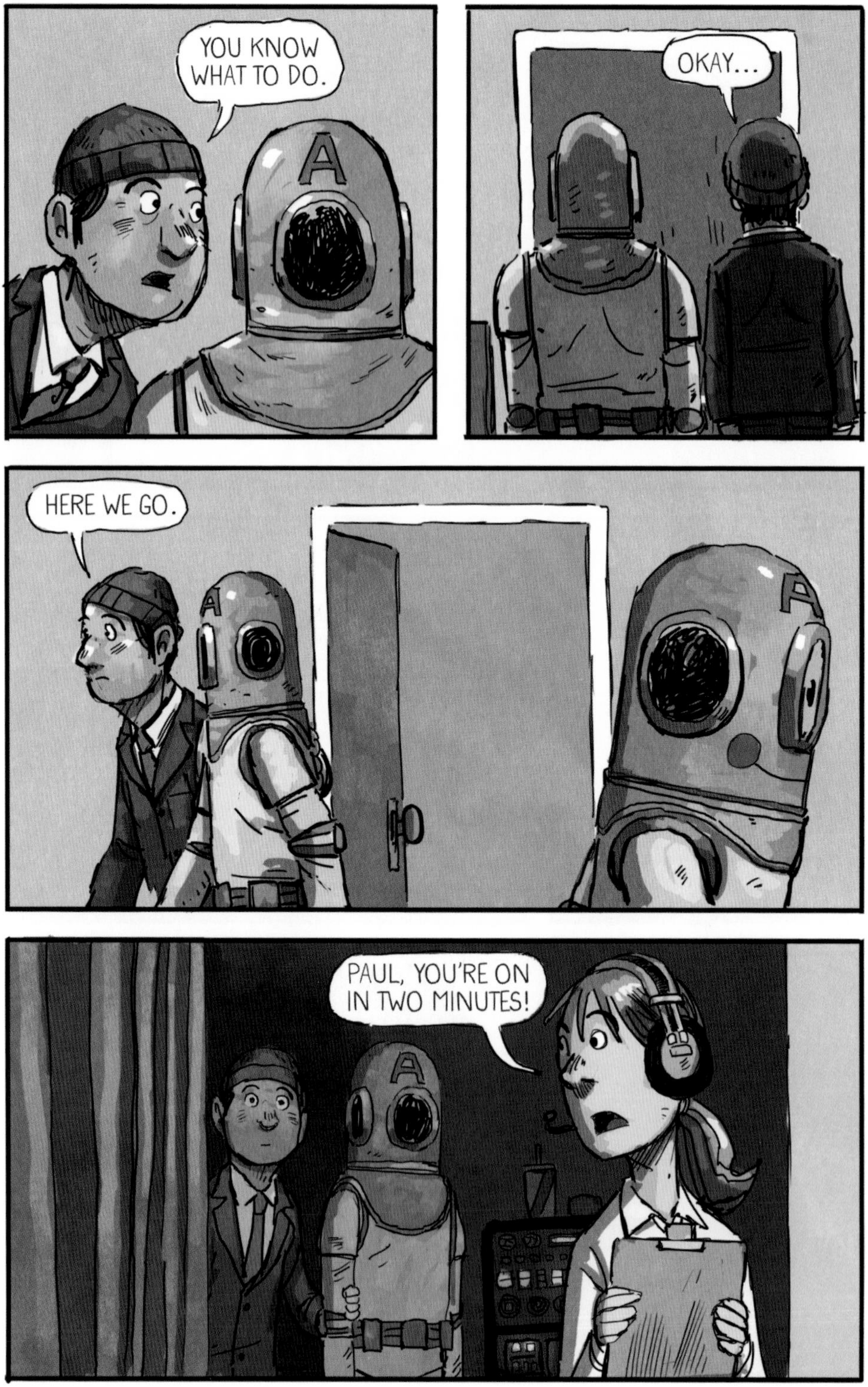
YOU KNOW WHAT TO DO.
OKAY...
HERE WE GO.
PAUL, YOU'RE ON IN TWO MINUTES!

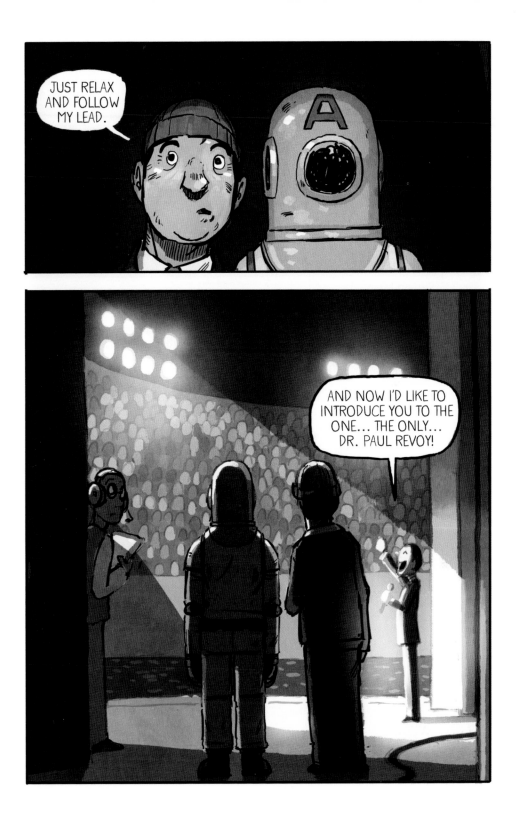

183

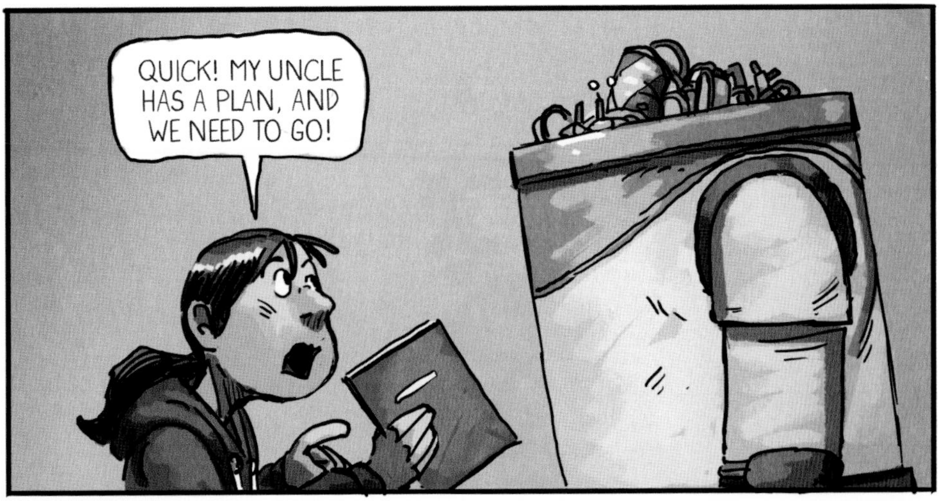
QUICK! MY UNCLE HAS A PLAN, AND WE NEED TO GO!

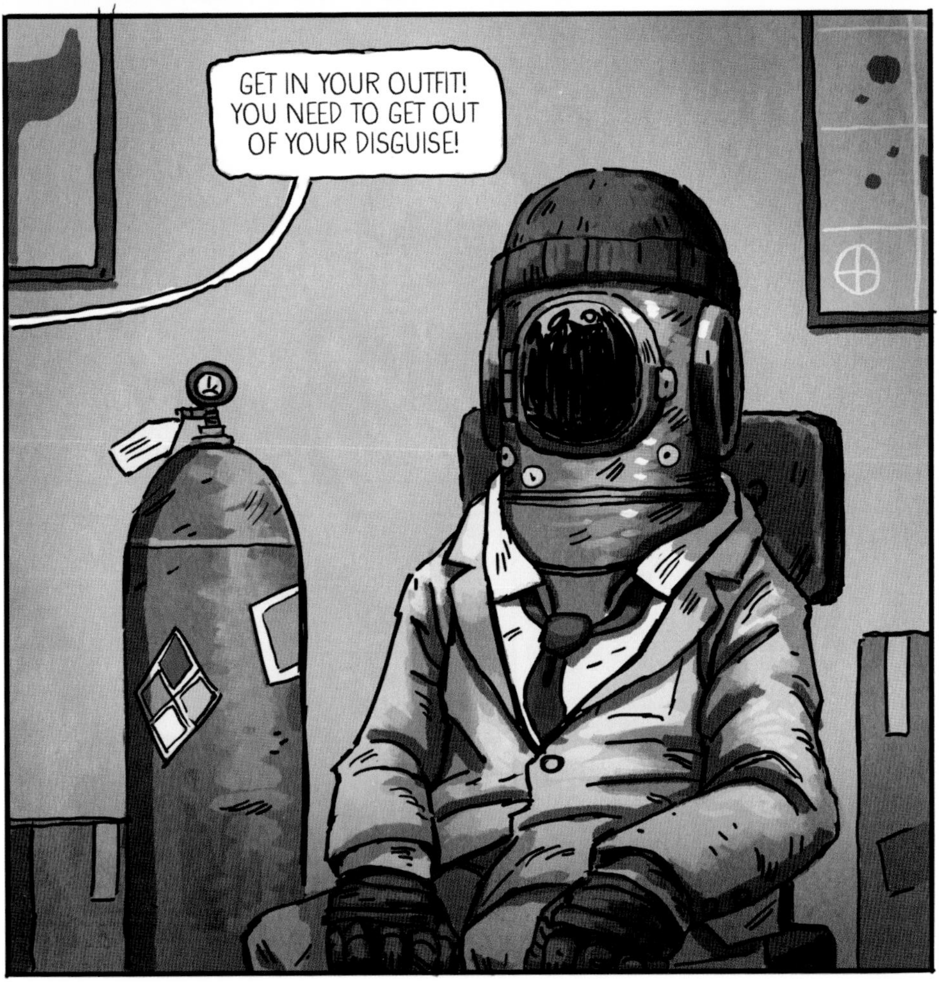
GET IN YOUR OUTFIT! YOU NEED TO GET OUT OF YOUR DISGUISE!

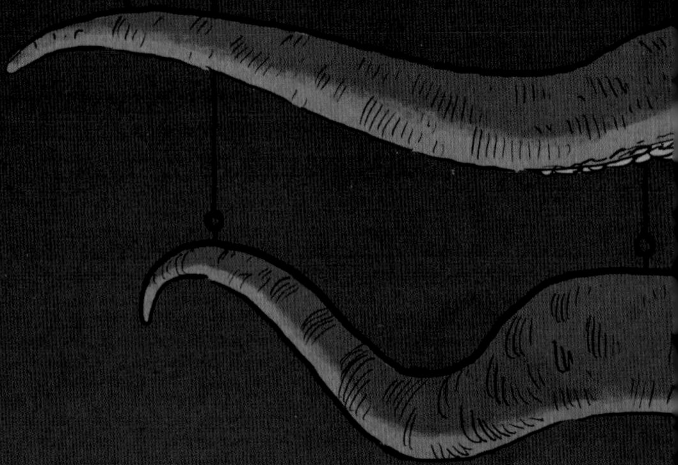

THE CREATURE FROM THE DEEP

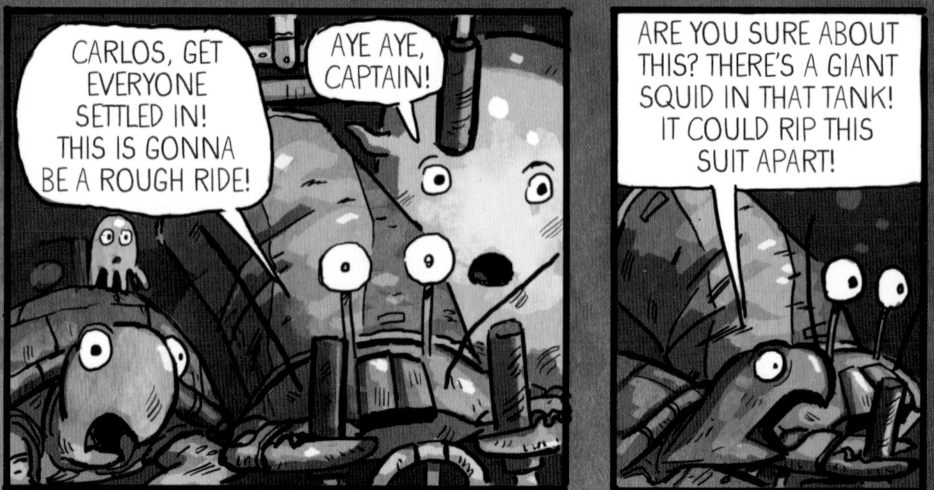
CARLOS, GET EVERYONE SETTLED IN! THIS IS GONNA BE A ROUGH RIDE!
AYE AYE, CAPTAIN!
ARE YOU SURE ABOUT THIS? THERE'S A GIANT SQUID IN THAT TANK! IT COULD RIP THIS SUIT APART!

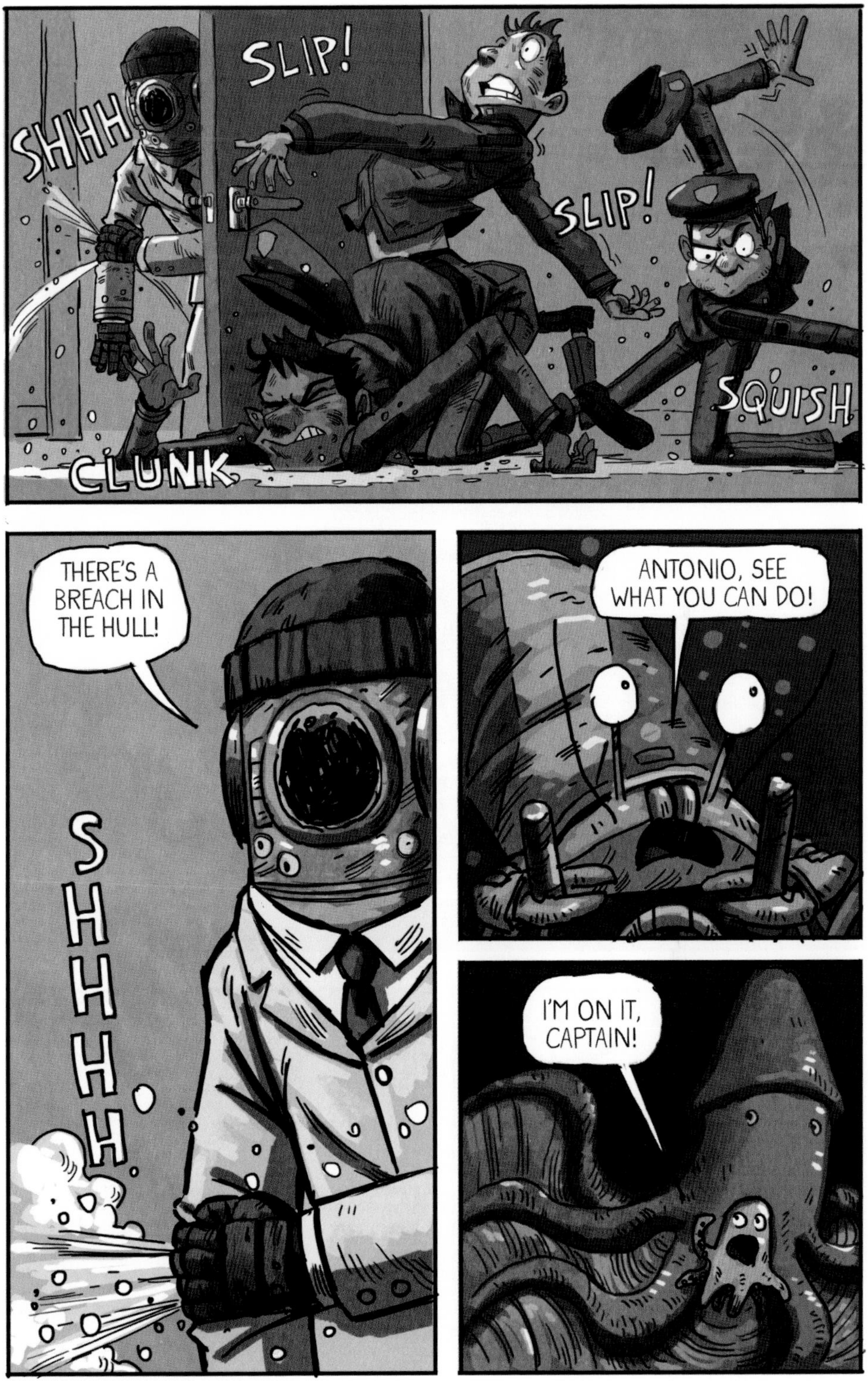
SHHH
SLIP!
SLIP!
SQUISH
CLUNK
THERE'S A BREACH IN THE HULL!
SHHHH
ANTONIO, SEE WHAT YOU CAN DO!
I'M ON IT, CAPTAIN!

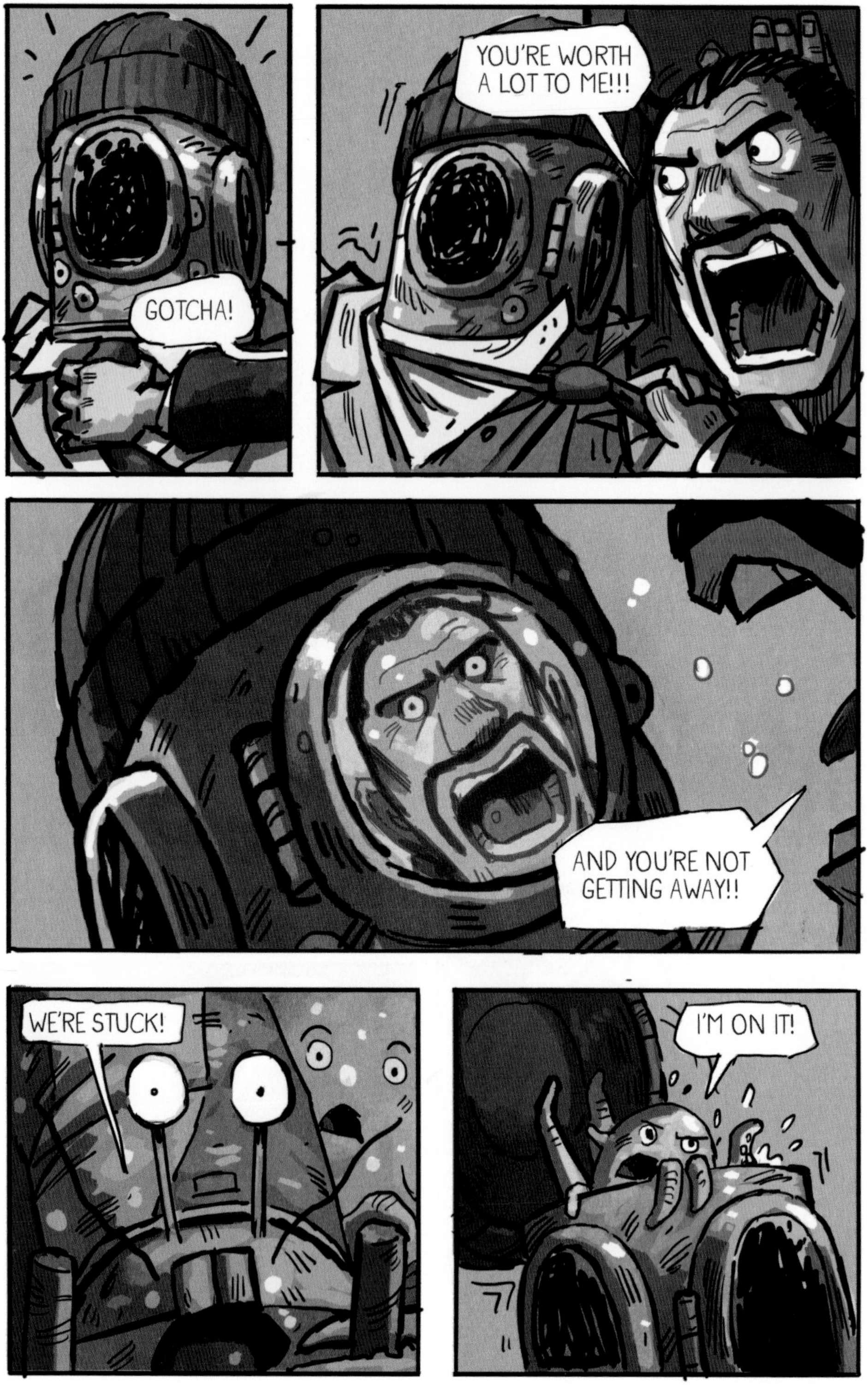
GOTCHA!
YOU'RE WORTH A LOT TO ME!!!
AND YOU'RE NOT GETTING AWAY!!
WE'RE STUCK!
I'M ON IT!

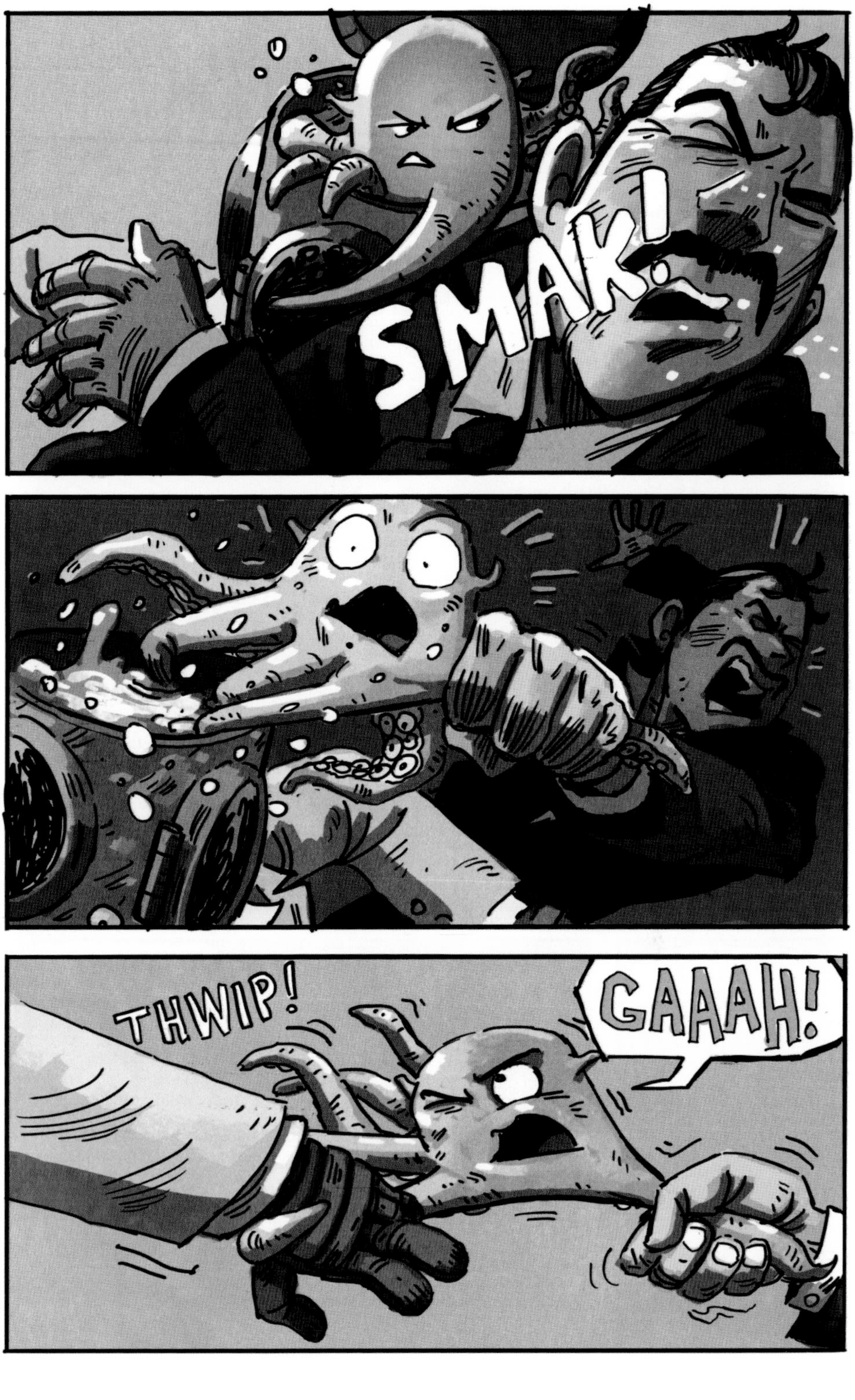
SMAK!
THWIP!
GAAAH!

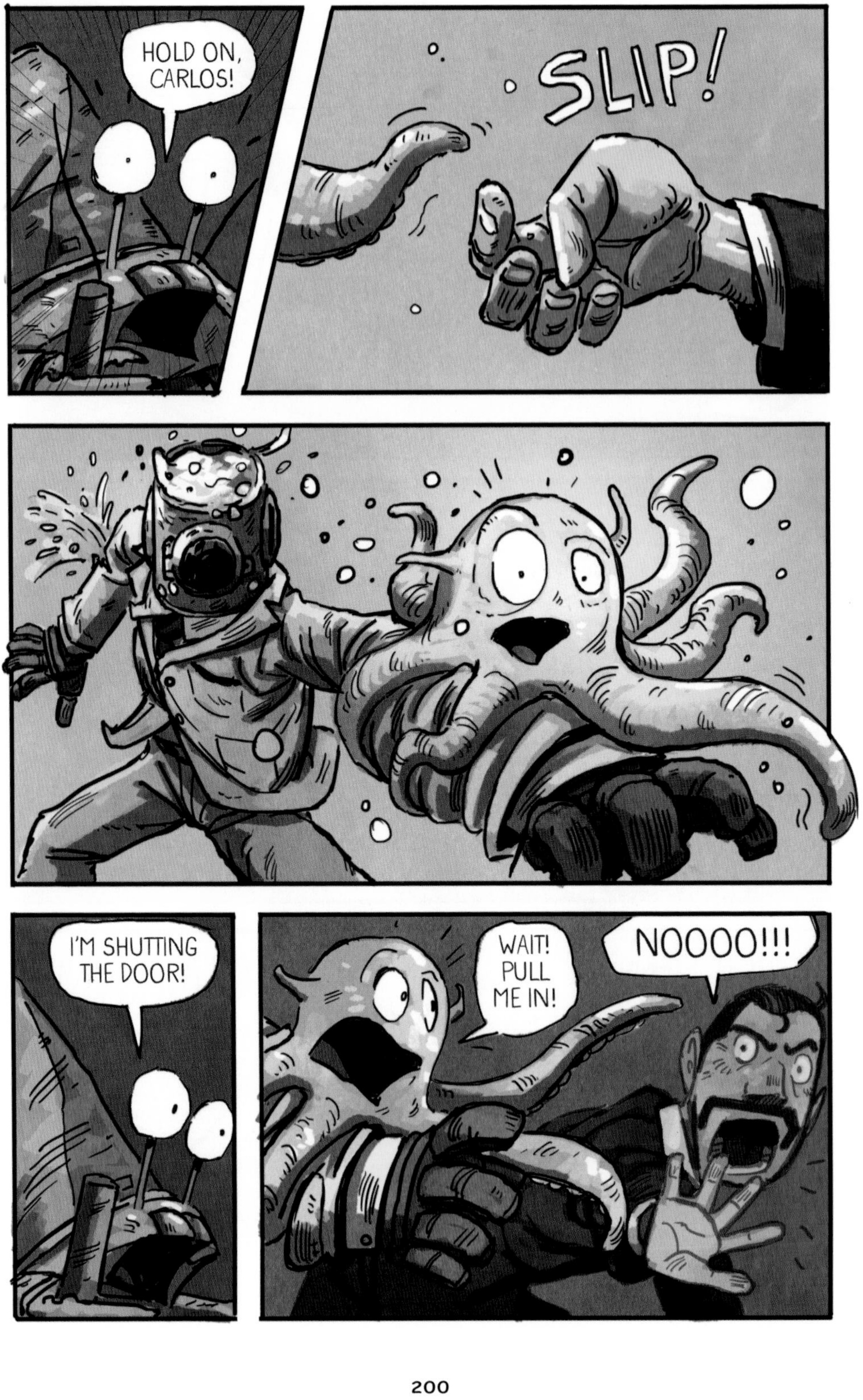
HOLD ON, CARLOS!
SLIP!
I'M SHUTTING THE DOOR!
WAIT! PULL ME IN!
NOOOO!!!

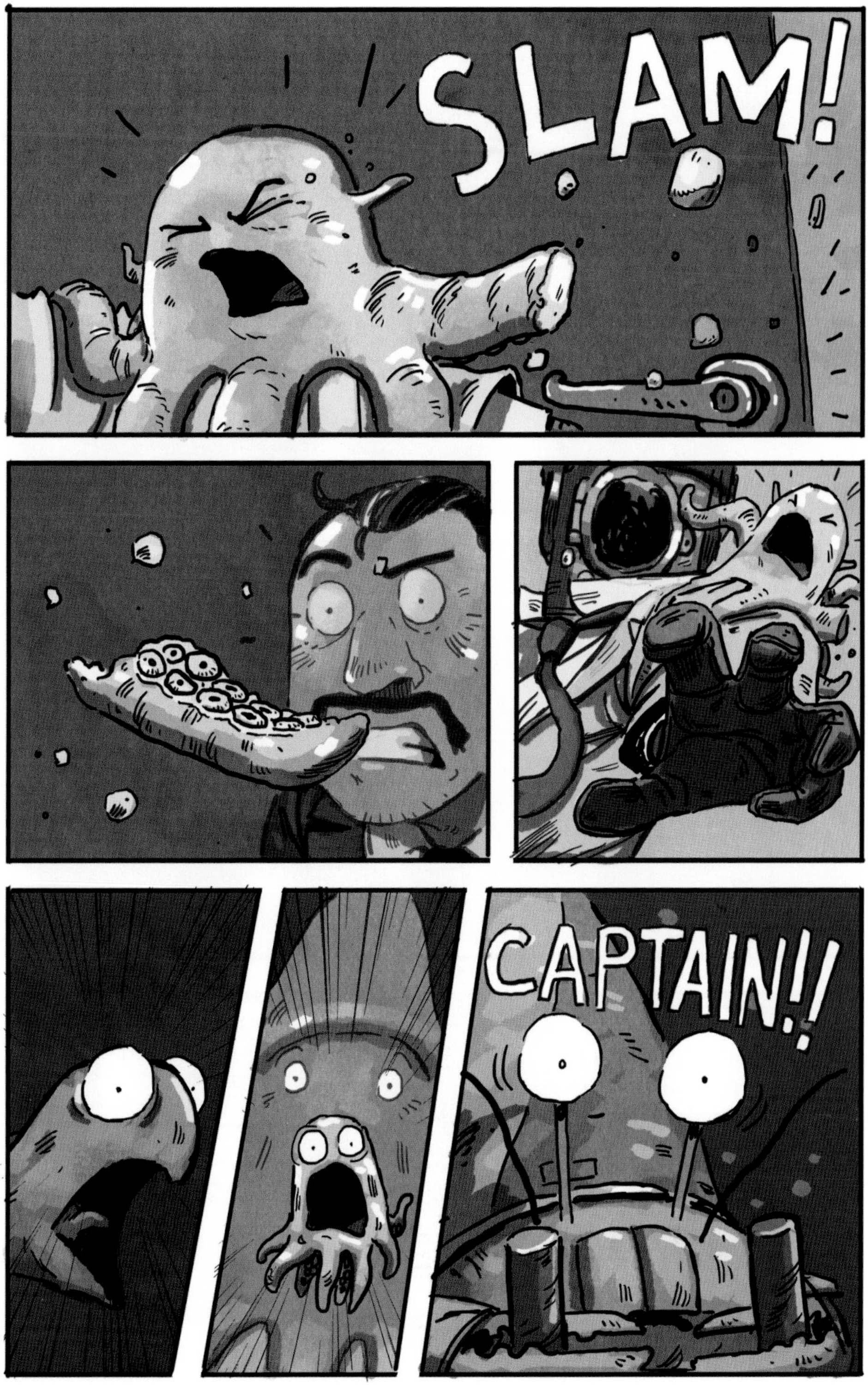
SLAM!
CAPTAIN!!

205

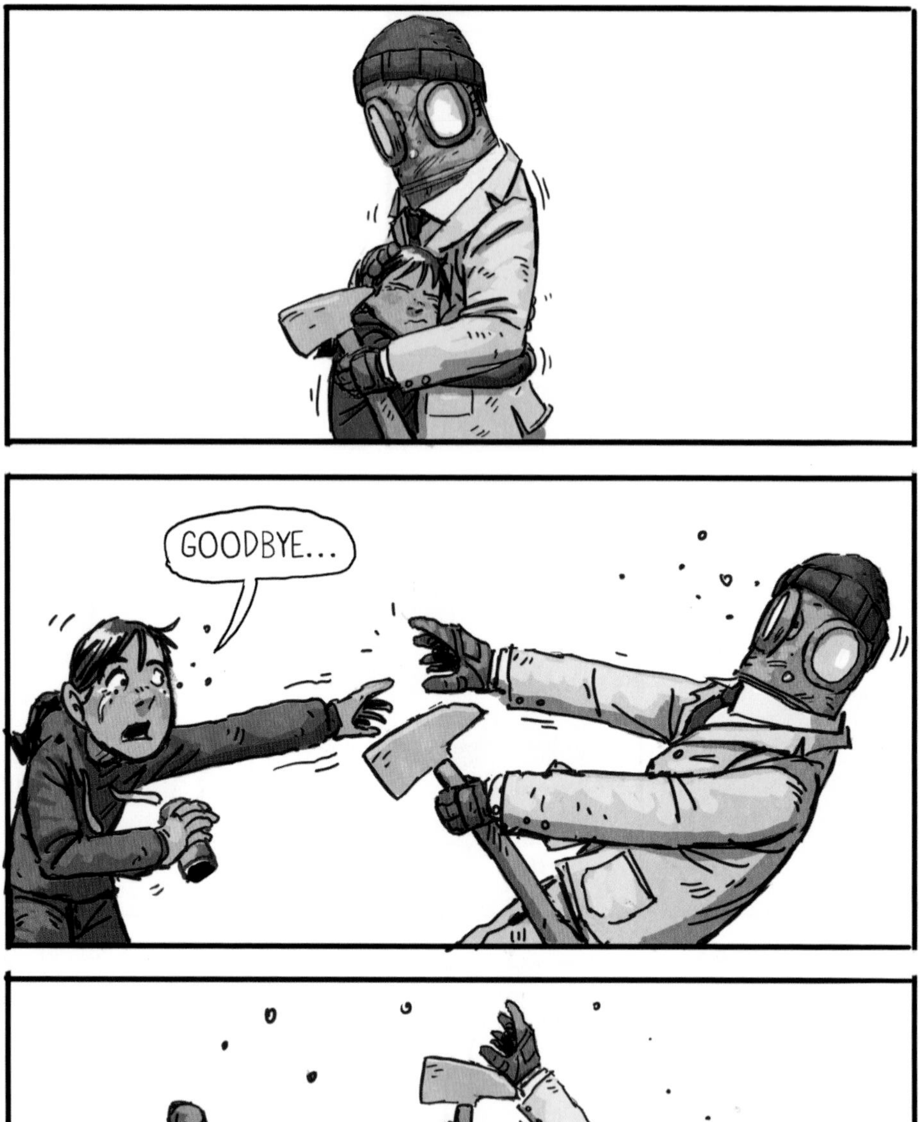
GOODBYE...

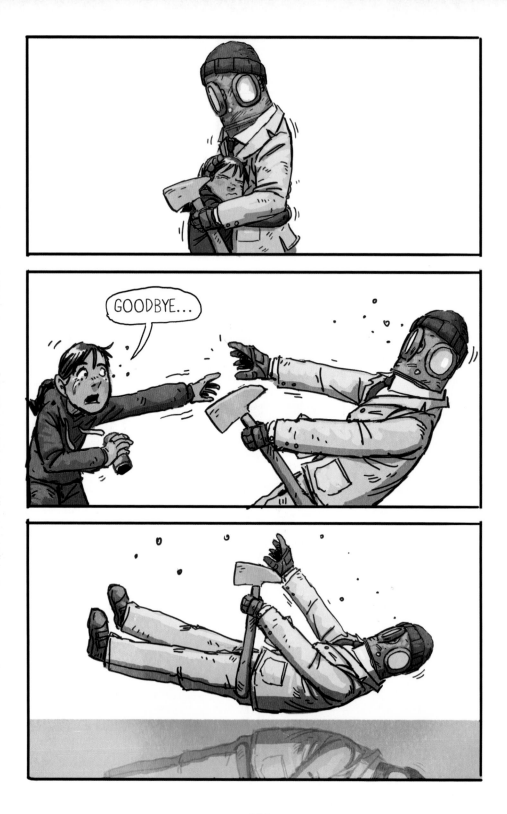

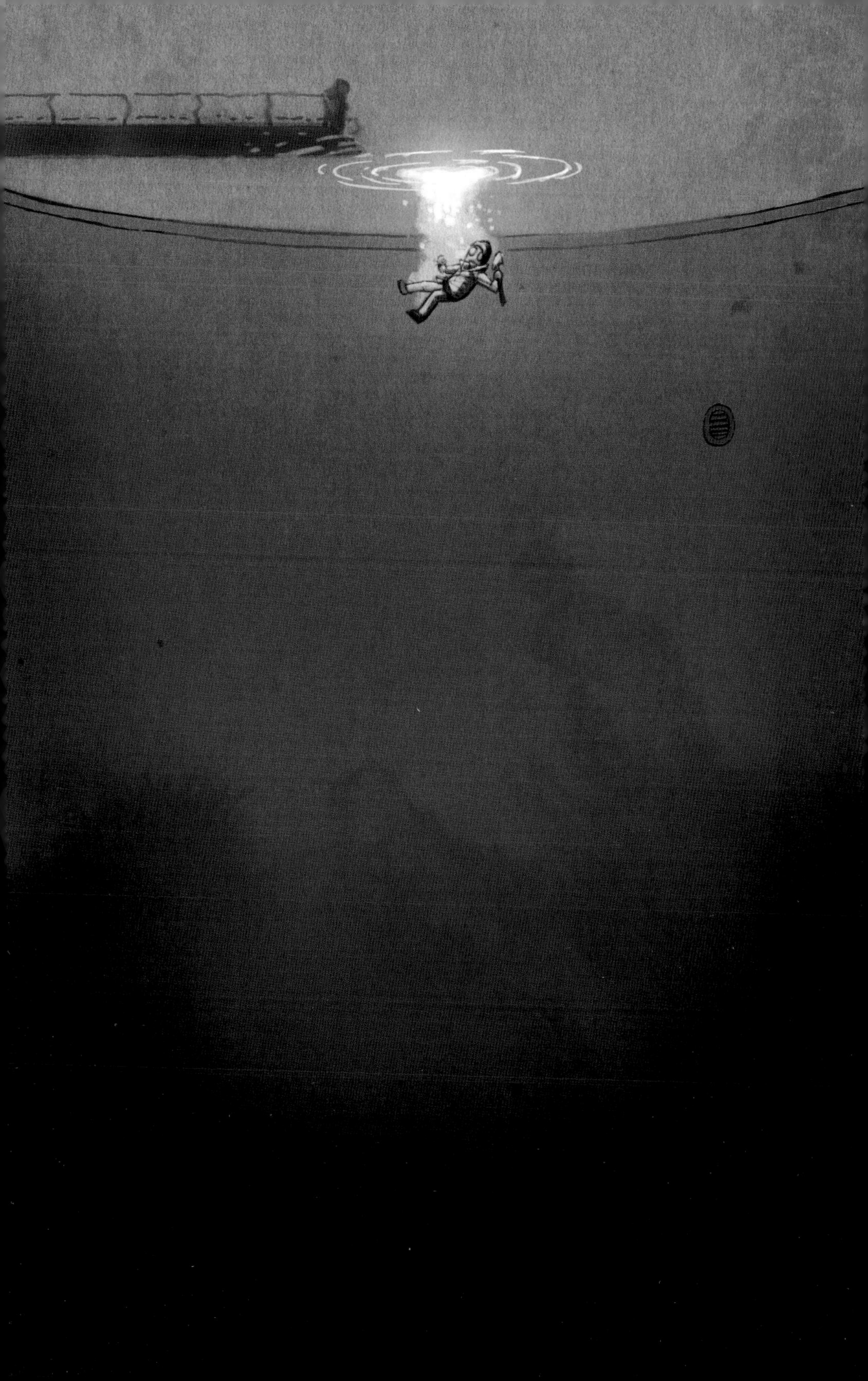

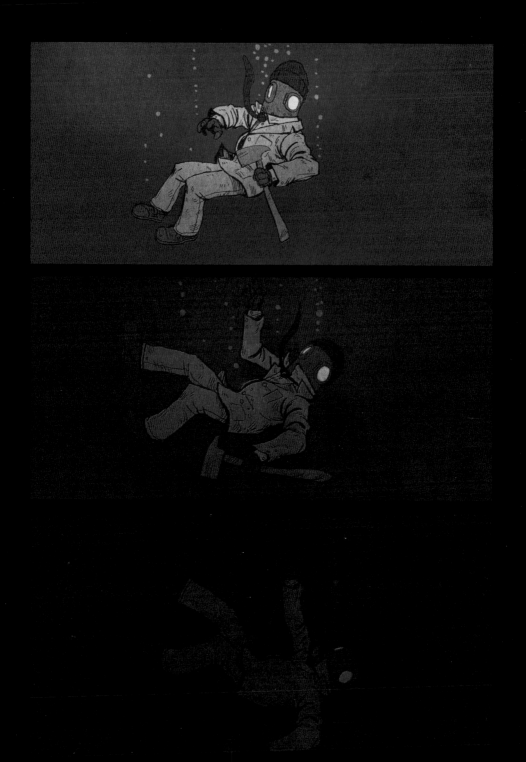

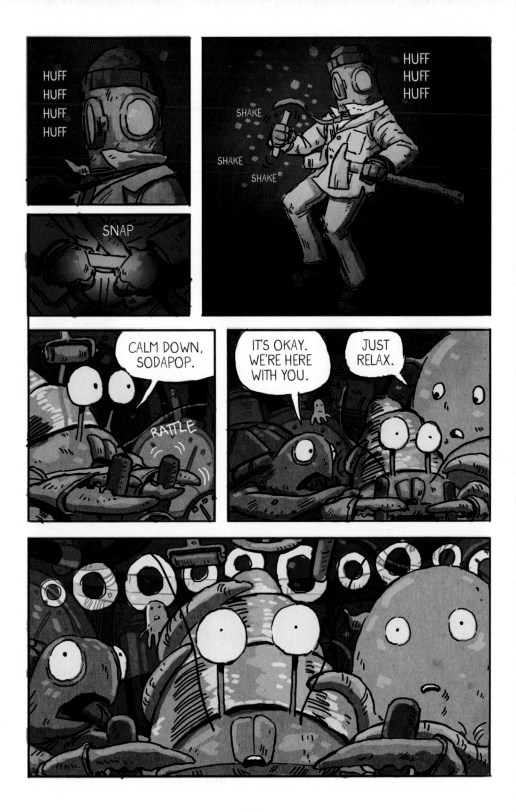

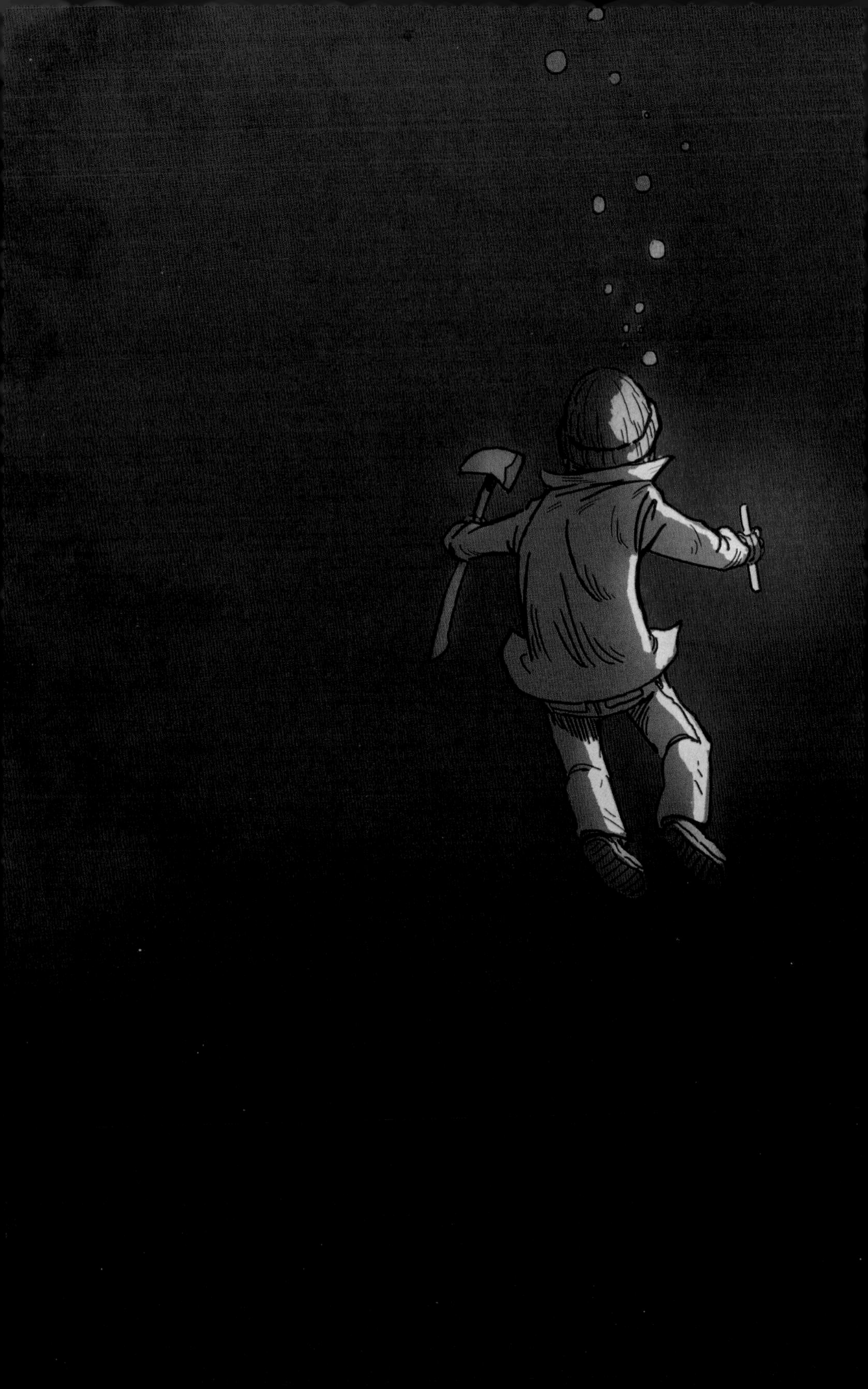

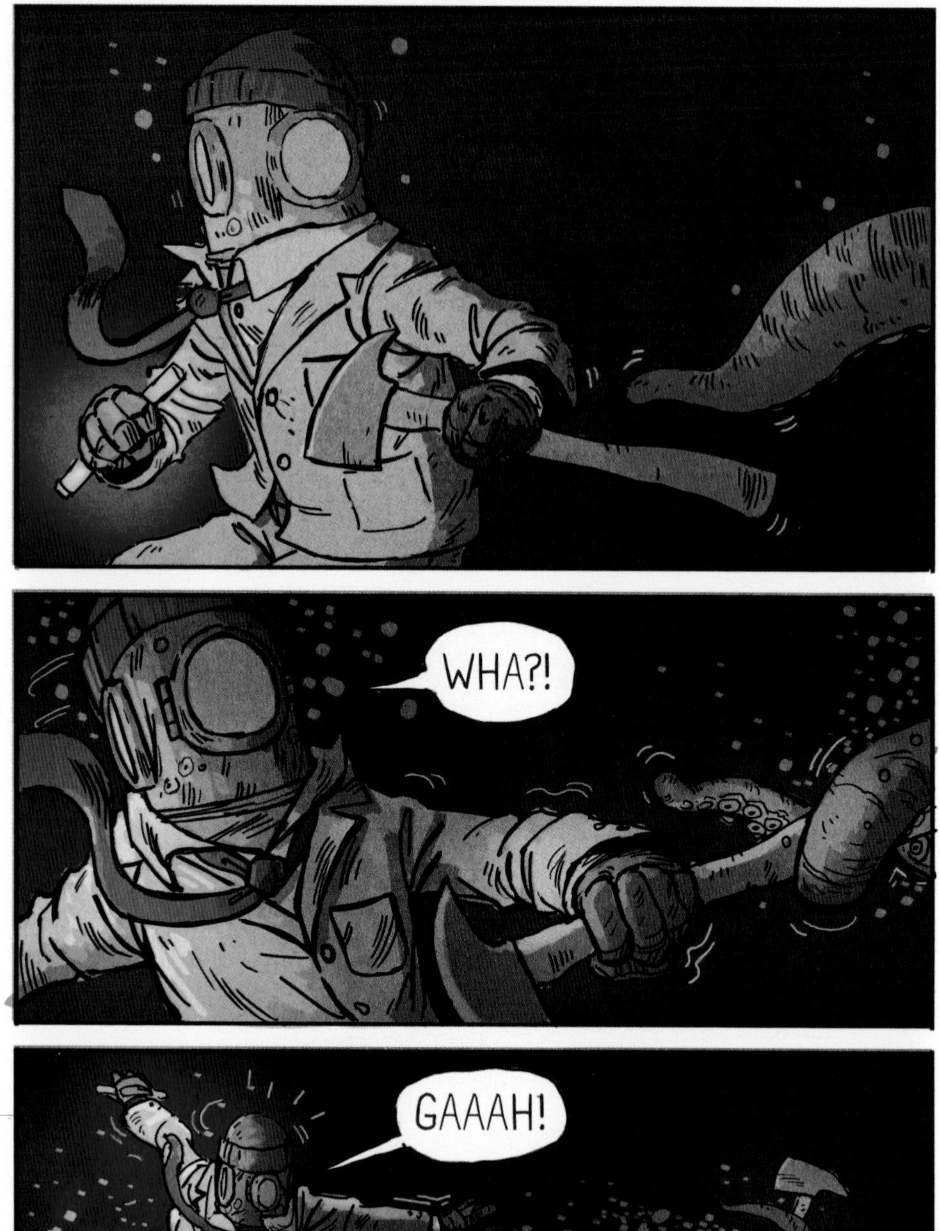
WHA?!
GAAAH!

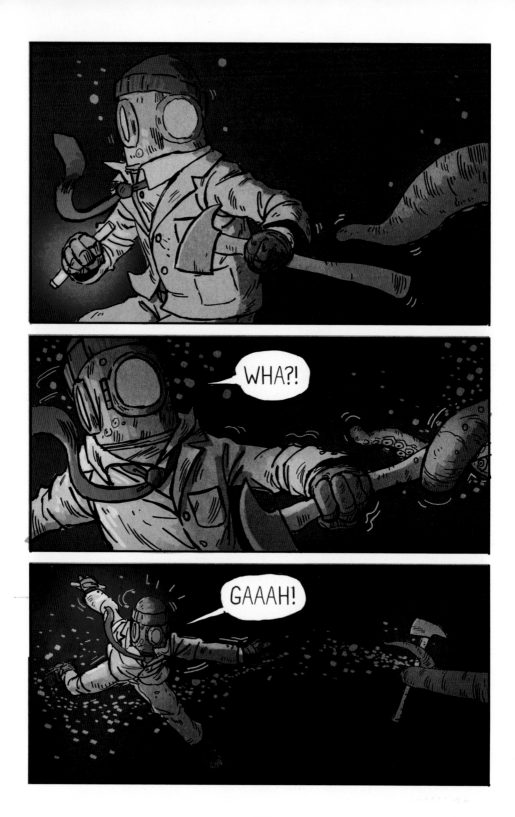

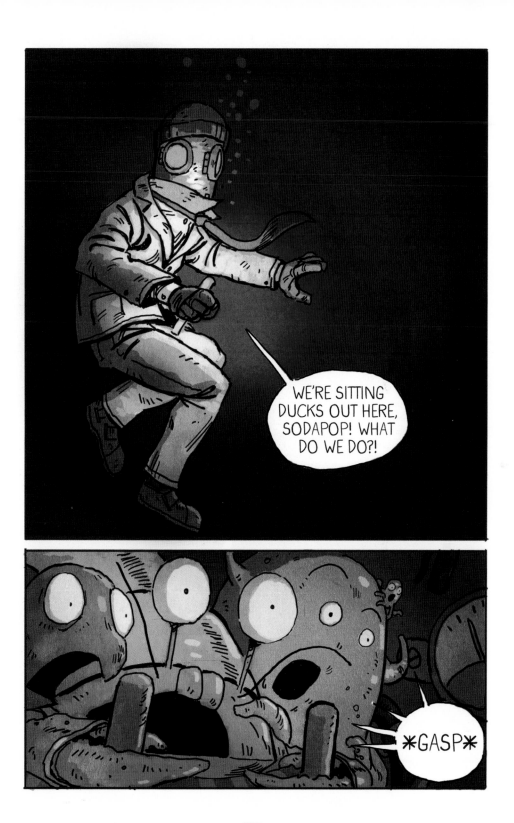

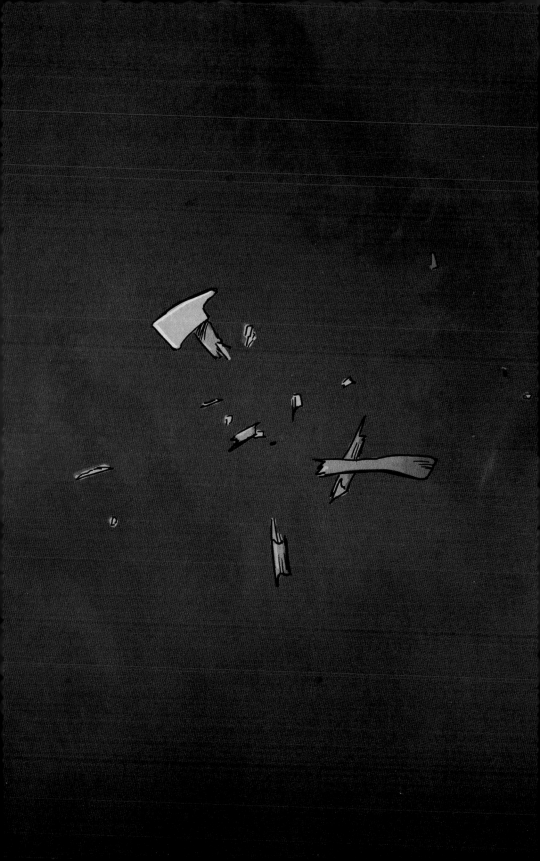

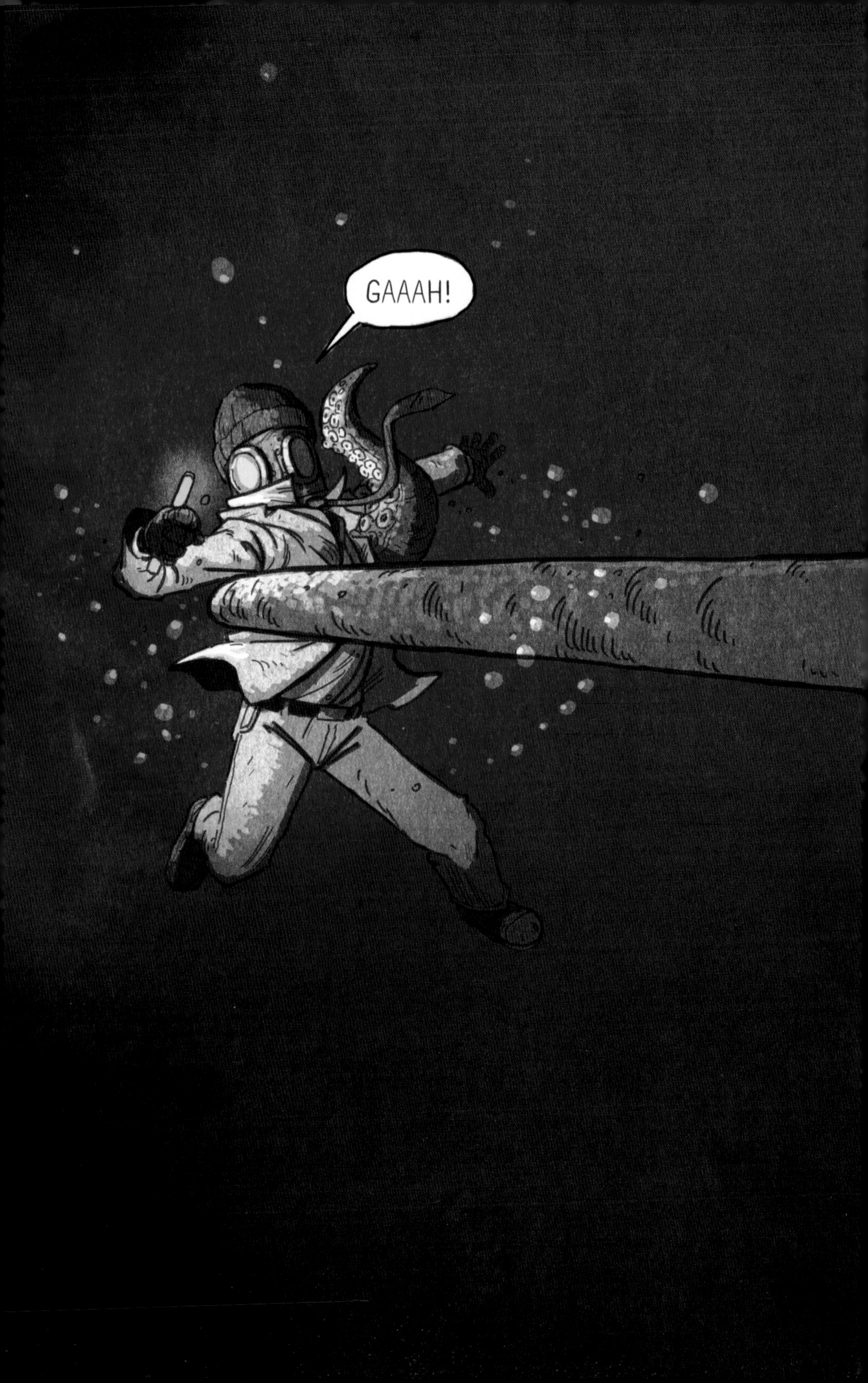
GAAAH!

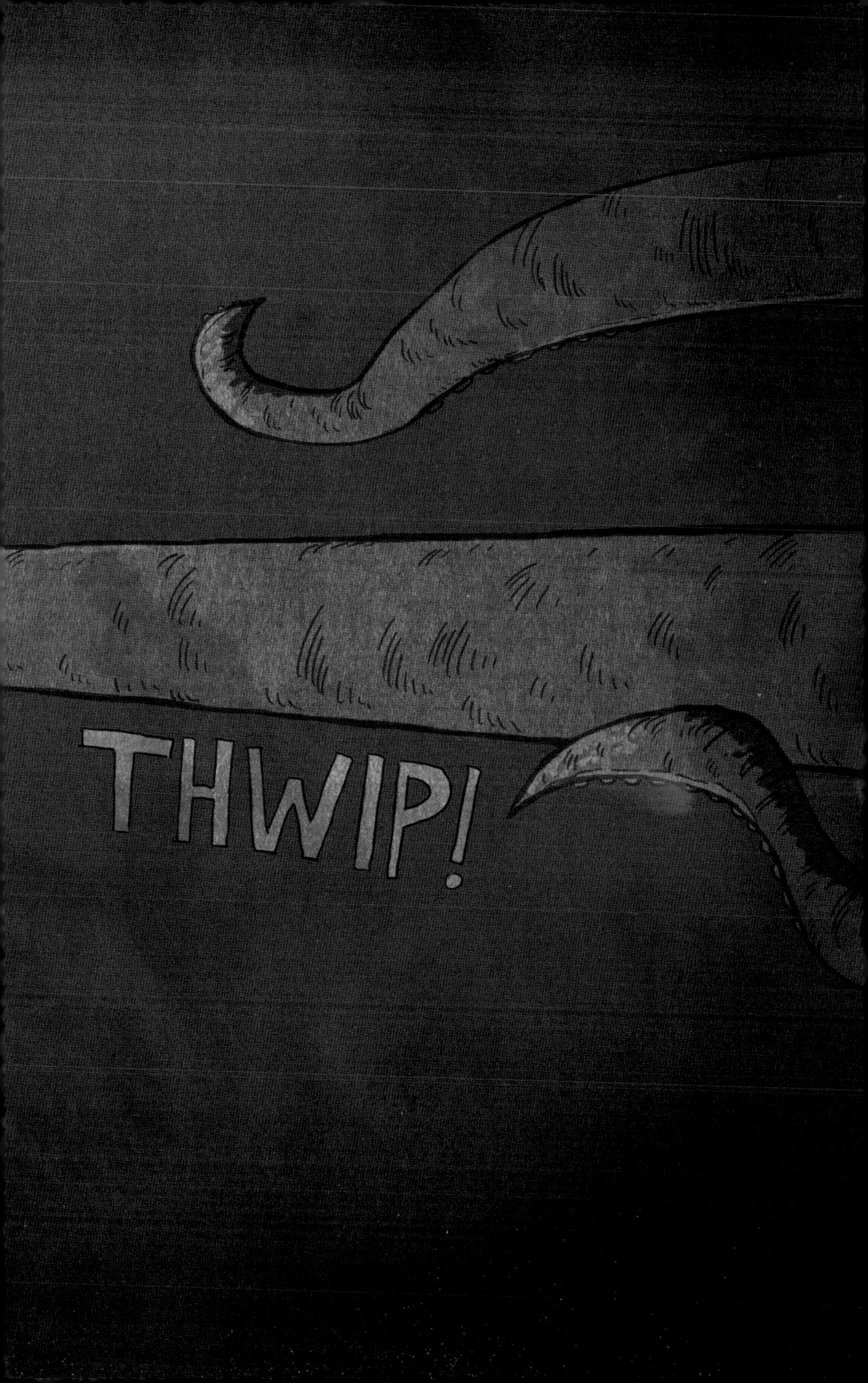
THWIP!

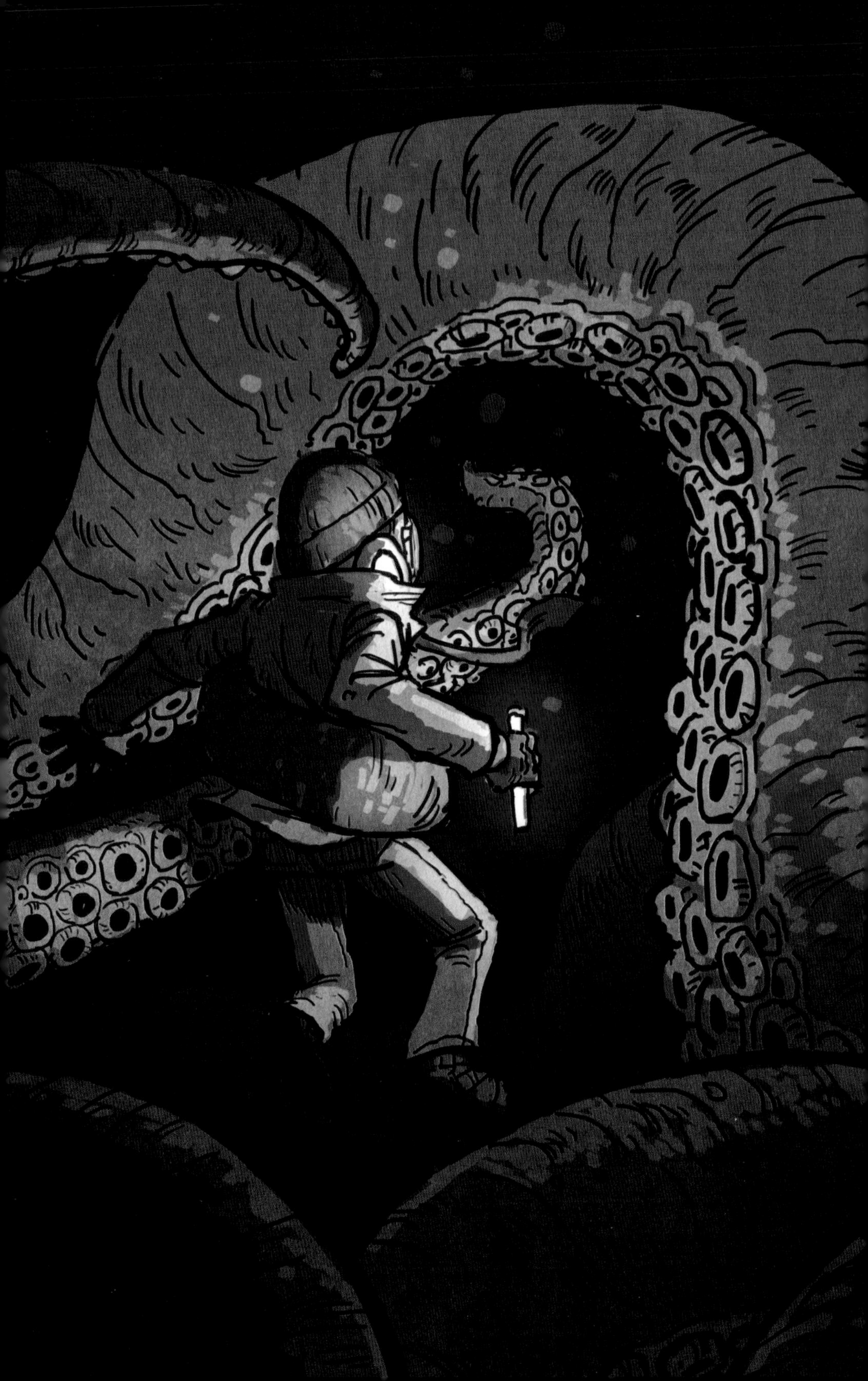

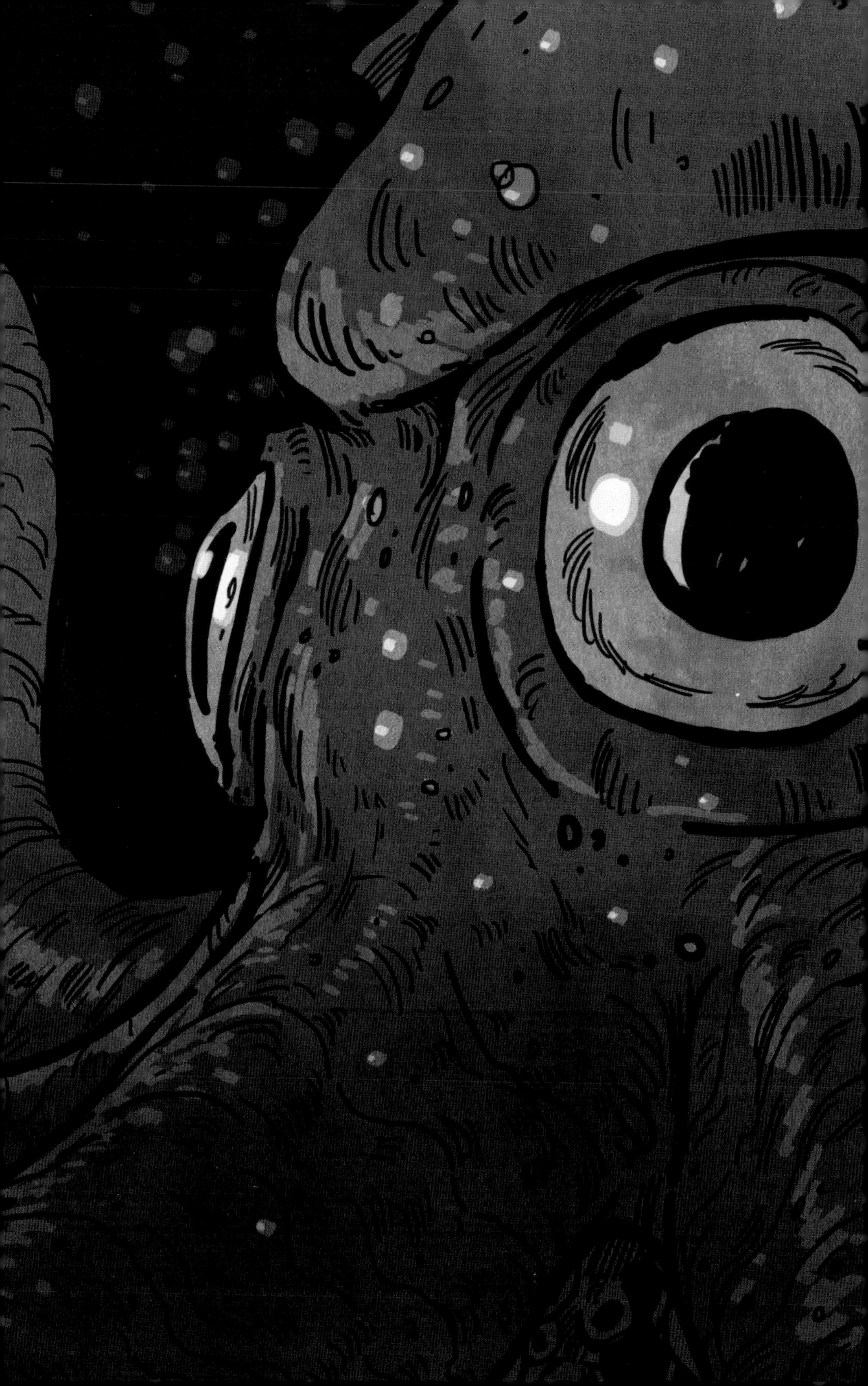

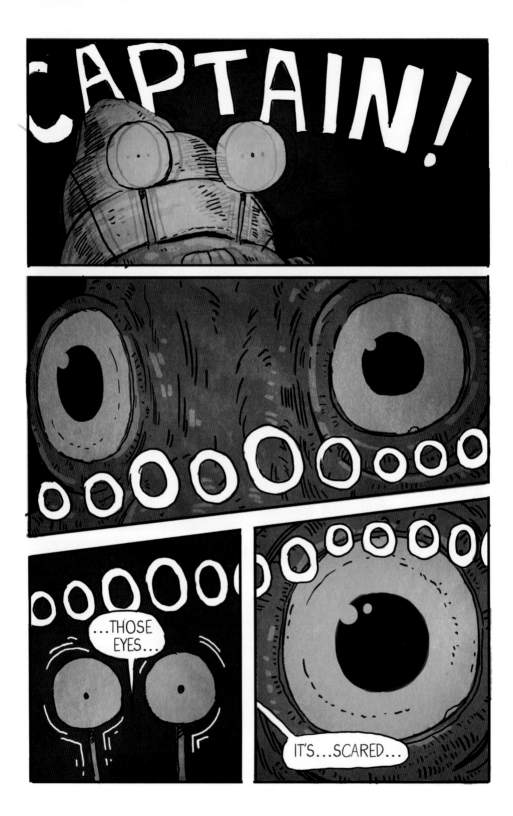

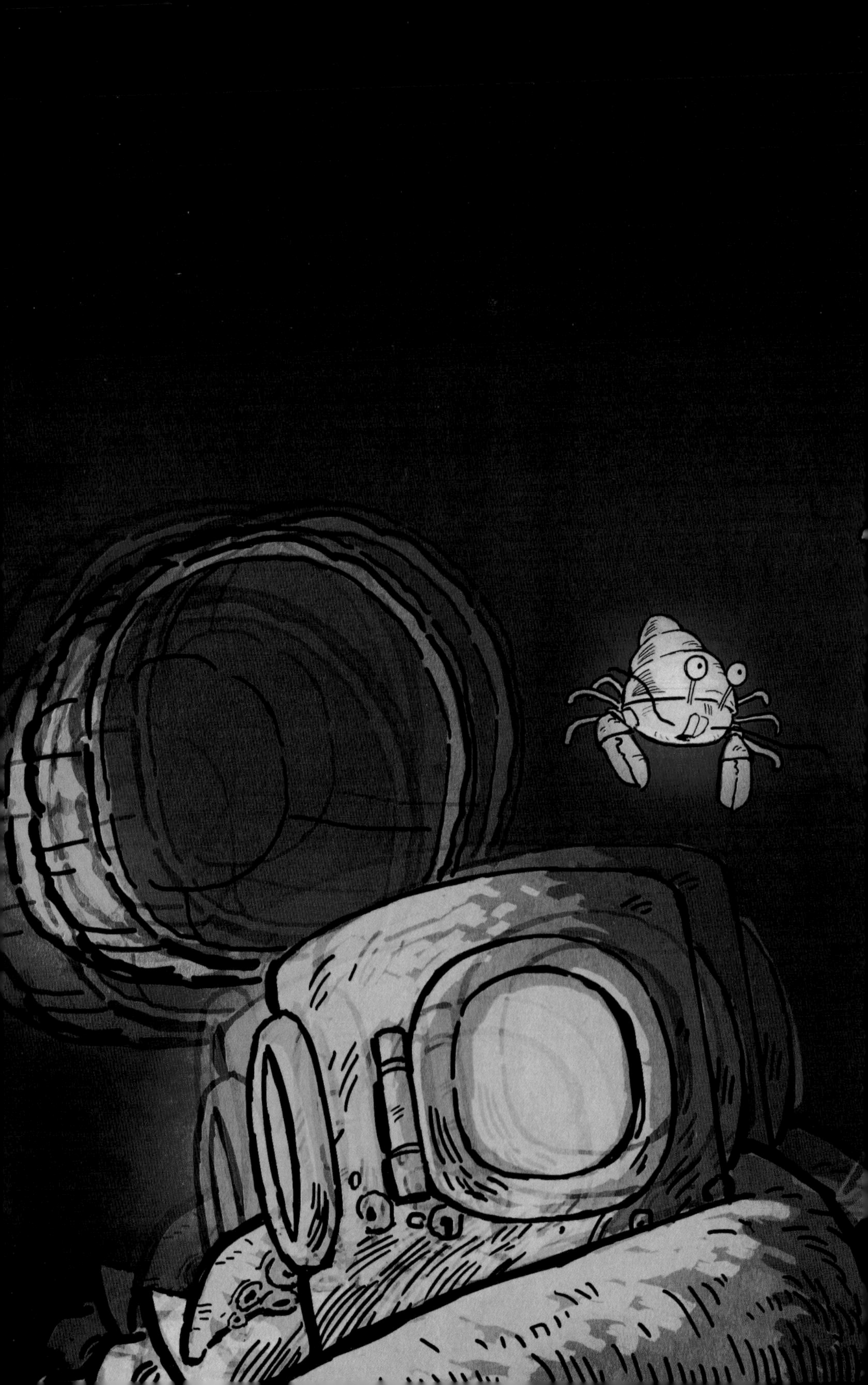

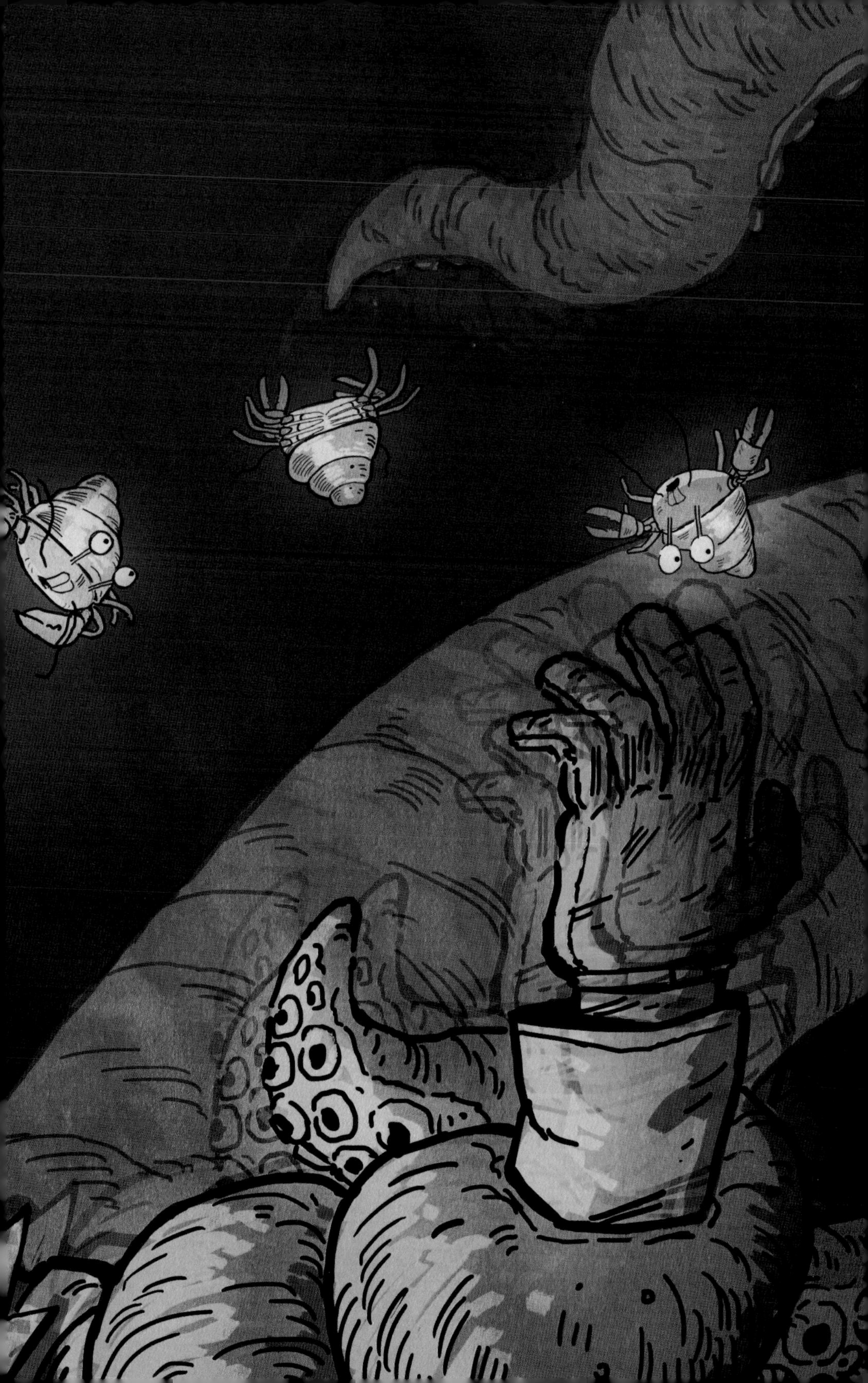

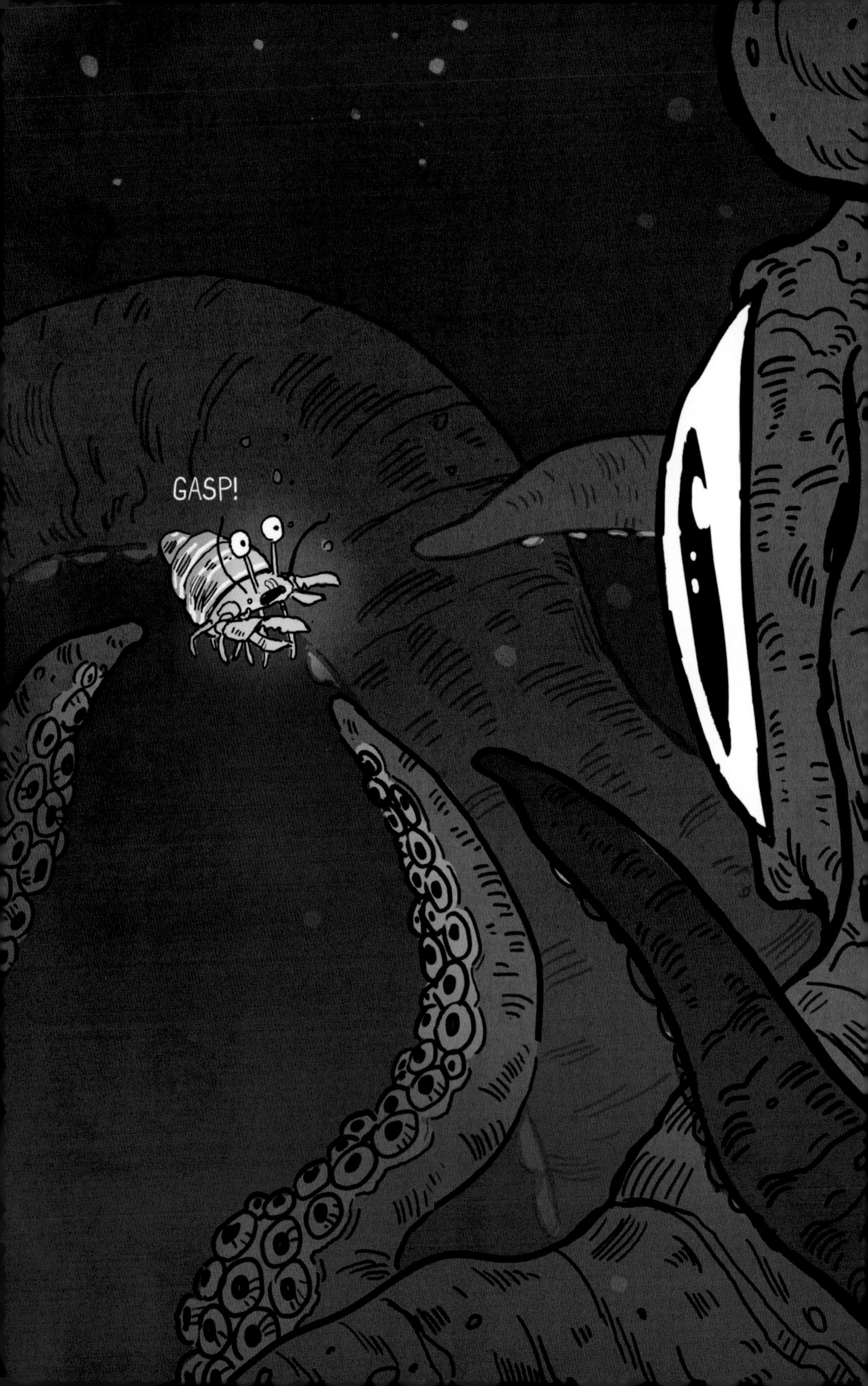
GASP!

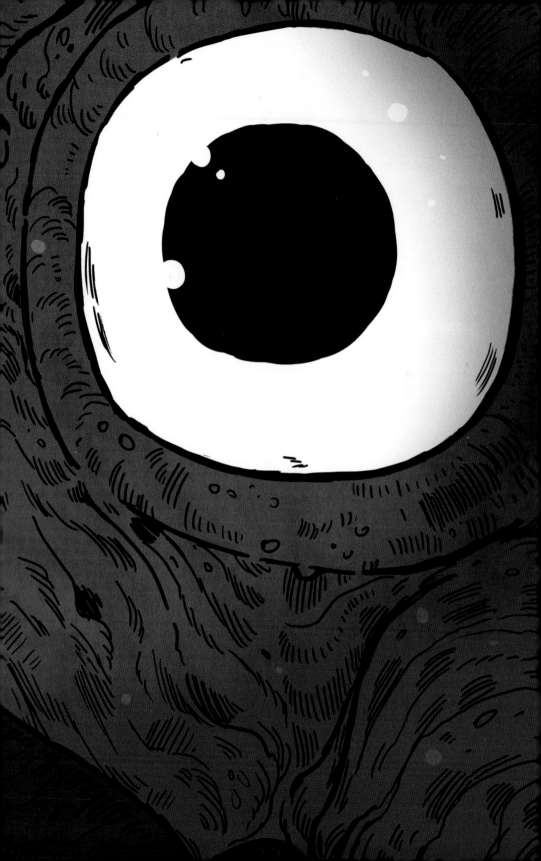

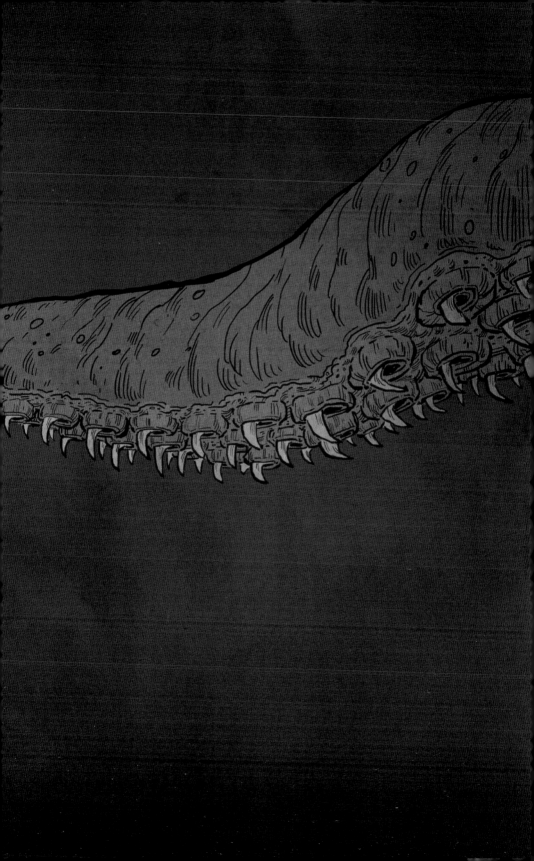

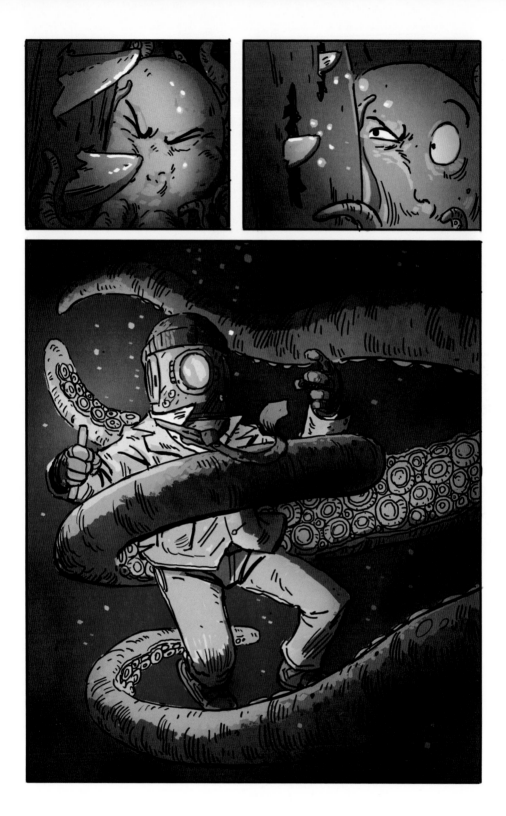

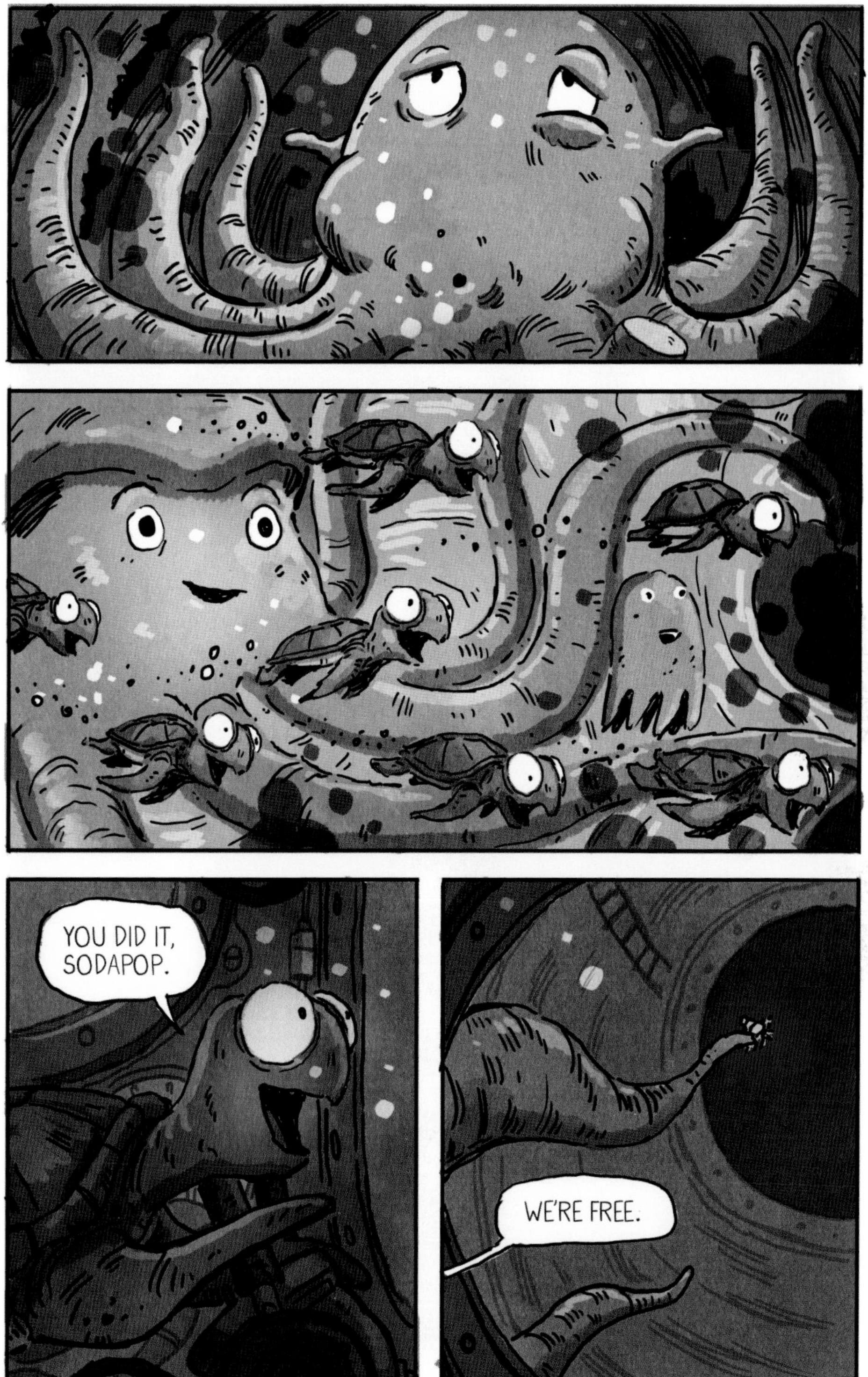
YOU DID IT, SODAPOP.
WE'RE FREE.

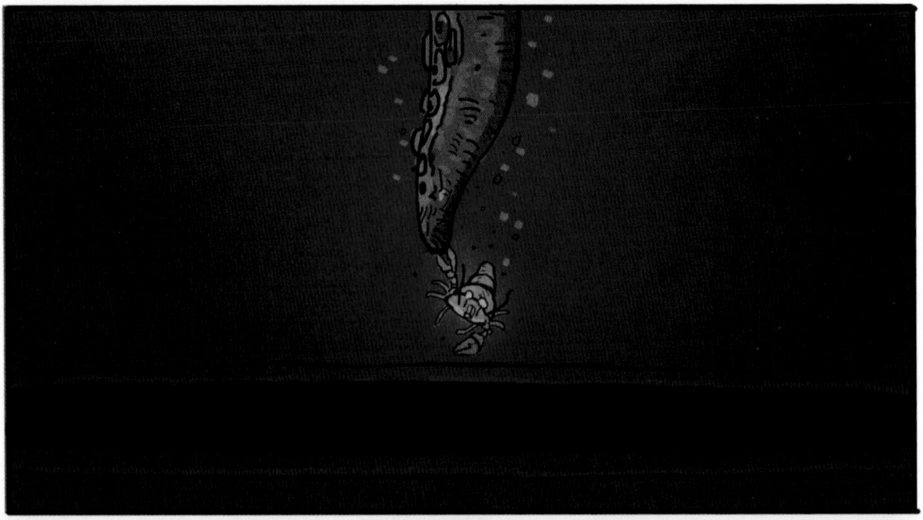

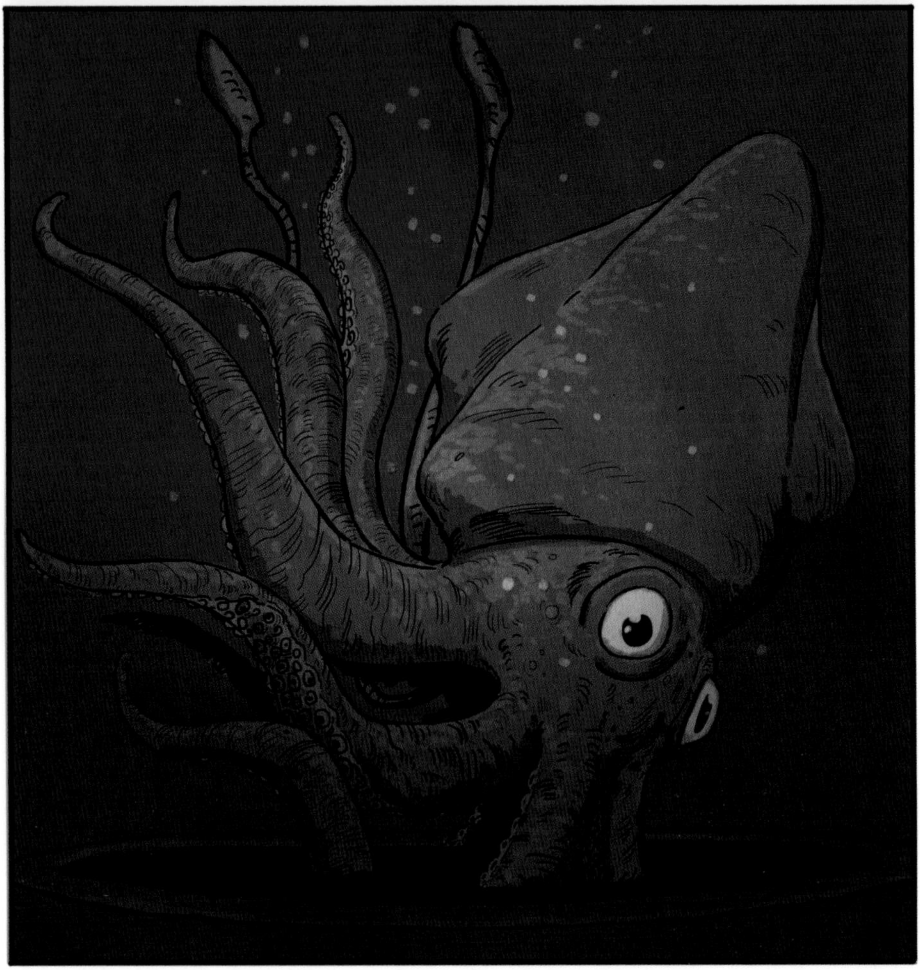

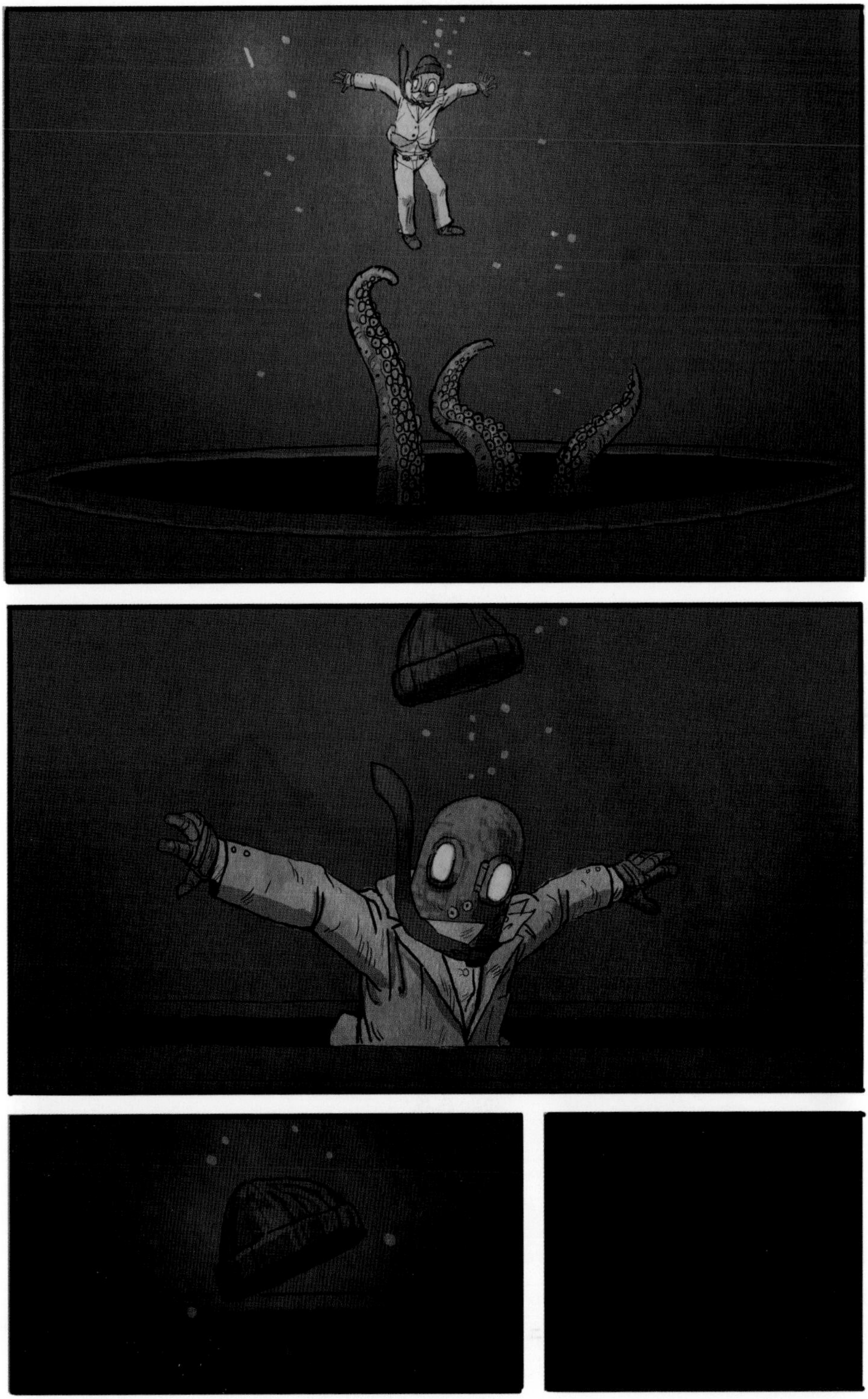

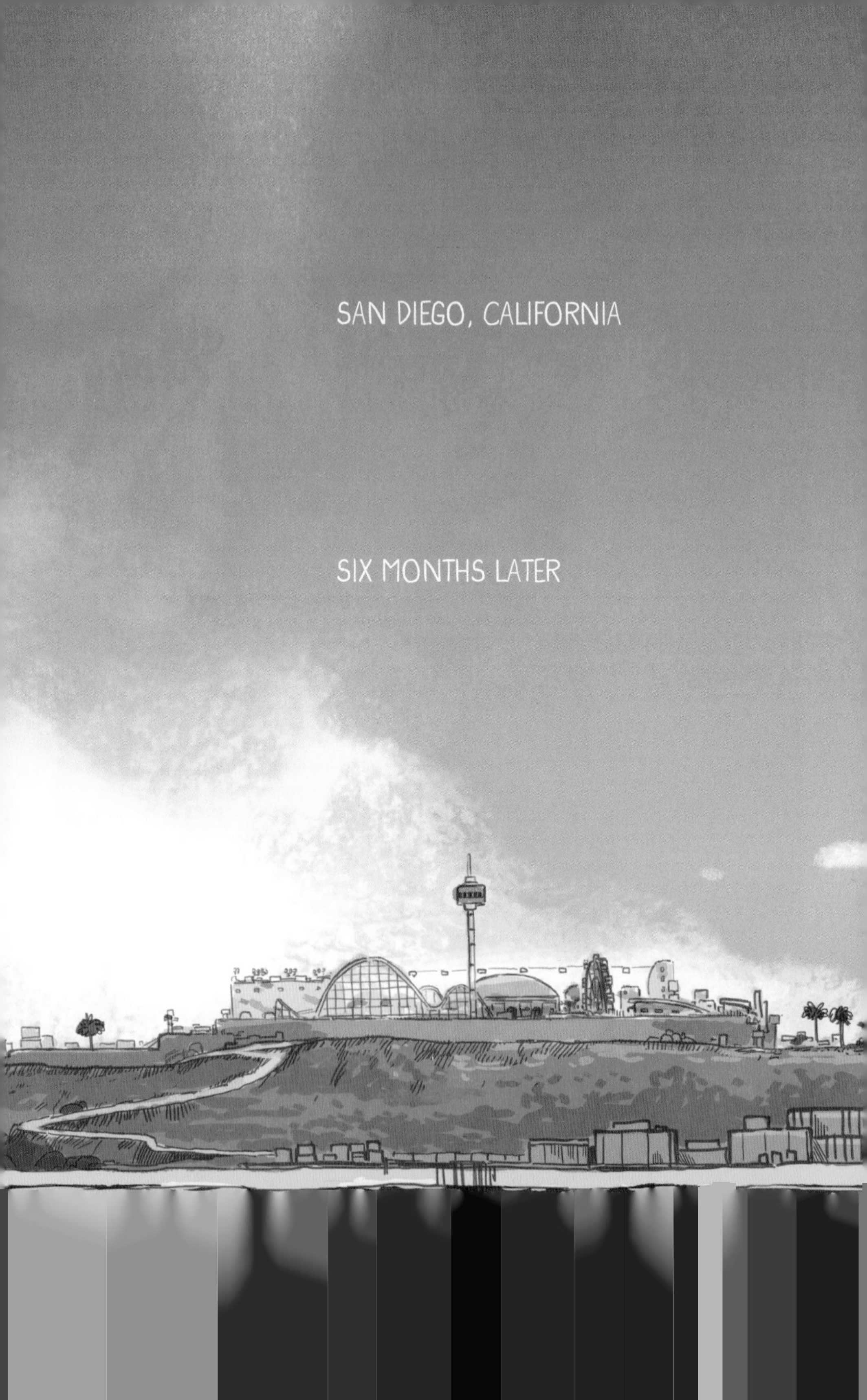
SAN DIEGO, CALIFORNIA
SIX MONTHS LATER

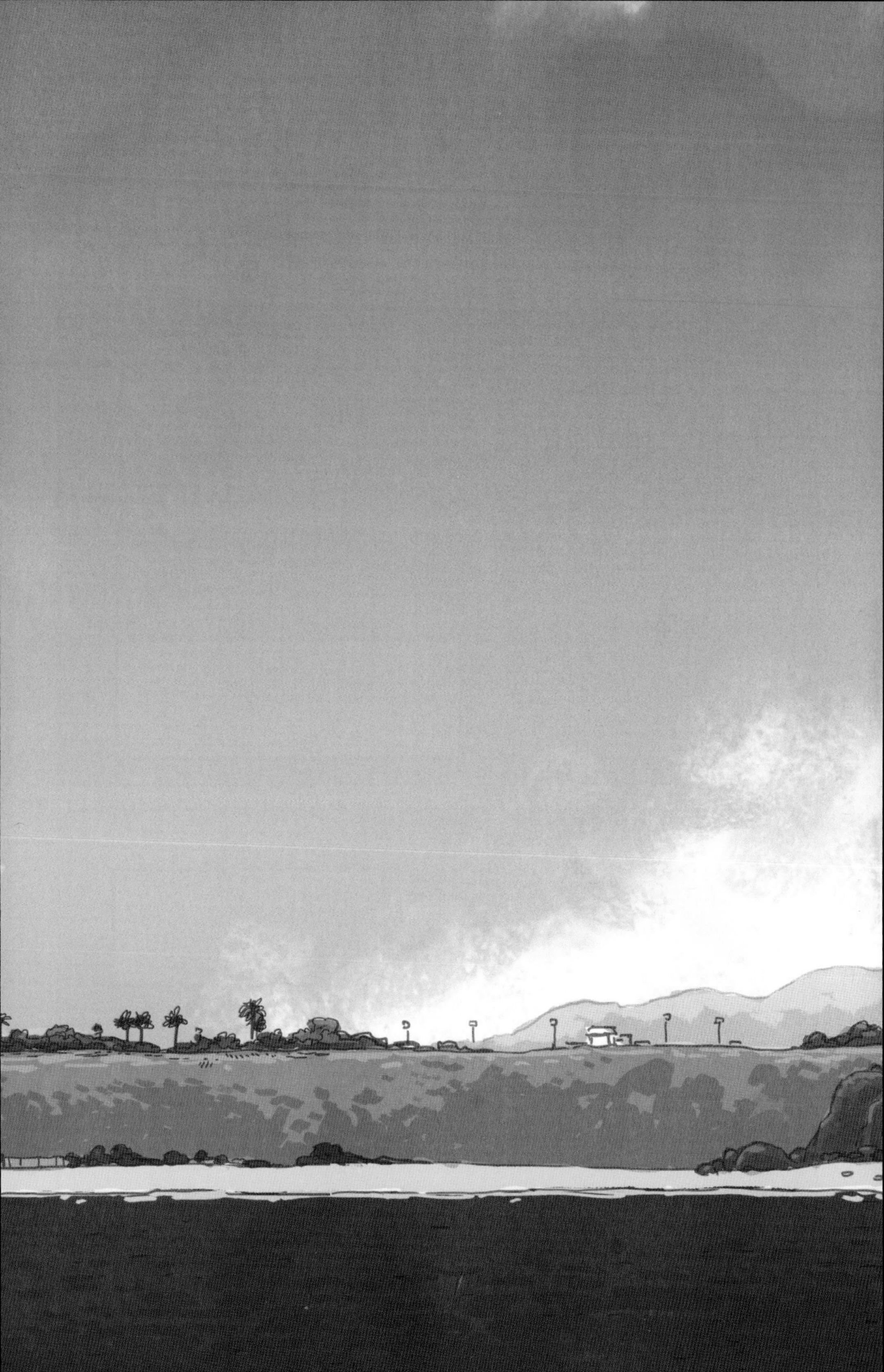

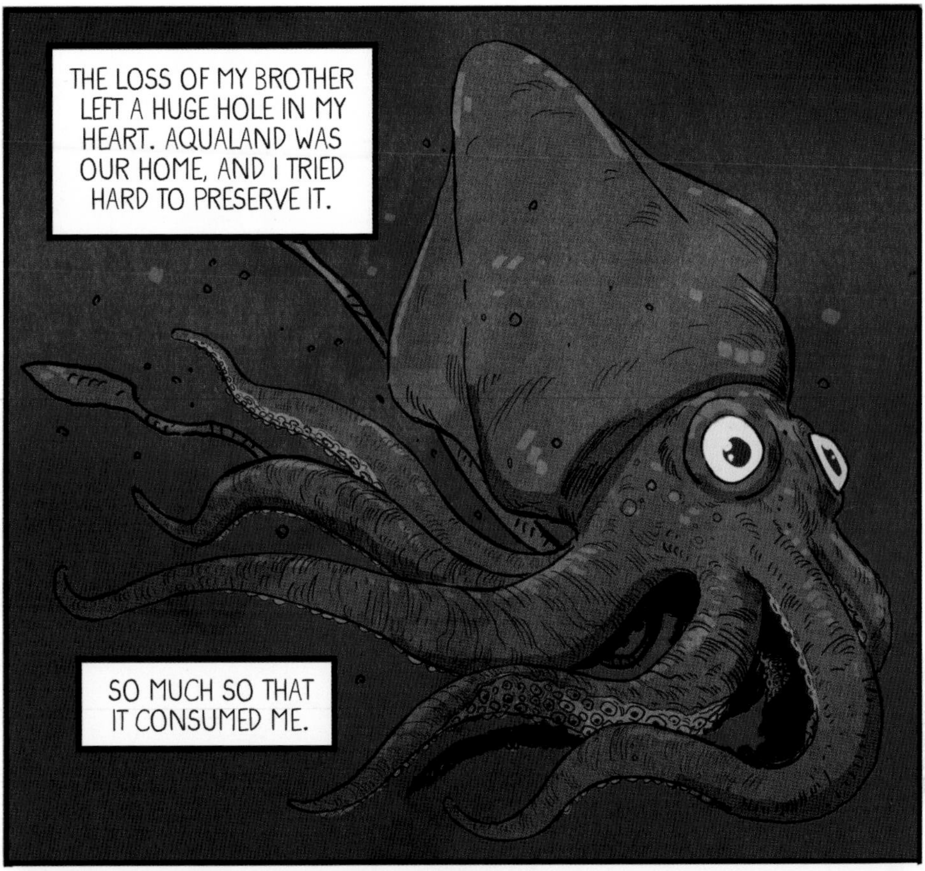
THE LOSS OF MY BROTHER LEFT A HUGE HOLE IN MY HEART. AQUALAND WAS OUR HOME, AND I TRIED HARD TO PRESERVE IT.
SO MUCH SO THAT IT CONSUMED ME.

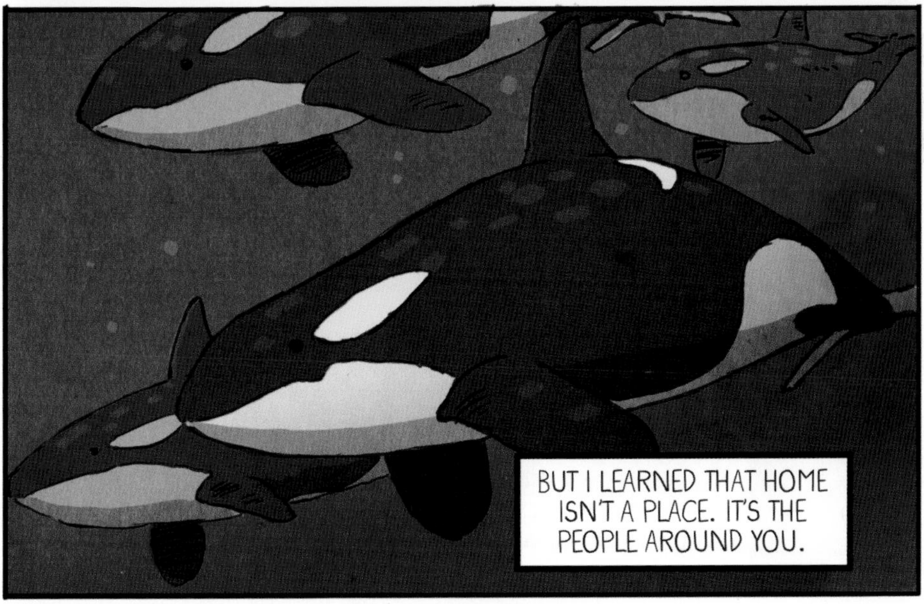
BUT I LEARNED THAT HOME ISN'T A PLACE. IT'S THE PEOPLE AROUND YOU.

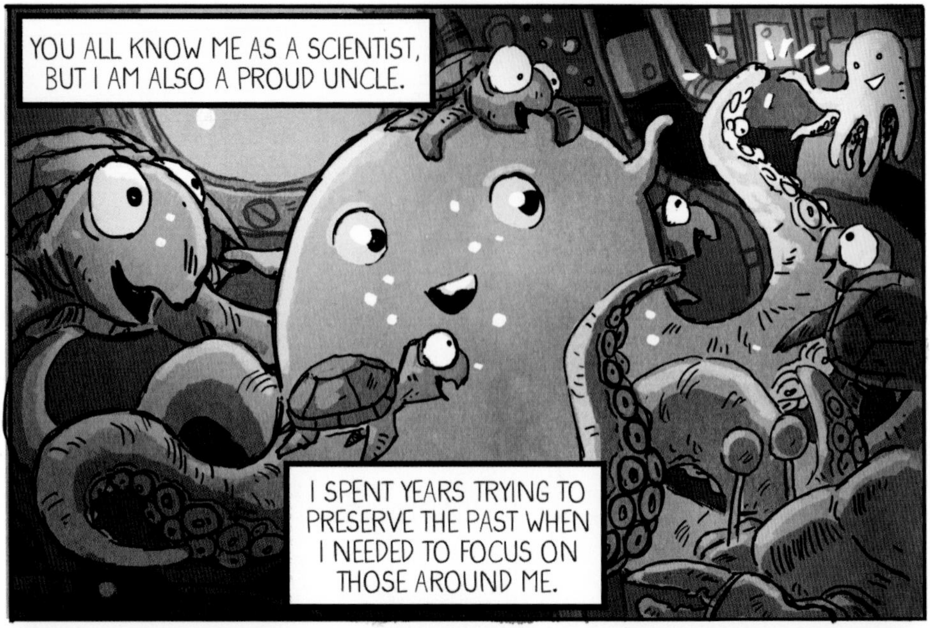
YOU ALL KNOW ME AS A SCIENTIST, BUT I AM ALSO A PROUD UNCLE.
I SPENT YEARS TRYING TO PRESERVE THE PAST WHEN I NEEDED TO FOCUS ON THOSE AROUND ME.

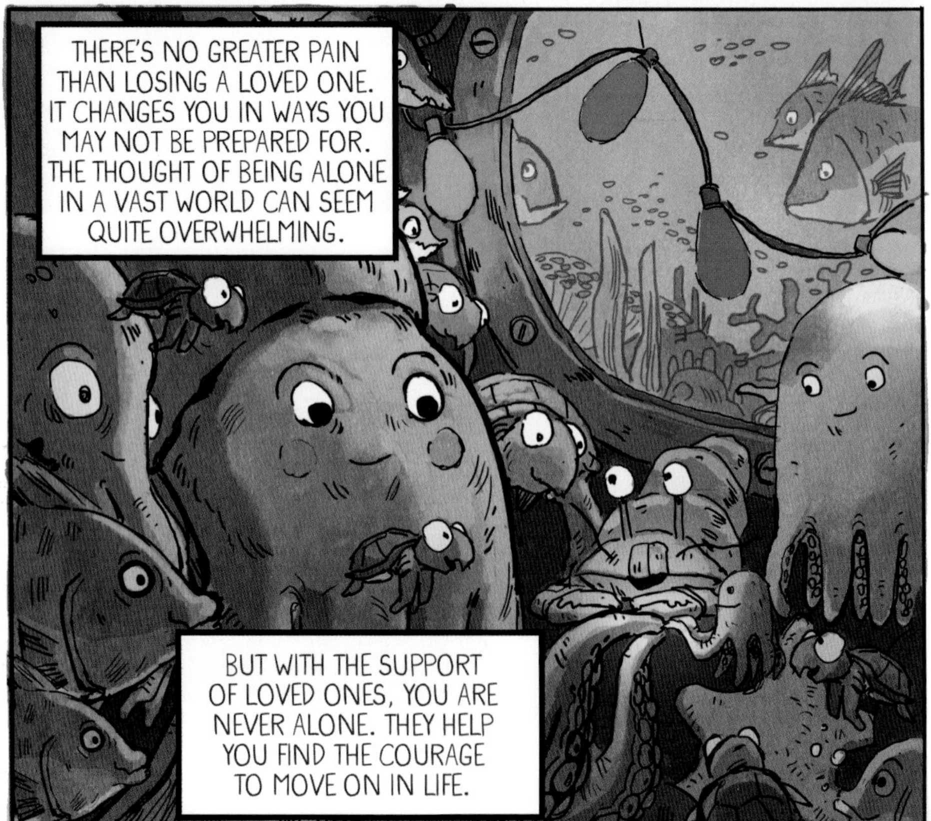
THERE'S NO GREATER PAIN THAN LOSING A LOVED ONE. IT CHANGES YOU IN WAYS YOU MAY NOT BE PREPARED FOR. THE THOUGHT OF BEING ALONE IN A VAST WORLD CAN SEEM QUITE OVERWHELMING.
BUT WITH THE SUPPORT OF LOVED ONES, YOU ARE NEVER ALONE. THEY HELP YOU FIND THE COURAGE TO MOVE ON IN LIFE.

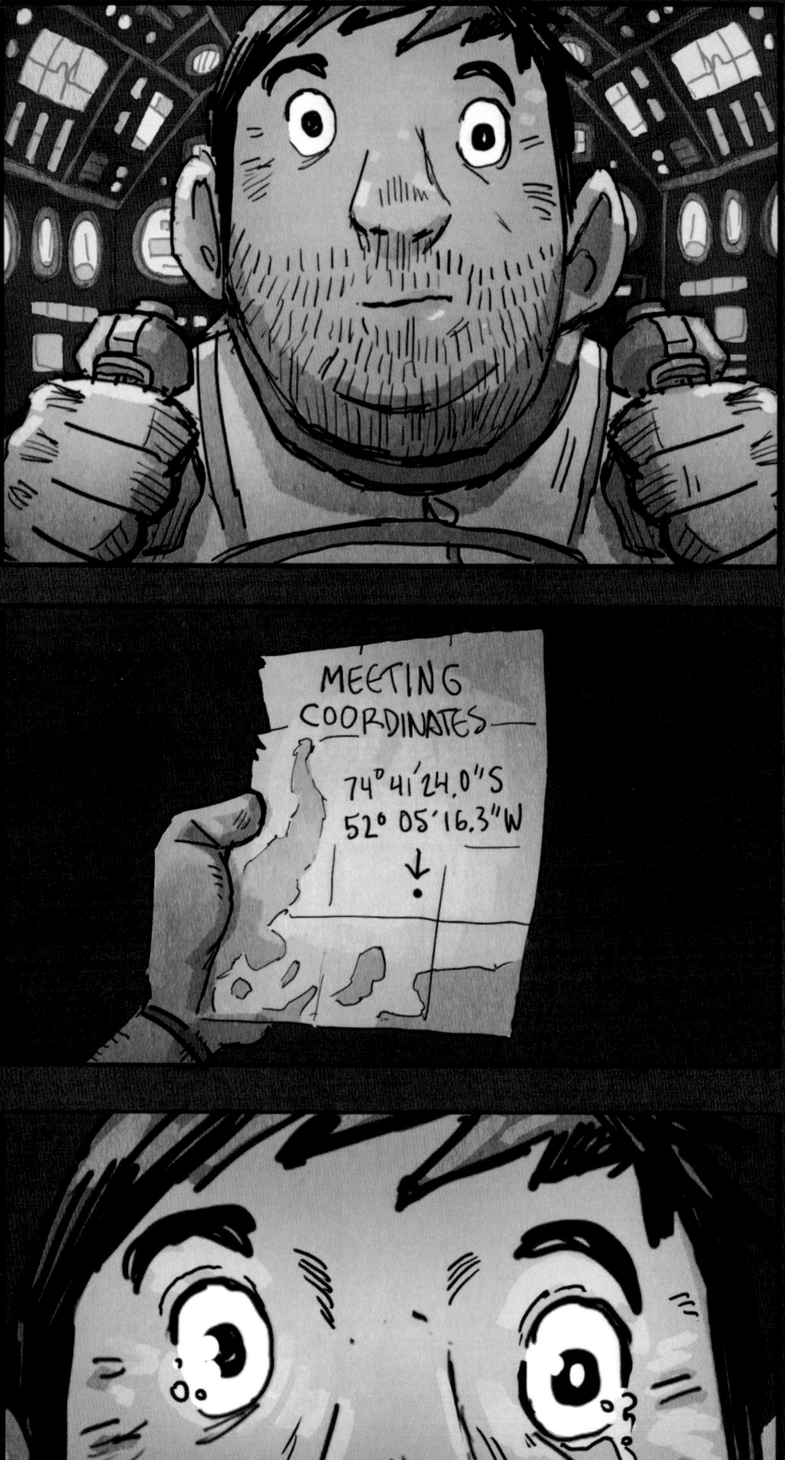
MEETING
COORDINATES
74° 41′ 24.0″ S
52° 05′ 16.3″ W

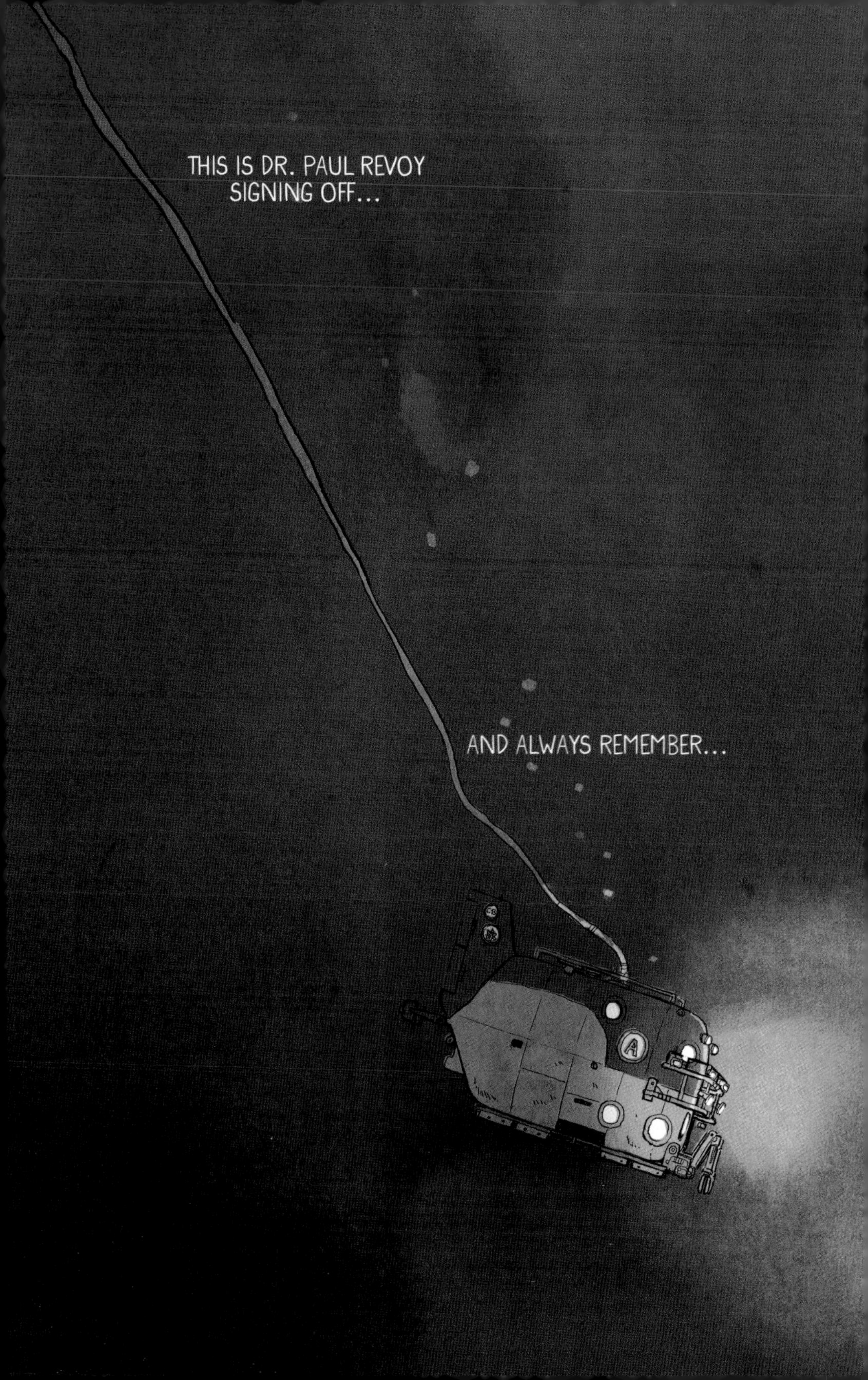
THIS IS DR. PAUL REVOY SIGNING OFF...
AND ALWAYS REMEMBER...

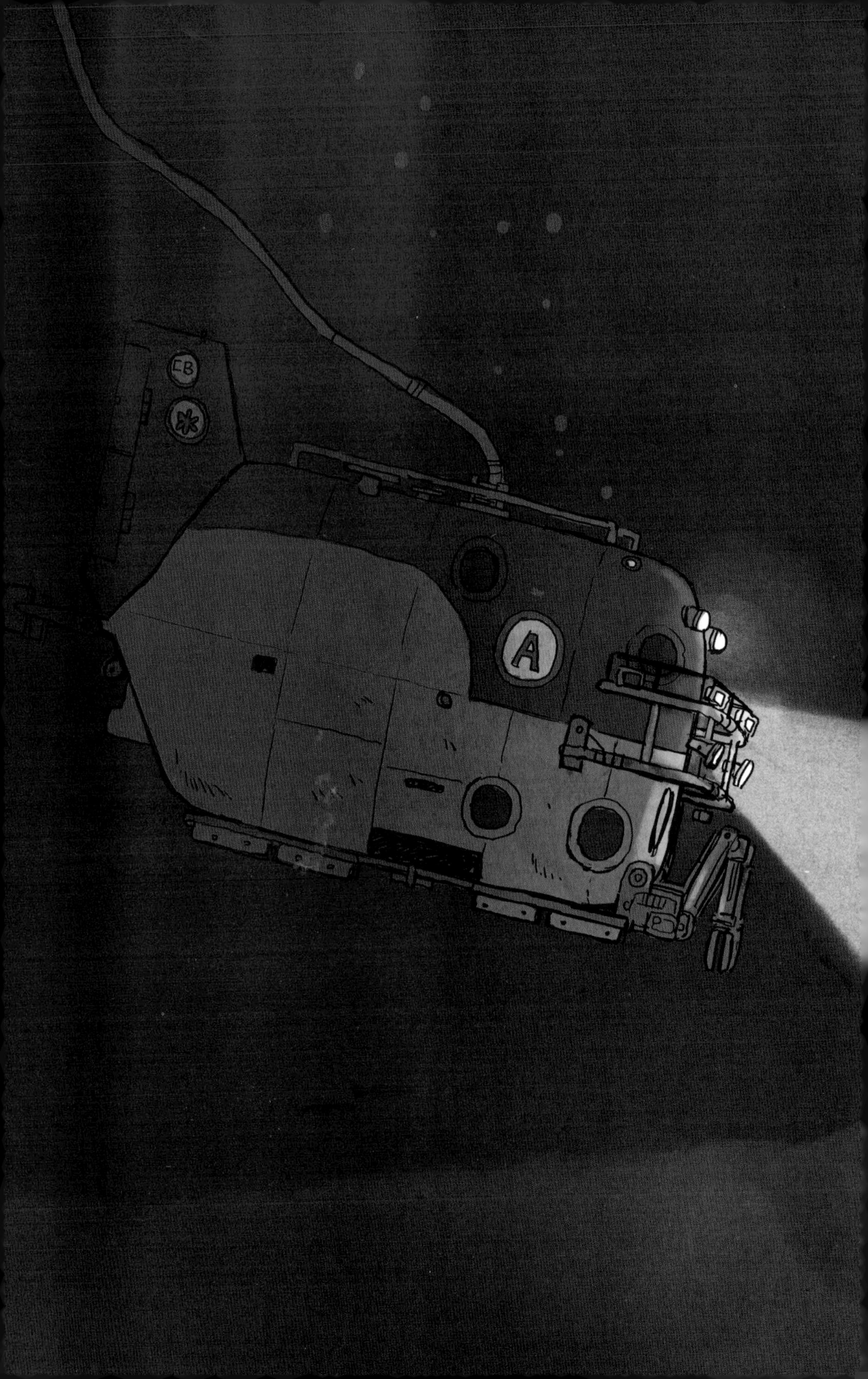
A

FAMILY COMES FIRST.

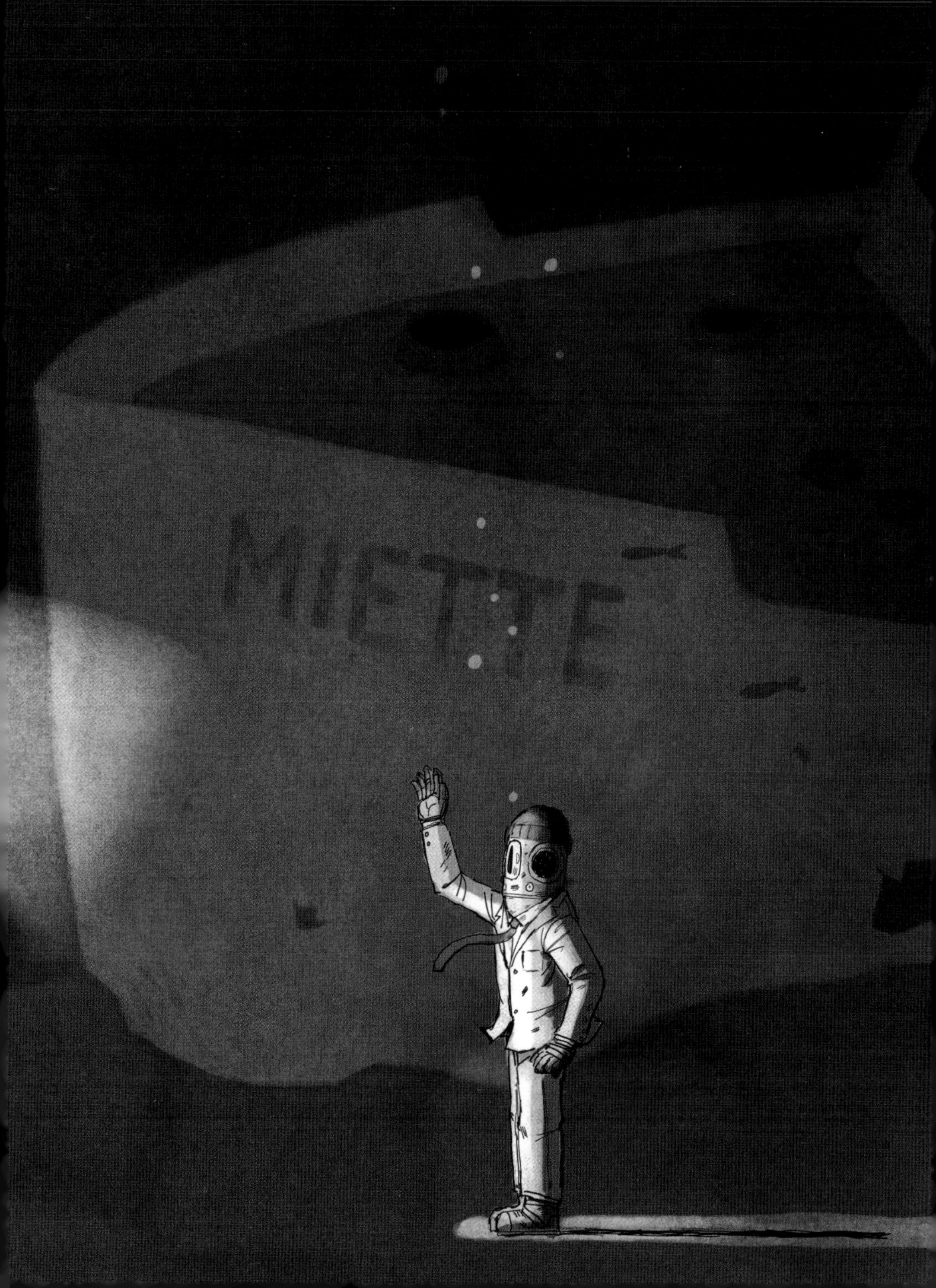
MIETTE

When I originally pitched *The Aquanaut* to my publisher, the simple premise was, "sea creatures that convert an old diving suit into a land walking device to find a paradise on land to escape all the dangers of the sea." But as the story evolved, it became much more heartfelt. *The Aquanaut* became a story about loss, preserving legacies, family, and holding on to memories. Ten years later, while wrapping up the final parts of this book, my own father lost his battle to liver cancer, and I suddenly found myself feeling all the feelings that these characters were experiencing in the story, and the project became even more personal.

The following images are development pieces that I had sketched early on with some notes that you may find interesting.

Hope you enjoyed the journey as much as I enjoyed making it.

Dan Santat

EARLY DEVELOPMENT AQUANAUT DIVING SUIT

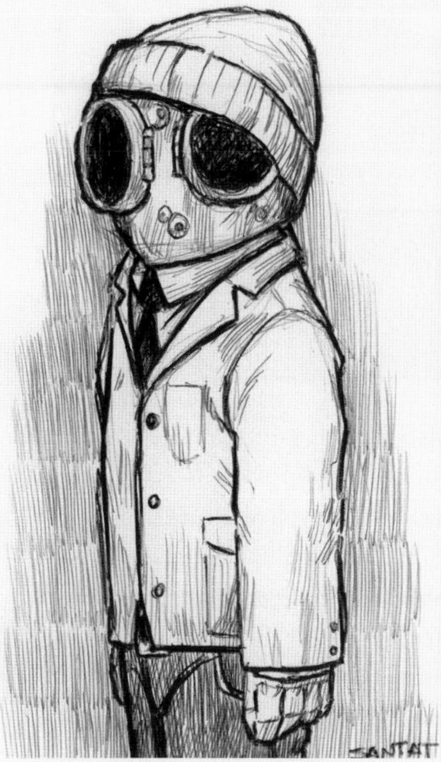
SANTAT

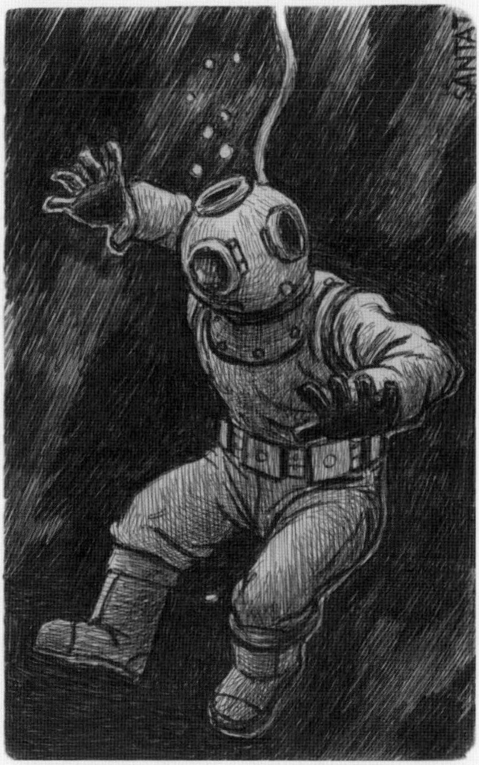
SANTAT

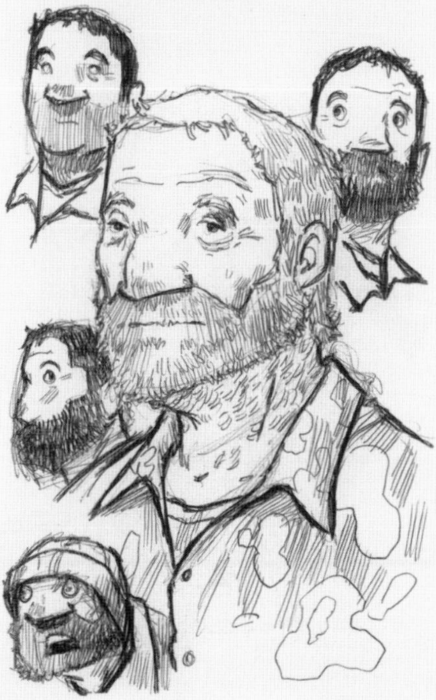

PAUL REVOY

Paul and Michel (pronounced Me-Shell) were both inspired by Jacques Cousteau and his marine research crew, who often wore iconic red wool beanies. I was always fascinated by old diving suits, and I was amused by the idea that sea creatures would attempt to use one as a fake human in an attempt to blend in with life on land, which I called "space" (the absence of water). In one scene that was deleted, I drew the sea creatures repurposing parts from a deep-diving submarine with robotic arms to build the Aquanaut.

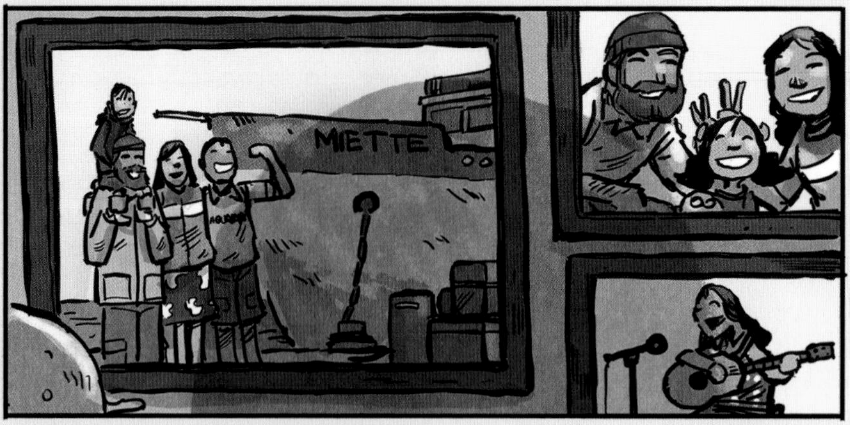
MIETTE

The names of the sea characters were also indicative of the backstory of Sophia's mother. In the second panel on page 56 you see a woman in the family photos. This was Sophia's mother, and as you can see, she was a singer, inspired by my love of the Brazilian singer, Astrud Gilberto. The names of Sodapop's three crew members, Antonio, Carlos, and Jobim (pronounced "Joe-Beam"), are named after the famous Brazilian composer Antônio Carlos Jobim who, along with Astrud Gilberto, created hit songs, such as "The Girl From Ipanema." Their names give a glimpse into the mind of Sophia's father, Michel, who named these exotic sea creatures as a way to memorialize his wife.

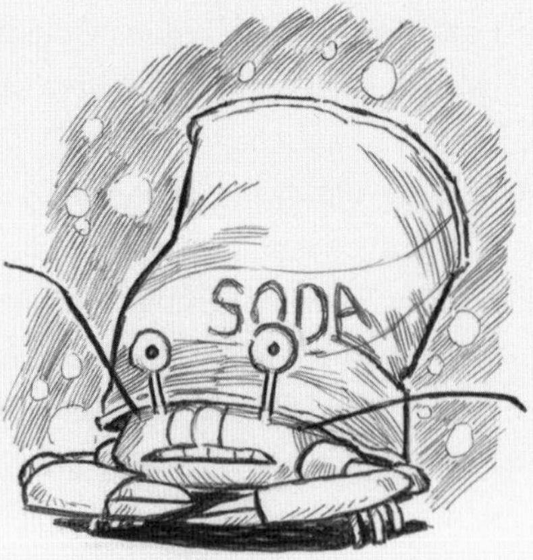
SODA

SODAPOP

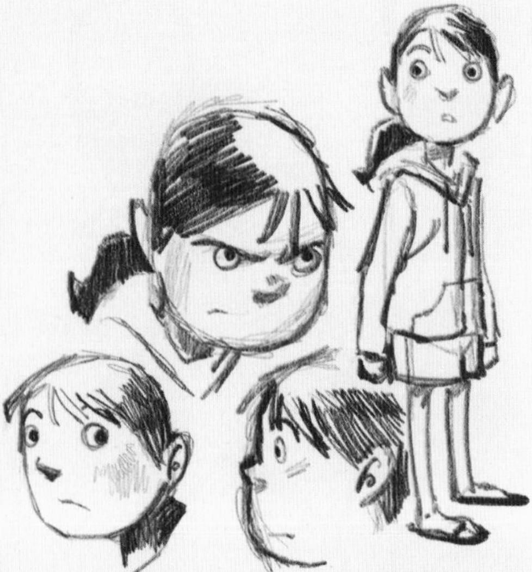

SOPHIA

CARLOS is the engineer of the crew, the one who operates the guts of the Aquanaut, and can multitask with all his limbs. I loved the idea that the crew consisted of all these rare and endangered sea creatures in search of others like themselves, who then realized that all the friends surrounding them were, in fact, their own adopted family.

ANTONIO is unique in the fact that a male Blanket octopus is 10,000 times smaller than a female and is extremely rare to find in nature.

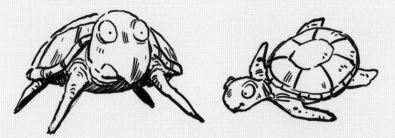

JOBIM, a Kemp's Ridley Sea Turtle, is the navigator of the bunch. He's more paternal than the rest in his instincts and keeps the crew in order. He's the Spock to Sodapop's Kirk.

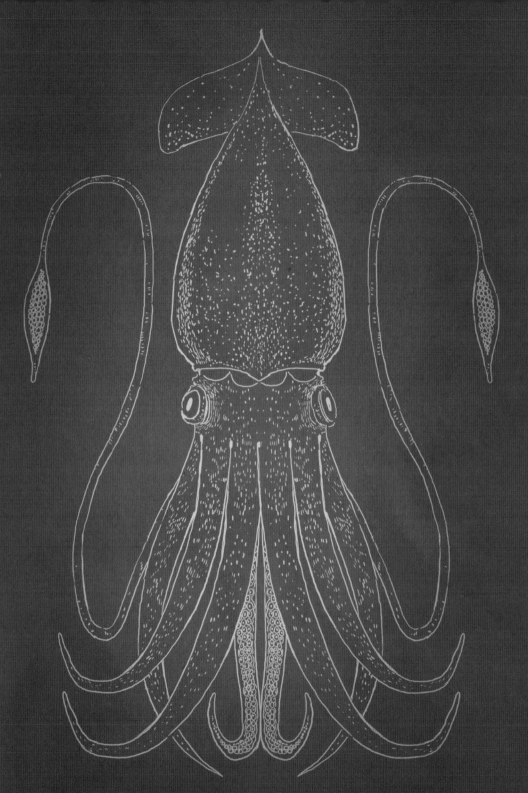

MESONYCHOTEUTHIS HAMILTONI

ACKNOWLEDGMENTS

The Aquanaut was a project that took over ten years to complete, to which there was no one to fault but myself, and within those years there are countless numbers of friends, family, and colleagues to thank.

Rachel Griffiths was the first editor of this book, and she waited patiently for five years for me to send her revisions while I was busy with a new family, a new home, and was juggling various other projects while setting my own off to the side.

Kait Feldmann was my second editor on this project, and for a year and a half she helped tighten up the story before she left to pursue greater heights in the publishing world.

David Saylor, the head of the Graphix imprint, helped finish the edits and kept the ship on the path toward completion.

Phil Falco, my art director, designer, and friend. You have always been my rock.

Mike Boldt, for coloring this book, and for his long-lasting friendship.

My friend, Arthur Levine, for giving me my big break in publishing and believing in this project.

My family, Leah, Alek, and Kyle for being my inspiration.

My agent, Jodi Reamer, for comforting me and telling me this book will be done when it's done.

And lastly, all my friends in the PBG. Renee, James, Ryan, Mike, Matt, Brett, Russ, Jess, Cale, and whoever decided to drop in on Skype.

Without all of you, this project would not have been possible. Without you I am nothing. You are all my family.

And family comes first.

DAN SANTAT

is a #1 *New York Times* bestselling author/ illustrator of over one hundred titles, which include *The Adventures of Beekle: The Unimaginary Friend*, the winner of the prestigious Randolph Caldecott Medal in 2015. Other titles include *Are We There Yet?*, *After the Fall (How Humpty Dumpty Got Back Up Again)*, and *Oh No! (Or How My Science Project Destroyed the World)*, which won the Silver Medal in book illustration from the Society of Illustrators in 2010. His first graphic novel, *Sidekicks*, was published by Scholastic/Graphix in 2011. He is also the creator of the Disney animated hit *The Replacements*.

Dan lives in Southern California with his wife, two kids, and various pets.

Visit him at beekleandfriends.com.

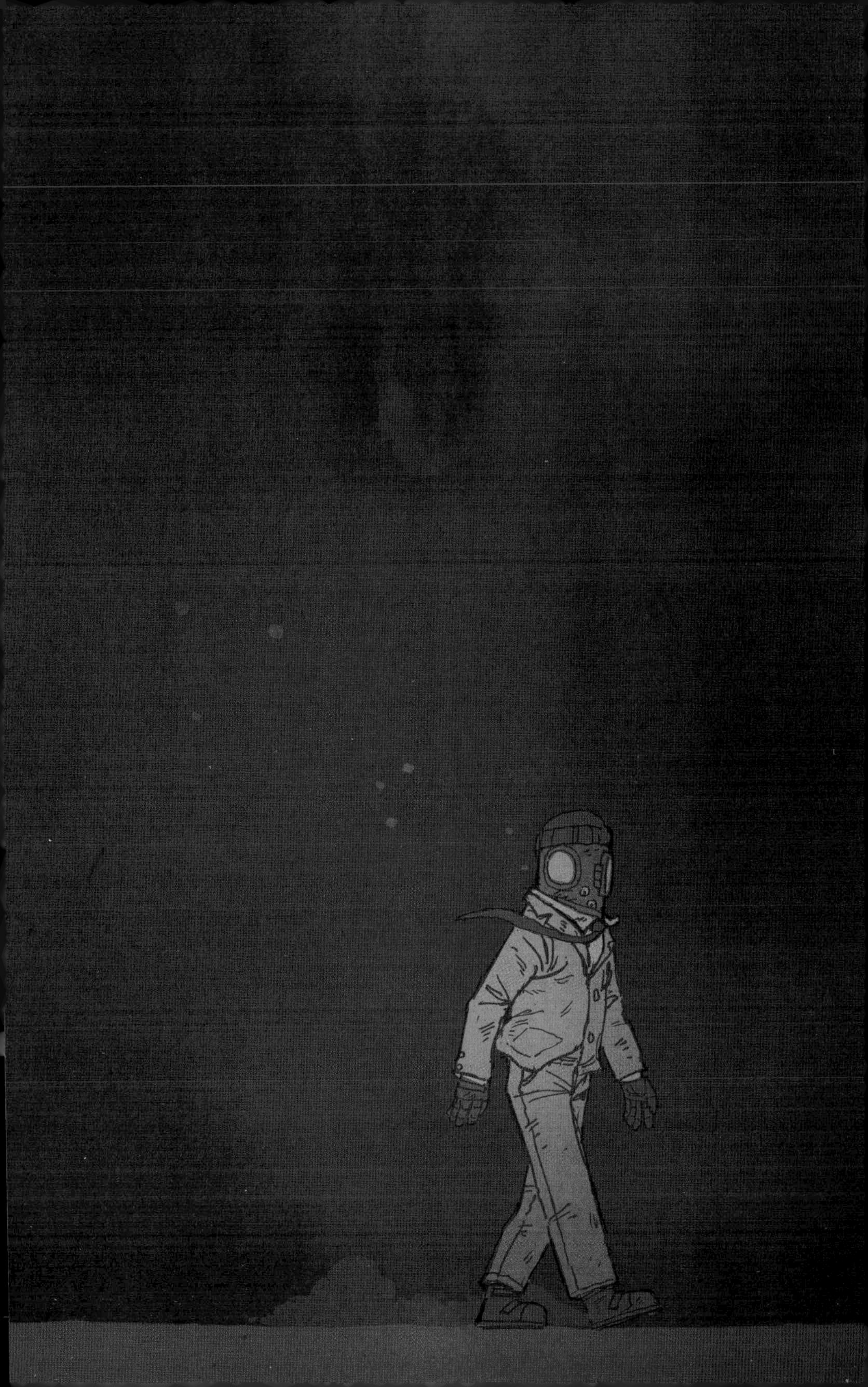

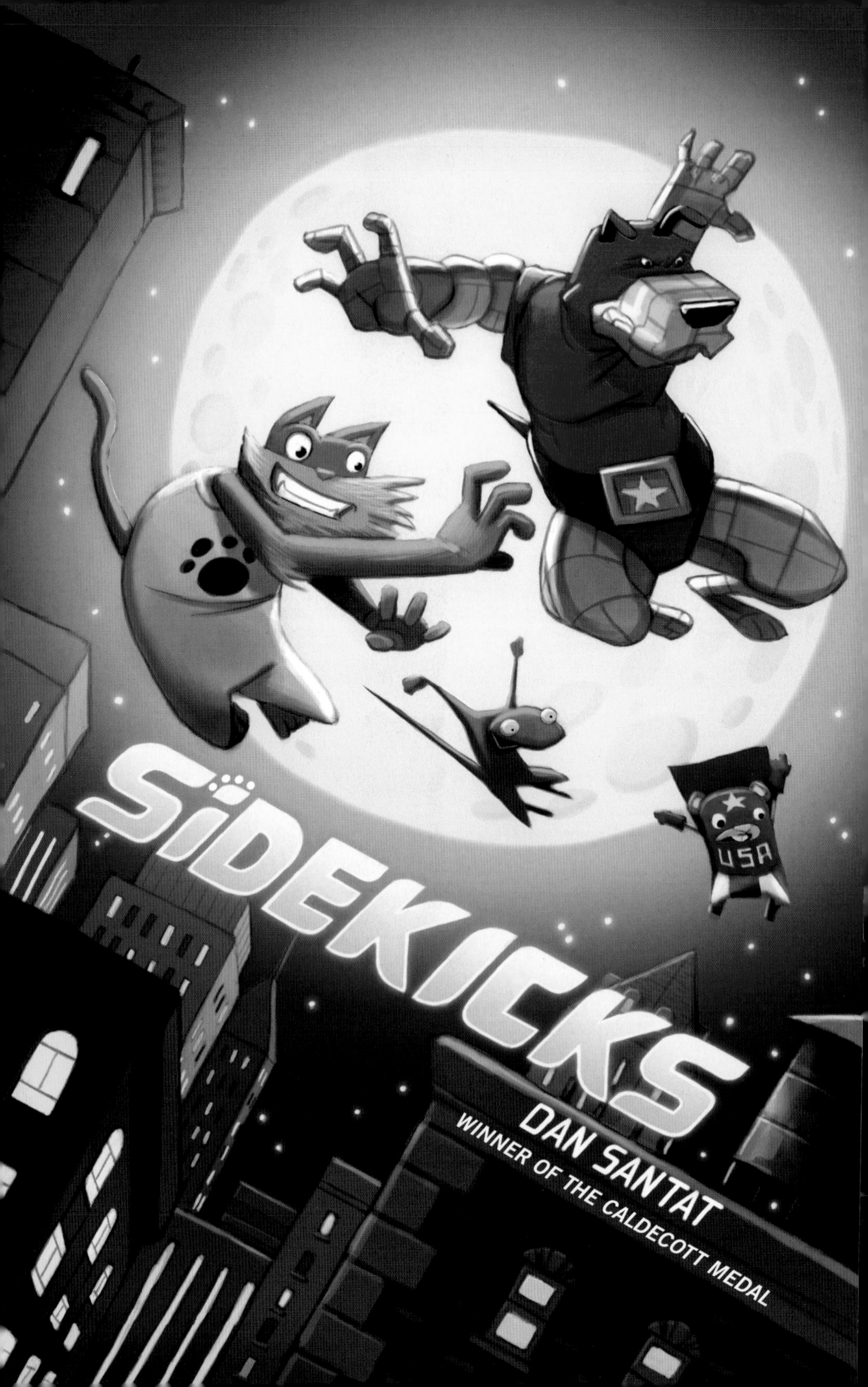
SIDEKICKS
DAN SANTAT
WINNER OF THE CALDECOTT MEDAL

Captain Amazing, hero of Metro City, is so busy catching criminals that he rarely has time for his pets at home. He doesn't even notice when they develop superpowers of their own.

So when he announces that he needs a sidekick, his dog, hamster, and chameleon decide to audition. But with each pet determined to win the sidekick position, the biggest battle in Metro City might just be at the Captain's house.

Then archvillain Dr. Havoc returns to town, and suddenly the Captain's in serious trouble. Can the warring pets put their squabbles aside? Or is it curtains for the Captain?

It's sit, stay, and save the world in this romp of a graphic novel by Dan Santat!

"Hilarious and heartfelt . . . a charming and well-told tale about friendship."
Kazu Kibuishi, creator of Amulet

"Lots of laughs and a boisterous and exuberant storyline."
Kirkus Reviews

"Lively, insightful, and just plain fun."
Bulletin of the Center for Children's Books

Library of Congress Control Number: 2021937540

ISBN 978-0-545-49760-2 (hardcover)
ISBN 978-0-545-49761-9 (paperback)

11 10 9 8 7 6 5 4 3 2   22 23 24 25 26

Printed in Mexico   189
First edition, March 2022

Edited by Rachel Griffiths and Kait Feldmann
Book design by Steve Ponzo
Creative Director: Phil Falco
Publisher: David Saylor